Henry Brodribb Irving

The life of Judge Jeffreys

Henry Brodribb Irving

The life of Judge Jeffreys

ISBN/EAN: 9783743349490

Manufactured in Europe, USA, Canada, Australia, Japa

Cover: Foto ©Raphael Reischuk / pixelio.de

Manufactured and distributed by brebook publishing software (www.brebook.com)

Henry Brodribb Irving

The life of Judge Jeffreys

The Right Hon.ble S.r George Jeffreys Kn.t & Baronet;
LORD CHEIF JUSTICE OF ENGLAND;
And one of his Ma.ties most Hon.ble Privy Council. Ano Dni 1684.

Jeffreys. ætat 36.
From an Engraving after Kneller.

THE LIFE OF
JUDGE JEFFREYS

BY

H. B. IRVING

M.A. OXON,

WITH THREE PORTRAITS

LONDON
WILLIAM HEINEMANN
1898

PREFACE

THIS book is an attempt, however imperfectly executed, to fill a gap in the biographical literature of the seventeenth century, and to reproduce the general features of a period during which the proceedings in the courts of law were intimately associated with the history of the nation.

After consulting all accessible authorities, both printed and manuscript, some of which have not been hitherto made use of, I have formed a rather different estimate of Jeffreys' life and character from that generally accepted. I venture to hope that my reasons for arriving at such an estimate may not appear unjustifiable.

Among many to whom I owe my thanks for help kindly given in the preparation of this book, I would select a few for special acknowledgment. To the officials at the Record Office, to Mr. Fortescue and Mr. Anderson of the British Museum Library, to Mr. Walkes of the Privy Council Office, to the late Mr. Alfred Morrison, and lastly to Mr. M. R. Jeffreys, who, with the greatest courtesy and kindness, placed at my disposal the few family papers in his possession relating to the career of Lord Jeffreys, to these I would express my especial obligation.

H. B. IRVING.

February, 1898.

CONTENTS

PORTRAITS OF JEFFREYS

I

THE BOYHOOD OF JEFFREYS

1648—1663

At Acton Park, in a beautiful green corner of the county of Denbighshire, near the town of Wrexham, George Jeffreys was born in the year 1648. Acton Park had been the family seat for a considerable period. Descended from a long line of distinguished ancestors, the house of Jeffreys could claim to be one of the oldest families among the gentry of Wales. But its historical importance had passed away with Tudor Trevor, Earl of Hereford, and other heroes of the national history ; and the Jeffreys had settled down as quiet country gentlemen, living in dignified ease, and sharing those responsibilities that usually fall to people in their station of life. The name of Jeffreys had attained local prominence in the persons of High Sheriffs and Welsh Judges, but its fame had not yet passed beyond the limits of its county.

The father whose son was destined to dissipate so rudely the unpretentious merit of the family achievement was Mr. John Jeffreys. He had proved no alien to the honourable traditions of his house ; and, at the age of eighty-four, when " Judge Jeffreys " had ceased to be anything but a hated name, this sturdy old gentleman felt justified in blessing God " that he had always studied the welfare and happiness of his children, and had never been guilty of an unkind or unjust act to any of them."[1] He had chosen a fitting wife in Margaret Ireland. This lady was the daughter of Sir Thomas Ireland, a Lancashire gentleman, erstwhile a Serjeant-at-law and learned editor of *Coke's Reports*. Mrs. Jeffreys was a pious good woman, if we are to believe the testimony of her friend Philip Henry, the eminent Dissenter, and one who did her best to bring up her children in a godly fashion. There is some reason for believing that Jeffreys' parents were themselves Dissenters, and it may well be that George's bringing up was unpleasantly austere to a child of his temperament. At any rate, it is admissible to suggest that in his early training and the religious tone of his father's household, Jeffreys found a primary cause for the lively hatred he evinced in later years towards the Nonconformists. It must not also be forgotten that Jeffreys' earliest years, 1648—1660, were passed during the period of Puritan ascendency, a period no doubt trying in many respects to vivacious children.

Of such estimable parents came " Judge Jeffreys." George was the fourth son. Three of his brothers grew to manhood, and, as far as we know, perpetuated the modest virtues of their parents, leading honourable if uneventful lives, and dying under circumstances that left nothing to be desired. John, the eldest, was a respectable High Sheriff, Thomas an amiable Consul, and James, the youngest, a very sufficient Prebendary. There is no reflection of either the abilities or the energy of the Judge in any of his immediate relatives. If his qualities are a reproduction of some remote ancestor, they cannot be traced at this distance of time. From his maternal grandfather he may have inherited some of his legal talents, and his paternal grandfather was a Welsh Judge. An unconvincing attempt has been made to establish the existence of a maternal grandmother with ambitious designs, but it remains unconvincing. It must not be

---

[1] Letter of Mr. John Jeffreys to the widow of his son, Dr. James Jeffreys, Prebendary of Canterbury, Jan. 18, 1690, in the possession of M. P. Jeffreys, Esq.

forgotten that "Judge Jeffreys" was a Welshman. Matthew Arnold has described wit, vivacity, an audacious love of excitement, a want of measure and steadfastness and sanity, as prevailing characteristics of the Celtic nature. Lord Justice Vaughan Williams has added disregard of personal liberty. These qualities have been for some time associated in the public mind with "Judge Jeffreys." Amidst the Teutonic moderation of his immediate relatives, it may not be unreasonable to regard George as a wilful protest on the part of the Celtic element in the family character against threatened extinction.

The memory of the Judge has not escaped that misrepresentation which is the everlasting portion of unpopular characters. There is a prevalent impression that he was a man of obscure and ignoble origin, an uneducated declaimer, violent and ignorant, whose shortcomings may be comfortably attributed to the mysterious consequences of want of breeding. Insinuations of this kind are very fatal to character, and, if there is any hope of mercy for Jeffreys, should be immediately corrected. It is impossible to calculate the enormous damage which the reputation of Scroggs (Jeffreys' only peer in judicial infamy) has suffered from the assertion of his enemies that he was a butcher's son, and the unfortunate support that questionable statement has derived from his cacophonous name. All that can be said with certainty of Jeffreys' boyhood amounts to this—he was considered by those who knew him a lad of exceptional talents, and, for that reason, received at the hands of his parents the best education possible to a gentleman of that period. Philip Henry examined the boy's learning at his mother's request, and found him remarkably proficient. He was first sent to Shrewsbury School, then the preparatory school for the gentry of the neighbourhood. Lord Campbell unmercifully accuses Jeffreys, even at this tender age, of cheating his schoolfellows at marbles and leapfrog; but adds that, in spite of these failings, he contrived to get himself elected Master of the Revels by

his long-suffering companions, whatever that may mean !
In his eleventh year Jeffreys was removed to St. Paul's
School in London, with the view, Lord Campbell has it,
of ultimately entering life as a shop apprentice.   Here
he became the pupil of Dr. Cromleholme, Pepys' " con-
ceited, dogmatic pedagogue Crumlum," who was at any
rate sufficiently in earnest to die of the loss of his library
in the Great Fire.   Jeffreys remained at St. Paul's two
years.   In 1661 he was removed to Westminster, at that
time under the Mastership of the awful Busby.   As
Jeffreys only remained in the school a year, he had not
time to benefit fully by the training which mellowed
Locke, Dryden, and many a divine, to the comfort of
succeeding generations.   Locke complains that at Westminster greater efforts were shown in directing tongues
to learned languages than minds to virtue.   Some may be
inclined to cite Jeffreys in confirmation of this charge.
They can, if they will, call Lord Campbell in evidence,
for he says that Jeffreys was occasionally flogged for
idleness and impudence.   This is another supposition
on Lord Campbell's part ; but the reputation of Busby
and the healthy failings of any well-constituted school-
boy lend it greater probability than falls to the lot of the
majority of the noble author's biographical inspirations.
Whilst at Westminster, Jeffreys is said to have had a
dream in which his rise and fall were graphically revealed
to him.   He is also said to have often narrated his vision
to his friends in the days of his success.   This may or
may not be true.   Dreams and prophecies in the case
of famous or infamous people are often invoked after the
event to lend a supernatural importance to their earthly
careers.   If Jeffreys was really in possession of this supernatural information it is surprising that he did not
manage his future more skilfully.   Lord Campbell has
introduced a gipsy into the story, for reasons not immediately obvious.

For reasons equally mysterious, Lord Campbell con-
ducts an unauthenticated correspondence between Jeffreys

and his father relative to the former's desire to adopt the profession of the Law. It is said in the contemporary accounts of the Judge's life that this desire on the part of George was very alarming to Mr. Jeffreys, and drove the unfortunate gentleman to prophecy. " George, George, I fear thou wilt die with thy shoes and stockings on," he is is reported to have said at the close of the arguments as to the lad's future. Seeing that not a few of George's ancestors had been engaged in the legal profession, and George himself educated on a liberal scale, Mr. Jeffreys' alarm is eccentric. But there were further difficulties in the way of fulfilling his son's wishes. An University training was then, as now, a frequent preliminary to entering on a legal career, and George would have liked to enjoy the experience. But, alas ! Mr. Jeffreys could not possibly afford to send his son to the University ; that was quite beyond his means. Lord Campbell treats us to quite a moving picture of the internal economy of Acton Park, in which he describes the anxious family seated in solemn conclave, striving as best they may, poor souls ! to gratify the ambitious cravings of a sinister youth. The University is quite out of the question ; ten pounds is all Mr. Jeffreys can possibly afford his son as an income during his years of studentship in the Temple. That sum being quite insufficient, the whole of the glorious project is about to be abandoned, when the maternal grandmother afore-mentioned, " pleased to see the blood of the Irelands break out," advances to the rescue, and out of a " small jointure " agrees to allow £40 a year to her delightful grandson. Rejoicing in her munificence and wrapt in dreams of future glory and Sir Richard Whittington, the poor and struggling Mr. Jeffreys advances upon London.

Having aspersed the son and impoverished the father, the historians of Jeffreys' boyhood may well rest content. They have had the first say ; and, if it is necessary to dispel their mists, there is very little to offer in return.

In the first place Jeffreys *was* sent to the University, to

Trinity College, Cambridge, in the March of 1662 ; and not only that, but soon after poor impecunious Mr. Jeffreys sent his youngest son, James, to Jesus College, Oxford, to prepare him for the Church. George Jeffreys remained at Cambridge a year, and in May, 1663, was entered as a student at the Inner Temple. How far the help of the grandmother was necessary seems doubtful. If not rich, Mr. Jeffreys seems to have been well enough off to educate his sons very liberally. His eldest son could afford to be High Sheriff, and there are other signs that his means were not so straitened as to be unable to afford £40 for George's maintenance at the Temple. In any case it is not very important to determine whether he could or could not ; but it *is* important to point out the way in which the scanty details of Jeffreys' boyhood have been filled out by a great deal that is either unreliable anecdote or pure invention.

It would no doubt be consoling to many who regard a traditional belief with uncompromising reverence, if it could be shown that the boyhood of " Judge Jeffreys " was one long record of petty misdeeds, in which the far-seeing might have detected the germs of greater crimes. Some such consideration may have impelled Lord Campbell and others to rely on their imaginations to supply the gaps in Jeffreys' early history, though they can hardly be congratulated on the ingenuity of their efforts.

The boyhood of Jeffreys, like the boyhoods of many greater men, remains, and will ever remain, a closed book to us. Perhaps if we had the book it would not be worth opening ; though the fact could not fail to surpass in value the rather pinchbeck fiction which has apologised for its absence. However, on the few scattered facts that have been left to us, it may fairly be assumed that some instruction, if not amusement, is to be derived from the career of a well-born, well-educated and gifted young man, who, in spite of his birth, his breeding and his gifts, has become one of the most vehemently detested memories in the history of his country.

STUDENT LIFE AND EARLY YEARS AT THE BAR

1663—1671

FOR five years, from 1663 to 1668, Jeffreys was a student of the Inner Temple. In those days the students resided actually within the precincts of their Inn, and led a life similar to that of an undergraduate in a University College. The Benchers took the place of Dons, and had a very bad time of it : if they resented the impertinences of the students, they got pumped on for their pains ; and if they complained to the Judges, who seemed to have exercised a kind of supervision over the discipline of the Inns, they were not infrequently snubbed, and on some occasions soundly rated. The students considered themselves quite competent to look after their own rights and privileges, as my Lord Mayor learnt to his cost. His coming into the Temple one night with his sword of state borne before him caused such an outburst of indignation that he had to run off to the King and send for the train-bands. In 1678, on the occasion of the fire in the Temple, the then Lord Mayor repeated the offence, and again had his sword beaten down before him. But this time he took a more effective revenge : he sent back the engine that was coming from the City to extinguish the flames, and made himself comfortably drunk in a neighbouring tavern.

A student's life in the seventeenth century seems to have been as long and merry as it is now short and colourless. How Jeffreys spent these five years can only be a matter for surmise. If we are to believe the few writers who have alluded to this period, we should be inclined to suggest that it was spent in getting drunk. Roger North, his elegant contemporary, says that " his beginnings at the Inns of Court were low." But from the outset it is necessary to receive anything North writes about Jeffreys with great caution. North was a prim, proper little person, with no sense of humour, timorous and diffident, but decided in his views and strong in his prejudices, as only people of narrow views and large affections can be. It was in this last respect that, apart from differences of temperament, Jeffreys offended him beyond all hope of pardon. Roger North loved his brother Francis dearly, with a great and impervious affection, and regarded him as all that a great lawyer and an upright man should be. How far Francis North deserved this adoration,—how far, if Roger North had possessed any sense of humour, he could have continued to adore,—we may have better opportunities of judging later on. At any rate Roger did adore his brother unspeakably, and Francis' enemies were his enemies. Of these Jeffreys was the foremost. The opposite natures of the two men made disagreement inevitable as soon as they were placed in a position where disagreement was possible. The occasion offered later in Jeffreys' career, and from that moment a mutual dislike sprang up between them. "All the men of law in England," says Roger North, "in place and out of place, mustered together," did not so much affect his brother's quiet as Jeffreys. In this sentence Roger North gives us the best test of the reliance to be placed on his views of Jeffreys. Even the great and good Sir Matthew Hale suffered at his hands for not sufficiently appreciating the virtues of Francis. What then would be the sufferings of Jeffreys, who not only failed to appreciate the virtues of Francis, but laughed at and made merry over them, and whose character, his most ardent apologist will admit, is not quite so proof against detraction as Hales's? Any writer concerned with the legal history of this period owes an invaluable debt to North for his quaint and attractive work ; but the very fact that in a life of Jeffreys that work must be constantly referred to makes it at the outset imperatively necessary to explain the circumstances under which it was written and their natural effect on Roger North's estimate of Jeffreys' career and character.

"His beginnings were low." By this Roger North must be taken to mean that his days were passed in drinking and keeping low company. It would be idle to pretend that Jeffreys was not a hard drinker ; and a hard drinker in those days meant a good deal. Even the virtuous Francis North took more than was good for him ; but then he could feel it coming on, and used to sit smiling and say nothing, "so harmless a thing of a petit good fellow was he." Judging by his portraits he must have looked rather idiotic at these times. Jeffreys was never of the "sitting smiling" order. He drank his fill, often more than his fill, with the frankness and freedom characteristic of his age. We know that he did so later in life ; it is therefore presumable that he did so with if anything greater freedom in youth. The Temple must have offered the same facilities to the indulgence of such habits of revelry in the young as the Universities offer to-day in a lesser degree in their wines and common rooms ; and Jeffreys no doubt availed himself fully of such opportunities. In London the company he would meet in the course of such revels would be mixed, though the tavern then was a higher place of entertainment than it is now. We may conclude that Jeffreys, in the matter of his amusements, offered no resistance to the lax habits of the age, and that perhaps the greater part of his time was given over to amusement. All this would be naturally very shocking to men like the Norths who were assiduous students and had been brought up in a manner that made the laxity of manners prevalent in their day distressing to them. But Jeffreys was very different to the Norths. He was no assiduous plodder, his brain was quick to apprehend, and he possessed, in the opinion of those best capable of judging, that instinctive penetration into the real merits of a question which seems to be the most essential characteristic of a great lawyer. He was never the ignorant man he has been represented ; he must have acquired some knowledge of law to merit the praise that has been bestowed on him ; but he probably acquired quickly, and without much effort—a facility always dangerous in a man of sociable habits. He was in all probability only too ready to fling away his books and betake himself to the dancing and fencing schools, those " rendezvous so dangerous and expensive to young gentlemen of the Temple." He may have believed that time spent in learning the arts of society was profitably employed, especially if he did not intend to rely too severely on book learning for his future success. However Jeffreys employed his spare time, in drinking or dancing or fencing or gaming, the voice of calumny, loudly as it has cried against him, has never been able to accuse him of that grosser immorality which disgraced the society of his day ; and it is very certain that had there been the opportunity of doing so, posterity would not have been long kept in ignorance. But these insinuations of North, whatever degree of faith may be placed in them, can only refer to one side of Jeffreys' life. Drink and low company cannot, even in Charles the Second's reign, explain the extraordinary rapidity of Jeffreys' rise. Three years only after his call to the Bar he was elected Common Serjeant of the City of London. To accomplish this he must have acquired a considerable interest in the City and a certain standing in his profession. To gain these in three years from his call to the Bar would be hardly possible unless he had by his abilities and personal advantages already made a reputation that preceded him and secured for him immediate employment. A young man in Jeffreys' station could not have come up to London friendless. The social position of his parents, his own education at public school and university must have launched him into some sort of society in which he might win favour and influence if he had the power to do so.

Until Jeffreys' portrait had been exhibited in the National Portrait Gallery it would have been difficult to induce well-instructed people to believe that " Judge Jeffreys " as a young man was possessed of a fair countenance, well formed in feature, and attractive in expression. His picture is the likeness of a refined and delicately made young man, the head small, and covered by thick brown hair, the eyes large and dark, the nose rather long and straight, the upper lip short, the mouth finely curved. His hands are peculiarly small and delicate in shape. If only a sufficient number of people visit the National Portrait Gallery there is likely to be a revulsion in favour of the Judge, such as no apologising or whitewashing can achieve. That specious thing known as the " verdict of history " has never received such a decisive and simple rejoinder as in this portrait of Jeffreys. Whether it will be effective depends on the popularity of the National Portrait Gallery.

Good looks, engaging manners and conspicuous talents are not such a frequent combination in the young men of any day as to fail to attract the attention of society, always on the look out for the promising sprigs of the rising generation. If we add to these gifts good birth and good breeding, the effect produced by the happy possessor of these advantages on the Aldermen of the City of London must have been peculiarly fascinating ; if his festive capacities were equally well developed, very complete. Jeffreys rejoiced in all these means to favour. It was in the City of London that he first found influential friends, and from the City of London came his first preferment. The City must have been the field in which during these five years he had chosen to push his fortunes. He did so to such good purpose that when on his call to the Bar he began by practising in the City Courts he reaped an immediate reward. One of his more influential friends was a certain Alderman Jeffreys, nicknamed the

" Great Smoker," because so much of his merchandise was burnt in the Great Fire.   He was not, as far as we know, related to Mr. George Jeffreys, but perhaps the similarity of name and the personal attractions of the young man drew them together.   The Alderman warmly espoused Mr. Jeffreys' fortunes, and placed his purse and his interest at his disposal.   An equally important friend of Jeffreys was Sir Robert Clayton, that prince of citizens, who from scrivener's boy had risen, by usury under royal and distinguished patronage, to a position of prodigious magnificence.   This was a friendship which, in spite of the gravest political differences, lasted till the end.   As Sir Robert Clayton was a highly respectable person, Jeffreys deserves some credit for having enjoyed the regard of that estimable man during the whole of his unpopular career.

We may assume then that during the five years of his novitiate Jeffreys was not wholly drunken and idle, his beginnings not altogether low.   He certainly did not lead a life that would commend itself to a sober student or an anxious father, but his pleasures were not so wholly engrossing as to prevent him from giving his charms and his talents every opportunity of showing themselves off to some advantage.   He never forgot he had a career to make.   If he had forgotten this as completely as some writers would have us believe, he would never have been heard of at all.   But we know that he was heard of, and that very quickly.   At twenty he was called to the Bar, and found plenty of work awaiting him.   Fortune smiled on the young man.   He had talents, he had friends.   He started full of promise which he fulfilled with precocious rapidity ; at twenty-three he was a Judge, —an object of wonder and envy to many, of admiration to a few.   But good fortune so signal and rapid as this is fraught with danger to a youth of a passionate and ambitious nature.   Premature success may spoil the best of us, and serve to bring out very wilful qualities in the headstrong and the confident.   Mr. Jeffreys had plenty of assurance, overwhelming ambition and very little self-control. If he has things too much his own way, it is to be feared that his assurance may swell to bursting, his self-control decline to vanishing point, and his ambition swallow up any good qualities remaining.

At the time of Jeffreys' call to the Bar (1668), the profession of the Law had recovered all the profits and emoluments which the disturbances of the Civil War had considerably diminished, and was regarded as the most promising field in which a young man who had little to help him save his own abilities might hope to win his way to distinction and prosperity. The class of men practising at the Bar numbered many of eminent and respectable attainment ; and the Bench was filled by some good lawyers and one of the greatest men who has ever adorned a seat of justice.

Sir Matthew Hale was at this time Lord Chief Baron of the Exchequer. The three attributes bestowed on him by Matthew Arnold no one will deny him : truthfulness of disposition, vigour of intelligence, and penetrating judgment. He was a man whose errors we can the more readily forgive in that they prove the humanity of his greatness. In 1671 he was to leave the Exchequer for the Chief Justiceship of the King's Bench, and to pass away in the fulness of his dignity from the honours he adorned, the giant before the flood ! Hale is remarkable as one of the very few men of his time who understood the function of a Judge as we understand it to-day. With him impartiality was fanatical in its scrupulousness ; and Roger North's list of prejudices to which he was subject only enhances the distinction of a mind that on the seat of justice emancipated itself from every unjust or unworthy influence. But North did not like Hale ; for Hale, whilst he recognised the abilities, did not relish the personality of brother Francis. Extraordinary as it may sound at the first announcement, the man who most gained upon him and won his ear and his friendship was Mr. George Jeffreys. Of course Roger North cites this partiality as a strange failing on the part of so great a man, and ascribes its origin to little accommodations administered to the Lord Chief Baron at Mr. Jeffreys' house in the shape of a partridge or two on a plate, and a pipe after, served up with the pleasing diversion of satirical tales and reflections on well-known men of the town. North, rather puzzled, can only explain such an intimacy as an example of Hale's extravagant love for " bizarre and irregular wits." True, Hale as a young man had once betrayed a sinful love for stage plays and merry-making, and Jeffreys may have served to kindle some smothered remnant of these wicked proclivities in the heart of the old Puritan. But Mr. North's elaborate explanation of the incident is just a little laboured ; and Lord Campbell's suggestion that Jeffreys won over Hale by an affectation of religion, a wanton supposition. Mr. Jeffreys was a bright, handsome and intelligent lawyer, winning a rapid success in his profession, sufficiently opposed in temperament to Hale to attract his regard and sufficiently clever to display his best qualities to so good a man. There is no reason to look with shame, surprise or suspicion on an intimacy which is as creditable to Jeffreys as it is in no way discreditable or " bizarre " on the part of Hale.

Among those to whom Mr. Jeffreys would look up as the leaders of his profession were certain men who in later years were to be called upon to play some part in his future career. Roger's estimable brother, Sir. Francis North, had just been appointed Solicitor-General. This amiable, worldly and accomplished man, of much negative virtue, has invariably succeeded in irritating any writer who has been obliged to notice his existence. He never did anything peculiarly bad, and he certainly never did anything peculiarly noble. The unfortunate man meant well in a timorous sort of way, and would have been glad to escape with a decent modicum of approval ; but his brother Roger, by exaggerating his eminently domestic virtues and exalting the respectability of a vestryman into the attributes of a Daniel, has rendered him eternally ridiculous. A splay-faced man with wily eyes. In 1673 North was promoted from Solicitor to Attorney-General, and two years later his talents and his assiduity were fitly rewarded by his being raised to the Bench as Lord Chief Justice of the Common Pleas. It would have been well had he ended his days in a position in every way suited to his legal ability and his moral worth, but in an evil hour he accepted the custody of the Great Seal, and never had a happy moment afterwards.

Of a very different stamp were the Serjeants Scroggs and Pemberton, two very considerable men of law at this period, who likewise played important parts in the story of Jeffreys' life. Serjeant Pemberton has claims to respectful consideration, if only for the fact that the worthy Evelyn describes him as "honest." He was one of those energetic beings who, after devoting their powers of earnest application to the reckless indulgence of their physical appetites, at a critical moment transfer them to more lasting pursuits, and achieve honour and renown in their new departure. In the sordid retirement of a debtors' prison, whither his extravagance had led him, Francis Pemberton came to his senses and, under sympathetic surroundings, commenced the study of the Law. It is not surprising that he emerged from this novel seat of learning a very sharper in his trade, and by the aid of his sobered talents acquired an extensive practice. Pepys' evidence leaves no doubt as to his remarkable success. Not only does he tell us how pretty it was to see the heaps of gold on the lawyer's table, but adds that the eminent counsel had never read the case on which he consulted him, and gave him perfectly incorrect advice. There can be no surer signs that he was indeed a famous leader and had risen from the ashes of a dissolute past a thriving and respected lawyer. In 1679 the Serjeant was appointed a Judge of the King's Bench.

In the character of Pemberton excess was an incident, a temporary ailment that departed as quickly as it came, without leaving any traces of its occupation. But it was quite otherwise with Mr. Serjeant Scroggs. In his disposition excess was constitutional, physically and intellectually inherent. He was a debauchee in thought as well as action, and indulged as recklessly in his principles as his pleasures. Whatever he undertook he performed with a violence to which the excellence or infamy of the actions mattered little. But, as in the case of Jeffreys, his only serious rival in the field of judicial villainy, he impudently refuses to consider the fitness of inaccurate romance and submit to be sketched as the conventional monster whose brutality is only equalled by his ignorance. We can dismiss the story of his butcher descent. He was educated at Oxford, where he took a Master's degree. After a probationary course of military adventure as an officer in King Charles's army during the Civil War, he was called to the Bar, and by his abilities soon achieved professional success. He became one of the City Counsel, distinguished for the wit and elegance of his speech. Pepys heard him plead in the House of Lords and declared him to be "an excellent man." His speech on his appointment as a Judge was so much admired that he published it, and the copies were speedily sold out. Loose principles and useful talents commended him to Lord Danby, a nimble wit and comely presence to the Duchess of Portsmouth. By the side of such sponsors wounds received for King Charles I in the Civil War were superfluous recommendations to King Charles II; and his future was assured.

This shining example of rapid advancement was to be closely followed a few years later by young Mr. Jeffreys, to whom in all but one respect the progress of Serjeant Scroggs might have served as a model. But the machinations of his detractors have failed to convict Jeffreys of a dissolute or immoral youth. Beyond shadowy indications of intemperance, he seems as a young man to have been almost unnaturally free from the prevailing tendencies of his period. It is a significant fact that Hale, the friend of Jeffreys, detested Scroggs. On one occasion, when the latter, arrested on a King's Bench warrant for assault and battery, pleaded to the Court his privilege as a Serjeant, the Chief Justice left him to his fate. But it must always be remembered, in dealing with the men of Scroggs' generation, that those who had fought and buffeted in the Civil War, who had endured the pains and perils of defeat and exile, and to whom wine and women had been the only occupations left under the stern *régime* of a suspicious Government, were very slow to settle down again into decent habits. The shameless immorality of Charles the Second's reign, the obvious desire to shock the ugly virtue that had so long oppressed them, the careless indulgence of the upper classes on the return of their Sovereign were the necessary outcome of a state of civil discord and a natural reaction against a preceding period of gloomy repression. The Puritan ascendency had oppressed but not extinguished the loose disposition of the Cavalier ; he carried with him into the summer of his prosperity the evil habits of his winter of discontent.

III

THE RISE OF THE COMMON SERJEANT

1671—1678

In 1667 Jeffreys had been guilty of an early marriage. The circumstances of it, if correctly given, are very much to his credit.

In the course of the formation of that large *clientèle* which the young student was winning to himself in the City of London, he chanced to visit the house of a certain wealthy merchant, who rejoiced in the possession of a daughter. The personality of the daughter is unimportant when we learn that she had thirty thousand pounds. Adopting this view of the situation, the handsome young lawyer laid siege to the maiden's heart ; and, to better further the gentle war that he was waging, pressed into his service one Sarah Neesham, the daughter of a clergyman, apparently acting as confidante or companion to the City maiden. In the latter capacity she was employed by the besieger to carry notes and messages of devotion to the besieged, a task she would seem to have performed so efficaciously that the fair garrison began to show signs of a speedy surrender. Alas ! on the eve of triumph the merchant father discovered all. The besieged was removed out of harm's way, the besieger routed from his entrenchments, and Miss Neesham cast upon the world with £300. In her distress she hurried to Mr. Jeffreys, and poured out the tale of her sorrow, thereby so powerfully affecting the heart and imagination of the impulsive youth that, without more ado, he offered her his hand and problematical fortunes as compensation for her misadventure.   The offer having been accepted, on May 22nd, 1667, George Jeffreys and Sarah Neesham were married in the church of All Hallows, Barking.   How the news was received at Acton, how the young couple contrived to provide for the early years of their married life, history does not relate ; but a home to support and a rapidly increasing family must have been powerful incentives to Mr. Jeffreys to apply himself with all the vigour he possessed to the task of furthering his professional ambitions.

For eleven years Mr. and Mrs. Jeffreys led, we may hope, a happy and what should have been a prosperous existence.   Sarah was a good wife, and repaid her husband's generous act by constant affection and six children.

In the case of Jeffreys this story is almost too favourable to his character to be an invention, and displays generosity and good humour on the part of the Judge. There is no reason to doubt that in private life he possessed these qualities, if in a rather excessive degree ; the Merry Monarch took pleasure in his society, and, in spite of the large sums that must have passed through his hands, he died with considerable debts and few friends.

In 1668 Jeffreys had been called to the Bar ; in 1671, at the age of twenty-four, he was elected Common Serjeant of the City of London.   Even in those days of precocious success the rise was phenomenally rapid.   Mr. Jeffreys was reaping with a vengeance the reward of his assiduous cultivation of a City interest.   In the City Courts the favour of such magnates as Clayton or the Alderman namesake gave him the best start possible ; whilst the " bold presence, fluent tongue, audible voice and good utterance " bestowed on him by his anonymous biographer, show that he possessed attributes far more potent than interest to advance his fortunes.   The fame of his advocacy spread with such rapidity that he was " courted to take fees, breviates were thrust into his hands in the middle of a case by parties who perceived that things were going ill

with them."   Roger North would have us believe that at
this period Jeffreys resorted to a certain theatrical expedient
for the purpose of increasing his reputation.   His custom
was to go to a coffee house and sit among his friends, when
the following little drama would be enacted for their
edification.   To Jeffreys enters his clerk, who informs him
that company attend him at his chamber.   Jeffreys huffing
replies, " Let them stay a little ; I will come presently ; "
and the clerk takes his departure, amidst the respectful
admiration of the uninitiated.   The story is an old one,
the device conventional, and, one would have thought,
superfluous on the part of an exceptionally gifted youth,
with the purse and interest of a rich Alderman at his
disposal, and the good wishes of many of the citizens in
whose Courts he practised.   There can be little doubt
that it was by the agency of these latter resources, rather
than the vulgar expedients suggested by North, that Mr.
George Jeffreys attained so early in his career to the office
of Common Serjeant.

Lord Keeper North, in the few notes he has left on the
subject of Jeffreys, describes him as commencing with a
turbulent spirit against the Mayor and Aldermen, and
taking the part of the burgesses against them.   No evidence
is adducible in favour of this version ; and Roger North
admits it was the very opposite of his subsequent practice
when he had become a highflier for the Mayor's authority.
It is at the same time conceivable that Mr. Jeffreys,
by giving the Court of Aldermen a wholesome taste of
his turbulent ability in opposition, may have obliged that
body to hasten as quickly as possible the closing of his
mouth by the conferment of the Common Serjeancy.

Until within comparatively recent times, the acceptance
of the offices of Common Serjeant or Recorder of London
was not the termination of a legal career, as it usually is
to-day.   The recipient was not expected to give up his
practice at the Bar, and whilst sitting as a Judge in the City
Courts could as an advocate in the King's Courts at Westminster continue his search after still higher honours.

Had it been otherwise, Mr. Jeffreys would never have consented to confine his tireless ambition within the narrow limits of the Mayor's Court or the Old Bailey. Once Recorder—an office to which in due course of time he might reasonably aspire—he was well aware that he must look elsewhere for further promotion ; that, having given him the best legal prize in their possession, the City could minister little more to his desires, and that circumstances might arise in which the patronage and favour of the Corporation would operate as a serious bar to his bolder aspirations. At the time of his appointment to the Common Serjeancy, Jeffreys may well have observed the first signs of the preponderance among the citizens of London of that popular party which viewed with jealousy and suspicion the designs of the Crown and Court, and which less than ten years later was to break out into the most undisguised hostility to their measures. Symptoms of ultimate divergence between Crown and City made one fact clear to the mind of the Common Serjeant,—the occasion might arise when he would be obliged to choose between devotion to his present employers and adherence to his Sovereign. If he were to solve this problem by considerations of self-interest his choice could be easily determined. The Crown was the supreme fountain of honour and emolument ; the Recordership was the limit of City preferment. Not to miss the latter he must continue to cultivate the good graces of the citizens ; but to be Lord Chief Justice or Lord High Chancellor he must attach himself to the fortunes of him from whom alone such prizes might be obtained, and, if possible, so ingratiate himself with his Majesty as to be able, in the event of an open rupture between Court and City, to pass with profit and advantage into the service of the former. At this period a double policy of the kind adopted by Mr. Jeffreys was far easier of execution than it would have been a few years later. The anger and distrust which culminated in the Popish Plot pandemonium had not yet openly ranked the City on the popular side, and though a large section among its leaders regarded with dislike the mysterious policy of the King and his high-minded advisers, a certain measure of cordiality subsisted between the parties, and there were those in their councils who, from various motives, enjoyed the favour of the Court.

At the same time, setting aside motives of self-interest, Jeffreys' temper and character would incline him to enlist in the service of the Court rather than the popular party. His was an arbitrary habit of mind ; he hated factious sentiment and religious fanaticism, both of which were present in large quantities among the extreme malcontent section of the popular party. If he had ever indulged in republican sentiments, as some writers would imply, he had come to loathe them as men will their youthful excesses.

When anybody of no particular dignity, but filled with an overmastering desire to employ his hand and heart in the service of his Sovereign, wished to bring such a desire under the notice of his august master, the one unfailing conduit pipe down which the aspirant might slide into the presence of the Monarch was Mr. William Chiffinch, page, Secretary and Keeper of the King's Closet. This gentleman, " who had carried the abuse of backstairs influence to scientific perfection," is represented by Roger North (whose version we are now adopting) as the means by which Jeffreys proceeded to carry out his schemes for the future. One common failing rendered a union between these two great men almost inevitable. Mr. Chiffinch was an impetuous drinker, who never let any one depart from him sober, and whose business as a spy depended for its success on the secrets he drew by means of " saltiferous drops " from his stupefied victims. Mr. Jeffreys, as far as drinking capacity went, was one of his few rivals. It merely required the tiresome formality of an introduction to inaugurate that close friendship which is apt to grow up between " immane drinkers ; " and, in the intervals of pleasure, Mr. Jeffreys, who pretended to main feats with the citizens, could furnish much useful information about the intentions of the City malcontents, among whom he was in the habit of ranting about with great vehemence and posing as a highflier for the authority of Mayor and Aldermen. Little did the simple giants dream what a viper they were nourishing in their capacious bosoms ! or that in these backstair revels were being sown the seeds of that immoral union between King and Common Serjeant, out of which was to spring, in the fulness of time, the terrible and immortal nightmare known to the vulgar as " Judge Jeffreys " ! that now for the first time, with copious libations, the supplicant implored the prize of treachery, and in the wild passion of the devotee strove to forget the pains of worship !

Some such heightened impression is left on the mind after reading North's narrative of the rise of Jeffreys. Fierce and unquiet, the Common Serjeant is represented as drinking himself into the notice of the Court ; the scanty jottings of the Lord Keeper on his enemy's career are copiously illuminated by Roger's luxurious imagination.

But, whilst cheerfully admitting that at no period of his short life was abstinence in any way a natural or acquired element in Mr. Jeffreys' disposition, it will be edifying to indicate a few subtler methods than intoxication by which the Common Serjeant strove to advance his fortunes in the direction of the Court.

It is very possible that Jeffreys may have used Chiffinch as a means of introduction to Whitehall, or at least, in company with many better men than himself, have found it expedient to accept the hospitalities of the Clerk of the Closet. But if Jeffreys was desirous of a closer acquaintance with the Court party, his official position in the City must have afforded him many opportunities of carrying out his wishes. The City during the reign of Charles II. was a factor of considerable importance in domestic politics. Its extent was still practically conterminous with London itself, it represented with tolerable accuracy the general political feeling of the capital, and exercised control over the order and well-being of the citizens. Nothing is more conclusive of the consideration attached by the Court to its political attitude than the frequent attempts of the King to obtain supremacy in its councils, and the deliberate attack that was made upon its independence during the three years of despotism which closed the reign of Charles II.

When Jeffreys entered on his new office the Recorder Howel was a lawyer whose share in public affairs was strictly limited to the duties of his place. If, then, the Common Serjeant displayed to those of the Court party with whom he must have come in contact at the various City festivals a broader sense of the possibilities of his situation than was compatible with the mere discharge of his official functions, so much the better. At the houses of his friends Clayton and the " Great Smoker " he must have found ample occasion to bring himself under the notice of those for whom he could offer to perform the most useful services ; nor was the Court likely to let slip the chance of acquiring so able an intelligencer within the territories of a suspected and suspicious power.

Jeffreys was not slow to make the most of these facilities. A letter preserved in the British Museum proves that as early as 1672 the Common Serjeant was employed by the Government in business of a very secret and mysterious nature. The letter is addressed to Sir Richard Browne, the old and faithful Clerk of the Council, at his lodgings at Whitehall, and is dated from the Inner Temple, April 5th.

" Sir,—I have caused diligent search to be made from the beginning of 1668 till this time, and you may be assured there is none ; fear not ; keep all things close, excuse haste and the rudeness of this address, made by
" Your most faithful servant,
" George Jeffreys."

For what purpose this " diligent search " was made,, what this peculiarly secret errand, why Browne is exhorted to have no fear and keep all things close, it is impossible to determine ; and, as Jeffreys' duties were eminently confidential and unofficial, it is not likely that light will ever be shed on the nature of the transaction. From the very beginning of this year the Cabal Ministry had been engaged in cynically outraging the most cherished feelings of the nation. In January, the closing of the Exchequer had violated public credit ; in March, the Declaration of Indulgence, following closely on the public reception of the Duke of York into the Catholic Church, had confirmed the worst suspicions of earnest Churchmen ; later in the same month the national hatred of France was provoked by the combined attack of Louis and Charles on Protestant Holland. There was no doubt plenty of work to be done on which it was quite inexpedient that the fierce light of publicity should be allowed to shed its inconvenient rays. Charles was at home in schemes hidden from the world, and always retreating deeper into secrecy. ·Under the respectable conduct of Browne, Jeffreys was invited to follow the King into the innermost recesses of his clandestine politics.

Having placed the Common Serjeant at so early a date as 1672 on an intimate footing among the confidential agents of the Crown, it is easy to account for his subsequent connections with certain distinguished members of the Court. Very possibly through the medium of Browne, who had known her honest Breton parents in France, Jeffreys first became acquainted with Louise de Querouaille. This lady was proclaimed mistress of the King by the title of Duchess of Portsmouth in 1673 ; and from that date until his death maintained, in spite of extensive competition and vicious unpopularity, a lasting influence over the mind of Charles. A pretty baby face, a decent carriage towards the desolate Queen, and a happy knack of summoning immediate tears in moments of emergency, were the principal resources of her power. She seems to have betrayed a penchant for handsome and witty lawyers. Scroggs was a personal friend ; but he was close on fifty when she came into office. Jeffreys, who added the charm of youth to his physical and mental advantages, must be reckoned her prime favourite. Her interest in his fortunes was a matter of public knowledge, to which a lampoon of the period describing the Duchess thus courteously refers :—

> " Monmouth's tamer, Jeff's advance,
> Foe to England, spy of France,
> False and foolish, proud and bold,
> Ugly, as you see, and old."

It was a matter of course that his intimacy with the Duchess, purely platonic as far as we can judge, should have brought Jeffreys into contact with the Minister who in 1673 had succeeded to the power of the Cabal, for Lord Danby was commonly believed to have enjoyed the utmost favours of the new mistress. Danby is a typical politician of the Restoration period. His projected revival of the old Cavalier principles of Church and State was a high-minded and reasonable intention ; but his conscientious fidelity to a King whose only purpose, if he ever possessed one for any length of time, was to dispense, as far as possible, with that integral feature of our Constitution known as parliamentary control, foredoomed it to failure. In close association with these statesmanlike ideals Danby combined the most unblushing indifference as to his choice of means, an unworthy jealousy of intellectual equals and the conventional laxity in private morals. The success of his policy was to a great extent dependent on a system of bribery and espionage by which he sought to maintain a subservient majority in Parliament, and it was no doubt as part of this system that he accepted at the hands of the Duchess the services of her handsome young lawyer. From his point of vantage in the City the Common Serjeant was able to give useful information as to the intentions of the popular leaders, who vented against Danby all the discontent stirred in their minds by the shifty conduct of the King, and to warn his patron of contemplated attacks in the Lower House.

On February 15th, 1677, Parliament had met, after a fourteen months' prorogation, in no very gentle mood. On February 28th, Mr. Jeffreys is thus moved to address the Lord Treasurer. :—

"My Most Honoured Lord,—I did design an earlier trouble to your Lordship rather than to be thought unmindful of returning my dutiful acknowledgment of the many favours you were pleased to confer upon me : but there fell nothing within the narrow compass of my intelligence worthy your consideration, or wherein I could imagine you were much concerned. Nor do I at present find any such momentous design against your Lordship as should need affect the meanest of your thoughts. I only beg the favour to acquaint you with, what I doubt not but you have already been advertised of, that to-morrow there are some few (for I cannot understand, though I have been inquisitive, that there are many concerned in it) that design to try some reflections on your management of the Excise, and have been inquisitive in that affair in order thereunto ; it is not hoped the success will be great, but desire to know how it will relish in the House. . . . . . Did I conceive it worthy your trouble I should be more large in the intimation, but I cannot perceive that you are materially aimed at. My Lord, I humbly beg your pardon for this great(?) and confidence, being emboldened thereto by your great consideration and favour towards me ; and I beg leave to assure your Lordship that I will with all zeal and industry embrace all opportunities wherein I may manifest myself to be a loyal subject to my King.

"My Lord,

"Your Lordship's most grateful, faithful,

"and obedient servant,

"George Jeffreys." [1]

---

[1] The original of this letter was in the possession of the late Mr. Alfred Morrison.

This letter calls for little comment. It is couched in the fulsome and elaborate style usually adopted at that time by a client in addressing his patron. It explains as clearly as possible the relations between Jeffreys and Danby. That a young man with a career to make should adopt the profession of a political informer was in no way shocking to the unscrupulous spirit of the age. It would be idle, taking into account the strange admixture of honesty and dishonesty, principle and interest so frequently observed in the actions of these seventeenth century politicians, to refuse to admit that principle as well as interest had some share in the alliance between these two men, that Jeffreys' lifelong attachment to the cause of personal government and the Church of England sprang from something more than a vulgar desire for self-aggrandisement. Though Jeffreys ultimately went to lengths which Danby could not approve, we find him as late as the reign of James II. in close communication with that statesman. In the absence of any definite testimony it may not be unfair to assume that from Danby Jeffreys received his first schooling in practical politics, or at least formed a youthful admiration for the Treasurer's abilities. The old Cavalier spirit, that loved the Church and loathed the Dissenters, was well-calculated to attract the young Common Serjeant, and the importance of a strong union of King and Church was always present to the mind of Jeffreys as the surest foundation of arbitrary power.

By means of the subtle management of Danby the Session of 1677 passed off quietly. Shaftesbury and other peers of the country party were sent to the Tower, and the inevitable subsidy voted ; though, as Reresby phrases it, " it was much feared that some votes were gained more by purchase than affection "—the calm before the storm.

In the meantime Jeffreys might reasonably expect some reward for his pains and dangers. Whether the country interest in the City had grown suspicious of the Common Serjeant, or the influence of the Lord Treasurer had proved insufficient, Jeffreys did not receive the Recordership which fell vacant on Howel's resignation in 1676. It was in all probability his age—he was not yet thirty—that determined the electors more than anything else ; and the post was given to William Dolben, a sound independent lawyer and a son of the Archbishop of York.

But in the following year the Common Serjeant was to experience the first of the many honours ultimately conferred upon him by a grateful Sovereign. In September, 1677, Mr. Jeffreys was appointed Solicitor-General to James, Duke of York, and received the honour of Knighthood at Whitehall. At this period the Duke of York, much to the annoyance of Danby, had obstinately espoused the cause of the French alliance,—a proceeding which must have brought him into some sort of union with the Duchess of Portsmouth, who was always regarded by the public as the evil genius of the national degradation involved in such a policy. The Duchess was not slow to present to the Duke the young and intelligent lawyer, whose sprightly talents seem to have immediately impressed the heavy James. From this appointment dates Jeffreys' period of service to the future King James, which only terminated with the fall of the dynasty and his own destruction, and to which the former, whatever his motives, adhered with fatal fidelity.

Lord Campbell, with his singular penetration into the psychology of the defunct—a penetration which triumphantly o'erleaps those bounds of evidence and authority that hamper the proceedings of more timorous historians—tells us Jeffreys was silly enough to be much tickled by these marks of royal favour ; and describes how he apologised to his friends in the City for the honours done him by the Court. There is of course no authority given for these revelations. Nor was there any need for apology. The time had not yet arrived when Court favours were displeasing to the citizens ; on the contrary, they would only enhance the consequence of the Common Serjeant with a great number of the Aldermen.

Another year was to pass by, to our knowledge unevent-

ful, in the life of Jeffreys, and Sir George received a mark
of personal favour from the King so unmistakable that it
soon became the talk of the town, and the popularity of
the Common Serjeant in Court circles was impressed as an
undoubted fact on the public mind.   So well had things
thriven with Sir George, professionally and otherwise, that
he had been enabled to purchase a house in Buckinghamshire, at Bulstrode, where he subsequently acquired the
manor.   There, in August, 1678, King Charles, accompanied
by the Duchess of Portsmouth, did Sir George the honour
of dining with him.[1]   The proceedings during the meal
were marked by the utmost cordiality.   The King caused
his host to sit down, and drank to him full seven times.
We may be sure the host was not behindhand in similar
demonstrations of devotion towards his distinguished
guest, and displayed qualities and capacities which must
have outshone in the eyes of the genial monarch all the
sober achievements of the past.   After an evening such as
this, Sir George might fairly cherish the hope that henceforth there would be no service too intimate or too
questionable to be entrusted to the hands of one whose
disposition was so happily coincident with all that was best
and truest in that amiable good humour which served with
the second Charles in place of heart.   This Bulstorde revel
with its seven toasts hardly confirms Macaulay's statement
that Charles II. always regarded Jeffreys with scorn and
disgust, in opposition to the revengeful and obdurate
James, who was pleased to become his patron.   Next
morning London was full of the honour done to the
Common Serjeant, and the rumour spread that Jeffreys
was to be Recorder or Lord Chancellor of Ireland.   Needless to say that, if he was offered the choice, he preferred
remaining in London to an honourable exile in Dublin ;
and accordingly the necessary steps were taken to gratify
his wishes at the expense of others.   In October the
venerable Mr. Justice Twisden, of the King's Bench,
received a complimentary quietus and a pension of £500,

1 *Verney Papers*, Hist. MSS. Comm.

Jeffreys as Recorder of London. ætat 30.
after the painting by Kneller.
in the National Portrait Gallery.

Jeffreys as Recorder of London. ætat 30.
after the painting by Kneller.
in the National Portrait Gallery.

and the Recorder Dolben was set in his place. In the same month, "freely, unanimously and by scrutiny," the Common Serjeant was elected over the heads of three other candidates to the vacant Recordership. Whatever their political differences, the faithful City was in all probability only too pleased to have as their Recorder a courtier who so obviously basked in the sunshine of royal esteem.

Shortly after his appointment as Recorder Jeffreys made another appearance before the King, which, if anything else were necessary, must have completed the fascinating impression he had already made on his royal master. Certain persons had printed a Psalter called the "King's Psalter," in violation of the rights of the Stationers' Company. The Company haled them before the Privy Council, retaining Jeffreys as their advocate. The King presided at the Board, and, in the presence of Charles, Jeffreys thus described the conduct of his opponents. "They" (the printers of the piratical Psalter) "have teemed with a spurious brat, which being clandestinely midwived into the world, the better to cover the imposture they lay it at your Majesty's door." This cheeky allusion to the promiscuous paternity of his Sovereign pleased the King, for to him the subject was always a source of pride. He turned to the Lords on his side and said, "This is a bold fellow, I'll warrant him." Bold certainly, but not indiscreetly so. Pleasant evenings at Bulstrode had placed the Recorder on a familiar footing with his King ; and, though the jest was of surpassing impudence, Charles II. enjoyed impudence if it was witty.

In February of the same year Sir George had lost his first wife. But with rather suspicious haste the void created in his heart was promptly refilled. In May following he married Lady Jones, the "brisk young widow" of a Welsh knight, and daughter of Alderman Sir Thomas Bludworth, M.P., who had been Lord Mayor of London in the Plague year. Occurring as it does some few months before his election as Recorder, this alliance must have considerably strengthened his chances and augmented his interest in that direction. Unfortunately, the common gossip of the day saw fit to blacken this incident in the private life of the Recorder. It asserted that the brisk young widow had so far forgotten her moral and artistic feelings as to allow herself to be consoled during coverture by one Sir John Trevor, familiarly known as " Squinting Jack," "than whom no man ever had a worse squint." This Trevor was a barrister and a cousin of Jeffreys, to whom he owed such success as he had hitherto obtained. He was a sordid, avaricious fellow, but not lacking in boldness and cunning. How far the second Lady Jeffreys had yielded to the wiles of this plain man there is nothing but scandalous rumour to inform us. But things were not allowed to rest tamely at this point. The story goes that, on the premature birth of a child as the fruit of her union with Jeffreys, it became evident to the most casual student of the almanac that there had been a mistake somewhere. When a year or two later Jeffreys had made himself thoroughly unpopular with the city malcontents the discovery was made a theme for popular doggerel in the shape of a ballad called *The Westminster Wedding, or the Town Mouth*,[1] *alias the Recorder of London and his Lady*, in which Jeffreys is loaded with the customary abuse, and he and Chief Justice Scroggs are represented as quarrelling in their cups on the subject of Lady Jeffreys' accident.

> " They railed and bawled and kept a pother,
> And like two curs did bite each other,"

and are eventually consigned by the author to the gallows.

The exact truth of this scandalous story, like that of the many tales and anecdotes that form almost the only material for the history of Jeffreys' early years, cannot be ascer-

---

[1] At the trial of Francis Smith for libel, Feb. 1680, Jeffreys had described himself in his capacity of Recorder of London as the " Mouth of the City of London."

tained ; **nor** is it important that it should **be**. These stories must be taken together, without placing any too great reliance on their value in fact, and out of their general tenor some conception may be formed of the character of the man whose life they profess to illustrate, and whose personality must to a certain degree be reflected in tales of which he is the hero. After his appointment as Recorder, Jeffreys is brought actually before us ; we can read his own words, and the words of others about him whose authority is unimpeachable ; his history moves on surer ground. The reader will then be in a better position to appreciate how far these early stories have truly described or are the legitimate outcome of Jeffreys' personal character.

IV

THE RECORDER OF LONDON

1678

As Recorder of London Jeffreys falls for the first time under the notice of Lord Macaulay. It is with reluctance that any writer of history finds himself obliged to differ from a great historian ; but in justice to the memory of Jeffreys it is impossible to allow Macaulay's sketch of the Judge to pass unchallenged.

Macaulay gives a long description of the career and demeanour of Jeffreys, and justifies the violence of his language by quoting two instances in which the innate brutality of the man is strongly brought out. In the first place Macaulay's description of Jeffreys' personality is taken entirely from two authorities provedly hostile to the man they are describing. The first is the " Life and Death of George Lord Jeffreys," prefixed to a book called the *Bloody Assizes*, the work of a scurrilous enemy, and a low-class publication without any claim to authority. The second is the sketch of Jeffreys given by Roger North in the life of his brother Francis, the Lord Keeper of the Great Seal. At the outset of this work the reader has been cautioned against the untrustworthiness of North ; and sufficient reason has been shown why his treatment of Jeffreys was bound to be unfriendly, to say the least of it. Macaulay, by melting these two exaggerated narratives together in the crucible of his own sensational rhetoric, has produced a picture of Jeffreys which may be not improperly styled a caricature. Of the two examples of Jeffreys' judicial conduct quoted by Macaulay to justify his indignation, the one he treats without any attempt at a historical appreciation of the real circumstances of the case, the other he garbles in a manner that is indefensible from the point of view of an impartial treatment of authorities. If Macaulay's history was not so greatly admired and so widely read, if his picture of Jeffreys was not the one that is in the minds of most Englishmen, there would be no need to undertake the thankless task of correcting it.

Macaulay's first instance is the trial of Lodowick Muggleton, the founder of the religious sect of the same name, which took place at the Old Bailey in 1677, whilst Jeffreys was still Common Serjeant. This Muggleton is a perfect example of the ludicrously malignant fanatic, the outcome of the extravagant religious tendencies of the Puritan ascendency. His high cheekbones, narrow eyes and long, straight, murky hair speak the fierce inanity of the uncompromising devotee, who rejoices in religious excess for the opportunities it affords him to get on familiar terms with his Maker and hurry large consignments of his enemies to hell-fire and everlasting damnation. Muggleton and a man called Reeve styled themselves respectively the cursing and blessing prophets designated by St. John in the Apocalypse. On Reeve's death his duties as bestower of blessings reverted to Muggleton, who proceeded to distribute blessings and curses with an unsparing hand and on the least provocation, though his capacity would seem to have lain most effectively in the latter direction. The unlovely profanity of his proceedings at length attracted the notice of the authorities ; his house was entered and searched on a warrant of the Chief Justice Rainsford, "a deadly enemy," and Muggleton delivered into the hands of Satan. So blasphemous were the books found in his possession that it was thought fit to put him on his trial, which commenced at the Old Bailey on January 17th, 1677. Of this trial Muggleton has left an account in his *Acts of the Witnesses of the Spirit*, from which we shall freely quote.

"Following the example of Christ," Lodowick disappointed the expectations of thousands by remaining perfectly silent throughout the proceedings. His counsel, "a deceitful knave and fearful fool," declared himself ashamed to plead on behalf of so blasphemous a cause ; whereupon Muggleton complains with some reason that a counsel who has taken forty shillings to plead and then says he is ashamed of his client's cause, "hath no truth in him." But it may well be that the zealous advocate considered forty shillings an insufficient wage for imperilling his salvation by defending such shocking profanities. He accordingly satisfied his professional conscience by urging a technical point with regard to the date of the publication of the books found at the prisoner's house. This plea Chief Justice Rainsford, who presided, overruled ; whereupon Muggleton expresses a pious wish "that God would have executed visible and immediate judgment on him ; " but bears up against the disappointment caused by the passive attitude of Heaven in the face of his calls for intervention by the pleasing reflection that God purposely waited until a time when "the worm of conscience and hell-fire" should bring the Chief Justice to a rude sense of his shortcomings. In the meantime, unmoved by the supernatural dangers gathering over his head, Rainsford charged the jury, and described the prisoner to them as pernicious, blasphemous, seditious and heretical. Not to be outdone in his art of denunciation, Muggleton briefly dismisses the subject by stigmatising the Chief Justice as a "cursed devil."

The jury retired to consider their verdict, and Muggleton was taken into a small room. On returning into court he found that "bawling devil" Jeffreys on the bench, who called him an "impertinent rogue" because he did not grow pale or ask favour of the Court. A verdict of Guilty having been delivered, the Common Serjeant proceeded to sentence. He said that the Court were sorry the laws were so unprovided with fitting punishment for Muggleton's crimes, and that therefore the Court had decided to give him what he was pleased to term an " easy, easy, easy punishment." This easy punishment consisted in three days in the pillory in three places from eleven till one, a £500 fine with the alternative of Newgate until payment, and the burning of his books in the prisoner's presence. Macaulay forgets to add that Jeffreys was not passing his own sentence on Muggleton ; it was the sentence of the Chief Justice and the other Judges who had tried the case. As Common Serjeant of the City of London, Jeffreys merely acted as the mouthpiece of the Court in passing sentence on those prisoners who had been convicted before the King's Judges.

In his capacity as prophet Muggleton concludes his narrative by a general denunciation of his enemies and a particular declaration with regard to their respective futures. A large proportion of them appear to have died shortly after the trial. In one case his wife Mary, who on occasions seems to have acted as his understudy, delivered the sentence of damnation, and the unfortunate recipient died six weeks after. Rainsford, a very estimable person in private life, happening to die in 1679, is despatched " to join King Saul in hell, rejected of God and of Muggleton the last true prophet of God, where the hottest fire will be his portion." Thither he was followed a few months later by the Lord Mayor, whom Muggleton had " for some time known to be a devil."

But it was on Jeffreys that the fiercest torrent of the fanatic's wrath was to descend. Jeffreys was the only one of those upon whom Muggleton had desired God to execute visible judgment who had had the temerity to survive any length of time the prophet's maledictions. The prophet describes the Common Serjeant as " one of the worst devils in nature, although his voice was very loud "—the antithesis is mysterious. After paying him an unconscious compliment as an advocate by complaining that, be a cause never so just, he would be sure to baffle it and make squabbles, and wrangle it out, he goes on to express satisfaction that the laws of Heaven have thoughtfully provided him with eternal torments. Before the trial Muggleton knew him to be a reprobate and appointed of God to be damned ; but the trial has proved him an absolute devil in the flesh. "And he is accordingly recorded in the tables of Heaven for a reprobate devil, and here on earth and to the end of the world a Damned Devil."

Having thus irrevocably disposed of all his enemies Muggleton terminates his relation, and cheers the hearts of the faithful by the sublime prospect of himself and the deceased Reeve sitting upon thrones and judging all true believers and wicked despisers.

To any modern reader such a creature as Muggleton is merely ludicrous. It seems absurd to punish him or to take any serious notice of his proceedings. Nowadays he would be allowed a square of grass in Hyde Park, where he might rave his fill to the amusement of the casual bystander. But in the days of the Second Charles a spectacle of this kind was no laughing matter. Fanatics were taken seriously indeed ; for to the loyal mind fanaticism was associated with nothing but treason, rebellion and civil war. Nor were the Crown-appointed Judges likely to be behindhand in their detestation of such excesses. The words of Chief Justice Kelyng in Messenger's case fittingly describe the point of view from which the Bench regarded religious extravagance. "We are but newly delivered from rebellion first begun under the pretence of religion and the law, for the devil has always this vizard upon it ; that rebellion began thus, therefore we have great reason to be very wary that we fall not into the same error ; but it should be carried with a watchful eye." His predecessor Hyde, in sentencing Twyn to death for high treason, expressed the same feeling when he said : "There is nothing that pretends to religion that will avow or justify the killing of Kings but the Jesuit on the one side and the Sectary on the other." Horror of the late King's murder, a haunting fear of the recrudescence of rebellion among the more violent of the Sectarian remnant, and an intemperance of thought common to all men in a period when the fierceness of political passion swayed even the impartiality of legal proceedings, impelled Judges to indulge in violent language and violent punishments against all kinds of religious or political fanaticism. This state of feeling among a certain class must be constantly borne in mind in order to a right understanding of Jeffreys' career.

When these prejudices are properly considered, the Common Serjeant's rebuke of Muggleton as "an impudent rogue" and his "easy, easy, easy punishment" are no extraordinary examples of judicial heartlessness and brutality, but, by comparison with some of his contemporaries, would seem to err rather on the side of leniency. When Muggleton's own hand has furnished us with a vivid portrait of the murderous fury of his hatred and the blasphemy of his familiar assumption of Divine co-operation it is senseless to wonder or revolt at the severity of his treatment. The horror and alarm which the diatribes of the prophet must have inspired in the judicial mind of the seventeenth century are fearful to contemplate. That he was nearly killed with brickbats when he did eventually stand in the pillory, instead of being a cause of reproach against Jeffreys (who was only delivering the judgment of the whole Court), as Macaulay by the juxtaposition of his sentences would imply, is rather a proof of the indignation and dislike which the malevolent disposition of the prophet had excited among the populace of London. The tailor-prophet has left to posterity in his own bloodthirsty narration of his acts a complete answer to any charges of exceptional persecution on the part of his opponents.

Two months after Jeffreys' appointment to the Recordership his manner of performing his judicial functions is illustrated by another contemporary document. In Jeffreys' time it was part of the duty of the Recorder to pass sentence at the end of the Old Bailey Sessions upon all the convicted prisoners, who appeared in batches before him to receive their punishments and such admonition as the Recorder might think fit to address to them. There exists in the British Museum a printed report of Jeffreys' speech in performing this duty at the close of the Christmas Sessions of 1678. This is the second authority used by Macaulay to justify his portrait of Jeffreys.

On the prisoners being put to the bar, the Recorder commenced with a general declaration, in the course of which he regretted to see youth "arrived at such a height of debauchery notwithstanding the frequent examples found in this place;" but when he saw among them so many who, in spite of mercy shown, "persisted in so vile a habit of wickedness, it seemed to him absolutely necessary that judgment be speedily executed upon them." After recommending them to seek Christ, and to make the utmost use of the very little time left for the advantage of their immortal souls, Sir George addressed himself specially to one Russell, a bailiff, who had stabbed to death the brother of a woman he was trying to arrest for debt, because he had stood in his way. "You stand convicted of that most horrid crime murder, blood which cries out to Almighty God for vengeance, ... not only an offence against the law of God but even against Nature. . . . For if there were no such thing as a God in Heaven or justice upon earth, Nature itself teacheth a man not to be barbarous to his own likeness. Therefore it will become thee to use all the tears thou canst shed to wash away the blood thou hast spilt, and that will not be enough to take off thy guilt; for nothing but the precious blood of our dear and blessed Lord and Saviour, the Lord Jesus Christ, can save a man that is guilty of so great and horrible a wickedness as shedding innocent blood."

From Russell he turned to a young man of the name of Bradshaw, who had been convicted of treason in clipping coin. The youth and modesty of the lad had evidently made some impression on the Recorder's heart, for he begins: " I am sorry, heartily sorry, and very much lament to see a youth, in whom there seems to be so much modesty, far from persuading any one to believe that any manner of villainy should lurk under so promising and so good a face, come under the guilt of so great an offence." But the truth of it is that the apprentices of London have got into a trick of clipping coins and abusing their masters in other ways, and it is time an example were made. "It is a disease that will run through the whole flock. And I am sorry to see you the first sad, lamentable instance of that justice, which must pass against offenders of this kind, whose modesty should have prevailed on you not only to look like a virtuous boy but so to have acted." And the Recorder goes on with the evident hope that the modest lad may avail himself of the opportunity he is about to offer him. "But inasmuch as thou hast offended the law, it will become thee, if thou hast offended thy master or anybody else, to make them what reparation thou canst by making confession of thy offence, and discovering the parties that were concerned with thee, whoever they are. For there can be no better means of salvation in the next world or hopes of mercy in this world, than by confessing thy crimes, and telling thy accomplices ; and 'tis my advice, tell all thou knowest." With which reasonable counsel the Recorder passed sentence of death upon him.

Three men and seven women convicted of petty larceny were the next to claim the Recorder's attention. His speech to this batch must be given in full, as it is the instance chosen by Macaulay to display the hideous brutality of the Judge. "You, the prisoners at the bar, I have observed in the time that I have attended here, that you, pickpockets and shoplifters, and you other artists which I am not so well acquainted with, which fill up this place, throng it most with women ; and generally such as she there, Mary Hipkins, with whom no admonitions will prevail. They are such whose happiness is placed in being thought able to teach others to be cunning in their wickedness, and their pride is to be thought more sly than the rest ; a parcel of sluts who make it their continual study to know how far they may steal and yet save their necks from the halter, and are so perfect in that as if they had never been doing anything else. But take notice, you that will take no warning, I pass my word for it, if ever I catch you here again I will take care you shall not easily escape. And the rest of these women that have the impudence to smoke tobacco and guzzle in alehouses, pretend to buy hoods and scarves only to have an opportunity to steal them, turning thieves to maintain your luxury and pride ; so far shall you be from any hope of mercy if we find you here in the future that you shall be sure to have the very rigour of the law inflicted on you. And I charge him that puts the sentence into execution to do it effectually, and particularly to take care of Mrs. Hipkins, scourge her roundly ; and the other woman that used to steal gold rings in a country dress ; and, since they have a mind to it this cold weather, let them be well heated. Your sentence is that you be taken to the place from whence you came, and from thence be dragged tied to a cart's tail through the streets, your bodies being stripped from the girdle upwards, and be whipt till your bodies bleed."

Contrast with this Macaulay's version taken from the very paper in the British Museum of which the above is an exact reproduction : " When he has an opportunity of ordering an unlucky adventuress " (the woman Hipkins was a confirmed thief and trainer of thieves, " with whom no admonitions would prevail ") " to be whipped at the cart's tail, ' Hangman,' he would exclaim, ' I charge you to pay particular attention to this lady ! Scourge her roundly, man. Scourge her till the blood runs down ! It is Christmas, a cold time for madam to strip in ! See that you warm her shoulders thoroughly ! ' "

It would have been unfair enough to have quoted isolated passages from a speech of which the whole must be considered in order to do adequate justice to the parties concerned. But it will be seen that Macaulay, not content with this, gives an entirely imaginary version of the address, puts words into Jeffreys' mouth which he never uttered, construes the formal language of the sentence into a violent exhortation to the hangman to draw blood, and euphemistically describes an habitual offender of an incorrigible type as an unlucky adventuress. Whatever Jeffreys' character he is entitled to fair treatment, and in this particular instance he can hardly be said to have experienced it.

What are the facts of the case ? Jeffreys had before him a gang of hardened thieves, who, not content with stealing themselves, taught the inexperienced to do the same. He had already sat as a judge at the Old Bailey some seven years, when London and consequently its criminal classes were a much smaller community, and had known these prisoners of old as incorrigible rogues. The sentence he passed upon them bears no trace of peculiar severity to any one who realises the difference in the treatment of criminals that divides the seventeenth from the nineteenth century. The only portion of the address which can at all claim to arouse any feeling of surprise is the Recorder's recommendation that Hipkins and the stealer of gold rings be heated in the cold weather by the congenial method of the scourge, a rather unnecessary aggravation of their plight. It is only fair in this connection to quote the words of Mr. Pike in his valuable *History of Crime.* " It would be as great an error to suppose that impartiality and independence were the chief characteristics of juries, as that consideration for prisoners was commonly shown on the Bench at any time before the Revolution." In those days the idea of flogging a woman did not present by any means the same repugnance as it would to the modern mind. Macaulay himself describes how gentlemen used to make up parties to go to Bridewell and see the women whipped.

It would have been better for Jeffreys throughout his career if, when he condemned deserving criminals, he could have subdued an unfortunate sense of humour that too frequently betrayed him into expressions of undue satisfaction at the opportunity afforded him of giving them their deserts.   But that is very far from the " fiendish exultation," the " voluptuous titillation," the " luxurious amplification " of harrowing details which Macaulay tells us the sight of human tears and human misery invariably excited in his brutal nature, a description he justifies by garbling his authority.

The gang of petty thieves was followed by a soldier of the name of Momford. This man in a fit of intoxication had boasted that he was a Papist, that he hoped to see all Protestants drowned and to be at the burning of them.   Such folly might at any other time have passed unnoticed, but at the end of 1678 when the fury of the Popish Plot agitation was at its height, the silly bravado of an inebriate was quite sufficient to hurry its utterer into the dock.   " You, prisoner at the Bar," said the Recorder, " see now the great inconvenience that comes upon the debauchery of some people ; you that seem to have no religion in the world but when you are drunk.   But you must not think drunk or sober to revile the Protestant religion and go un-punished for it.   Let the times be thought never so dangerous, yet I hope it will always be seen that the magistrates of this City and Kingdom dare tell all mankind they do and will own the Protestant religion and dare curb the proudest He who shall presume to transgress our Laws or offer to reproach our religion.   And all the priests and Jesuits they shall never blow up any man to that height of impudence, as to dare to do anything in contempt of the government . . . . And so you shall find out who when you were drunk could brag you were a Papist and hoped to see Protestants burnt.   You are an excellent man no doubt at a faggot.   Your contempt is very great, and the Court is very sensible of it ; and that all the world may take notice how sensible they are and that you may see it shall not be sufficient excuse to say you were drunk when you did it," he fined him £100, committed him to

Newgate till payment, and ordered him on release to find sureties for good behaviour for seven years. Momford's revel cost him dear, but his case has a touch of comedy by the side of the dark events that were passing around him.

The last to claim the attention of Sir George were the brothers Johnson, who had signalised their enterprise and fraternal affection by proceeding in company to steal lead off the top of Stepney Church. In this instance the Recorder's sense of humour is pleasingly exploited for the benefit of these aspiring thieves. "You are brethren in iniquity, Simeon and Levi. I find you are not Churchmen the right way. But you are mightily beholden to the Constable ; if he had given you but half an hour time longer, you had been in a fair way to be hanged. Your zeal for Religion is so great as to carry you to the top of the Church. If this be your way of going to Church, it is fit you should be taken notice of. It is but a trespass, it is true, but I assure you one of the rankest that ever I heard of, it is Cozen-German to Felony. Are you not ashamed to have offered at the commission of such an offence in a Place whereto, if you were men that had any regard to a future state, you would pay a great reverence, because good men meet there to pray against such offences, not to commit them as you did." They were accordingly fined £20 each with commitment and sureties to follow.

This case concluded the business of the session. I have quoted the report of these proceedings at some length because they afford an excellent illustration of the manner in which Jeffreys performed the ordinary functions of his position, when his mind was undisturbed by any political or religious prepossession. By considering the report in its entirety, Jeffreys appears in a distinctly favourable light. It is not too much to say that, excepting in the one instance we have mentioned which is more offensive to our modern taste than to our reason, the Recorder's speech is unexceptionable. Its tone is moderate ; it is not, in one case at least, without a certain sympathy ; it is marked by much good sense and a powerful and original eloquence. The vehemence of expression, exaggerated in later years, is free from any violence or intemperance. It must be remembered that we are considering a century when the whole style of judicial language must appear unnecessarily fervid to a less passionate generation. The sedate and moderate Hale thought nothing of calling a man whose perjuries had excited his indignation, a "devil." The different tone adopted by Jeffreys towards the different prisoners as they came before him displays an insight into character, which he undoubtedly possessed ; and on one or two occasions he uses his sense of humour with wholesome and decent effect.

Henceforth, in following the fortunes of Sir George Jeffreys, it becomes necessary to follow the history of his time with which his success or failure is inextricably involved. Hitherto we have traced him by a faint and overgrown path of unreliable anecdote through the secrets of his advancement, which have been in a great part sufficiently clandestine to elude detection. It has been easier to correct misapprehension and falsehood than to establish new facts of great consequence. Excepting its rapidity his career, judged by the standard and the morality of his day, is neither remarkably noble nor strangely base. A man of his parts and temperament would have made his way quickly in any age, decently and respectably as things go in the nineteenth century, recklessly and questionably as things went in the seventeenth century. That Jeffreys should have joined the Court party was inevitable in a man of his disposition of mind ; that he should have acted in the secret service of the Crown was consistent with the air of mystery that clouds the proceedings of Court and country alike. That he chose the wrong side in the light of subsequent events accounts for much of the obloquy with which every portion of his career has been loaded. It is at the hands of Whig historians that Jeffreys has suffered most unmercifully. His victims, mostly Whigs, have been extravagantly canonised, whilst he, their judge,

has been **as** extravagantly damned as a violent Tory who
used the judgment seat to vindicate his political principles.
Jeffreys may be deserving of censure, even allowing for the
period in which he lived, and that censure may well come
most vigorously from the pens of Whigs. But no man
deserves misrepresentation, whatever his offences against
public feeling. During the agitations of 1678 and the
three following years the Whigs afforded Jeffreys an example of unscrupulous injustice in the cause of party
politics which unfits Whig writers, unless they are capable
of entirely emancipating themselves from an undue
attachment to their political party, to sit in judgment
even on Jeffreys.

V

THE POPISH PLOT

1678, 1679

WITH the commencement of the Popish Plot agitation in the August of 1678, the courts of law entered on a period of political activity which, if it has degraded them in the eyes of posterity, has given them an historical interest such as they have never enjoyed at any other time. Whilst party politics were still in a state of nature, whilst plot and counter-plot were the ordinary weapons of respectable statesmen, and political failure only too frequently implied exile or death, the courts of law were the convenient instruments by which the successful party procured the punishment of its opponents. The Crown, from its position of vantage, naturally had the best right to profit by the exertions of its chosen judges. But the sword was two-edged, and, when grasped by the hands of popular passion, could be wielded with irresistible effect even against its master. That the courts should have laid down their independence before influences of this kind was, from the nature of the case, inevitable. The independence and impartiality of the bench, even at the best of times, can only be secured by certain material guarantees, which were denied to the judges of the seventeenth century. No substantial wage, no impregnable independence subsidised their probity and braced their impartiality. Appointed by the King, at his will and pleasure they held their places : and on the convenience of their decisions depended their earthly salvation.   But it would be a serious error to suppose that upon this account the proceedings of the judges derived no consistency or sincerity from an honest indulgence in principles of some kind.   Principles they had in abundance ; but they were principles diametrically opposed to our modern conceptions of judicial conduct.   King's men, chosen from among the faithful, looking to the Crown as the fountain of all honour and authority, they regarded the maintenance of the royal supremacy against the dangers and perils of faction as a sacred duty, which the law imperatively called on them to fulfil.   The tone of the bench was almost invariably the tone of the Court, and the country-party were regarded as the sworn foes of law and order.   Thus His Majesty's judges were enabled to achieve that happy combination of principle and expediency which must be the harmless ambition of every conscientious man.   If it is kept in mind that the judicial ideal of Hale, to-day the rule, was in the seventeenth century the exception, the difficulty of a complacent understanding of the period about to be described is considerably diminished.

In the September of 1678 Titus Oates laid his first batch of revelations before the Privy Council, and told how the Papists were plotting the murder of the King, the burning of London, and the subjection of the realm to Papal authority.   Danby at first mistrusted the narrative, Charles treated it with the contempt of a man who knew the real truth.   Prompt action might have stifled the horrid development of the fabrication.   But the minister paused to consider the possibilities of the incident as political capital ; and two days after Oates's appearance the King went off gaily to Newmarket.   In the meantime Coleman, the Duke of York's Jesuit confessor, had been arrested on the strength of Oates's denunciation, and the discovery of certain incriminating letters, which he had neglected to destroy, roused the already apprehensive multitude to a pitch of terror and excitement that tore from the uncertain hands of Charles and his minister the further control or conduct of the agitation. It was "as if the very cabinet of hell had been laid open ; one might have denied Christ with less content than the Plot." The murder of Godfrey, the Justice who had taken Oates's depositions in October, stirred the populace to the last degree of fury. All the flimsy safeguards that two hundred years ago protected the reason and humanity of mankind against the fierce invasion of passion and prejudice were swept from men's minds, and the nation clamoured for vengeance against its imaginary foes.

To check the outbreak was impossible ; to neglect it, fantastic. Charles, on whose secret negotiations with Louis XIV. and the vague mistrust his duplicity had inspired lay half the blame of the popular frenzy, bowed before the storm and generously left to others more worthy than himself the honour of martyrdom for a faith which he seemingly preferred to any other form of worship. But there were those to whom an attitude of inert acquiescence was for different reasons inexpedient. Shaftesbury welcomed the fury of the outbreak as a powerful weapon of offence against the perfidious Court. Danby had at length made up his mind to combat his growing unpopularity and check the French intrigues of the King by joining the cry against the Papists. With all the arts of skilled intriguers, these two statesmen leant their countenance to the " Oatesian " disclosures, whose precise degree of truth or falsity they were probably unable or did not trouble to determine.

Towards the end of November, when the general excitement had laid hold of every class in the community, the trials of the prisoners arrested on the information of Oates and his disciples commenced in the Court of King's Bench. To the presidency of that court, as Lord Chief Justice of England, had succeeded Sir William Scroggs. His dissolute past and his professional ability have already been described. On the recommendation of his patron Danby, he had been appointed in 1676 a puisne judge of the Common Pleas. In the customary speech he delivered on taking his seat in court for the first time, he had enunciated with such force and eloquence the principles of loyalty, according to which he conceived it to be the duty of a judge to act, that Lord Northampton, present on the occasion, hurried from Westminster to Whitehall to assure the King that not one of the many hundred sermons he had caused to be printed since his restoration taught the people half so much loyalty as Sir William Scroggs' speech. Such a notable confession of faith and the continued favour of the Treasurer raised Scroggs to the Chief Justiceship of the King's Bench on the discharge of Rainsford in 1678. The character of this judge has generally received at the hands of posterity treatment only equalled, hardly surpassed, by that accorded to Jeffreys. The same violent maledictions, the same heedlessly inaccurate assertions have been his everlasting portion. Some of these inaccuracies, his vulgar birth, his lack of ability or education, have been already exposed. It only remains to inquire how far he has really deserved the indignation excited by his proceedings at the Popish Plot trials.

To the temperament of Scroggs the excitement of the Plot was a severe temptation to indulge his worst and exploit his choicest gifts. He possessed none of the qualities of a judge, but in an extreme form all the more passionate attributes of the advocate or the demagogue. The influence of judicial office, in a day when all judges were more or less political partisans, could exercise no control over his impetuosity. In his large build, his broad and comely visage, his wit and sagacity, in the wealth and boldness of his eloquence, Scroggs irresistibly suggests a seventeenth century " Stryver." His careless and dissolute habits, his " true libertine principles " were all encouraged with the same intense energy with which he had flung himself into the service of the King in the Civil War. Every day in his house was a holiday ; he was the equal in dissipation of the highest Court rakes. His love of wine amounted to a passion. He cannot live without claret, he can write of nothing else to his friend

Hatton, he rails against his women-kind because they drank up so passionately whatever wine is sent to him.[1] "He could not avoid extremities," says Roger North. "If he did ill, it was extremely so, and, if well, extremely also." This last admission of North argues that he cannot have been wholly bad ; very few men are, fewer than are vulgarly imagined by those who judge character from the sheer examples furnished in novelette or melodrama. Scroggs was a sturdy supporter of the royal cause from his earliest years, and had been ready to lay down his life for his sovereign. If he adhered on the bench to the same conception of duty, he can at least claim the merit of consistency, by no means too common a failing among his brethren. But, though his obtrusive loyalty has not enhanced his popularity with the good Whigs who have rent him so distressfully in their stately pages, it is not in this respect that he has to face the most serious charges. The real substance of the accusation against him is that he deliberately hastened to death with brutal and frequently illegal violence certain persons upon the strength of evidence which he must have known to be false ; and that he did so in order to secure himself in the office he was holding or to obtain yet further advancement. That Scroggs seized on the Plot agitation with indecent fervour is undeniably true ; but it was a passionate fervour ludicrous in a man who was acting a part from motives of self-interest or to win popular applause. He could have effected both these objects with half the rant and display which were as injudicious as they were superfluous. If he was consciously playing a part, then it was a most senseless piece of over-acting, and Scroggs, whatever his shortcomings, was no fool. To our ideas his treatment of the prisoners is shocking, his tirades cruel and indecent in a judge or advocate, but that Scroggs sincerely believed from the outset in the existence of the Plot, and that with all the strange vehemence of his ill-balanced judgment, it is impossible to doubt. At the

<hr>

[1] *Hatton Correspondence*, Camden Soc.

beginning of the agitation a belief in a widespread and malignant Popish conspiracy was universal and, under the circumstances, by no means unreasonable. There was hardly a judge on the bench who did not share that belief. With Scroggs such a belief speedily degenerated into a passionate and ruthless creed. If with this faith there mingled certain elements of vanity and self-interest, it must not be forgotten that such alloy has infected natures of a far purer and finer metal than that of the Chief Justice.

From the outset Scroggs threw himself with feverish energy into the detection of the reputed conspiracy. When in October Oates detailed his narrative to the eager and ready ears of the House of Commons, the Chief Justice was sent for to further examine the witness and take such depositions as might be offered. He at once fell in with the temper of the Commons and assured the House that he would use his best endeavours in the prosecution of the Jesuits, for he feared the face of no man, where King and country were concerned. The doors of the House were locked, and no one was suffered to go out. The Speaker's Chamber was placed at the disposal of Scroggs, whither he proceeded and took informations and issued warrants with becoming vigour. There is a smack of the martial ardour of the ex-cavalier captain in the militant activity of the Chief Justice.

The first of the Plot trials is that of Edward Coleman, the Duke of York's confessor, which took place in the Court of King's Bench at Westminster on the twenty-seventh of November, 1678. But, before entering upon the details of the proceedings, the reader should be furnished with some notion of the salient differences of criminal justice and procedure which separate the seventeenth from the nineteenth century. Without some notion of this kind the conduct of the actors cannot be rightly judged.

Sir James Stephen in his *History of the Criminal Law*, in criticising these trials, admirably sums up the conditions under which they took place. " The prisoner was looked upon from first to last in a totally different light from that in which we regard an accused person. . . . . In nearly every one of the trials for the Popish Plot, and, indeed, in all the trials of that time, the sentiment continually displays itself, that the prisoner is half, or more than half, proved to be an enemy to the King, and that, in the struggle between the King and the suspected man, all advantages are to be secured to the King, whose safety is far more important to the public than the life of such a questionable person as the prisoner. A criminal trial in those days was not unlike a race between the King and the prisoner, in which the King had a long start, and the prisoner was heavily weighted. . . . . The prisoner as soon as he was committed for trial might be, and generally was, kept in close confinement till the day of his trial. He had no means of knowing what evidence had been given against him. He was not allowed as a matter of right, but only as an occasional favour, to have either counsel or solicitor to advise him as to his defence, or to see his witnesses and put their evidence in order. When he came into court he was set to fight for his life with absolutely no knowledge of the evidence to be produced against him. . . . . That the prisoner's witnesses were not permitted to be sworn was even in those days considered as a hardship, and the jury were told in all or most of the trials to guard against attaching too much weight to it." There was in the seventeenth century an entire absence of any sort of conception of the true nature of judicial evidence. There seems to have been a prevailing impression among lawyers that, if a man came and swore anything whatever, he ought to be believed, unless directly contradicted. The principle that the uncorroborated evidence of an accomplice should not be acted on, was practically unknown. Judges considered them as bad men, but necessary to the discovery of crime ; juries attached a mechanical value to their oaths. "The inference suggested by studying the trials," adds Sir James, "for the Popish Plot is not so much that they show that in the seventeenth century judges were corrupt and timid, or that juries were liable to party spirit in political cases, as that they give great reason to fear that the principles of evidence were then so ill understood, and the whole method of criminal procedure was so imperfect and superficial, that an amount of injustice frightful to think of must have been inflicted at the assizes and sessions on obscure persons of whom no one ever has heard or will hear. A perjurer in those days was in the position of a person armed with a deadly poison, which he could administer with no considerable chance of detection."

Under these circumstances, so little conducive to the administration of perfect justice, and in an atmosphere charged with the popular terror and exasperation, the unfortunate Papists were haled to the bar to take their trials.

Scroggs had already given a foretaste of the spirit in which he proposed to direct the due course of law. Six days before Coleman's trial he had disposed of one Stayley, a Catholic goldsmith convicted upon bare but uncontradicted evidence of threatening to kill the King. In his charge to the jury, after dealing with the facts of the case, the Chief Justice violently and irrelevantly assailed the Jesuit doctrines, and laid particular stress on the fact that, " when a Papist once hath made a man a heretic, there is no scruple to murder him," a conception of Romish doctrine much relied upon at the time to explain the murderous schemes attributed to apparently inoffensive Roman Catholics. Scroggs dearly flattered himself on his insight into the subtleties of Jesuit casuistry and never lost an opportunity of expatiating on the mischievous fallacies of the Romish faith. He goes on to ask to be excused if he is a little warm, " when perils are so many and murders so secret," but reflects with some show of sense that " it is better to be warm here than in Smithfield." Papists, who murder heretics, think they become saints in heaven. " I hope I shall never go to that heaven, where men are made saints for killing kings." The extraordinary thing is that in another part of his summing up the Chief Justice had told the jury to pay no attention to the rumours or disorders of the time, but to let their verdict depend on the evidence alone. On that evidence alone he could have easily obtained a conviction, so that his theological discourse served no purpose whatever. But Scroggs was one of those men cursed with what is vulgarly known as "the gift of the gab," and no sense of justice or propriety could prevent him, once started, from plunging headlong into the excitement of an oratorical parade.

Coleman's trial was to derive additional interest from the fact that on this occasion Titus Oates was to make his first public appearance as a witness. Oates is perhaps the most entirely hideous nightmare that the distraught credulity of man has ever evoked from the depths. His fantastic turpitude provokes at times a suspicion of insanity. In his distorted nature sexual and moral perversion joined in friendly rivalry. From earliest youth his passion for notoriety found expression in the invention of startling falsehoods ; in various ways he rendered himself impossible to all who came in contact with him. It was in revenge for his expulsion from the Jesuit College at St. Omer's, which had taken him in out of pity and charity, that he invented the Popish Plot ; for his hatred knew no bounds. He invariably covered with lewd and blasphemous abuse any who happened to offend him ; the English, the Romish Church, all alike suffered at different seasons. But perhaps the most remarkable circumstance about Oates, was the mirthful confirmation which his moral ugliness derived from his physical aspect. "He was a low man, of an ill cut, very short neck ; and his visage and features were most particular. His mouth was the centre of his face ; and a compass there would sweep his nose, forehead and chin within the perimeter." North's mathematical process admirably defines his long flabby countenance.

At the present juncture Oates had every reason to be content. His passion for notoriety and his arrogant vanity were simultaneously gratified. Hailed as a saviour by nation and Parliament, he lodged at Whitehall, surrounded by guards, at an annual pension of £1,200. He had assumed the robes and title of a doctor, preached to enthusiastic congregations, got a blazon from the Heralds' College, and gave sumptuous entertainments on his blazoned plate. At his elbow stood his robed counsel learned in the law ; Dr. Jones was honoured with the care of his health. His indiscretion knew no bounds ; in his usual discourse he abused the Duke of York and the King's wife and mother to whomever he met. No one dared to contradict him ; for at such a season the power of the wanton perjurer was limitless.

So inspiring a prospect as that of Oates's glorious regeneration was bound to induce others to follow his example. But none of the disciples approached the master's original personality. Bedloe, a man of magnificent appearance, was indeed the merrier, though not the greater rogue of the two. He was a vulgar sharper, whose whole life had been spent in cheats of different kinds. "His life," says L'Estrange, "had been that of a wild Arab upon the prey and the ramble. It was a congruous preparatory to the consummated state of a flagitious miscreant." The plot perjuries were but the climax to a career of progressive crime. He also was lodged and guarded in Whitehall, gave out that his father was a major-general of good Irish family, and lent his name to a dramatised version of his lies, entitled *The Excommunicated Prince, or the False Relique.*

The evidence of these two rascals was to form a portion of the case against Coleman. But the unfortunate man had himself furnished the Crown with far stronger evidence of his guilt. The intellectual power of Coleman was by no means commensurate with his lofty ambitions. Filled with misplaced confidence in the prospects of a Catholic restoration in England and his own ability to assist in effecting the same, he entered into a lengthy correspondence with Père La Chaise, the French King's confessor, on the subject, and, as a prospective Secretary of State, drew up elaborate documents by which Parliament was to be dissolved and other necessary measures carried out, when the supreme moment arrived. Some of these letters and drafts, which he had omitted to destroy at the time of his arrest, were mainly instrumental in causing his conviction. Worn out by the excesses of his religious observances, his sad sunken eyes and lean withered countenance set off with ghastly pallor by his black peruke, Coleman would have filled impartial minds with nothing but pity for a weak misguided zealot. But the excited Court that professed to judge him, saw in his wasted features nothing but the bloodless ferocity of the unscrupulous Jesuit.

The conduct of the prosecution was entrusted to Sir William Jones, the Attorney-General. "Bull-faced Jonas" was a profound lawyer, with a great opinion of his own learning and a supreme contempt for the ignorance of others, "so that in speaking as counsel one might mistake him for the Judge." His disposition was rough, sour and suspicious, though at bottom he was a good and faithful friend. A steady opponent of the Court, he threw himself with apprehensive zeal into the prosecution of the Plotters, and ordered all the billets of wood in his cellar to be removed into the yard, lest they should serve as fuel for the fireballs which he fondly believed the Papists intended to fling into his house.

The Solicitor-General, Sir Francis Winnington, Serjeants Maynard and Pemberton, and Mr. Recorder Jeffreys, also took part in the prosecution. High in the favour of the Court, Sir George was briefed for the Crown in the greater number of the Plot trials, excepting those which took place at the Old Bailey. There in his capacity as Recorder of London he sat on the bench with the Lord Mayor and the other Judges.

The trial commenced at nine o'clock in the morning. The Recorder having opened the indictment, and Maynard recapitulated the facts of the case, the Attorney-General addressed the jury. By way of exciting them to an impartial hearing of the case, he suggested that ever since the Reformation the Jesuits had been plotting against the peace of the realm ; but that now they had definitely directed their efforts against the life of the King. "No doubt they would have been glad that the people of England had had but one neck ; they knew the people of England had but one head, and therefore they resolved to strike at that." He remarked with considerable truth on the foolish vanity of Coleman who, he said, had saved them much labour ; "he hath left such diligent and copious narratives of the whole design under his own hand, that reading them will be better than any new one I can make."

At the conclusion of the speech Coleman asked the Court to allow him counsel, but according to the custom of the time was refused. He then called attention to the violence of the prejudice raging against all Papists, and the consequent difficulty that justice had "to stand upright and lie upon a level." Scroggs answered that he should have a "fair, just and legal trial," the fairness and justice of which he proceeded to ensure by boasting that they were not going to do to Coleman as he would do to them, "blow up at a venture" and kill people because they are of a different persuasion. "We seek no man's blood, but our own safety."

After some vain attempts of the Chief Justice to draw certain admissions from the prisoner, Oates was called. Jeffreys rose and desired that the witness should not be interrupted in his evidence, to which the Court consented. But, before Oates commenced, Scroggs with great earnestness exhorted him to speak the truth. "You are to speak the truth and the whole truth ; for there is no reason in the world that you should add any one thing that is false. I would not have a tittle added for any advantage or consequences that may fall, when a man's blood and life lieth at stake ; let him be condemned by truth ; you have taken an oath, and you being a minister, know the great regard you ought to have of the sacredness of an oath, and that to take a man's life away by a false oath is murder, I need not teach you that." Grateful no doubt for the admonition and the excellent intentions that prompted it, Oates did not see his way to alter his previous determination, and entered confidently on his narrative.

His first acquaintance with the prisoner had begun in the November of 1675. At that time he had carried a letter from Coleman to Père La Chaise acknowledging certain instructions from La Chaise relative to the employment of the sum of £10,000 in a design for cutting off the King of England. Three years passed and Oates saw nothing more of Coleman until the April of 1678, when he found his friend in a condition of the most bloodthirsty activity. On the 24th of April the London Jesuits held a consult at the Whitehorse Tavern in the Strand. There it was decided that two men of the name of Pickering and Grove should be hired to shoot the King. Grove was to have £1,500 for the job; but Pickering " being a religious man " preferred thirty thousand masses at twelve pence a head. Coleman was not present at the consult, but a few days later received the news of their spirited resolution with great satisfaction. In sundry letters on the subject he suggested that it would be an excellent thing to trepan the Duke of York into the plot for murdering his own brother. In the same month Oates again met Coleman in the chambers of a Mr. Langhorne, a barrister in the Temple. Langhorne was an honest and learned lawyer and a very bigoted Catholic. In his room Oates saw a number of commissions from Paulus d'Oliva, the General of the Society of Jesus. These commissions were addressed to all the chief Catholics in England and appointed them to the various offices they were to hold when the plot should have been successful. Lord Powis, who was perpetually ill of the gout, was to be Lord Treasurer; Lord Bellasis, who was so infirm that he could hardly keep his feet, Lord General. The army was entrusted to the most efficient hands. Mr. Howard, a brother of Lord Carlisle, was appointed a Colonel; at the time of his appointment he was playing cards every day and dying of gout at Bath. "Major-General" Sir Thomas Ratcliffe, in spite of the honour done him and the apparent responsibilities of his position, had never left his home in the North all the summer. In Oates's presence Langhorne handed Coleman his commission as Secretary of State, the latter remarking it was a good exchange. Coleman considered that he must show some return for the "good exchange," and accordingly in July he is found once more plotting the removal of the King. This was at the house of Mr. Ashby, an ex-rector of St. Omer's. Mr. Ashby was on the point of removing to Bath to join "Colonel" Howard in the gout cure. On the eve of departure he sent for Coleman and told him that if Pickering and Grove missed fire, Sir George Wakeman, the Queen's physician, was to be offered £10,000 to put poison in the royal physic. However, for some unexplained reason July passed and nothing happened. Coleman grew restless at this inaction. In August he was present at a consult of Jesuits and Benedictine monks at the Savoy. It was then resolved that four Jesuits should go over to Dublin and murder the Duke of Ormond, the Lord Lieutenant. But this was not enough for the eager Coleman. He wished to make assurance doubly sure, and proposed that a desperate Irishman of the name of Fogarthy should be sent over to poison the Duke, in case the four Jesuits miscarried. Fogarthy's services were ultimately declined, and Coleman was compelled to seek other means of carrying out his murderous intentions. Fogarthy agreed to hire four ruffians, his fellow-countrymen, who should go down to Windsor and kill the King. Arrived there the hired assassins would seem to have been for the moment in a position of financial embarrassment. With a liberality that would have done credit to any melodrama, Coleman sent them £80 by special messenger. But in spite of this liberal aid the attempt broke down and, by the end of August, Oates had divulged the conspiracy.

Oates concluded his interesting testimony by impudently remarking that he could give other evidence, but would not, because of other things not yet fit to be known. The Court allowed the statement to pass unchallenged. Scroggs certainly subjected Oates to a searching cross-examination, and seems at times to have seriously doubted his credibility. But as he had little to go upon save the uncontradicted inventions of the witness himself on a subject the real truth of which could only be known to a few incriminated persons, it is not surprising that he was unsuccessful in seriously shaking the informer's evidence. His attempt only serves to demonstrate the unfortunate circumstances that in those days hampered the detection of the simplest perjury.

Coleman fared better in his essay at cross-examination, for though he had shown little ability in the conduct of his defence, he knew something of the facts Oates professed to reveal. The chief point he established was that when on the 30th of September he was confronted with Oates before the Privy Council, the latter swore he did not know him, and had not then volunteered any of the evidence he now gave against him. Oates retorted that his sight was bad by candle light, that he was very tired at the time, and that he was not going to give Coleman a chance of supplanting his evidence by letting him know it beforehand, a most convincing reason ! Sir Robert Southwell, a member of the Council, came to Oates's rescue and said that in Coleman's presence Oates had mentioned before the Council the offer of money to Wakeman to poison Charles. But it is strange that when put to it, Oates should not have recollected the circumstance for himself. Scroggs however seemed to consider Southwell's evidence as a striking proof of the informer's veracity.

Bedloe, following Oates, swore to having carried letters between Coleman and La Chaise in 1675. Further, he said that in May 1677 he was at Coleman's house behind Westminster Abbey. Coleman was standing at the foot of the staircase talking to Harcourt, the Jesuit Rector of

London, and Bedloe heard him say that, if there were a hundred heretical Kings to be deposed he would see them all destroyed.

Coleman in answer contented himself with solemnly protesting that he had never seen Oates or Bedloe before they had been produced as witnesses against him. Bedloe insolently replied:—"You may ask that question, but in the Stone Gallery in Somerset House, when you came from a consult, where were great persons, which I am not to name here, who would make the bottom of your plot tremble ; you saw me then." Somerset House being the residence of the Queen, herself a Papist, this veiled declaration was dangerously impudent. To such a pitch had the unwonted elevation of the informers excited their presumption that, when crossed or contradicted, they did not hesitate to vent their spleen upon those whose proximity to the throne might have been expected to screen them from their accusations.

This evidence was followed by the reading of Coleman's letters and papers. It is unnecessary to reproduce them in full ; for they are long and tedious. They consist of certain letters to Père La Chaise, imaginary declarations with regard to the dissolution of Parliament drawn up by Coleman in his capacity as a prospective Secretary of State. One quotation will be sufficient to show to what extent they justified his conviction. " We have here a mighty work upon our hands, no less than the conversion of three Kingdoms, and by that, perhaps, the utter subduing of a pestilent heresy which has domineered over a great part of this Northern world a long time. There never were such hopes of success since the death of our Queen Mary as now in our days, when God has given us a Prince who has become (may I say a miracle ?) zealous of being the author and instrument of such a work. That which we rely upon most, next to Almighty God's providence and the favour of my master the Duke, is the mighty mind of his most Christian Majesty." When this letter is considered, the bigotry of its tone and the hopefulness of its assertions, the confirmation it must have given to the worst suspicions of the nation and the revelation it contained that there were traitors even in the highest places, much of the cruelty and violence that followed its publication is rendered not only intelligible, but, in the temper of the times, excusable. Coleman had dealt with his own hand the most fatal blow at the security and liberty of his co-religionists, and lent the most convincing support to the lies of Oates and Bedloe. After the reading of the letters, Coleman tried feebly to prove an alibi, which only made his case worse. He followed up this failure by joining in a weak and irritating argument with the Chief Justice. Scroggs, evidently considering that after the letters there was little more to be said, impatiently exclaimed, " What kind of way and talking is this? You who have such a swimming way of melting words, that it is a troublesome thing for a man to collect matter out of them, you give yourself up to be a great negotiator in the altering of Kingdoms, you would be great with mighty men for that purpose, and your long discourses and great abilities might have been spared." Coleman still stuck to the alibi and asked the Chief Justice to send for a certain entry book. Scroggs, unwilling to uselessly prolong the case, replied : " If the cause turned upon that matter, I would be well content to sit until the book was brought, but I doubt the cause will not stand on that foot, but if that were the case it would do you little good."

Scroggs turned to the jury. He commenced his charge by dealing with the letters, and told them that only one construction could be put upon them, and that fatal to the prisoner. Having disposed of all relevant topics, he invited the jury to follow him in a short theological discourse on his favourite subject, the folly and villainy of the Romish Church. He said that nowadays any cobbler could baffle in argument any Romish priest, and that only two things could make a man give up the Protestant for the Catholic faith, interest or gross ignorance. As Coleman was an educated man, the former motive had prevailed with him. "Your pension was your conscience and your Secretary's place your bait." Then followed an eulogy of King Charles the First, who, he said, could have defended the Protestant religion against any of the Cardinals at Rome. "And when he knew it so thoroughly and died so eminently for it, I will leave this characteristic note. Whosoever after that departs from his (King Charles's) judgment, had need have a very good one of his own to bear it out." After stating the faggot and the dagger to be the Papist methods of conversion, and treating the jury to two Latin quotations he concluded : "Our execution shall be as quick as their gunpowder, but more effectual. For the other part of the evidence which is by the testimony of the present witnesses, you have heard them. I will not detain you longer now, the day is out."

Mr. Justice Jones filled up the Chief Justice's omission by adding, "You must find the prisoner guilty or bring in two persons perjured." Scroggs offered to wait for the verdict of the jury, if they would not be long. It was now five o'clock, and the trial had lasted eight hours, without an interval of any kind. The jury answered : "We shall be short," and withdrew from the bar. After a brief space they returned with a verdict of "Guilty," and Coleman was put back, to come up for judgment the following morning.

On his re-appearance before the Court next day the Chief Justice addressed the prisoner in a speech remarkable for the dignity and consideration of its feeling. The earlier portion of it contained comments on the grievous sins of Popish doctrine but no personal reflections on the prisoner himself, only an exhortation to further confession. The latter part of the address extorted from Coleman a sincere expression of gratitude for its charitable and Christian spirit ; but the unfortunate man, whilst humbly confessing himself guilty of many crimes and some failings and defects, swore as a dying man that he had no more to confess. This, Scroggs said,

he could not believe, but that in any case his own papers
had convicted him.   On Coleman asking permission to
see his wife and friends in prison, Scroggs answered him
in words which perfectly illustrate the condition of the
Chief Justice's mind, and no doubt the minds of all those
concerned with him in the trial.   " You say well, and it
is a hard case to deny it ; but I will tell you what hardens
my heart, the insolencies of your party (the Roman Catholics, I mean) that they every day offer, which is indeed a
proof of their plot, that they are so bold and impudent,
and such secret murders committed by them as would
harden any man's heart to do the common favours of
justice and charity, that to mankind are usually done.
They are so bold and insolent, that I think it is not to
be endured in a Protestant kingdom, but for my own
particular, I think it is a very hard thing for to deny a
man the company of his wife and friends, so it be done
with caution and prudence.   Remember that the Plot is on
foot, and I do not know what arts the priests have, and
what tricks they use ; and therefore have a care that no
papers nor any such thing, be sent from him.   But for
the company of his wife and friends, or anything in that
kind that may be for his eternal good, and as much for
his present satisfaction, let him have it, but do it with
care and caution—Mr. Richardson (addressing the keeper
of Newgate), use him as reasonably as may be, considering
the condition he is in."

On the third of December, firm in his faith, and, it is
said, grievously disappointed that his great friends had
not found it in their hearts to obtain his pardon, Coleman
was hanged, drawn, quartered and disembowelled according
to law.

If all the Popish trials had been conducted in the spirit
of Coleman's, if all the convictions had been as justifiable
as his, there would be little ground for surprise or indignation.   Under his own hand the foolish vanity of the
prisoner had written his own condemnation.   In the
absence of all cross-examination and in the then defenceless

condition of an accused person, deprived of all legal assistance and ignorant of the evidence to be given against him, the weak points in Oates's testimony could only be laid open as his story was made more public, and his narrative exposed to more searching criticism. It has been suggested that Scroggs, in omitting to notice Oates's and Bedloe's evidence to the jury in the course of his charge, implied thereby a disbelief in their veracity. But it must be remembered that it was late when the Chief Justice commenced his summing up, that the Court had been sitting without intermission for eight hours, and that Scroggs had frequently remarked that he considered the prisoner's letters as quite sufficient evidence to ensure conviction. In sentencing Coleman, he went so far as to cite Oates as establishing certain facts against the prisoner. He had moreover subjected the witness to a severe cross-examination without appreciably shaking his testimony, and regarded Coleman's successful exposure of Oates's inconsistency as in a great measure discounted by Southwell's evidence.

If to the Chief Justice or any man further confirmation was needed for the wildest fabrications of the impostor, was it not found in the dangerous menaces, the sanguine treason of Coleman's fatal correspondence? Was it any longer possible to doubt the extent and extravagance of a plot that presumed to look for its accomplishment to him in whose name its conspirators were being hurried to the scaffold? Could the Chief Justice have lighted upon a more righteous or legitimate theme for the exercise of his oratorical energy? Little wonder that in the presence of his own and the public indignation he hewed the Catholics " as Scanderberg the Turk."

The conviction and execution of Coleman only served to feed the public passion which cried with a loud voice for unremitting vengeance on the murderous Papists. " The populace," says Roger L'Estrange, " mellow as tinder to take fire on the least spark, ran amuck at Christianity itself and bore down everything that stood in their way betwixt this and hell. There never was such a competition betwixt Divine Providence on the one hand and the World, the Flesh and the Devil on the other for the preserving or destroying of a nation." The Commons in a burst of sweeping apprehension ordered all Papists to be secured, and Oates with a force of constables at his heels laid hold of as many as the capacity of his inventive powers would allow. As a fruit of his zeal at the December sessions at the Old Bailey, a batch of five Jesuits charged with attempting to murder the King and introduce Popery into the realm presented themselves for a fair trial. Jeffreys attended on the bench in his capacity of Recorder, but Chief Justice Scroggs with the Chief Baron Montagu and his brothers Bertie and Atkyns came down from Westminster to conduct the business. The agitation was thriving merrily. It was a veritable season of believing. Oates was declared the "Saviour of the Nation," people fled from him as from a blast, " for whom he pointed at was straightway taken up." Robed in silken cassock, he sat at the tables of bishops and prated of all persons, high and low, with insufferable insolence. His coarse virulence was hailed as the candour of a plain blunt man, his saucy impudence as the pardonable eccentricity of a hero.

Of the five prisoners, one of them, Ireland, was a Jesuit priest and a member of an old Yorkshire family. He was related to the Penderells of Boscobel who had sheltered Charles II. after the battle of Worcester, and one of his uncles had been killed in the Civil War fighting for King Charles I. But such antecedents availed him little against the violence of the times. Oates laid hands on him and with Whitebread, the Jesuit provincial, two other priests of the names of Fenwick and Pickering, and a Catholic gentleman of the name of Grove, he was flung into Newgate. There the unfortunate men were entrusted to the loving care of the keeper, Captain Richardson, who, in his anxiety for their safety, loaded them with bolts and chains to such an alarming extent that Fenwick was very nearly obliged to have his leg amputated. In vain Ireland's sister used every exertion of which a woman was capable to prepare her brother's defence. Seeing that the prisoners were not permitted to see anybody or send for any witness, her efforts were not unnaturally attended with little success. Oppressed by every disadvantage that could beset an accused man, unassisted by knowledge or experience, these five prisoners were expected to combat all the manifold resources which await the service of passion and injustice when they select the due process of law for the destruction of their victims.

Oates's story at this trial was similar to that he had told at Coleman's, but was embellished by certain lively details which had happily occurred to his mind during the interval. Pickering and Grove were the men who at the now famous consult of April 24th, at the tavern in the Strand, had been told off to murder the King. After all the prisoners had, in Oates's presence, signed the resolution which had been passed to effect that object, Pickering and Grove had hallowed their bloody emprise by taking the sacrament. Not that these two gentlemen were seriously disturbed in mind by the hazard of their attempt. For years they had followed the monarch with fell intent, but ill success. At last in the March previous to the consult, a favourable opportunity had presented itself, but alas! at the supreme moment of realisation, which was to crown with achievement these years of lurking ambush and fruitless search, Pickering discovered something wrong with the flint of his pistol and durst not fire. When he got home, his excuse was considered quite insufficient, and Whitebread prescribed for him thirty strokes of discipline. During May and June, Oates said he had often seen the assassins skulking about in St. James' Park with their huge screwed pistols, cumbrous weapons of a size between an ordinary pistol and a carbine. Out of compliment to the victim these pistols were loaded with silver bullets, which Grove, in merciless mood, had wished to have champed, that they might inflict incurable wounds. In

June, Oates was in the full confidence of the plotters, and Ashby, the gouty rector, had done him the honour to consult him as to the relative merit of pistol, dagger or poison as means of removing Charles. Oates, whose leanings were always rather towards the subtle than the artless, recommended poison. July passed by uneventfully ; but in August the good faith of Oates began to be questioned in the Jesuit camp, and one evening in that month the informer had the imprudence to call on Whitebread at his lodgings. He found the Provincial at supper, but the latter rose immediately from his meal, welcomed him with reviling and affront and gave him a sound thrashing. A subsequent attempt to assault and murder the false disciple unfortunately miscarried.

These were the most important details with which Oates now clothed the skeleton of his original narrative. Scroggs, who was full of his usual assurances of a fair trial, invited the prisoners to answer the witness. Grove protested that he had only met Oates two or three times in his life, and that his chief recollection of their meeting was confined to a temporary advance of eight shillings which he had made to Titus, and which Titus had apparently omitted to refund. Fenwick, however, reimbursed Grove for his loss ; the rest of the transaction may be quoted from the report of the trial.

Lord Chief Justice.—Were you of his (Oates's) acquaintance, Mr. Fenwick ? Speak home, and don't mince the matter.

Fenwick.—I have seen him.

Lord Chief Justice.—I wonder what you are made of ; ask an English Protestant a plain question and he will scorn to come dallying with an evasive answer.

Fenwick.—I have been several times in his company.

Lord Chief Justice.—Did you pay eight shillings for him ?

Fenwick.—Yes, I believe I did.

Lord Chief Justice.—How came you to do it ?

Fenwick.—He was going to St. Omers.

Lord Chief Justice.—Why, were you treasurer for the society?

Fenwick.—No, my Lord, I was not.

Lord Chief Justice.—You never had your eight shillings again, had you?

Fenwick.—It is upon my book, my Lord, if I ever had it.

Lord Chief Justice.—Did Mr. Oates ever pay it again?

Fenwick.—No, sure; he was never so honest.

Lord Chief Justice.—Who had you it of then?

Fenwick.—I am certain I had it not from him; he did not pay it.

Lord Chief Justice.—How can you tell you had it, then?

Fenwick.—I suppose I had it again, but not of Mr. Oates.

Lord Chief Justice.—Had you it of Ireland?

Fenwick.—I do not know who I had it of, nor certainly whether I had it.

Lord Chief Justice.—Why did you not ask Mr. Oates for it?

Fenwick.—He was not able to pay it.

Lord Chief Justice.—Why did you lay it down for him?

Fenwick.—Because I was a fool.

Lord Chief Justice.—That must be the conclusion always: when you cannot evade being proved knaves by answering directly, you will rather suffer yourselves to be called fools.

Fenwick.—My Lord, I have done more for him than that comes to; for he came to me in a miserable poor condition, and said, "I must turn again and betake myself to the ministry to get bread, I have eaten nothing these two days;" I gave him five shillings to relieve his present necessity.

Mr. Oates.—I will answer that; I was never in any such straits. I was ordered by the provincial to be taken care of by the procurator.

Fenwick.—You brought no such order to me.

Mr. Oates.—Yes, Mr. Fenwick, you know there was such an order, and I never received so little in my life as five shillings from you; I have received twenty, and thirty, and forty shillings, at a time, but never so little as five.

Lord Chief Justice.—You are more charitable than you thought for.

Fenwick.—He told me he had not eaten a bit for two days.

Mr. Oates.—I have indeed gone a whole day without eating, when I have been hurried about your trash; but I assure you, my Lord, I never wanted for anything among them.

Lord Chief Justice.—Perhaps it was fasting day.

Lord Chief Baron.—Their fasting days are none of the worst.

Mr. Oates.—No; we commonly eat best on those days.

Popish villainy was an established fact. Chief Justice and Chief Baron girded and jested at the distresses of the prisoners. On the Bench, in the Parliament, as well as in the streets and coffee houses, there was no place left for moderation or sobriety; truth, justice, humanity, honour and good nature were all Popishly affected. Oates, retiring to partake of some refreshments kindly ordered for him by the Chief Justice, was succeeded by Bedloe. His evidence was uninteresting. As it only incriminated Ireland, Pickering and Grove, Whitebread and Fenwick for want of a second witness against them were put back, to be tried at some future time on a different charge. Poor Ireland then tried to prove an alibi. For want of sufficient preparation the attempt was unsuccessful, and did him more harm than good. In vain he begged for further time to bring together his evidence. His prayer was refused. "Then," he cried, "we must confess there is no justice for innocence." He was right; there was not in the seventeenth century. But it was the law rather

than the judges that was at fault. Scroggs turned to
Pickering and asked him what he had to say. "I will
take my oath I was never in Bedloe's company in all
my life," answered the prisoner. "I make no question
you will," retorted Scroggs, "and have a dispensation for
it when you have done." It was not altogether the fault
of Scroggs and his brethren that such a view of Romish
theology could be flung with annihilating force against
any attempts of these wretched victims to speak the
truth. Useful and necessary as the doctrine of dispensation may be under certain circumstances, the English
Protestant of the seventeenth century saw in it only
the glaring abuses of that doctrine that had contributed
among other causes to bring about the Reformation.

At this point, Ireland's indefatigable sister called as a
witness on his behalf Sir Denny Ashburnham, Member
for Hastings. She asked him to produce an indictment
for perjury which had been drawn up against Oates in
that town. He did so, but, as though to apologise for
his effrontery in reviving a youthful indiscretion of that
excellent man, irrelevantly remarked : "I think truly that
nothing can be said against Mr. Oates to take off his
credibility." It was certainly unlikely that at that moment
anything would be said to impeach the signal veracity of
the Doctor, and Ireland gained little by the attempt to
blacken the credit of the national saviour.

"Have you any more witnesses, or anything more to
say for yourselves?" asked Scroggs.

Ireland.—If I may produce on my own behalf pledges
of my own loyalty, and that of my family.

Lord Chief Justice.—Produce whom you will.

Ireland.—My sister and my mother can tell you
how our relations were plundered for siding with the
King.

Lord Chief Justice.—No ; I will tell you why it was : it
was for being Papist, and you went to the King for
shelter.

Ireland.—I had an uncle that was killed in the King's

service : the Pendrels and the Giffards that were instrumental in saving the King after the fight at Worcester are my near relations.

Lord Chief Justice.—Why, all those are Papists.

Pickering.—My father, my Lord, was killed in the King's party.

Lord Chief Justice.—Why then do you fall off from your father's virtue ?

Pickering.—I have not time to produce witnesses on my own behalf.

Ireland.—I desire time to bring more witnesses.

Grove.—As I have a soul to save, I know nothing of this matter charged upon me.

Lord Chief Justice.—Well, have you anything more to say ?

Ireland.—No, my Lord.

Scroggs recapitulated the evidence to the jury, and concluded his review by saying : " But when the matter is accomplished with so many circumstances which are material, and cannot be evaded or denied, *it is almost impossible for any man either to make such a story or we to believe it when told. I know not whether they (the Papists) can frame such a one ; I am sure no Protestant ever did, I believe, never would invent such a one to take away their lives.*" The Chief Justice rises to heights of tragic irony, hardly surpassed in the gloomiest flights of Attic drama.

Leaving the relevant issues of the case, Scroggs swept on to his wonted homily on Romish doctrine, determined to make the best of the great opportunity afforded him of gratifying his rhetorical and theatrical leanings. The noisy mob that beset the court stimulated his boisterous nature, and fired his vigorous eloquence. With unbounded generosity he launched at his excited listeners the richest periods of passionate prejudice that his turbulent intellect could summon up from a teeming vocabulary and an unstable mind, and, sword in hand, " hewed down " his defenceless victims. He began by saying that the

Plot and Popish villainy were self-evident, and then, with a warmth considerably augmented since Coleman's trial, proceeded : " We know their doctrines and practices too well to believe they will stick at anything that may effect those ends.   They must excuse me if I be plain ; I would not asperse a profession of men as the priests are with hard words if they were not true, and if at this time it were not necessary.   If they had not murdered Kings I would not say they would have murdered ours. But when it has been their practice so to do ; when they have debauched men's understandings, overturned morals, and destroyed divinity, what shall I say?   When their humility is such that they tread upon the necks of emperors, their charity such as to kill princes, their vow of poverty such as to covet kingdoms, what shall I judge of them?   When they have licenses to lie and indulgences for falsehoods, nay, when they can make him a saint that dies in one, and then pray to him as the carpenter makes an image, and worships it, and can think to bring in that wooden religion of theirs amongst us in this nation, what shall I think of them?   What shall I say to them?   What shall I do with them ?   If there can be a dispensation for the taking of any oath (and diverse instances may be given of it, that their Church licenses them to do so) it is a cheat upon men's souls, it perverts and breaks off all conversation amongst mankind; for how can we deal or converse in the world when there is no sin but can be indulged, no offence so big, but they can pardon it, and some of the blackest be accounted meritorious ? What is there left for mankind to lean upon if a Sacrament will not bind them (unless to conceal their wickedness) ?   If they take tests and Sacraments, and all this under colour of religion be avoided, and signify nothing, what is become of all converse ?   How can we think obligations and promises between man and man should hold, if a covenant between God and man will not ?

" We have no such principles nor doctrines in our

Church, we thank God. To use any prevarication in declaring the truth is abominable to natural reason, much more to true religion ; and it is a strange Church that allows a man to be a knave. It is possible some of that communion may be saved, but they can never hope to be so in such a course as this. I know they will say that these are not their principles nor their practices, that they preach otherwise, they print otherwise, and their Councils determine otherwise. Some hold that the Pope in Council is infallible ; and ask any Popish Jesuit of them all, and he will say the Pope is infallible himself in Cathedra, or he is no right Jesuit. If so, whatever they command is to be justified by their authority ; if they give a dispensation to kill a king, that king is well killed. This is a religion that quite unhinges all piety, all morality, all conversation, and is to be abominated by all mankind. They have some parts of the foundation, it is true ; but they are adulterated, and mixed with horrid principles, and impious practices. They eat their God, they kill their King, and saint the murderer. They indulge all sorts of sins, and no human bonds can hold them." Real or feigned the indecency of this tirade would be singular at any other time and from any other man than Scroggs. Proceeding out of his mouth and addressed to the sympathetic and bloodthirsty audience it is merely the response of the sensational advocate to the enthusiasm of the crowd, the indignation of the ex-Cavalier roused to the defence of Church and State against the machinations of foreigners and heretics. Its eloquence is enviable and worthy of a saner cause.

But this speech has a more than personal significance. It is only by the prevalence of such a conception of the doctrine of the Romish Church that the alarm and inhumanity of the Plot agitation can become intelligible, and it was the misfortune of the Romish Church to have given only too good cause in the past for such a disastrous view of its perverted dogma. Excited as is its tone, the Chief Justice's harangue accurately describes the Popish terror

which possessed the minds of men of far more sober
intellect than Scroggs, which had beguiled the nation to
receive into her bosom its unholy brood of informers and
perjurers, and imposed on the judicial intelligence or
smothered the judicial conscience by its horrid suggestions.

Fired by the heat of Scroggs' address the jury promptly
returned a verdict of " Guilty" against the three prisoners.
" You have done, gentlemen," cries the Chief Justice,
" like very good subjects, and very good Christians, that
is to say, like very good Protestants ; " then turning to
the prisoners, he flings at them a parting taunt, " And
now much good may their thirty thousand masses do
them ! "   Little enough in this world !   The Court adjourned till four o'clock.

Jeffreys, though sitting upon the bench, had taken
little part in the trial. But now that the prisoners had
been convicted, it became his duty as Recorder to
pass upon them the sentence of death. At five o'clock
Jeffreys, accompanied by some of the City Justices,
re-entered the Court, and the prisoners were set before him. Ireland pleaded once more that he might
have further time to call his witnesses, a request the
Recorder was bound to refuse. He urged his loyalty,
his relations' fidelity to the King. " I believe, Mr.
Ireland, it will be a shame to all your relations that you
should be privy to the murder of that good King whom
your relations served so well," was the Recorder's answer.
The executioner was called to tie up the prisoners. After
some delay and a reproof from Jeffreys this functionary
appeared and proceeded to perform his duty. Pickering
submitted in silence, Grove with the exclamation, " I am as
innocent as a child unborn."

Captain Richardson having pointed out the three
prisoners from among the others awaiting the Recorder's sentence, Jeffreys addressed himself to them. He dwelt, in
more temperate language than Scroggs, on the immorality of
a religion that encouraged the murder of Kings that violated
not only the law of the land but the law of God Almighty

Himself. "But," he hastened to add, "this I speak to you not vauntingly; 'tis against my nature to insult upon persons in your sad condition. God forgive you for what you have done! and I do heartily beg it, though you don't desire I should. Poor men, you may believe that your interest in the world to come is secured to you by your masses, but do not well consider that vast eternity you must ere long enter into, and that great Tribunal you must appear before, where his masses" (speaking to Pickering) "will not signify so many groats to him, no not one farthing. And I must say it, for the sake of those silly people whom you have imposed upon with such fallacies, that the masses can no more save thee from a future damnation than they do from a present condemnation." After protesting that there were many Catholics in England worthy men abhorring such crimes, the Recorder reminded the prisoners that the very fact that they were Roman Catholic priests residing in England was punishable with death. He was sorry with all his soul that men educated in England, surrounded by the good examples of others, could hold such mischievous principles and debauch others to do the same; and then, turning to Grove, "I am sorry also to hear a layman should with so much malice declare that a bullet if round and smooth was not safe enough for him to execute his villanies by; but he must be sure not only to set his poisonous invention to work about it, but he must add thereto his poisonous teeth; for fear if the bullet were smooth it might light in some part where the wound might be cured. But such is the height of some men's malice, that they will put all the venom and malice they can into their actions. I am sure this was so horrid a design that nothing but a conclave of devils in hell, or a college of such Jesuits as yours on earth, could have thought upon."

Once more as a Christian, in the name of the great God of Heaven, the Recorder begged them, for their own souls' sake, not to be over persuaded by the doctrines of their religion. "I know not, but as I said, you may think I speak this to insult, I take the great God of Heaven to witness, that I speak it with charity to your souls, and with great sorrow and grief in my own heart, to see men that might have made themselves happy draw upon themselves so great a ruin." He assured them that they had been fairly tried and convicted. Ireland had complained he had not been given sufficient time to call his witnesses. "But," answered Jeffreys, "he had a kind sister, who took care to bring his witnesses, an indulgence rarely allowed to men in his situation. Not that I blame her for it, I commend her ; it was the effect of her good nature, and deserves commendation. . . . . "I once more assure you, all I have said is in perfect charity. I pray God forgive you for what you have done." .

"And then came from his delighted lips," writes Lord Campbell, "the hurdle, the hanging, the cutting down alive, and other particulars too shocking to be repeated." In other words he passed upon the prisoners the customary sentence of death in cases of treason in precisely the same words in which Lord Campbell, had he been Chief Justice in 1848 instead of 1850, would have been obliged to condemn any traitor convicted before him. There is not one expression in Jeffreys' address that shows the least delight in the performance of his painful duty.

The year 1678 was drawing to its close. It had witnessed the discovery, the development and the complete establishment of the Plot. It left the nation in a condition of fearful and credulous excitement. Rumours, portents, suspicion and apprehension combined to brutalise and infuriate the public mind. A reverend divine wrote exhorting the citizens of London not to slumber like snails until the Papists had burnt or demolished their houses. "Let them banish this fatal stupidity. For his part he would not lie in the same bed with his own brother if he thought him a Papist. It was easier to chain up the damned spirits of hell than such bloodthirsty monsters." Citizens slept with watch-lights at their beds' heads, fearful at any moment of being roused by the cry of fire, and finding London once more a prey to Papist incendiaries. From the provinces came rumours that Spanish galleons filled with soldiers were bound for Milford Haven ; from Purbeck it was reported that great numbers of armed men had landed, whereupon the whole county of Dorset flew to arms only to find themselves deceived. In London, people were searching for reputed treasure hid by the Jesuits in the Savoy. Servant maids were committed in all directions on suspicion of setting fire to their masters' houses; and one, more ingenious than the rest, was only too pleased, when accused, to lay the blame upon the Papists. But on the 12th of January in the new year a portent transpired which put all others to shame. The 12th was a Sunday, and about eleven o'clock on that day during Divine service a prodigious darkness overspread the sky for half an hour, so that the church services could no longer be conducted without candle-light. The ghost of Sir Edmundbury Godfrey availed itself of the prevalent gloom to appear during mass at the Queen's Chapel in Somerset House. Roger North unkindly attributes the miraculous darkness to a combination of mist and common smoke, which, he says, must frequently occur in towns and is very rare out of town. Whatever the explanation of the phenomenon, it has in later times become so frequent that its terrors have materially decreased. In 1679 it was a prodigy to the Plot believers, an accident to the sceptical. As the former were the most numerous, its effect must have been very encouraging to Dr. Oates.

But even among the more intelligent of the community, though by methods less prodigious, judgment was dismayed and reason blinded. "I cannot without horror and trembling reflect upon the many mischiefs and inconveniences we have been run into," said Jeffreys seven years later, when called upon to sit in judgment on the arch-deceiver. Meanwhile, the arch-deceiver, by the will and grant of the High Court of Parliament and the contributions of the godly, dwelt in plenty and luxury at Whitehall. He preached to thronged congregations, and though to Evelyn he seemed bold and furiously indiscreet, everybody believed what he said. Among the wise and learned Oates could count well nigh as many and as ardent supporters as among the thoughtless and the ignorant. All was imputed to a special providence of God. The evidence was so bold and positive, the fact so horrid, there were so many conspirators of quality to countenance the tale and formalities of law in favour of the witnesses, that it is easy to believe how many were the Lords and Commons, the Judges and Bishops drawn into the net of the delusion.

To Jeffreys' ambitions the year 1678 had been most gratifying. His Inn at the Temple had recognised his successes at the Bar by electing him a Bencher. The City had unanimously promoted him from the Common Serjeancy to the Recordership. The Crown had shown its goodwill by briefing him in all the Plot prosecutions ; he had been talked of as Attorney-General or Lord Chancellor of Ireland. At home, though he had lost his first wife, the befriended confidante, in the early part of the year, he had repaired the loss in a manner very conducive to the furtherance of his interests in the City of London. Fortune continued to smile on the young Recorder : he was only thirty-one ; a favourite apparently with all parties, he might hope to win in course of time the highest offices in his profession. But troublous days were ahead of him, as the astute young gentleman cannot fail to have observed. Court and Parliament were drifting farther apart, and the majority of the citizens was more likely to side with the latter than the former. All the wariness in the world could not avert the moment when Sir George would be obliged to choose between his two masters, and build his hopes of further preferment on the ardour of his attachment to one of the great political parties.

Lord Campbell professes to fathom the unscrupulous wiles by which Sir George was endeavouring to better himself in the midst of the confusions of the time. He tells us how in the first place the King called for Sir

George at the outbreak of the agitation and took counsel of him as to what course he should adopt. Thereupon, Jeffreys recommended that Charles should for awhile profess a belief in Oates and his confederates, allow the popular fury to exhaust itself and then, when the people were weary of blood, fall upon Shaftesbury and his crew and smite them hip and thigh. It would have been difficult for any man to give Charles advice more congenial to his easy, heartless disposition ; indeed, the course of conduct suggested is so peculiarly characteristic of the King, so creditable to his head and so discreditable to his heart, that one is loth to deprive him of the credit of having originally conceived it. Jeffreys, intimate with the King's favourite mistress and certainly a *persona grata* at Court, may well have been consulted by Charles as to the state of public feeling, the intentions of the City and such matters of which he would have special cognizance ; but that at so critical a moment the King would have framed his policy on the advice of the Recorder of London is possible—Charles was not particular as to the dignity of his advisers—but not very probable.

However, Lord Campbell, undeterred by the absence of authority, goes further. Not only was Jeffreys guiding the King with immoral counsels, but on the Bench he was playing the tempter to the gullible Scroggs. He was beguiling that worthy with tales of the King's complete faith in the existence of the Plot, and thereby whetting his fury against the luckless Papists. What Jeffreys would have been likely to have gained by this manœuvre Lord Campbell does not condescend to explain; the evidence on which he bases the assertion is paltry and garbled. An inflammable being like Scroggs cannot have wanted much coaxing to break out into a flaming fire of denunciation ; and it must be remembered that even had Jeffreys wished, for some mysterious reason or in wanton malice, to excite the Chief Justice, he was not in a position of such prominence as to seriously sway the mind of Scroggs. Jeffreys played a very unimportant part in most of these trials, and at many of them was not on the Bench at all, or, if he was, would not have sat at the elbow of the Chief Justice. It is, of course, striking from the point of view of the popular historian to represent Jeffreys as a youthful Mephistopheles urging poor mortals to damnation by insidious counsels and lying hopes. But so much has been done in this way with Jeffreys that it may be equally interesting to reduce him to his natural proportions again. And these, physically and morally, are more comely than has been popularly supposed. The quotations so far given from his public utterances are quite undeserving of the heated language that has been bestowed indiscriminately on all portions of his career, and hardly justify the historical misrepresentations it has been his privilege to enjoy from the lavish hands of a successor, whose historical injustice has not even that sense of humour which lightens the darkest passages of his predecessor's misdoing.

VI

THE TRIAL OF SIR GEORGE WAKEMAN

JULY, 1679

It would be an improper tax on the patience of the reader to expect him to follow at length all the Plot trials in which Jeffreys took part. In many of them the Recorder's share was insignificant, and the accounts already given of the trials of Coleman and Ireland will suffice to place the reader in possession of the outlines of Oates's story and the evidence supporting it.

In February, Jeffreys was made a Serjeant-at-Law, an honour which his position as an advocate thoroughly justified. But the young Recorder was about to lose a valued friend and patron. Parliament met in March. The country party, backed by French gold, were well in the ascendant ; and whatever hopes Charles and Danby may have built on the improved temper of a new House of Commons were immediately shattered. Not only did the House attack the Papists with renewed vigour, but it straightway fell upon Danby with impeachment and attainder, and he was committed to the Tower in April. Though his connection with Jeffreys was by no means severed by his imprisonment, the fallen Minister ceased to be any longer effective in forwarding the Recorder's fortunes.

It was to Danby that Jeffreys owed his first employment in the mysterious services of the Court, and his close alliance with the Duchess of Portsmouth. On Danby's fall the

Duchess had transferred her political affections to Robert Spencer, Earl of Sunderland ; and Jeffreys, as part of the stock in trade, was included in the transfer. A man of infinite subtlety, an accommodating disposition and an irresistible address, Sunderland had much in common with the Recorder. They were both young men, Sunderland not yet forty, Jeffreys thirty-two, both in the enjoyment of good spirits and easy principles ; all the elements of a lasting political alliance combined to draw them closer together. The changes and chances of King Charles's reign were to be many ; but, secure in the support of the favourite mistress, it would have been difficult for men far less adroit than these two to miss power and preferment. In replacing Danby by Sunderland, Jeffreys had made the best exchange possible under the circumstances.

In June of the same year the Recorder was called upon to pass sentence on another batch of convicted Jesuits. They had been tried in the now customary fashion, sneered at by the Judges, stormed at by Scroggs, their witnesses beaten by the mob. Among them was a barrister, one Richard Langhorne, a very extraordinary man in all respects, learned and honest in his profession, but bigoted and of a dismal countenance prophetic of a violent death. He had some acquaintance with Jeffreys, and in fitting terms the latter expressed sorrow at finding his friend in such sad condition. He spoke charitably to the prisoners of the justice of their trials and the irreproachable character of the evidence on which they had been convicted. " There is not the least room for the most scrupulous man to doubt of the credibility of the witnesses that have been examined against you." Jeffreys subsequently admitted that he was at this time one of those who had been surprised into a belief in the truth of Oates's story, a surprise which he never forgave that unscrupulous impostor. " Gentlemen," he concluded, " with great charity to your immortal souls, I desire you, for the love of God, and in the name of His Son, Jesus Christ, consider these things ; for it will not be long before you are summoned before another tribunal about them. And great and dreadful is the Day of Judgment at which you and all men must appear."

As Jeffreys closed his address with the customary sentence of drawing and quartering, a great acclamation in the Court testified to the lively satisfaction which these convictions afforded to the public mind.

But at Whitehall it was otherwise. The day Whitebread and his fellows were condemned, the King was not well pleased, and only by the advice of others persuaded to keep his feelings to himself. Even in the Council differences broke out. Halifax was so irritated by some adverse comments which Sir William Temple made upon the convictions, that he threatened to tell the public that Temple was a Papist, and so far lost his head as to exclaim that the Plot must be handled as though it were true, whether it was so or not. This must have been pleasant hearing for even the complacent Charles. It is with some justice that James in his " Memoirs " speaks of his brother at this time as that " unfortunate Prince, for so he may well be termed in this conjuncture ; " though Charles' sufferings were by no means so acute as might have been expected in a man who was allowing others to be put to death in the name of a conspiracy of which he was the most guilty member. But to an ordinary onlooker, like Henry Sidney, these trials were the clearest things that ever were seen ; and it would have required a person of far stronger purpose and nobler heart than Charles II. to have saved these unfortunate prisoners, whom even calm and rational men looked upon as the most flagrant criminals.

However, at a subsequent Council, Charles took great pains to obtain a reprieve for Langhorne, which distressed h s friends exceedingly. Lord Anglesey, the Privy Seal, warmly seconded his efforts, but Shaftesbury violently and successfully withstood them.

Langhorne and his companions suffered ; and the public interest turned to the approaching trial of Sir George Wakeman, at which it was rumoured Oates was to involve in his accusations not only the Queen's physician but Queen Catherine herself.

In November of 1678 Oates had appeared at the bar of the House of Commons, and exclaimed, in his ugly voice, "Aye, Taitus Oates, accause Catherine, Quean of England, of Haigh Traison." The treason consisted in a plot formed by the Queen and her physician to murder the King. Charles had refused to have anything to do with this monstrous accusation, except to disappoint by his indignation those who had reckoned on his infidelities as likely to tempt him to lend a willing ear to such a charge. But it was otherwise with Parliament. Sir George Wakeman, the Queen's physician, was clapped into the Gatehouse, there to await his trial, virtually the trial of the Queen and the crowning achievement of the supporters of the Plot. So great was the success that had hitherto attended Oates's efforts in the courts of law, so complete appeared to be the faith of Judge and jury in whatever he might please to allege, that the informer may well have felt the moment had arrived when he ought to play his trump card. In any case the public undoubtedly regarded the approaching indictment of Wakeman as the most important event that had occurred since Oates first made his revelations. July had been fixed for the trial. It was to take place before Scroggs, than whom Oates may well have thought he boasted no more ardent advocate. There was no reason to believe that the public craving for Popish blood was in any degree diminished. The astonishing boldness and impudence of the charge, the high position of the lady implicated, these may have provoked some misgiving among the more respectable ; but to the partizans of the good Doctor, flushed with a succession of bloody victories, misgiving appeared almost fantastic.

On July 18th, Wakeman, a Catholic gentleman called Rumley, and two priests, Marshal and Corker, were charged at the Old Bailey before Scroggs and a full Bench, including Mr. Recorder Jeffreys, with conspiring to murder the King. Evelyn, the diarist, was in Court. He had determined to come and see for himself what these trials were like. He found the Bench crowded with innumerable spectators. The air was full of strange rumours. The trial was to be postponed, the Judges had been down to the Council at Windsor on the subject of the trial. When the new Attorney-General, Sir Robert Sawyer, after a little preliminary evidence, turned to the prisoners, and said: "Now, gentlemen, it behoves you to take notes. We shall come home to you! Dr. Oates!" every one felt that the good Doctor had reached the most supreme and critical moment of his great career.

In June, 1678, said Oates, Ashby, an octogenarian, chronically incapacitated by gout, but, according to the Doctor, one of the most energetic and vigorous of the Catholic conspirators, wrote to consult Sir G. Wakeman about his malady. Wakeman, in replying, recommended the patient a milk diet and the Bath pumps, and, by way of further invigorating the old gentleman, added that the Queen had kindly consented to assist him in poisoning the King. Full of the glad tidings Ashby left for his gout cure. A few days after, Oates, as a promising disciple, and one in whom great trust was reposed, was invited by Fenwick and Harcourt to accompany them to Somerset House to see the Queen. Oates went with them and waited in an antechamber while his companions entered the Queen's apartment. The door being open, Oates listened to their conversation. The Queen was complaining of her husband's infidelities. The recollection of them apparently so preyed on her mind that she at length agreed to help Wakeman to murder the King. Well satisfied, Fenwick and Harcourt rejoined Oates in the antechamber. Oates asked them if they would be so kind as to present him to the Queen. They did so, and after Her Majesty had bestowed a gracious smile on the young novice they all three took their departure. Wakeman was again approached and offered £10,000 to do the job. He asked for fifteen, and got it. Oates saw the receipt for that sum in his handwriting.

This was all Oates said that he could recollect at present. Wakeman immediately taxed him with having failed altogether to recognise him when he and the Doctor were confronted before the Privy Council, and with having said on that occasion that he had never seen him before in his whole life. Oates had the old excuse of Coleman's trial ready at hand. He was so ill and tired and indisposed, in respect both of his "intellectuals" and anything else, that he could not charge him home ; and the light was so bad. "This is just Coleman's case," said Wakeman ; "the light was in your eyes." Oates immediately claimed the protection of the Court against such a daring reflection. Wakeman also remarked with some force that all Oates's reputed interviews with him took place in the presence of Ireland and Fenwick and others whose silence had been ensured by their previous executions. Scroggs, to the astonishment of all, took up Wakeman's point, and himself asked Oates why he had not given all this evidence against the prisoner before. "I can by and by give an answer to it, when it is proved by him what I said," was the imperfect reply. After some further cross-examination, Oates suddenly recollected some fresh evidence with regard to the prisoner Marshal, whom he had hitherto failed to implicate in his narration. Marshal, a very strenuous and rhetorical person, had according to Oates, in company with three of his co-religionists, indulged in speculation as to the probabilities of King Charles II. ever again partaking of Christmas pies. The speculation had become so intense that Marshal and another went halves in a significant wager that Charles had enjoyed these pies for the last time. Marshal asked Oates to be more specific about the date of this occurrence. "It is a great privilege. I tell you the month," answered Oates, with transcendent impertinence. "It was the beginning or middle of August." After a few more questions Oates unbent further, and condescended to fix the Feast of the Assumption as about the date of the unholy wager. But he did not deign to bestow many more privileges of

this kind. To his intense surprise Scroggs had been
questioning him with pertinacity for some time, and the
Doctor was growing weary of the sudden interest that the
Chief Justice had developed in the details of his story.
" My Lord, I desire I may leave to retire, because I
am not well," asked Oates. Scroggs told him he must
stay till after the prisoners' defence. Jeffreys offered
the Doctor some refreshment by way of consolation.

Bedloe swore that he had met Wakeman at Harcourt's.
—it is curious that he had not given the following
evidence at Harcourt's trial in the previous June,—where
the priest and the physician were discussing the usual
subject, the removal of the King. Wakeman was somewhat unwilling, but Harcourt cheered his fainting heart
by giving him a bill for £2,000 from the Queen. It was
then agreed that, if the Windsor Plot failed, Wakeman
was to try poison ; and, if that failed, the deed was to be
done at Newmarket.

Wakeman in reply called God to witness that he had
never seen Bedloe before. " If I had been acquainted
with Mr. Bedloe I should have known him to be a great
rogue, which is but what he has said of himself ; and I
should not have thought fit to have trusted such an one
with such a great secret as this." " It may be," retorted
Scroggs, " he calls himself a great rogue for that which
you would have applauded him for, and canonised him
too. It may be he thinks he was a rogue for going as
far as he did ; but perhaps you are of another opinion."

But Scroggs, in spite of some licks with the rough side
of his tongue which he had occasionally bestowed upon
the prisoners, was not receiving the evidence of the
informers with that warm confidence which his previous
bearing had led them to expect ; and at the conclusion of
Bedloe's evidence, the Chief Justice suddenly called Sir
Robert Sawyer's attention to the fact that Bedloe had
sworn nothing against Wakeman except the receipt of
£2,000 from the Queen for no particular object. Sawyer
reminded the Chief Justice that Harcourt and Wakeman

had spoken of the design in Bedloe's presence, and mentioned Windsor and Newmarket ; upon which Scroggs broke out : "What is all this ? We are now in the case of men's lives, and pray have a care that you say no more than what is true upon any man whatever. I would be loth to keep out Popery by that way ; they would bring it in by blood or violence ; I would have all things go very fair." Bedloe was recalled, and repeated his evidence. "He says now quite another thing than before," cried Scroggs. "No, no," echoed North, Jeffreys and Sawyer. Scroggs had been a little too previous. He had probably taken no notes of the evidence, and his tactless impetuosity was quick to betray him into the premature exposure of his intentions.

Wakeman then called the attention of the Court to the prescription Oates said he had given to Mr. Thimbleby, alias Ashby, when he sent him to Bath. Sir George pointed out that it was ludicrous to order a man milk and the Bath waters at the same time, as the waters made the milk curdle. Oates, with practised ingenuity, got out of the difficulty by saying that the milk was only to be taken while he remained in town. On this point a long argument arose. Mr. Justice Pemberton and Mr. Justice Atkyns showed themselves strongly in favour of Oates, and thoroughly accepted his explanation. Whatever change was to take place in the opinion of their Chief, the two "puisnes" had lost none of their faith in the Plot and its exponents.

But a more serious blow was struck at the Doctor's reputation when the Court proceeded to hear evidence of what took place in the Privy Council when Oates first accused Wakeman. It was very clearly proved that on that occasion he had not laid to Wakeman's charge the greater part of the evidence which he now gave against him. He had merely alluded to a letter which he had seen in Fenwick's hands proving Wakeman's complicity in the attempted poisoning of the King. But of the prescription to Ashby, of the interviews with the Queen and the other facts with which he now adorned his narrative, he had said nothing. It further transpired that as soon as he had heard Oates's story the King had sent for Wakeman, and the Lord Chancellor had informed the physician of Oates's accusation. With an indiscretion only too frequent among the innocent, Wakeman, instead of categorically denying his guilt, had entered into a long recital of the various services he had rendered the Crown. Thereupon Oates was recalled. Asked if he had anything more against Sir George, he had replied : " No, God forbid that I should say anything against Sir George Wakeman, for I know nothing sure against him."

The Doctor could not have given a more positive reply. And yet here he was at the trial bristling with new found proofs of the physician's guilt ! When Sir P. Lloyd was called and bore testimony to the scene just described, Oates coolly exclaimed, " I remember not one word of all this." " But this is a Protestant witness," was Wakeman's pointed retort. Oates then declared that his failure to charge Wakeman fully had been due to weakness and fatigue, he had been so hurried up and down that he was hardly " compos mentis." But Scroggs would have none of the Doctor's customary excuses. " What ! " he cried, " must we be abused with we know not what ? It did not require such a deal of strength to say, ' I saw a letter under Sir George's own hand.' " Oates, nettled by this unwonted opposition, sneered at the Privy Council : " To speak the truth, they were such a Council as would commit nobody." " That was not well said," exclaimed Jeffreys. " He reflects on the King and all the Council," cried Wakeman. And the Doctor's discomfiture was completed when Scroggs turned to him with the sharp rebuke : " You have taken a great confidence, I know not by what authority, to say anything of anybody." The injured Doctor gave no further sign of animation during the rest of the trial. Scroggs's sudden and pronounced want of consideration for the " Nation's Saviour " had produced painful surprise among his audience. His brother Judges, ready enough to fall upon any impertinence or presumption on the part of the prisoners, refused to second the efforts of their Chief when they were directed against the Doctor. In attempting to disparage the credit of Oates, Scroggs was on a fair way to upsetting his own.

However, the indiscreet flourishes of Marshal's rhetorical defence gave Scroggs an opportunity to recover some measure of his popularity. Marshal, who seems to have modelled his style on that of the Chief Justice, indulged in a telling denunciation of the Plot witnesses. They were " villains in print, preferment tickles them, rewards march before them, and ambition, which greedily follows, beckons them, to lie, though God and conscience tell them they are unjust." .... " England is become a mournful theatre, upon which such a tragedy is acted as turns the eyes of all Europe towards it ; the blood which has been already spilt has found a channel to convey it even to the remotest parts of the world. Though it inspires different breasts with different resentments, yet it may speak a language that none who are friends of England will be willing to understand. Our transactions here are the discourse and entertainment of foreign nations ; without all doubt will be chronicled and subjected to the censure of ensuing ages. I have great reason to believe that not any one of those honourable persons that sit Judges over us would be willing to have their names written in any characters but those of just moderation, of profound integrity, of impartial justice, and of gracious clemency. Though we would not be all thought to be well-wishers to the Roman Catholic religion, yet we would be all thought friends to religion ; though we exclaim against idolatry and new principles of faith, yet we all stand up for old Christianity ; whereas if the testimony of living impiety be applauded and admitted, the cries of dying honesty scoffed and rejected, what will become of old Christianity ? If any voice, cry, or protestation of dying men pass for truth and obtain belief, where is our new conspiracy ? The question comes to this, the belief of Christianity in Roman Catholics and the appearance of their innocency are so fast linked together by those solemn vows and protestations of their innocency, made by the late executed persons, that no man can take up arms against the latter, but must proclaim war against the former. Nor can our innocency bleed but our Christianity must needs by the same dart be wounded. Nor can any tutelar hand stretch itself forth——"

Lord Chief Justice North : " You speak ' ad faciendum populum,' and should not be interrupted, but I think you lash out a little too much."

North's mild attempt to check this torrent of eloquence proving ineffectual, Scroggs intervened. " Your defence has been very mean, I tell you beforehand, your cause looked much better before you spoke a word in your defence, so wisely have you managed it." " But really for your particular part, Mr. Marshal," remonstrated Jeffreys, " you abound too much in flowers of rhetoric, which are all to no purpose." " I hoped it would be no offence to insist," pleaded the harassed orator—but he could get no further. Rhetoric is contagious, Scroggs scented battle and plunged wildly into the fray. " Papists," he cried, " were all that is lying, cruel and bloody. Therefore never brag of your religion, for it is a foul one, and so contrary to Christ that it is easier to believe anything than to believe an understanding man to be a Papist. If we look into the Gunpowder Treason, we know how honest you are in your oaths, and what truth there is in your words ; to blow up King, Lords and Commons, is with you a merciful act, a sign of a candid religion : but that is all a story with you ; it is easier for you to believe that a saint, after her head is cut off went three miles with her head in her hand, to the place where she would be buried, than that there was a Gunpowder Treason." It apparently never occurred to Scroggs that he was now dealing in the same popular rhetoric which he and his brethren had so censured in poor Marshal.

The audience received the Chief Justice's harangue with a loud shout. But Marshal was undaunted, and continued the struggle. Scroggs threatened him with another har-

angue if he did not take care.   Even this menace left him
undismayed.   At length, Pemberton, coming to the rescue
of his Chief, told the prisoner not to teach the jury and
repeat things again and again.   Realising the futility of
further effort, Marshal subsided into a reluctant silence.

Scroggs's summing up is a peculiar piece of work.   It
is very much in favour of the prisoners, and free from
any of his habitual tirades against Popery.   For that
reason it lacks all the tempestuous vigour of his previous
performances, and seems rather the unwilling utterance
of one who is performing an uncongenial task.   He
remarks, in the middle of his charge, that he cannot
undertake to repeat every word of the evidence, but only
so much as he can remember to be material, and hopes
his brothers will help him out.   But the brethren sat
mum ; they had by this time discovered the change in
their Chief's sentiments, and firmly declined to follow
him in his apostasy.   They regarded with ill-concealed
dislike the sudden doubts he was launching against the
credit of the Saviour of the Nation, and were not unnaturally surprised that these doubts should come from the
mouth of one who had in the immediate past so rampantly
denounced Catholic villainy.   If they were to be convinced
that they had hitherto been wrong in attaching such credit
to Oates, the conviction would hardly be borne upon them
by the abrupt recantation that now fell from the lips of
the Lord Chief Justice.

Scroggs must have felt this unsympathetic attitude of
his brethren.   But, by summoning up a few of those
strong eloquent sentences of which, whatever its faults,
his oratory seldom stood in want, he contrived to bring
off his unpopular performance with some show of dignity.
He is speaking of Oates's failure to recognise Wakeman
in the Council Chamber.   "Sir Thomas Doleman did
indeed say, Mr. Oates was very weak, so that he was in
great confusion, and scarce able to stand ; weigh it with
you how it will, but to me it is no answer.   I tell you
plainly, I think a man could not be so weak but he could

have said he saw a letter under his hand. It was as short
as he could make an answer, and it is strange that he
should go and make protestation that he knew nothing.
And so I pray you weigh it well. Let us not be so amazed
and frighted with the noise of plots as to take away any
man's life without reasonable evidence. These men's
blood is at stake, and your souls and mine, and our oaths
and consciences are at stake ; therefore never care what the
world says, follow your consciences : if you are satisfied
what these men swear is true, you will do well to find
them guilty, and they deserve to die for it ; if you are unsatisfied, upon these things put together, and they do
weigh with you that they have not said true, you will do
well to acquit them."

The Chief Justice had no sooner finished than Bedloe
rose and complained that his evidence had not been
rightly summed up. Whatever the inconveniences of
his position, Scroggs was not going to suffer such impudence as this. "I know not by what authority this
man speaks," was the stern, almost biblical, answer of the
Chief Justice. "Make way for the jury there ; who
keeps the jury ?" called the usher of the Court. Scroggs
and his brethren left the Bench to sup, but the Recorder
remained to take the verdict. In an hour the jury returned, and asked Jeffreys if they could convict the prisoners of concealment of treason only. Jeffreys told them it
must be high treason or nothing. "Then take a verdict," answered the foreman, and a verdict of "Not
Guilty" was returned for all the prisoners. "Down
on your knees," said Captain Richardson, the keeper of
Newgate, to Wakeman ; and, in all sincerity, the fortunate
man knelt down and prayed the blessing of God on the
King and honourable Bench. Wakeman and Rumley
were immediately released ; but Corker and the flowery
Marshal were detained in custody, to take their trial as
being Romish priests exercising their functions in England
contrary to the Statute of Queen Elizabeth.

The acquittal of Wakeman was as "a thunderstroke to

the ' Plotters.' " It was Oates's first public check, and it was a check from which that good man may be said to have never recovered. More Papists were to be done to death on foul testimony, Oates was to be heard again in the courts of justice, and Dangerfield was to foist yet another elaborate perjury on the confiding nation ; but Oates never enjoyed after Wakeman's trial the consideration or repute he had enjoyed before it. The verdict was not only a victory for the Court, but it was a sign that, with the letting of blood, the anti-Papist fever of the country was gradually abating. Though everything was done by its adherents to keep the belief in the Plot fresh by sensational discoveries and occasional executions of innocent Catholics, from the acquittal of Wakeman dates the gradual decline of the imposition, and the victory of Charles's policy of sufferance and inaction.

In the courts of law the unexpected result of the trial was productive of much confusion and distrust. The sudden revolution in the attitude of Scroggs caused dismay and indignation among the public and ill-concealed disgust among some of his colleagues on the Bench. It was openly said that the " ungodly " jury had been tampered with, that the briefs of the Crown counsel were imperfect, and that Scroggs had had good store of gold for his share in the business. Two facts certainly tended to justify the indignation of the public. Wakeman, after going down to Windsor and kissing the King's hand, left the country ; and the Portuguese ambassador committed the inconceivable indiscretion of calling on Scroggs after the trial, to thank him for so loyally preserving the fame and honour of Catherine of Braganza. When, in August, Scroggs went the Oxford circuit, the public expressed their opinion of his conduct by throwing half dead cats into his carriage window, and crying in a loud voice, " A Wakeman ! A Wakeman ! " In London he was made the subject of libel and lampoon under the name of " Clodpate." So gross had these attacks become that on the first day of the Michaelmas term of 1679, the Lord

Chief Justice publicly answered his traducers. His speech was fearless, solemn and dignified. The " hireling scribblers " he did not deign to notice, except to warn them of impending punishment ; but, lest any sober and good man should be misled by their lies, he solemnly declared from his seat of justice, " where I would no more lie or equivocate than I would to God at the Holy Altar," that he had followed his conscience according to the best of his understanding in Wakeman's trial, without fear, favour or reward. Even Lord Campbell, in a footnote, finds himself sufficiently impressed by this eloquent and powerful rejoinder to acquit the Chief Justice of pecuniary corruption ; but, he goes on to say, " I believe that he was swayed in this instance by a disinterested love of rascality." This is not a very convincing criticism. There is no real ground for believing that up to the time of Wakeman's trial Scroggs was otherwise than sincere in his denunciation of the Papists. Violent and over-heated he certainly was ; but that all his vehemence was assumed to prop up a story he believed to be false is a conclusion for which there is no warrant. His sincerity first comes in question at Wakeman's trial, when he begins to harass a witness he had previously courted and approved. The motives that urged him to this course can only be conjectured from a few of the attendant circumstances that have come down to us.

In the first place Scroggs went to Windsor just before the trial. The King, determined to save the Queen's honour, may have enlightened the Chief Justice on points in Oates's evidence of which he alone could expose the falsehood. Scroggs may also have learnt, what he did not know before, that these Papist prosecutions and executions were not so gratifying to Charles as he had imagined. Scroggs was always a loyal follower of his King ; and a hint from Charles that he might abate his excessive ardour would be quite enough for the Chief Justice. Roger North gives an anecdote of his brother, which is intended to further enlighten posterity on Scroggs's sudden conversion. Scroggs was driving back from Windsor with Sir Francis North, his brother Chief Justice, when he suddenly asked North whether Lord Shaftesbury, the leader of the Plot supporters, really had great power with the King. "No, my lord," replied North; "no more than your footman hath with you;" at which Scroggs hung his head and sat silent and thoughtful for some time. From this incident Roger North dates Scroggs's disparagement of Oates. He also represents the Judge as a friend of Shaftesbury. That statesman, always ready to win over any adherent of the Court, may well have cultivated the society of the Chief Justice, who could be very useful to him in fostering the belief in the Popish Plot. They certainly used to dine at each other's houses, and one night Scroggs mightily offended the Tory, Francis North, by inviting him to meet the great Whig leader. Scroggs's vehemence at the outset of the agitation was no doubt prompted and excited by the wily statesman, who found excellent material for his cunning in the inflammable disposition of the Chief Justice. The latter, thoroughly excited, ranted on until he discovered, either from the King or some other source, that Shaftesbury's agitation was by no means single-minded, and that he was being made use of as a tool to serve the personal ends of that statesman. From that moment his ardour cooled; and though he did not one whit abate his conviction of the existence of a dangerous Plot and the villainy of the Roman Catholics, he began to regard the evidence on which they were prosecuted and the characters of Oates and his colleagues with a calmer and more judicial eye. He even went so far as to admit that he was troubled about the justice of Langhorne's conviction, an admission which, if not sincere, could have no purpose at all. A more lenient view of his conduct is supported by Anthony Wood in his *Athenae Oxonienses*. He is the only author who has spoken of Scroggs in anything approaching to favourable terms, and would seem to have been personally acquainted with him. He tells us that the Chief Justice mitigated his zeal in the Plot when he saw that he was to be made a "shoeing-horn to draw on others." At any rate, Scroggs's speech against his libellers is a powerful and impressive utterance ; and it suggests that, having come to his senses and realised the use to which he had been put by an unscrupulous party leader, he determined to resume the true functions of a Judge, which he had in his passion abdicated, and do his best in the future to check the insolent witnesses and giddy-headed rabble.   But it is easy enough to excite the giddy-headed ; it is quite another thing to control them.   This Scroggs learnt to his cost when he attempted to do so.

VII

THE FIRST ABHORRER—THE PARLIAMENTARY RECKONING

1679—1680

THE acquittal of Wakeman was a turning point in the career of Jeffreys. Hitherto few had doubted the existence of a Plot and the relative truth of Oates's depositions. Jeffreys, when Chief Justice, admitted at Oates's trial that all had at first been " surprised into a belief." But, after Wakeman's trial, that belief was, in the minds of many, at an end. Henceforth, the Plot became a party matter ; two camps were formed of believers and non-believers, not only among politicians but among the Judges also. Scroggs, and those of his brethren imbued with Court principles, suddenly recognised the villainy of Oates and the deception he had practised upon them. Pemberton, Atkyns and such of the Judges as leant to the popular side, ignored Wakeman's acquittal, censured his jury and continued to warmly support the Doctor whenever he appeared to give evidence before them. North alone, if we are to believe his brother, had from the first recognised the absurdity of the whole story. But in this instance Roger's anxiety to vindicate the Chief Justice's intelligence can only be successful at the expense of his integrity. North in the course of one of the trials remarked that the Plot was " as clear as the sun." Roger explains this as an example of his brother's " shining irony." If this is a correct explanation and not a rather fantastic apology, it is monstrous that a Chief Justice should have made use of such "shining irony," when he must have been well aware of the sense in which his irony would be received by the excited multitude. Roger's zeal for his good brother's infallibility is fatally indiscreet at times.

But it was not in his judicial capacity that Wakeman's acquittal affected Jeffreys. He had taken little part in the trials, and, though no doubt at first " surprised into belief," he had come, by his familiarity with Court affairs and his own perspicacity in detecting a scoundrel, to regard Oates with suspicion. It was in respect of his position in the City, his office as Recorder, that the result of the trial touched him most nearly. To trim between his master at Court and his masters in the Court of Aldermen was no longer possible. The acquittal had fired with indignation those malcontents who regarded the policy of Charles with hatred and misgiving ; and Shaftesbury's supporters did their best to feed the discontent. Pamphlets virulently attacking the King, the Duke and Scroggs were secretly printed and sold by the City booksellers. In the Council the majority of the Aldermen unhesitatingly declared in favour of the exclusion of the Duke of York from the succession to the throne. To Jeffreys, as Recorder of London and the Duke's Attorney-General, such a decision was very pertinent and called for immediate action on his part. He did not hesitate in his determination. In spite of the powerful opposition he would have to encounter and the peril in which his Recordership was placed, he declared straightway for the cause of the King—to him the cause of law, order and good government—and publicly denounced the seditious proceedings of the popular agitators. Jeffreys has been reproached with treachery on this occasion, but it is difficult to establish the charge. It is not treacherous to try and stand well with all parties as long as some sort of agreement is possible, neither is it treacherous when discord becomes inevitable to choose the unpopular side. Without claiming for Jeffreys any very high measure of sincerity or principle,

he may well have honestly preferred the government of
the King to the factious clamour of the populace, the
arts of the Court to the arts of Lord Shaftesbury. If
the duel was to be fought out in the courts of law it would
be more congenial to his character and conscience to assist
in the punishment of the King's seditious enemies than in
the convictions of unoffending Papists on the testimony of
Dr. Oates. Now, for the first time, men began to realise
with what recklessness Shaftesbury was prepared to use
the Doctor and his unlovely gang for the destruction of
his enemies. It is less surprising that Jeffreys should have
opposed himself to such devices than that Judges such as
Atkyns and Pemberton should have continued to support
them. A mortal struggle had been entered upon between
the King and Shaftesbury. It had commenced by the
shedding of blood, and in the shedding of blood it was to
terminate. Shaftesbury killed Papists ; the King, when
his time came, killed Whigs. Jeffreys, if he was obliged as
a lawyer to take part in such proceedings, preferred Whig-
killing. The latter could be cleanly, legally and conscien-
tiously removed; treason was an elastic term, and Whiggism
full of dangerous possibilities. But to put people out of
the way on the evidence of such a rascal as Oates and the
clamour of an unscrupulous faction, was in every way
distasteful to his character.

The Exclusion Bill had to a great extent taken the
place of the Plot as the avowed cause of the public excitement ; the indignation of all true Protestants now vented
itself against the Duke of York. As James's Attorney-
General Jeffreys was prepared to stand by his master. In
the August of 1679 the King had fallen seriously ill, and,
on his recovery a few weeks later, the Mayor and
Aldermen went down to Windsor to offer an address of
congratulation. The Recorder, who accompanied them
in his official capacity, proposed that, after waiting on
his Majesty, the deputation should also wait on the
Duke of York. This the deputation declined to do, and
though the Duke was present at his brother's side when

the King received them, the Aldermen ignored his presence altogether. Jeffreys, unabashed, remained behind after the deputation had withdrawn, and, with his father-in-law, Sir Thomas Bludworth, who seems to have been one of the small party in the Council that still followed the Court, had an audience of James. Such conduct cannot have been pleasing to the Aldermen, but it was very pleasing to the King. When Sir William Jones resigned the Attorney-Generalship Jeffreys was spoken of as a possible successor ; but the post fell to Creswell Levinz, an efficient and respected lawyer.

In the meantime Parliament, still bent on the Exclusion, was prorogued by Charles in October, and a not unreasonable supposition got abroad that the King intended for the future to govern without one. Fears of this kind lent fresh strength to the public agitation and, being well manipulated by Shaftesbury and his creatures, threw London into a ferment of apprehension. " Agitants and sub-agitants " went about among the people inciting them to draw up petitions to the King, praying him to call a Parliament. The public responded with alacrity to the invitation and overwhelmed Charles with petitions, some genuine, others covered with unmeaning hieroglyphics like " vermin in the bed of Nile." To crown all, the Mayor and Aldermen presented a petition, copies of which they had ordered to be printed and posted about the City. For this they were summoned before the Privy Council and charged to put an immediate stop to this craze for seditious and tumultuous petitioning. Clayton, the Lord Mayor and a member of the country faction, tried to evade obedience to the command by saying he did not know how he could legally put a stop to it. The Recorder, with mischievous readiness, suggested a very easy method of helping my Lord Mayor out of his difficulty. " Let the King," he said, " issue a proclamation forbidding the framing and printing of such petitions." But this advice was a little too bold even for the Council. Luckily, Chief Justice North was at the board, ready with

a more cautious and subtle method which should be quite
as effective and less startling to the legal mind. So
Jeffreys' bolder counsels were not adopted ; but neither the
King nor the Aldermen, from their respective points of
view, were likely to forget Mr. Recorder's kind suggestion.
The next year was to be a critical one for that aspiring
lawyer. His future now depended on the success of the
King's policy or that of his opponents. As long as the
former could manage his own affairs without parliamentary
assistance, Sir George Jeffreys, now his declared adherent,
might hope to keep his place, for the Aldermen would not
dare get rid of their Recorder in the face of an independent
King. But let Charles fail in his attempt and be obliged
to summon a Parliament, and Mr. Recorder might look
for very short shrift from his aggrieved employers.

Whether Mr. Recorder was aware of these circumstances
or not, he made no concealment of his intentions, and with
increasing zeal threw himself heart and soul into the
service of the King. He gave up all attempts at compromise, and risked everything in his opposition to the
factions of the City.

These were in a state of great activity, printing and
publishing under seemly titles attacks upon the King and
his Government. One Benjamin Harris, a bookseller,
published, under the specious title of *An Appeal from the
Country to the City for the Preservation of His Majesty's
Person*, a book in which the King was accused of neglect-
ing to prosecute the Plot and the Duke of Monmouth
recommended as his successor in the place of the Duke of
York, on the ground that having the worst title he would
make the best King and " humour the people for want of
a title."

For publishing this pamphlet, Harris was brought
before Scroggs at the Guildhall in the February of 1680.
Harris had boasted before his trial that in what he did
he had " thousands who would stand by him." Some
portion of these thousands thronged the court, and by
clamour testified to their enthusiasm for the prisoner.

Jeffreys, who appeared to prosecute for the King, undaunted by this show of popular favour, expressed a hope that the crowd had come to blush for Harris not to encourage him, and deplored the rebellious spirit of the age. As to the book "it was as base a piece as ever was contrived in hell, either by Papists or the blackest rebel that ever was." If it had been written about a tradesman, he went on, the writer would long ago have had to hide his head, but nowadays one could do anything "under the dissemblance of a pretence for the Protestant religion."

The evidence against Harris was very clear. All his counsel could do was to call "a neighbour," who said Harris was very quiet and peaceable. "A bookseller that causes a factious book to be printed, or reprinted if it was printed before, is a factious fellow," was Jeffreys' trite and unimpeachable retort. "You say right," added Scroggs.

But the jury were reluctant to convict. They tried to find the prisoner guilty only of *selling* the book, an attempt greeted by a clamorous shout from the adherents. Scroggs said they must find a plain "Guilty" or "Not guilty." Still they hesitated, until Jeffreys suggested they should give their verdict one by one, by the poll : at which the good men and true all "cried out together," and returned a hurried "Guilty." Harris escaped with a fine and the pillory. Scroggs, smarting under similar attacks, would have whipped him, but Pemberton interceded.

Harris had been tried on February 5th. Two days later Jeffreys undertook the prosecution of another libellous bookseller. This time Scroggs had been the object of attack. The Lord Chief Justice had been having a very bad time since Wakeman's acquittal. Not only had dead cats been flung at his head, but in his own Court his " puisnes," Pemberton and Atkyns, sneered covertly at his treatment of Oates and lauded the Doctor's veracity in his presence. At a banquet at the Guildhall Shaftesbury and his confederate Lords openly taunted him with his change of front ; and in January of 1680 Oates exhibited articles against him before the Privy Council, in which, besides his legal misdemeanours, the Chief Justice was charged with swearing and drinking to excess at the house of a nameless gentleman of quality. Scroggs, in reply, called for the name of the unknown, and in short made such sport of the Doctor's high misdemeanours that the Council would hear no more of them. The Chief Justice's only consolation came from the King, who sent for him to his bedside and told him not to mind. "They have used me worse," he said, "and I am resolved we will stand or fall together."

As a result of this happy union, Francis Smith, book-seller, was charged on February 7th with a libel on the Chief Justice. Mr. Justice Jones presided. Sir Thomas Jones was a fellow countryman of Jeffreys, of a red countenance and a heated disposition, but "grave, reverend and impartial" according to Roger North, and a stern upholder of the royal prerogative. Smith's libel consisted in a book called *Observations upon the Late Trial of Sir George Wakeman, &c.* by a certain *Tom Ticklefoot, the Tabourer, late Clerk to Justice Clodpate.* "Justice Clodpate" was no other than the old Scroggs of Coleman's and Ireland's trials ; and in the pamphlet the doings of the new Scroggs of Wakeman's trial were facetiously compared with the former conduct of "old Clodpate." The most daring passage was that in which the author hinted at the report that Scroggs had been "approached" before the trial of Wakeman. "But by all that is good it was my old master Clodpate's desire, peace be with him ! always to sham up an evidence when anybody had been with him the morning before."

Smith was defended by a Mr. William Williams, a barrister and member of Parliament. He was a prominent member of the country party, and appeared in most of the cases in which the fortunes of that party were however indirectly concerned. He was a Welshman by birth, and consequently a mutual dislike and rivalry soon sprang up between Jeffreys and himself. Jeffreys contrived to quarrel with all his fellow countrymen. His cousin, Trevor, Williams and Mr.

Justice Jones,—they all seemed mightily jealous one of another, but were naturally united in feelings of greater animosity towards Sir George, as by far the most successful Welshman in the legal profession. Williams continued to be a thorn in the side of Sir George during the greater part of his career ; but, in spite of an act of gigantic apostasy perpetrated in the following reign, his achievements against the peace of his fellow countrymen met with little success.

Jeffreys, in opening the prosecution, attacked the license of the time with no less bitterness than in Harris' case, and vigorously denounced the seditious uses to which the agitation against Popery was being turned. " I know," he said, " that every word I utter is taken in short-hand to be commented on as persons' humours shall steer them ; but I do think, as being the mouth of the City of London, it is my duty to speak thus much, that I hope, nay, I may dare confidently affirm, that the generality of the City of London, all good men and men of abilities, are for the King and the Government as it is now established by law "—at which there was a general " hum " through the Court, testifying to the unpopularity of the Recorder's loyal sentiments.

However, Mr. Williams, who appeared for Smith, admitted that his client's libel was " sufficiently infamous," but was proceeding to demur to the information when Jeffreys interrupted him, " Sir, do you admit the record ? " " Sir, if you will give me leave you shall hear what we will admit," answered Williams. " Come, come, sir, if you do not admit the record, we will have none of your anticipation," says Mr. Recorder. " What do you call your speech but anticipation ? " retorted Williams ; and he went on to urge the languishing, sick and dying condition of his client (who lived, however, till 1688, and was only at the beginning of his troubles). He was about to admit Smith's guilt when up jumped a Mr. Fettiplace, counsel on the same side, and said he had no order from his client to admit anything. But nobody heeded Fettiplace, and the

Judge urged submission. "I am for a sinner's repentance with all my heart," echoed Jeffreys invitingly. The Judge spoke soothingly of Scroggs's pity and compassion. At last Mrs. Smith appeared, and agreed on her husband's behalf to a verdict of "Guilty" being taken. "You have done well," said Mr. Justice Jones, and he promised to intercede with Scroggs, "a person that loves no man's ruin, but delights rather in the universal welfare of all people." Jeffreys promised to do the same, but never did, according to Smith. The latter was let off with a small fine, but, being an incorrigible Anabaptist, will be heard of again shortly.

Not only in the courts of law did Jeffreys give public expression to his political sentiments. In every possible way he advertised his devotion to the Court. On the return of the Duke of York from abroad he waited on him with congratulations. In April he took part in a proceeding by which the methods of the Petitioners—as the agitators for the summoning of Parliament were now known—were called into the service of their opponents, and a nickname found for the Court party for which they must have been very grateful at such a season. On April 17th Mr. Francis Wythens, member for Westminster, and Sir George Jeffreys brought addresses to the King, one from his constituents, the other from the loyal citizens of London wherein they declared the method of petitioning then abroad to be the method of 1641, and intended to bring Charles II. to the block as his father before him, all which doings they "*abhorred*." "The train took," says Roger North, "and the frolic went all over England," so that from every town addresses of Abhorrence poured in, and "Abhorrer" became the answering nickname to Petitioner.

The next day Mr. Wythens was rewarded for his loyalty by the honour of Knighthood. Sir George Jeffreys in the course of a few days received a long-coveted prize for his share in the business. Denbighshire, the county in which Jeffreys was born and his family had long been established, was part of the Palatine Earldom of Chester. Among other privileges the Palatinate had its own courts of law presided over by a Chief Justice and "puisnes" whose jurisdiction extended over North Wales. It would be very pleasant to a successful young man like Jeffreys to hold such an office as that of Chief Justice of Chester for many and obvious reasons. As a stepping stone to higher things, as a means of receiving honour in his own country, and as a well paid, easy and comfortable employment Jeffreys looked on the place with longing eyes. And now he had arrived at a point in his career when he might not unreasonably aspire to such an honour. Young as he was, about thirty-two, his success and present position gave him a sufficient claim. But there was an obstacle in his path, and that an awkward one—the place was already occupied. Sir Job Charleton, a loyal old Cavalier, and a very reverend, deserving gentleman of sixty-five, had been Chief Justice now eighteen years. And the worst of it was, the old gentleman was very comfortable in his office. He belonged to an old Shropshire family, and was anxious to stop at home and die in his own country. But Jeffreys meant to have the place, and now seemed a fitting opportunity to seize it. Through the Duke of York and the Duchess of Portsmouth, brother and mistress, it was suggested to the King that Jeffreys' devotion should be acknowledged, that the Chief Justiceship of Chester would be to him the most pleasing form of acknowledgment and that, if it were conferred upon him, Sir Job could easily be consoled by a puisne Judgeship in the Court of Common Pleas. The King yielded, and an intimation was forwarded to poor old Sir Job to that effect. The latter, in great distress at this abrupt disturbance of his repose—for "it was like taking out the eyes of the good old gentleman," says Roger North—hurried up to London to see the King himself and ask the reason of his dismissal. In vain he sought an audience of Charles. At last one day he sat him down in St. James's Park, like "hermit poor," and waited at a spot where the King returning from his walk must pass him by. But Charles espied him from afar and fled his reproaches;

whereupon some say Sir Job pitied his poor master and
gave up hope and buckled to his business in the Common
Pleas ; others, that he did at length succeed in seeing his
master, who promised he should keep his place, and in true
Stuart fashion kept his promise by giving it to Jeffreys.
In any case on April 30th Jeffreys was gazetted Chief
Justice of Chester, and Charleton sat in the Common Pleas.
In the following month Sir George was promoted to be
one of the King's Serjeants.

Honours were falling thick upon him ; he was gathering
a worthy reward for his devotion to the King's employment.   But such marked success was fraught with danger
to a man of Jeffreys' temperament.   He possessed one of
those extreme dispositions that charm us in the artist but
depress us in the Judge,—a temperament passing in a
moment from the height of self-satisfaction to the utmost
depths of gloom and depression, over-confident in success,
unduly prostrate in failure, intemperate, emotional.   In
the artist, emotion of this kind is translated into his work
and lends it passion and intensity.   But Jeffreys was a
lawyer, not an artist, and, had he confined himself strictly
to the exercise of his profession, might have learnt to sub-
due his dangerous tendencies towards an emotional expression of life.   Unfortunately, he belonged to that class of
lawyers who were politicians first and men of law afterwards, ambitious of power and preferment, using their legal
career as a stepping stone to the great places in the State.
The furious excitement of politics in Charles the
Second's reign had much in common with the artistic
temperament, or the Celtic nature, or the want of moral
sense, or whatever we like to call the absence of the more
stolid virtues.   For that reason its effect on Jeffreys
would be exciting in the extreme, and serve to kindle a
zeal and intemperance of action, highly improper and
disastrous in a lawyer and of very questionable value in a
politician at any other period than at the end of the
seventeenth century.   Jeffreys too was a young man,
prematurely successful, ardent, attractive, a great favourite

in high quarters, arbitrary in character and principles ; the consequence of which was that, at this point of his career, he gave way to an undue elation of spirits which took unpleasant forms, made him very unpopular, drew on him public rebuke and lost him his Recordership. Certainly Jeffreys had by now so far committed himself on the King's side that he could not have expected much mercy at the hands of a refractory Parliament ; but we find evidence that about this time the undue elation of spirits, consequent on his rapid advancement in the esteem and confidence of his party, developed an arrogance which may have been temporarily effective with the seditious but was unwelcome to his seniors and very much resented by his opponents. Jeffreys always wanted keeping in order ; he could behave very well if he chose, and had an unexpected habit of rising worthily to great occasions, but, towards the end of 1680, he rather lost his head and conceived himself to be a little more powerful and secure than he really was.

The government was still bent on suppressing the seditious temper of their opponents in the City. At the beginning of July another bookseller, one Henry Carr, was arraigned before Scroggs at the Guildhall on the charge of publishing a *Weekly Packet of Advice from Rome.* The libellous passage was one reporting the discovery of a " wonder-working plaister truly catholic in operation," which " made justice deaf and blind, took spots out of the deepest treasons, helped poisons and those who used them, and stifled a plot as certainly as the itch is destroyed by butter and brimstone." The drift of these insinuations is obvious ; the pamphlet was a thinly veiled attack on the dubious attitude of the Government towards the Plot. Jeffreys and Wythens, the original Abhorrers, appeared for the King. The former in opening his case touched very appropriately on the methods of Carr and his party. " He thinks," he said, " he can scratch the itch of the age, and that he may libel any man concerned in the Government if he can but call him a Papist or popishly affected." Such unpalatable truth as this was very unwelcome to the audience ; they had come to hear quite another story. When Sir Francis Winnington, who defended Carr, spoke of the methods of the prosecution as those by which an angry Papist might hope to convict an innocent Protestant, a loud "Hem !" from the people testified their approval of the insinuation. "You see what a case we are in," cried Scroggs ; "you see what a sort of people we are got among." The witnesses against Carr were evidently affected by the popular feeling, and it was only with great difficulty and no little ingenuity that Scroggs and Jeffreys could get the truth out of them. The latter neatly turned the tables on these unwilling Protestants. Formerly, he said, they had complained of the difficulty of getting the truth from Popish witnesses. "Now," he went on, alluding to the printer of Carr's book, a very obstinate witness, "I must say, if ever anything were an instance of Popery, then that man is one of the Jesuitest fellows that ever was ; for he does cant so like them that a man can't tell how to govern himself." He concluded with a dig at the "Hems" of his audience. "Whoever it is that after this evidence shall acquit this man, he must be a man of humming conscience indeed !" The Chief Justice followed the Recorder's lead. In his charge he taunted the rabble with humming and making a great noise during the trial but after a conviction doing nothing for the unfortunate men they had cheered to their punishment. Poor Benjamin Harris, he said, had written to him from his prison that all his party had forsaken him and no man would give him anything to help him to pay his fine. "And therefore these fellows, these hummers, let them all know, whenever they come to espouse a cause of public concern against the Government, they spoil it ; and when they are taken, they ruin one another." The jury, after an hour's consultation, found Carr guilty. "You have done like honest men," quoth my Lord Chief Justice. "They have done like honest men," echoed Mr. Recorder.

Confident as Jeffreys was becoming with the apparent success of his efforts, he showed how well, on occasions, he could "become the seat of justice." The trial of Giles, a Papist, charged with the attempted murder of a Protestant magistrate, at which Jeffreys presided as Recorder, has been commended by the late Sir James Stephen as one of the only two Plot trials that were conducted with "conspicuous fairness and decency." Like most impartial proceedings in courts of law the trial is tame and uneventful. Jeffreys, with an open mind, cannot help becoming conventional. His gifts were essentially militant in character, and required the stimulant of indignation or prejudice to show them off in their most fanciful and characteristic fashion.

Too fanciful and characteristic for Mr. Baron Weston! This learned and resolute Judge, a stern prerogative lawyer, fearing neither man nor Parliament, presided at Kingston Assizes in the July of 1680. If treated reasonably, Roger North says, there was no gentleman " more obliging, condescensive and communicative; " but, being insupportably tormented by gout, his temper became so touchy that any unreasonable opposition made him appear as if he was mad. He was evidently in no very amiable mood this month at Kingston, for he opened the Assizes by a fierce attack on Zwinglius and Calvin *à propos* of the conduct of petitioners. Before him in this mood appeared Jeffreys, on *his* side unduly elated and inclining to the masterful. A spirit of this kind in a powerful advocate usually leads to an improper interference with his opponent's case. Jeffreys at once took the whole matter in hand, and examined and cross-examined all the witnesses, and interrupted his learned friend's questions with the usual exclamations and side comments. This was too much for the gouty Judge, who told the Serjeant to hold his tongue. Some words passed between them; Jeffreys complained that Weston did not use him like a counsellor, curbing him in the managing of his brief. "Ha!" exclaimed the angry Baron, "since the King has thrown his favours upon you, in making you Chief Justice of Chester, you think to run down everybody; if you think you are aggrieved, make your complaint. Here's nobody cares for it." Jeffreys again protested, and was again told to hold his tongue, whereupon he sat down and wept with anger. Some have made these passionate tears at Kingston a cause of reproach and disgrace to Jeffreys. But be it remembered, Jeffreys was at this time the spoilt child of legal fortune; he had had everything his own way, he had only to ask and receive, he had a Welsh temper and probably kept late hours. No wonder he exhibited a momentary weakness at the pointed violence of the Baron's repartee. Jeffreys always had a nice sense of affliction, though he was sufficiently unselfish to control it when it conflicted with the just deserts of other people.

The report of this proceeding at Kingston soon reached London, and served with another matter to give the Recorder an unenviable notoriety. In the Verney Correspondence one writing from London in August says "Jeffreys is extremely cried out against, about Justice Doughty's being covicted of murder. Some say he and Mrs. Wall, the Duchess of Portsmouth's woman, lay their heads together to have it so; others he and Strode, Bailiff of Westminster, agreed to it. Either was very bad if true."

The mystery contained in this paragraph can never be solved, and there is no entirely trustworthy evidence to show how or from what motives Jeffreys acted in this affair.

The facts are these. Philip Doughty, Esq., of Chesham, is included in a recusancy list of Papists drawn up for the House of Lords in the December of 1680, but is stated to be still in Newgate at the time. In July or August of that year Doughty had been convicted at the Old Bailey of the murder of a hackney coachman by the name of Capps. On September 9th Doughty addressed a petition to the King in Council asking for a reconsideration of his conviction on the following grounds :—

That the wounds were proved to be accidental, and not dangerous.

That the wounds were cured, and Capps went about his business again.

That he died of malignant fever, in the course of which ignorant people had mistaken his vomiting for blood.

That being assaulted by Capps the petitioner had been obliged to draw.

That the jury gave a rash and hard verdict, considering no malice was proved.

The King referred Doughty's petition to the Lord Mayor (Clayton) and the Recorder (Jeffreys), to report upon ; and in a few days they reported, recommending the petitioner to the King's mercy, owing to the differences of the witnesses as to the cause of Capps's death.

But in December of the same year we find Doughty presenting another petition to the Council. He complains that, though pardoned, he has never received a warrant to that effect, that he is still in prison and has been told that he will have to give money for a pardon if he wants it. The King in answer ordered the warrant to issue, and declared that in passing a pardon no one was to demand more than the usual fees.

Doughty was presumably released after this, and the matter ended.

What share Jeffreys had in these transactions it is impossible to say. His name only appears in them officially as recommending Doughty's pardon. Whether he had in the first instance pressed unduly for a conviction from interested motives or to please Mrs. Wall, the confidante of his protectress, the Duchess of Portsmouth ; or whether he had acted in collusion with Strode, a man of some violence in his office, who was about the same time tried for breaking into an Ambassador's house ; or whether he had had any share in the delay in the execution of Doughty's pardon ;—these questions cannot be answered.

Jeffreys was undoubtedly very intimate with the

Portsmouth faction at this time, and his familiarity with Mrs. Wall had already been made a theme of popular verse. It is alluded to in some lines dealing with his desertion of the popular party :—

> "But though they fret and bite their nails and brawl,
> He'll slight them and go kiss dear Nelly Wall."

Doughty's case is also alluded to in an indecent poem on "the Duchess of Portsmouth's Looking Glass," ascribed to Lord Rochester, in which occur the lines:—

> "Learn'd Scroggs and honest Jeffreys
> A faithful friend to you who e'er is ;
> He made the jury come in booty,
> And for your service would hang Doughty."

Had Jeffreys betrayed his judicial functions to gratify some spite of this lady against Doughty, or is the story merely an outcome of Jeffreys' growing unpopularity in the City and his known alliance with the Court ? Doughty certainly seems to have been unfairly treated in more ways than one, and rumour has credited Jeffreys with some share in his ill-treatment.

In any case both these incidents—Weston's rebuke and Doughty's conviction—went to swell the discontent against the Recorder that was daily rising in the City. It found vent in personal attacks on Jeffreys circulated in broadsheets about the town ; and the usual anonymous letter was not wanting. This took the form of a letter from "A Liveryman of London," in which he told Sir George how he had been defending his reputation against the attacks of an imaginary detractor. The old scandal about the second Lady Jeffreys was repeated ; Jeffreys was accused of having bragged that, as long as Mrs. Wall was mistress and the Duchess of Portsmouth was her mistress and her master's mistress, he could have what he would at Court ; and was warned by the author that, if he put his head in the pillory as Harris had, he would never get it out again.

Jeffreys however seems to have been singularly unaffected by these attacks. If we are to believe Francis Smith, he had in September of 1680 lost none of his vigour. The incorrigible Anabaptist had been at it again. This time he had not attacked the King's Government ; he had turned his attention to more domestic matters, and published a telling indictment of the gross expenditure of the Mayor and Sheriffs in the way of eating and drinking. He complained, with some show of reason, that the office of Sheriff had now become such an expensive one that no poor man could hold it ; and he cited an Act of Philip and Mary for retrenching the expenses of the Mayor and Sheriffs, which, he said, those whose duty it was to check such expenditure refused to put into action. For these modest incitements to civic economy, Smith was charged at the Guildhall with "maliciously, scandalously, seditiously, wickedly printing a malicious, etc., etc., book, to the great scandal and contempt of our lord the King, to the disturbance of his peace and against his crown and dignity." The indignation of the lavish aldermen had apparently quite mastered their sense of humour ; but the grand jury at the Guildhall, failing to appreciate how Smith's publication could rationally be construed into an intent to disturb the King's peace, threw out the bill. This did not suit Jeffreys at all. He seems to have considered that anything bearing the name of Francis Smith must be wicked, malicious and calculated to disturb the royal peace ; indeed, if we are to believe Smith, so firmly was this general conviction rooted in his mind that he had not troubled to read the particular work specified in the indictment. " Francis Smith ! " that was enough for Jeffreys, and ought to be enough for the grand jury. Accordingly he sent them back three times to reconsider their decision ; but they could not see their way to gratify his wishes. Then they should see his face. The terror of Jeffreys' countenance when moved to indignation has become a household story ; he was himself quite aware of the power he enjoyed in this respect, and frequently resorted to it in extreme cases. "God bless me from such jurymen," he exclaimed ; "I will see the face of every one of them and let others see them also. I will hear them repeat every man of them their own sense of this bill, thus exposing them to all possible contempt." The Bar was cleared, and one by one the seventeen reluctant gentlemen passed before the Recorder. But even the fierce glance of that great man failed to shake their conviction. "Ignoramus," they answered one after another, until, transported with rage, Jeffreys dismissed them with the assurance that God Himself would find it impossible to pardon their perjury.

He then called for Smith. "Mr. Smith," he said in bland tones, "you have the countenance of an ingenious person. Here are two persons that this jury have brought in ' Ignoramus' besides yourself, and yet they are so ingenious as to confess the indictment against them, and for their ingenuity in confessing they shall be fined but twopence apiece. Well, come, Mr. Smith, follow their examples. Show yourself as you seem to be an ingenious person and confess and try the grace and favour of this Court, and shame the jury that hath brought in a verdict contrary to plain evidence." To this gentle invitation Smith made the following reply : "Sir, my ingenuity hath sufficiently experienced the reward of your severity already formerly ; and besides, I know no law commands me to accuse myself, neither shall I ; and the jury have done like true Englishmen, and worthy citizens ; and blessed be God for such a just jury ; " to which Mr. Recorder, without more ado, politely retorted by recommitting Mr. Francis Smith to Newgate.

In three hours, however, Mr. Smith was released on bail, and ultimately the matter was allowed to drop ; but not before Smith had had a good deal more trouble with the Recorder in his attempts to get a copy of his indictment from the Judge's clerk. The Anabaptist concludes his narrative of these episodes with the following devout prayer : "From such a Judge (Scroggs) and such a Recorder of London and such judgment, good Lord deliver me, and may every true citizen and right Englishman say Amen."

So I am sure they will if they read Smith's narrative, which is, unfortunately, the only extant account of these proceedings. There is no official report of the trial. According to Smith's account, Jeffreys certainly treated the prisoner with scant justice, but, he probably considered, with not undue severity. In the Recorder's opinion, severity was perhaps more important than strict justice in dealing with such as Smith. The latter was a very determined foe of the Government, who spent most of the next six years in prison for various literary offences. It was Smith rather than Smith's particular crime that Jeffreys resented. That he had trouble with the grand jury is not at all surprising. About this time the juries of the City packed by the Whig Sheriffs were showing themselves very reluctant to proceed against members of the popular party, and Jeffreys had probably already experienced this on more than one occasion in his capacity as Recorder. The political battle was raging with ever-increasing vehemence as the time for the meeting of Parliament drew nearer. Which party would find itself uppermost when that time arrived was as yet uncertain. Meanwhile, the Government, who were above all anxious for a Parliament that should not concern themselves with the old agitations of the Plot and the Exclusion, was not likely to spare men like Smith, whose business was to keep these very questions alive by means of book and pamphlet. Jeffreys may also have thought to please his friends in the Court of Aldermen, Clayton, a very munificent man, and others, by resenting Smith's criticisms on their extravagance. In justice to Jeffreys, it must not be forgotten that he promised to forgive Smith for a crime for which a grand jury refused to "present" him, at the small cost of twopence; and that Smith in reply took up a most provoking stand on his undoubted legal rights. We only need add to this the evidence of his own writings to show that Smith was a very irritating person. Jeffreys' conduct to Smith was made one of the charges against him before the Committee of Parliament appointed two months later to enquire into his behaviour as Recorder, but the circumstances do not seem to have evoked much resentment. Perhaps Smith was too well known to them.

Smith's jury, however, was not unnaturally indignant with the Recorder. Rightly or wrongly, he had called them perjurers, a criticism for which they sought to be revenged. Under the leadership of Mr. Elias Best, they waited upon Scroggs and asked permission to indict Jeffreys. The Chief Justice told them that they had better defer their charge until the next Old Bailey Sessions, as it could not be tried till then, and he did not like to leave so high a man as the Recorder so long a time under an imputation of that kind. The jury agreed to this; but when the next Sessions came round, their prey had escaped them; Jeffreys had ceased to be Recorder. But that thoughtful man did not forget Mr. Elias Best and his kindly zeal on his behalf. The latter, being convicted some time later of drinking a treasonable health, absconded to avoid his punishment. In 1684 Jeffreys, then Chief Justice, happened to go the Northern circuit. Best, who had retired to these parts, heard of this, and, filled with a romantic idea that great men forget injuries done to them in their early days, waited upon Jeffreys and desired his service to his lordship. The Chief Justice, unaware of his identity, suffered him to depart. Unfortunately, some kind friend enlightened the Judge as to the identity of his respectful visitor; and, to his intense surprise, the well-satisfied Best found himself, in a very short space of time, lodged in York gaol. A little later he was removed to London, and in the Court of King's Bench had an early opportunity of once again desiring his service to his lordship, of which condescension his lordship marked his gracious appreciation by fining Mr. Elias Best £1,000, and affording him in the pillory a public opportunity of testifying to the thoughtful gratitude of Sir George Jeffreys towards old friends.

The proceedings against Smith were the last of Jeffreys' many notable appearances as Recorder of London. Retribution, or, more properly, vengeance, was at hand. At the end of October the long prorogued Parliament met, and, evil omen for Mr. Recorder, proceeded to elect as their Speaker his fellow-countryman and constant antagonist in the law courts, Mr. William Williams. Charles, who had quarrelled with Louis XIV and was accordingly in want of money, hoped, by supporting an anti-French policy abroad, to divert the attention of the country party from home affairs ; but the latter, now in receipt of French gold themselves, firmly declined to follow his Majesty's invitation, and returned to Popery and the Exclusion with a fierceness aggravated by a long silence and all manner of affronts. From its very first sitting Parliament showed its determination to revive all the distasteful questions which had disgusted the King before, and to punish with all possible severity those who in the interval had, as they thought, unduly or unlawfully violated the rights of the subject or improperly extended the prerogative of the Crown.

Of the Judges, Scroggs, Jones and Weston were immediately attacked, and articles of impeachment presented against them. Sir Francis Wythens, who shared with Jeffreys the honour of being the first Abhorrer, was expelled the House of Commons, and received his sentence kneeling at the bar of the House.

It was not likely so notorious an offender as Jeffreys would be excepted at such a time. His enemies in the City seized the opportunity to present a petition to the House of Commons at the very opening of Parliament, praying for his removal from the Recordership. At the same time the Common Hall of London petitioned the Lord Mayor and Court of Aldermen to similar effect. In the latter petition Jeffreys was spoken of as " of infamous memory" ; he was charged with falsely accusing the Council and misrepresenting them to the King, of menacing and threatening juries, affrighting and confounding witnesses, and being, in short, "most obnoxious and insupportably burdensome" in his office, "a person dangerous and destructive to public peace, unity and prosperity."

On October 27th, the House of Commons appointed a Committee to enquire into the charges against Sir George Jeffreys. On November 13th the Committee presented their report, upon which a debate ensued. The prevailing temper of the House was encouraged by Lord William Russell, who opened the proceedings by calling Jeffreys a great criminal, accusing him of countenancing the Plot and asking for an exemplary punishment. The debate is most remarkable for Mr. Booth's (afterwards Lord Delamere's) speech describing Jeffreys' conduct as Chief Justice of Chester. These were his words :—

" The county for which I serve is Cheshire, which is a County Palatine, and we have two Judges peculiarly assigned us by his Majesty : our puisne Judge I have nothing to say against him, for he is a very honest man for ought I know ; but I cannot be silent as to our chief Judge, and I will name him, because what I have to say will appear more probable : his name is Sir George Jeffreys, who I must say behaved himself more like a jack pudding than with that gravity which beseems a Judge ; he was mighty witty upon the prisoners at the bar ; he was very full of his jokes upon people that came to give evidence, not suffering them to declare what they had to say in their own way and method, but would interrupt them, because they behaved themselves with more gravity than he ; and, in truth, the people were strangely perplexed when they were to give in their evidence ; but I do not insist upon this, nor upon the late hours he kept up and down our city ; it's said he was every night drinking till two o'clock, or beyond that time, and that he went to his chamber drunk ; but this I have only by common fame, for I was not in his company ; I bless God I am not a man of his principles or behaviour ; but in the mornings he appeared with the symptoms of a man that over night had taken a large cup. But that which I have to say is the complaint of every man, especially of them who had any lawsuits. Our Chief Justice has a very arbitrary power in appointing the assize when he pleases ; and this man has strained it to the highest point ; for whereas we were accustomed to have two assizes, the first about April or May, the latter about September, it was this year the middle (as I remember) of August before we had any assize, and then he despatched business so well that he left half the causes untried, and, to help the matter, has resolved that we shall have no more assizes this year."

Booth's description of Jeffreys, even Lord Campbell admits, must be rather highly coloured. Sir William Jones, the ex-Attorney-General, who spoke later in the debate and against Jeffreys, opposed Booth's suggestion to remove him from his office at Chester, not considering the speech of the latter a sufficient proof on which the House could fitly act in the matter. Booth is known as a very violent party politician, extreme in his language and of an inflammable temper. " A little thing puts him in a passion," says Clarendon in his diary. That Jeffreys as Chief Justice of Chester may have been dissipated in his habits and occasionally jocular in the exercise of his functions, his conduct on certain occasions as Chief Justice of England might well incline us to believe ; but it may also be safely inferred from the subsequent conduct of Mr. Booth that where he was dealing with a political enemy we must not look for impartial consideration or temperate language at his hands. His smug blessing of God that he is not a man of Jeffreys' principles gives a Pecksniffian tone to his denunciation ; and it is evident from Jones's comment that his self-advertising tirade had not been altogether convincing to the House. It will be seen later on that the excellent Bishop of St. Asaph, Dr. Lloyd, was very far from sharing Mr. Booth's opinion of the conduct of the Chief Justice of Chester.

The real weight of the charges against Jeffreys seems to have lain in his conduct before the Privy Council in the matter of petitioning, when, in the presence of the Mayor and Aldermen, he advised the King how to direct them to suppress all petitions.   No other charge of any consequence was mentioned in the debate, though many others had been made before the Committee.   One man spoke in his defence—his cousin, John Trevor, who owed to Jeffreys his present prosperity.

"A man that is accused of many great crimes and can wipe off some of them is happy.   He (Jeffreys) stands fair as to his carriage relating to the libel and the rape. There is no evidence against him that he ever packed a jury, or has gone about to clear a person nocent.   He has been counsel for the King in the Plot and behaved himself worthily, and, if I may say, he was too forward in prosecuting ; if so, that may make some atonement for his forwardness in other matters.   His carriage in the matter of petitioning was an error of judgment.   He is a gentleman that hath raised himself in his profession. There is nothing said that he hath done wrong to any person in estate or life.   He said, ' He would submit his case to the House,' and I hope in some measure you will take pity on him.'

But they would not, for all that " Squinting Jack " might urge.   " What sticks with me," reiterated Jeffreys' constant friend, Sir Robert Clayton, " is his officiousness at the Council Table."   Jeffreys had on that occasion made Clayton, then Lord Mayor, and his colleagues look very foolish, and such impertinence from their own Recorder not unnaturally rankled in the hearts of Mayor and Aldermen.   The House of Commons readily took up their grievance, and saw in Jeffreys a most pernicious and irregular servant of the prerogative.   In spite of Trevor the House resolved on an address to his Majesty to remove Sir George Jeffreys out of all public offices.   On November 20th Charles sent back a message that he would consider of it.   On November 23rd, the Court of Aldermen received the resolution of the Commons, and ordered Sir Henry Tyler and Sir James Smith to acquaint Mr. Recorder with it.   On December 2nd, Mr. Recorder saved any further trouble by resigning his office ; but the

King declined to remove him from the Chief Justiceship of Chester.

Jeffreys' detractors have sought to make his fall unduly ignominious. Strict inquiry shows that, on the contrary, his removal was purely political, and that he received milder treatment at the hands of his enemies than was accorded to others of equal guilt with himself. Roger North has said that, in addition to the resolution passed against him in the Commons, Jeffreys was reprimanded on his knees by Mr. Speaker Williams before the whole House. There is no record of any such proceeding in the official journals of the House.[1] Had any such proceeding taken place, it would certainly have been recorded, as it is in the case of Sir Francis Wythens, Peyton and others. Why the House did not proceed to this extremity may be variously explained. Jeffreys probably had many friends among the members, men like Clayton, who would be anxious to spare him any great indignity. Many charges had been brought against him, but the greater number had not been established. Jeffreys had shown a desire to submit himself to the House, and the marked favour with which he was regarded in the highest quarters may have disinclined the Commons to offend the King by showing excessive severity towards one of his chosen servants. Unpopular as Jeffreys had made himself in the City by his political attitude, he was not allowed to resign the Recordership without receiving from the Aldermen substantial testimony to their appreciation of the services he had rendered in his exercise of that office. On the day that he announced his resignation the City Chamberlain was ordered to pay him £200, the residue of a sum voted to him in acknowledgment of his good services to the City, and a Committee was appointed to consider what compensation should be allowed him for the great sums he had disbursed in fitting up his official

---

[1] A witness at Colledge's trial certainly taunted Jeffreys with having been "on his knees" before Parliament, but there is no evidence to show that his words are to be taken as conveying the literal truth.

residence in Aldermanbury. With these tokens of mutual good-will, Jeffreys parted with his old employers. Political differences had come between them and made a longer union impossible ; but it was not without some regret that they lost an entertaining companion and an efficient Judge. Save in one or two instances, Mr. Recorder Jeffreys had shown himself to be a worthy occupant of an office in which eloquence, severity and a sense of humour will always be appropriate and desirable.

" Upon troubles in Parliament he would not stand his ground, but quitted his Recordership in fear and great entreaty." Such is Sir Francis North's note upon Jeffreys' retirement, and upon this note Roger has dutifully founded his incorrect history of the incident. His story about the reprimand is sufficiently contradicted by the silence of the Commons' Journals on the subject. He goes on to tell us—probably from his brother's information —how Jeffreys, alarmed by the action of the Parliament, begged and entreated the King to allow him to resign his place, and so put an end to the proceedings ; how Charles, loth to lose so valuable and influential a supporter among the citizens, for some time refused his permission ; and how at length yielding to his entreaties the King laughingly exclaimed that Sir George was not Parliament-proof and never had any real value for him afterwards. Charles II. never had any real value for anybody. His own character was too dubious, his perception too acute, his insincerity too constitutional to allow him to value any man save for his immediate utility. But that Charles can have seriously expected Jeffreys to hold on to his Recorder-ship after the meeting of Parliament is very unlikely. If Sir George had been a decorous trimmer like North, he might have been expected to do so ; but a man who had as openly avowed his sentiments as he, could not have retained his post ; it had become untenable to a person of his political sympathies. The City, by the choice of Jeffreys' successor, showed how absolutely foreign to their requirements had been the late Recorder. Sir John Treby, who took Jeffreys' place, was, according to a Tory writer, a fanatical Whig, the trusty confidant of faction, a free-thinker who made the Scriptures and religion a jest and shared with his predecessor but one qualification for the office, that of hard drinking. Jeffreys was a fanatic but not a Whig fanatic, he was the trusty confidant of a faction but not the Whig faction, and he had strong religious principles. He resigned the office quietly and submissively, because it would have been silly, if he had to go, to have been kicked out with ignominy ; he bowed to the storm because it would have been futile to have withstood it ; and if Charles thought the worse of him for doing so, he must have possessed less good sense than has been generally attributed to him.

Burnet, in opposition to North, says that Jeffreys was rather " raised " than depressed in the eyes of his master by the proceedings of Parliament against him. This is the more likely story. Charles's subsequent employment of Jeffreys in his most important legal concerns is directly contradictory of North's account.

Jeffreys fell at the end of 1680, because it was an hour of Whig victory. The victory was short-lived. When the tide turned once more, Jeffreys resumed his former influence, and enjoyed in a full measure the confidence of his own party. As a lawyer, circumstances were about to give him a greater share in the political history of his times than has ever before or since fallen to a person in his situation ; but it was an influence he had better have exercised in any other capacity than that of a lawyer, an influence that has been disastrous to his reputation if salutary to his country, an influence too severely felt even at this distance of time to be candidly or impartially considered. Jeffreys is now (1680) in his thirty-third year—he has eight more years to live. In these coming eight years he is to establish his reputation, his claim to historical notice. He has already plunged deeply into the politics of his day ; he has seen a political party put to death innocent Papists on the evidence of villains ; he has seen the courts of law used as the instruments of faction, the Judges swayed by passion and prejudice on the one side and the other ; he has felt the pains of defeat and the merciless accompaniments of political victory ; he has witnessed the unscrupulousness of statesmen, the brutality of the mob. One day he hopes to grasp power and authority in his own person. Trained in a reckless school, the servant of heartless masters, he will be predisposed by his character to fall in too readily with the violent passions of his times. His gifts, which at another period might have charmed and rejoiced all but the ever jealous and depressed, will now only serve to sharpen the sting of his resentment, tempt him to aggravate the distresses of his enemies, and draw down upon him that rich measure of exasperation only enjoyed by those whose misdeeds are enlivened by a striking personality and an unamiable attitude towards religious dissent.

VIII

THE JUDICIAL WAR

1681—1683

KING CHARLES endured his acrimonious Parliament until the March of 1681, when, having once more arranged to become a pensioner of Louis XIV., he was enabled to dissolve it, and never summoned another as long as he was King. The Whigs, by the unscrupulous violence of their methods, had to a great extent alienated public opinion ; so that when Charles took them by surprise at Oxford and sent his Commons about their business, public feeling was neither shocked nor alarmed. Deprived of Parliament as an arena, the courts of justice and the City Council became the new fields of battle where the contest between Whig and Tory was continued. But in the former field the Whigs were soon worsted. For a time they contrived, by means of friendly Sheriffs, to pack the Middlesex juries ; but as soon as the Court had taken over the appointment of the Sheriffs for itself, resistance was hopeless. Judge and jury in the King's hands, there was little chance of salvation for any Whigs who might fall into the clutches of the Crown lawyers.

Immediately after the dissolution in March the " judicial war " began. In such a war Serjeant Jeffreys would naturally be one of the foremost warriors. If the King had lost confidence in him, he had not lost the necessity of his services. He was briefed for the Crown in almost every State trial, until his elevation to the Bench in

1683. In spite of his fall he remained one of the King's chief adherents in the City, and was put into positions in which his influence, always considerable, could be best exerted. The King, as leader of the City Militia, was pleased to turn out certain of his officers, Whigs such as Sir Robert Clayton, and to replace them by Tories such as Sir George Jeffreys and his Alderman namesake Sir Robert Jeffreys. In the Lieutenancy of the City also Patience Ward, the late Lord Mayor, and Clayton, made way for Sir George Jeffreys and Sir John Chapman, a future Lord Mayor, who played a tragi-comic part in the drama of Jeffreys' downfall. Jeffreys was beginning to enjoy a very satisfactory revenge on his old masters. When he and his father-in-law Bludworth waited on the King with petitions, they were commended for their seasonable loyalty ; whilst the Mayor and Aldermen who followed them were reprimanded for meddling, and told to go home about their business. The King after dissolving Parliament had put forth a declaration, giving his reasons for the step. From all parts of the country addresses poured in—some sincere, some affected—thanking him for his conduct. One came from the apprentices of London, whose joy was so great that they gave a dinner at Sadlers' Hall to celebrate their loyalty, on which occasion Sir George Jeffreys was an honoured guest.

These were the pleasures of victory ; but there was the business of victory also, which had to be attended to in the courts of law. Besides his services as King's Serjeant, Jeffreys was appointed Chairman of the Middlesex Sessions held at Hicks's Hall, where he was able to gratify his undying dislike of religious dissent. But his services in the cause are best recorded in the reports of the State Trials in which he took part as counsel for the Crown. In some of them he took the leading part, in spite of the presence of the Attorney and Solicitor-General. It is in this respect that he is most closely associated with the history of the period ; for from the dissolution of Parliament in 1681 to the death of Charles in 1685, the history of the commencement of the Whig and Tory struggle is to be read, almost entirely, in the volumes of the State Trials. In their pages we may read how the methods of the Whigs in 1678, the violent convictions of unoffending Papists on infamous testimony, the coercion of judge and jury by popular frenzy, and the unscrupulous use which Shaftesbury and his party made of the weapons of the law, were turned against their authors ; and how, on better evidence and with more justice, the Whig leaders paid with death the penalty of their past excesses. Whig writers have deliberately blinded us to the retributive element in the so-called martyrdom of their heroes in the cause of English liberty, and have attacked the conduct of those whose duty it was to work out this retribution with an intemperance that less biassed judges have been unable to approve or justify.

In order to give an appearance of impartiality to his intentions, Charles, in the April of 1681, removed Scroggs from the Chief Justiceship of the King's Bench. He was consoled by a pension of £1,500 a year and a knighthood for his son ; but he was surprised nevertheless at his dismissal. Posterity cannot share his feeling of astonishment. Scroggs had made himself ridiculous ; his ill-judged vehemence, his extravagant eloquence, his preposterous, even if sincere, revulsion of feeling, all combined to arouse contempt ; and, as he never seems to have inspired fear, he had become useless and dangerous. Scroggs was a man who can never have " become the seat of justice " as Jeffreys did, on the admission of his warmest enemy. Jeffreys, if heated in temper, had a well-balanced and a legal mind, and a sense of humour which in his hottest moments always saved him from making a fool of himself ; moreover he inspired genuine feelings of terror in the hearts of men. All these advantages in a strong judge were denied to Scroggs : his mind was intrepid but blatant; he had none of the true instinct of a lawyer ; he had wit, perhaps, but little humour ; and he never seems to have terrified any man, in spite of the violence of his tongue. But he was not a butcher's son, and has probably incurred the wrath of posterity more by his folly than his villainy. Charles appointed Sir Francis Pemberton to succeed Scroggs. Pemberton had already been a puisne Judge of the King's Bench, but had been dismissed soon after Wakeman's trial for showing too much zeal against the Papists and too great faith in Oates. In both these respects he had certainly proved himself in no way superior to the popular prejudice, and his conduct towards the Papists in whose trials he took part was as harsh as that of Scroggs, though less violently expressed. When the latter veered in his opinions, Pemberton openly sneered at him on the Bench, and was accordingly dismissed. But he carried away with him the reputation of being a sound and honest lawyer, and, in spite of his conduct towards the Papists, a man comparatively free from political prejudice. If he had any leanings, they would seem to have been towards an interpretation of law more compatible with royal prerogative than popular government. In recalling him to the bench, Charles regarded him as a man respected by both parties, whose decisions in his favour would be more acceptable as coming from a reputedly impartial Judge.

Soon after his appointment as Chief Justice, Pemberton was able to satisfy both Whigs and Tories. He secured the conviction of Dr. Oliver Plunket, the Romish Archbishop of Armagh and Primate of Ireland, on evidence of the usual dubious kind, for plotting a Popish rising in that country; and he also condemned to death FitzHarris, a dangerous libeller of the Court, whom it was for many reasons expedient to punish. In both of these trials, Serjeant Jeffreys was among the prosecuting counsel, but his share in the proceedings was of a very secondary nature.

He took a much more prominent part in the trial of Stephen Colledge, which was held at Oxford on August 17th. This man was known as the " Protestant joiner." By trade a joiner, his superior abilities and fanatical enthusiasm in the Protestant cause had attracted the notice of Lord William Russell and other Whig politicians. He was the author of most of the squibs and pamphlets which appeared at the time of Wakeman's acquittal, attacking the King, the Duke and Chief Justice Scroggs. The meeting of Parliament in 1680 encouraged his intemperate violence, and he openly threatened the Court if they attempted to defeat the ends of the country party. When Charles alarmed the Whigs by removing the meeting place of Parliament to Oxford, apprehension only stimulated the joiner's energies to more violent resistance. He arrived at Oxford armed and accoutred with pistol, carbine, coat-of-mail and headpiece. When an angry politician of the opposite party hit him on the nose and made it bleed, he exclaimed: "I have lost the first blood in the cause, but it will not be long before more is lost." He also brought with him a large stock of green ribbons, with "No Popery," "No Slavery" woven on them, which he presented to those willing to become members of the "Green Ribbon Club"; and distributed caricatures, in one of which the King was represented as carrying Parliament on his back in the shape of a raree-show box, with a view to drowning it in a ditch; in another, the Duke of York, half bushman and half devil, was depicted, booted and spurred, riding the Church of England to Rome.

Such flagrant proceedings were bound to attract the unfavourable regard of the Government. In the hour of victory, when the King had decided to revenge himself on those who had been hounding him to the executions of innocent men and furnish an example to the turbulent and seditious, Colledge found himself clapt into the Tower on a charge of treason. On the 8th of July, he was arraigned at the Old Bailey, but a Whig grand jury threw out the bill. "If anything of Whig or Tory comes in question," says Luttrell writing at this time, "it is ruled according to the interest of the party," and the Tories had not yet secured Tory Sheriffs who would have made such a mischance impossible. But the Government was not to be defeated. It was decided that as at present a conviction in London seemed impossible, Colledge should be indicted at Oxford, where he could be proved to have made use of many treasonable expressions. To Oxford accordingly he was removed.

The approaching trial caused the most intense excitement. As the first real step taken by the Crown to suppress the pseudo-Protestant agitation which had now developed into an unconcealed attack upon the authority of the King, it was fraught with significance and painful foreboding to the outmanœuvred Whigs. There was another circumstance that gave it additional interest. With an almost pardonable cynicism, the chief witnesses on whom the Crown relied to prove their case against the prisoner were Dugdale, Turberville and " Narrative " Smith—three of the Plot witnesses who had recently served the Whigs by their evidence against Lord Stafford and other of their Popish victims. These were critical days for the Plot witnesses ; their profession was threatened with extinction, they must either look forward to neglect and destitution, if not worse, or secure the mercy of the King by the betrayal of their former associates. The lesser rascals such as Dugdale and Turberville did not hesitate to avail themselves of the latter alternative. But Oates from an obstinate fortitude or the consciousness of the irredeemable character of his perjuries, held firm to his principles. The Court had already shown an unpleasant disposition towards the Doctor by reducing his pension of £1,200 per annum to 40s. a week. Curtailed in his emoluments, deserted by his co-mates, the Doctor still, however, hoped for the best, believing the triumph of the Court to be but temporary, and another hour of parliamentary reckoning close at hand. Accordingly, he determined to confront his faithless confederates and, on behalf of Colledge, pit his testimony against theirs. Booted and spurred the Doctor came down to Oxford, followed by a train of his adherents, and the public looked forward to the choice spectacle of the once united witnesses swearing as hard as they could against each other.

To try Colledge a Special Commission had been issued, at the head of which was Lord Norreys. But the real business of the trial was to be in the hands of Chief Justice North and three others of his brethren, the ruddy Welshman Jones, Creswell Levinz and Raymond. North had no doubt been selected to preside as a trusty adherent of the King, one who had never had great faith in the Plot, and so could, with less indecency, accept the evidence of Dugdale and Turberville when they told another story. Pemberton would never have done the business, for he was reported honest and had supported Oates in the past with all the decision of honest conviction. It was a very difficult situation for any judge, and could only be supported by courage and boldness. Unfortunately, North lacked both these qualities, with the result that he was unable to conceal his uneasiness, performed his duty in a half-hearted and insufficient spirit, and has been heartily censured for his behaviour ever since.

The Attorney-General Sawyer, the Solicitor-General Finch, a son of Lord Chancellor Nottingham, Serjeant Jeffreys and Serjeant Holloway led for the King. With them was Mr. Roger North, who through his brother's influence was getting some employment at the Bar.

Chief Justice North and Mr. Justice Jones, who had been sent for from the Western Circuit, arrived in Oxford on the 16th. As North stepped from his coach a paper was thrust into his hand on which was written : " You are the rogue the Court relies on for drawing the first innocent blood." The Judges also learnt that one Aaron Smith, a Whig solicitor, had, in an interview with the prisoner, smuggled certain papers into his hands, intended to serve him in his defence. These were taken from him.

The Court sat next morning at ten o'clock. The heavy-faced joiner at once demanded the return of his papers, and for a long time refused to plead until satisfied. This, however, he was at length prevailed on to do. He then renewed his demand for the papers. Upon this, the Court sent for Aaron Smith, the solicitor who had put them into Colledge's hands. Roger North, in his Tory indignation, says this man was a "monster," and that his friends were accustomed to excuse his conduct by saying he was mad. At any rate, he was a bold Whig; for on coming into Court he cried out: "It is high time to have a care when our lives and estates and all are beset here." The Judges were much shocked at his presumption, and took recognizances of him to attend the Court during the session. Jeffreys exclaimed: "It is time indeed for Mr. Smith to have a care."

Smith disposed of, the Judges next considered Colledge's papers. Some they at once refused to return to him as being libellous speeches, "spitting venom upon the Government in the face of the country." The others, which were instructions for his better defence, furnished to him by Smith, were objected to by the Crown as being an indirect method of assigning counsel to the prisoner contrary to law. "To allow you those papers is to allow you counsel by a side wind," said Jeffreys. North took this view, but consented to a compromise suggested by Mr. Justice Jones: "These papers Colledge shall not be debarred of for his defence, nor you, Mr. Attorney, from prosecuting upon them;" and that Mr. Attorney might have more time to avail himself of the privilege of anticipating Colledge's case by a careful study of the joiner's documents, the Court adjourned until two o'clock.

On the re-assembling of the Court, the jury was sworn, and the trial proceeded. Dugdale, "Narrative" Smith (no connection of Aaron's, but one of the Plot witnesses so nicknamed from a pamphlet he had published), and Turberville swore that Colledge had often spoken of arming against the King and seizing his person. The prisoner attacked them with much spirit. Smith he described as the "falsest man that ever spoke with a tongue." Haynes, an Irish witness for the Crown, roused in him that contempt which Englishmen are too apt to cherish towards the individuals of that hapless nation. "Is it probable," he asked, "I should talk to an Irishman that does not understand sense ? " to which the Irishman retorted, with rather damaging effect : " It is better to be an honest Irishman than an English rogue." Jeffreys calmed the indignant witness. " He does it but to put you in a heat, do not be passionate with him."

The prosecution put into the box two witnesses who were not informers. One was a Mr. Masters, an old acquaintance of Colledge, who swore that the joiner had spoken approvingly of the Parliament of 1640 and recommended their example to that of 1680 ; and that when he one day called the prisoner jestingly " Colonel Colledge," " Marry, mock not," answered the latter ; " I may be one in a little time." Colledge did not ask this witness any questions. Jeffreys invited him to do so : " Have you anything to ask Mr. Masters ? you know he is your old acquaintance, you know him well." But the joiner did not respond to the Serjeant's invitation. The other witness was Sir William Jennings, who swore to the bloody nose incident at Oxford. He spoke with every appearance of truth and some reluctance ; Colledge vainly attempted to reduce the pointed character of his threat ; Jennings was sure of his own accuracy.

This closed the case for the Crown. Colledge proceeded to call his witnesses : they were of two kinds, —those who deposed to Colledge's character, and those who deposed against the truth of the Crown witnesses. The former were for the most part immaterial, the latter very decided in their tone. As the law forbade a prisoner's witnesses to be sworn, they seem to have consoled themselves for not being allowed to take an oath themselves by putting some good strong ones into the mouths of others. A fellow-lodger deposed that Haynes, the Irishman, was overheard saying to his landlady : " God damn me, I care not what I swear, nor who I swear against ; for it is my trade to get money by swearing." The reckless candour of Haynes was modest compared with that of

Smith and Turberville, if Oates was to be believed. "God damn" would seem to have been a kind of trade mark for the Crown witnesses, a watchword, the invariable preface to the bursts of ill-judged confidence drawn from them by the persuasive integrity of the good Doctor. Oates deposed that he had met Turberville as he was riding in his coach, and expostulated with him for giving evidence against Colledge ; to which Turberville politely replied : "God damn me, I will not starve ! " "Narrative" Smith, who was about to become a minister of the Gospel, had caused the good Doctor even greater pain. Smith had, according to Oates, been angered by Colledge in the course of an argument, and, on leaving the coffee-house where it took place, exclaimed : " God damn me, I will have his blood ! " The Doctor heard of this and remonstrated with the wayward man ; such words, he said, did not become a minister of the Gospel. " God damn the Gospel ! " replied his reverend friend. The Doctor's answer to Dugdale resolved itself into an argument as to whether the latter had ever suffered from a disease, the consequence of his profligacy ; and the result was fatal to Dugdale's veracity in that respect.

This encounter of the rival witnesses had been as dignified and admirable as their best friends could have desired. Where the truth lay it is not easy to determine, but we would incline to the opinion that on the whole probability is in favour of the Crown witnesses. Independent evidence shows Colledge to have been a man violent in speech and action. As a fanatic in the Protestant cause he must have been well acquainted with Dugdale and the others during the time they were swearing against the Papists, and may well in their presence have uttered the threats of violence against his opponents that they now reported. The evidence Colledge brought against them, if true, shows them to have been bigger fools than knaves. " Is it likely," asked North, in his summing up, " that after witnesses had sworn a thing, they should voluntarily acknowledge themselves to be forsworn, and that without any provocation they should at several times come to this one man (Oates) and declare themselves rogues and villains?" They certainly swore nothing against Colledge that is not consistent with the instances of his temper given by Masters and Jennings. Liars as they most undoubtedly were, there are circumstances about Colledge's case that make it more than likely that on this occasion they were able to square their interest with the demands of truth and justice. At any rate Oates' attempt to gainsay them was as far fetched and improbable as most of the productions of his imaginative mind.

Oates's appearance at this trial is memorable as being the first of his personal encounters with Jeffreys. Twice the two men faced each other in public, but the occasions were so divergent in their character, so unequal in the relative situations of the two antagonists and the latter so bloody in its termination, that they must always be reckoned among the most exciting personalities of English history. Jeffreys first made use at Colledge's trial of his fanciful custom of addressing Oates as " Doctor." " If there be any subordination relating to Mr. Turberville or any other of the witnesses against Colledge, make it out, Doctor," was the Serjeant's mocking encouragement, that irresistibly reminds us of the familiar intercourse of Mephistopheles and Faust. In the course of Oates's evidence the Attorney-General remarked : " Mr. Oates is a thorough-paced witness against all the King's evidence." " And yet, Dr. Oates had been alone in some matters, had it not been for some of these witnesses," sneered Jeffreys. Oates always rose to the occasion when impudence could avail. " I had been alone, perhaps, and perhaps not," was the reply ; " but yet, Mr. Serjeant, I had always a better reputation than to need theirs to strengthen it." " Does any man speak of your reputation?" answered the Serjeant. " I know nobody does meddle with it, but you are so tender."

The next passage was more pointed in its character. Oates had been alluding to a certain Mr. Savage, with whom he was in the habit of discussing the immortality of the soul and other subjects of divinity and philosophy. In the course of his statement he mentioned an Alderman Wilcox as being able to confirm his story, and was misguided enough to call in Jeffreys to his assistance. "I think Sir George Jeffreys knows Alderman Wilcox." "Sir George Jeffreys does not intend to be an evidence, I assure you," sharply retorted the Serjeant. Oates was nettled : "I do not desire Sir George Jeffreys to be an evidence for me. I had credit in Parliaments, and Sir George had disgrace in one of them." It was a home thrust, but Jeffreys was equal to it. With ironical submission he bowed before Oates, "Your servant, Doctor ; you are a witty man and a philosopher."

Yet one other—Jeffreys had angered Oates by repeating in disparagement of his evidence the rule of law that refused to allow a prisoner's witnesses to be sworn. Whilst Oates and Dugdale were wrangling heatedly over the latter's state of health, Jeffreys exclaimed : "Here is Dugdale's oath against Dr. Oates's saying." "Mr. Serjeant, you shall hear of this in another place," was Oates's menacing reply. The Doctor was no doubt thinking of a coming Parliament, where Jeffreys should hear of his presumption towards the "Saviour of the Nation." But fate decreed otherwise. In the Court of King's Bench, three years hence, Dr. Oates was to attend on my Lord Chief Justice Jeffreys and hear of something to his advantage, which that good man could hardly be expected to have foreseen in the days of his power and glory. It is interesting to note Jeffreys' early antipathy to Oates, forming as it does one of the most pleasing and commendable traits in the character of the future Chancellor.

Space forbids us to give further instances of Jeffreys' share in the cross-examination of the witnesses ; suffice it to say that it was considerable and in some cases very successful. He had one or two passages with the prisoner, who complained of his affronts and flourishes, and of his whispering with his fellow-counsel. If Jeffreys was severe with the prisoner, the Crown witnesses did not escape his censure. An irrelevant person called Stevens, who had searched Colledge's house, he frequently rebuked for his garrulity.

At the close of the case the Solicitor-General addressed the jury. His address was dull, and probably for that reason Jeffreys was put up after him, to impart concluding vigour to the case against Colledge. He opened by attacking the pseudo-Protestant agitation fomented by the prisoner, interspersing his remarks with some thrusts at the latter's trade as a joiner. " This gentleman, whose proper business it had been to manage his employment at London for a joiner, is best seen in his proper place, using the proper tools of his trade. I think it had been much more proper for him, and I believe you will think so too, than to come with pistols, and those accoutrements about him, to be regulating the Government ; what have such people to do to interfere with the business of the Government ? God be thanked, we have a wise Prince, and God be thanked he hath wise counsellors about him, and he and they know well enough how to do their own business, and not to need the advice of a joiner, though he calls himself ' the Protestant joiner.' "

His arguments he lightened by many pleasing reflections. He paid an ironical deference to the evidence of Oates. " Mr. Oates, I confess, has said *in verbo sacerdotis* strange things against Dugdale, Smith and Turberville : I have only the affirmation of Mr. Oates, and as ill men may become good men, so may good men become ill men ; or otherwise I know not what would become of some part of Mr. Oates's testimony." Are we to believe, he asked, that these men are " such great coxcombs " as to have confessed to Oates their intention to forswear themselves ? He vindicated the Irishman Haynes against the indignation of Colledge. " God forbid it should be affirmed that the country is an objection to any man's testimony, for truth is not confined to places nor to persons either, but applies to honest men, be they Irishmen or others." Of two witnesses whom he had in cross-examination a good deal shaken by some discrepancies in date, he said : " You may bring the north and south together as soon as their two testimonies, they are so far apart. I will conclude to you, gentlemen, and appeal to your consciences ; for, according to the oath that has been given you, you are bound in your consciences to go according to your evidence, and are neither to be inveigled by us beyond our proof, nor to be guided by your commiseration to the prisoner at the bar against the proof; for as God will call you to an account if you do an injury to him, so will the same God call you to account if you do it to your King, your religion and your own souls." The insinuation of the souls' salvation of the jury being involved in their giving a verdict for the King is adroit, and gives just the touch of the advocate to the almost judicial exhortation that preceded it.

It was two o'clock in the morning when North commenced his summing up. The lateness of the hour and the protracted character of the trial, seemed to justify in North's mind the most casual and incomplete charge, perhaps ever delivered by a Judge in a case of such moment. He did not conceal the faultiness of his recollection of the evidence given, and the absence on his part of any notes. He cursorily reviewed the evidence, and expressed his confidence in Dugdale and Turberville. Colledge at its conclusion begged the Chief Justice to look at his notes and remind the jury of certain points in his favour which he had passed over. "If there be any, I refer them to the memory of the jury ; I can remember no more," was North's answer. The jury were given two bottles of sack, which they drank in court, and sent to consider their verdict. At three in the morning they returned a verdict of "Guilty." This was greeted by a shout of remonstrance, and one of the more vehement remonstrants was immediately committed to prison, after which the Court adjourned till ten o'clock. At that hour next morning Colledge was sentenced to death. The execution was delayed until August 31st, as the Government were uncertain how his condemnation might be received by the public, and how far it might be expedient for the King to exercise his prerogative of mercy. But the fate of the fanatical joiner did not inspire that outburst of popular indignation which his friends had hoped for, and he was left to pay the penalty of his indiscretion. He suffered with becoming fortitude, or obstinacy, according as Whig or Tory judged him.

The execution of Colledge, and the indifference with which it was received by the public, mark two important changes in the feeling of the nation at large—disgust at the Popish Plot and its odious accompaniments, and alarm at the intemperate conduct of the Whigs. There can be no doubt that, on the sudden dissolution of the Parliament, the Whig party, confounded and indignant, began to meditate schemes of regaining by force the power which they perceived they could never regain by peaceful methods, as long as the King persevered in his intention of ruling without the assistance of a Parliament. They numbered among their party a certain section of desperate adherents of whom Colledge was a type, reckless partisans prepared, if only they could obtain the sympathy and encouragement of their leaders, to resort to arms as a means of recovering from their political defeat. These men proved the temporary ruin of their party ; it was their violence that was to a great extent answerable for the ultimate catastrophe of the Rye House Plot. They forgot that the one thing dreaded by the nation at large was another outbreak of civil war ; and that, as long as the King could turn to them for support against those who threatened him with rebellion, the nation would acquiesce in any measures, however severe, that he might take against those who sought to disturb the general peace.

Colledge's conviction was the death-knell of the Plot witnesses. The cynical use made of them by the Crown set the seal upon their complete disgrace. Turberville, Dugdale, and "Narrative" Smith, were thrown aside and left to whatever fate might befall them ; Turberville, to die within the same year a Papist ; Dugdale, to die of drink, a victim to the visions and torments of inebriate remorse, in the year 1682 ; and Smith, to achieve the distinction of narrowly escaping a conviction for murder in 1687. Dugdale, whose wretched end we have briefly noticed, was a singular figure among the rascals of the Plot. His remorse alone entitles him to peculiar distinction. At the time of the plot he had just left his employment as bailiff to Lord Aston, a Catholic peer, living on his estates in Staffordshire. Profiting by his situation and the reception accorded by the public to any one in the shape of an informer against the Papists, he hurried up to London with a pack of sensational stories about the machinations of the Staffordshire Catholics. Though the wickedest man on the face of the earth in the opinion of those who knew him—he had cheated Lord Aston's workmen of their wages, and been discharged for various embezzlements— there was an air of good sense and decency in the man's deportment that disposed people to give him credit. He told his story with such modesty and good taste that even the King, who from the first expressed to his particular friends his entire disbelief in the Plot, was for a moment shaken in his opinion. Dugdale is quite the gentleman of the " Oatesian " crew. He had none of the vulgarity of Oates and Bedloe, and executed his villainy with a refined and amiable subtlety that disarmed criticism. But, lacking the coarser fibre of his associates, he had not the good fortune to enjoy that brutal insensibility which guarded them so effectually against all the assaults of conscience. Dugdale died a pitiable victim to remorse. A man devoid of Oates's sturdy faith in his own villainy cannot carry per- jury beyond certain limits without feeling the ill effects.

Not that Oates was to escape all sense of disappointment and disgust. For the present his dwindled allowance was wholly withdrawn, he was turned out of his lodgings at Whitehall, and forbidden to approach the Court. The Doctor retired into the City, where he continued to flourish in the regard of many, until four years later an ever-mindful and arbitrary Government pressed him, in a manner that would brook no refusal, to come out from his retirement, and reappear once more on the scenes of his former triumphs.

The "judicial war" which, in the words of Lord Anglesey, had happily taken the place of the old civil war, promised to be an exciting struggle. So far victory had been with the Crown. Now, however, the Whigs advanced their most formidable engine, the "Ignoramus," which they discharged with tremendous effect in the faces of their opponents. In vain the Government set about the prosecution of Shaftesbury and others of his faction. The grand juries, packed by Whig Sheriffs, returned "Ignoramus" to the bills. Shaftesbury, emboldened by these successes, brought actions for conspiracy against certain of his enemies. The defendants met these attacks by getting the venue of trial changed from Middlesex, where they complained that they could not find an impartial jury. Serjeant Jeffreys was busy in making applications to the King's Bench to this effect. As Chairman of the Middlesex Sessions—an office he had obliged the Government by accepting shortly after his surrender of the Recordership—Sir George led a spirited attack on the Dissenters, whom the Government now associated with the faction as the declared foes of Church and State. Constables were despatched from Hicks's Hall, where the Middlesex justices sat, to find them out and break up their meetings. At the same time Jeffreys was not perhaps sorry to indulge in a passage of arms with the Whig Sheriffs. To meet the difficulty in regard to the grand juries, the Attorney-General Sawyer had discovered a Statute of Henry VIII., by which judges and justices had a right to reform the grand jury panels, and compel the Sheriffs to return the panels so reformed under pain of a heavy fine. Jeffreys caught at the weapon offered to him by Mr. Attorney, and at Hicks's Hall commenced the work of reformation. He took exception to many returned in the Under-Sheriff's panel, and ordered Pilkington and Shute, the two Sheriffs of London, to attend before him. They declined. Thereupon Jeffreys fined them £100.

The Mayor and Aldermen retorted by voting the Sheriffs' fine to be paid out of the City stock. The dispute was to have been carried before the Court of Exchequer, but it soon became merged in the greater contest. In the meantime Jeffreys was rewarded for his zeal by a baronetcy conferred on him in the November of 1681.

In 1682 the Government, weary of a struggle that was bound to be unsuccessful on their side as long as the Whigs could baulk them by their unfailing "Ignoramus," that "monster engendered in the filth of faction" which even the Attorney's device was powerless to crush, resolved upon two measures which should strike at the very root of the Whig resistance, and, if successful, would make the King, as Jeffreys expressed it, not only King of England but King of London also. In the first place, the Court determined that at all costs the next Sheriffs of London should be Tory Sheriffs who would, of course, as in duty bound, return Tory juries. In the second place, a writ of "Quo Warranto" was delivered in the name of His Majesty's Attorney-General to the Sheriffs of London, calling upon them to give an account of the liberties of the City and the validity of the Royal Charter by which they enjoyed them. This was merely the legal preparation to the compulsory surrender of the Charter into the King's hands, and its return to the citizens on the King's conditions.

The election of the new Sheriffs began in the Midsummer of 1682, and was not finally concluded till the end of September. It was a fierce contest. Dudley North, a brother of the Chief Justice, and one Box, who retired after a time in favour of a Mr. Rich, were the Court nominees, Papillon and Dubois the Whig. It is unnecessary to enter into the details of the election. That it was warm work Roger North's description leaves no doubt: "Midsummer work indeed, extremely hot and dusty, and the partisans strangely disordered every way with crowding, bawling, sweating and dust; all full of anger, zeal, and filth on their faces, they ran about up and down stairs, so that any one not better informed would have thought the place rather a huge Bedlam than a meeting for civil business. And yet, under such an awkward face of affairs as this was, the fate of the English Government and Monarchy depended but too much on the event of so decent an assembly." The last sentence gives no exaggerated idea of the importance which both parties attached to the issue : it was a life and death struggle in a very literal sense. Jeffreys, still a person of great influence with his own party in the City, lent all the help he could to the Tory candidates. He placed his house, situated near the Guildhall, at their service, and himself appeared on the hustings at critical junctures. But it was to the Lord Mayor that the Court chiefly owed their ultimate victory. Sir John Moor was one of those cautious, faint, secretive creatures who offend no one, and for their suspected weakness and amiability are thrust into positions where both parties hope to find in them a pliant tool. To the defeat and mortification of the Whigs, Moor, after his accession to office, showed himself a firm and ingenious servant of the Court, and by boldness and cunning won the day. With the election of North and Rich the "Ignoramus" perished ; and Shaftesbury robbed of his "monster," after vainly struggling to raise up another yet more hideous, fled the country in the month of November.

In the midst of the Sheriffs' election Jeffreys had been called away to hold his circuits as Chief Justice of Chester, but not before he had fired a parting shot at the City by committing to prison Mr. Goodenough, the Under-Sheriff and a violent Whig, for failing to provide him and his brother justices with their dinner at Hicks's Hall. His visit to Chester was timely. He followed closely on the Duke of Monmouth, who had been making one of his progresses—"*opportunities*," as Shaftesbury called them— through this part of England. The King had viewed this progress with considerable alarm, for it was to be made the opportunity of gatherings of Whig gentlemen who were rallying round the handsome, brainless youth with desperate intent. Luckily Absalom made no use of his "opportunity," much to the disgust of Achitophel ; and at the end of his progress was greeted by a warrant officer from David, charged to bring back his disobedient son at once to London. But Jeffreys found Chester and its neighbourhood very much disturbed by the recent visit. From Wrexham, whither he had probably gone on a visit to his father before commencing his judicial work, he writes to Leoline Jenkins, the Secretary of State, an account of the Duke's proceedings (September 18) :—" The excuse of his honouring these parts was, you know, a race ; and the loyal gentry, to divert company which that design aimed at, ordered another meeting, and published enclosed paper, which had this good effect, that there were ten to one of our side ; but his Grace won the plate, to the great joy of all true Protestants, for which bonfires have been made in Chester, and most of the honest men's windows broke, and the plate bestowed on the Mayor's child which his Grace hath christened by the name of Henrietta." Fearing further clamour, and that " the honesty of the town may not be dispirited," Jeffreys makes a suggestion with regard to the punishment of the rioters. Chester, he says, has not power to try treasons, but he is ready with an " useful accident " to help his Majesty's service. There are at present " three fellows in the city gaol " for clipping the coinage, a crime in those days classed among treasons. If Mr. Secretary will send him a Commission of Oyer and Terminer to try these fellows, that can cover any other cases of treason that may arise. He also gives the names of those who should be joined with him in the Commission. Jenkins evidently jumped at the happy accident ; for on September the 15th Jeffreys writes from Chester, where he has arrived to hold his Assize, thanking him for the Commission, which has reached him " truly in the nick of time." Jeffreys adds that he has been well received by most of the loyal gentlemen ; but he expects some trouble with the Mayor and Recorder (evidently Whigs) about the Commission, and wishes Jenkins had not included Alderman Streete in it, a " pestilently troublesome fellow." The parsons, he says, have done their parts, and the Mayor is angry with him for having thanked them. He concludes with an allusion to the Sheriffs' election in London, then raging at its height: "Sir, I wish all good success on Friday; my house is yours."[1]

As he feared, Jeffreys had some trouble with the Recorder when the Assize began. The latter first objected to the Commission, and then tried to go to the grand jury in person and prevent them from returning true bills. But, in spite of these factious manœuvres, Jeffreys, armed with his Commission, was able to perform the King's service; and we will hope that when he left Chester the "honesty of the town" had recovered from its temporary depression.

Jeffreys did not leave these parts without giving some proofs of amiability, particularly in his dealings with the Dissenters, who were now at the beginning of their sufferings under the new Government. At Flint Assizes he rebuked some officious persons who in distraining for a conventicle had been guilty of an illegal act; and he showed his gratitude to an old friend and his respect to his mother's memory by discountenancing any attempt to proceed against her friend Philip Henry, who at this time enjoyed the unenviable distinction of being the only Dissenter in all Flintshire.

In October he had returned to London for the beginning of the Michaelmas sittings, during which he was to appear as counsel in one sensational case. As Chairman of the Middlesex Sessions and the enemy of the Dissenters, he may have been instrumental in the arrest of the excellent Richard Baxter, which took place on the 21st under the Five Mile Act.

It was on the 23rd of November that Serjeant Jeffreys appeared with the Attorney-General Sawyer and Mr. Solicitor Finch to prosecute on the King's behalf Ford Lord Grey of Wark for "debauching" Lady Henrietta

---

[1] The originals of these letters are to be found in the Record Office among the Domestic State Papers.

Berkeley, daughter of the Earl of Berkeley. The chief culprit—for Grey was charged along with the creatures who had assisted him in his outrageous proceedings—was remarkable to the public not only for his social position but as one of the boldest and most reckless of the Whig leaders. A close friend of the Duke of Monmouth, he was active in inciting that luckless youth to those schemes of violence that ultimately brought him to the block, if he was not guilty of actually betraying him ; he was also a leading member of the Green Ribbon Club, one of the most determined associations of the Whig politicians, and along with his fellow members had taken a foremost part in the tumults attending the late election of the Sheriffs. The boldness of his schemes and the violence of his counsels were only equalled by the baseness of his principles and the cowardice of his character. In any other times the infamy of his public conduct would have doomed him to perpetual disgrace ; but along with Titus Oates the Whig regeneration of 1688 washed him of his sins : he became Earl of Tankerville under William III., and by an excellent Whig oration delivered in the House of Lords during that reign so far touched the hearts of the Whig historians that his seduction of his sister-in-law has never been exposed in all its baseness and perfidy, which in some respects transcend the poor morality of his day.

Lady Henrietta was Grey's sister-in-law, the latter having married a daughter of Lord Berkeley. In spite of their relationship, these two had carried on a passionate intrigue for four years. According to Grey, he had vainly endeavoured to stay his guilty love by courting, in a less restricted sense than is usually applied to that term, two other ladies of his acquaintance ; but even their utmost favours were fruitless to quiet his passion. So he had reconciled himself to four years of clandestine intrigue, and to being by the necessities of his situation frequently locked up for two days in the young lady's chamber on a diet of sweetmeats. At length Lady Berkeley discovered all, and passionately upbraided Grey with his conduct. The noble lord wept copiously, avowed his guilt, begged her not to tell her husband and swore repentance. A few days later Lady Berkeley allowed the penitent lover to spend a night at Durdans, her husband's place near Epsom, *en route* for his own seat in Sussex, but on a strict promise that he would not interfere with Lady Henrietta. Grey stayed from Friday night to Saturday afternoon. On the Saturday night Henrietta fled from her father's house and was taken by Grey's man, Charnock, to lodgings in London, where Grey visited her as his mistress and kept her concealed from the eager search of her parents. As the last means of discovering her whereabouts, Lord Berkeley determined to brave exposure and bring Grey to trial. The Crown, no doubt, was only too glad to lend a helping hand to the disgrace and punishment of so turbulent an opponent. On November 23rd, 1682, Grey and his confederates were indicted in the King's Bench before Chief Justice Pemberton, Mr. Justice Dolben and Mr. Justice Jones. Grey was represented by Mr. Williams, the ex-Speaker, Mr. Thompson and Mr. Wallop, three well-known Whig advocates who were generally briefed for any members of that party, whatever the nature of their offences. Williams and Thompson were old opponents of Jeffreys in the Smith, Harris and Carr trials. Mr. Wallop, who now appears for the first time on the stage of history, has been rendered eternally famous by Jeffreys' treatment of him at Baxter's trial in 1685.

The case against Grey was proved up to the hilt, and all the principal defendant could do was to stand in Court with his friends and endeavour to frighten the witnesses against him by steadfastly gazing on their countenances, an impertinence for which Pemberton and Jeffreys were obliged to rebuke him. Lady Berkeley swooned more than once in giving her evidence, and her husband standing by constantly broke out into fierce reproaches against the seducer. The Judges had very early made up their minds as to the prisoner's guilt, and treated the defence—poor enough from the nature of the case

—with scant endurance. Mr. Williams must have raised a smile when he remarked at the opening of his speech for Lord Grey that he "could not justify in strictness everything that my Lord Grey had done." Mr. Wallop cut a very sorry figure. With an indiscretion which strongly reminds a modern reader of the immortal Mr. Phunky, at the very end of the case he addressed the Lord Chief Justice as follows :—" We do hope in your lordship's observations upon the evidence to the jury, you will please to take notice that there is no colour of evidence of any actual force upon the lady which is laid in the information, that my lord did ' vi et armis abducere,' &c." Pemberton, one of the foremost lawyers of his day, made short work of this lengthy interruption. " Oh, Mr. Wallop, fear not I shall observe right to the jury ; but you have read the book that is written concerning juries lately, I perceive." Jeffreys rejoiced at this sudden exposure of the fount of Wallop's learning. " He has studied such books, no doubt, and has learned very good counsel of Whitaker," was the Serjeant's derisive comment.

But the sensation of the case was the appearance of the Lady Henrietta herself. She came into Court just as Jeffreys had finished his opening speech for the Crown. By the time that Mr. Williams rose and proposed to put her in the box, the Court had formed the most unfavourable opinion of the young lady's character. It was evident that she fully shared Grey's passion, and had not hesitated to gratify it to the agony of her parents and the dishonour of her house. For some time the Crown lawyers endeavoured to resist Williams' application that she should be heard in evidence, but the Judges could not see their way to refuse it ; whereupon Jeffreys sat down, with the apologetic augury, "Truly, my lord, we would prevent perjury if we could." His forecast was justified, for Lady Henrietta went into the box and perjured herself to the dismay of all. In vain did Mr. Justice Dolben exhort her : " Madam, for God's sake consider you are upon your oath, and do not add wilful perjury to your other faults." She persisted in her intention, until the Lord Chief Justice rebuked her. "You have injured your own reputation," he said, "and prostituted both your own body and your honour, and are not to be believed."[1] With that he turned to the jury, and charged them to convict the prisoners.

No sooner had the jury withdrawn to consider their verdict than Lord Berkeley, who had with difficulty suppressed his rage during the trial, rose and asked the Court that his daughter should be delivered to him. Lady Henrietta met her father's request by stating, to the general surprise, that she was married ; and a Mr. Turner was produced, who claimed the unenviable distinction of being her husband. "What are you ?" asked the Chief Justice of the apparition. "I am a gentleman," was the extravagant reply. "Where do you live ?" "Sometimes in town, sometimes in the country." "Where do you live when you are in the country ?" "Sometimes in Somersetshire," was the still indefinite reply. "He is, I believe," said Mr. Justice Dolben, "son of Sir William Turner that was the advocate; he is a little like him." Jeffreys offered the Court some further information. "Ay, we all know Mr. Turner well enough ; we shall prove that he was married to another person before that is now alive and has children by him." "Ay, do, Sir George," says Mr. Turner, "if you can ; for there never was any such thing." "Pray, sir," pursued the Serjeant, "did you not live at Bromley with a woman as man and wife, and had divers children ; and, living so intimately, were you not questioned for it, and you and she owned yourself to be man and wife ?" But Turner was firm, Lady Henrietta was his wife and no other, and he could produce witnesses. "I will go with my husband," said the lady. "Hussey ! you shall go with me home," cried the angry Earl. "I will

---

[1] It will perhaps hardly be credited that Campbell, in his anxiety to blacken Jeffreys' character, speaks of Lady Henrietta as a lady of "undoubted veracity" !

go with my husband."   "Hussey, you shall go with me, I say!" and so on till Lord Berkeley cried to his friends to seize his obstinate daughter ; but the Chief Justice sternly forbade them.   The Court broke up, but in the hall without swords were drawn by the rival parties and a scuffle ensued, until Pemberton, coming by, sent Lady Henrietta Turner to the King's Bench prison.

Next day the jury gave in a verdict of "guilty," but the matter was settled during the next vacation, and a "nolle prosequi" entered by the Attorney-General.   On her release from the King's Bench prison Lady Henrietta Turner disappeared ; but in the following year when Lord Grey fled the country on the discovery of the Rye House Plot, Lady Henrietta accompanied him to Holland as his mistress, much to the scandal and distress of the Scotch section of the exiles.

The day after the Berkeley case Jeffreys was busy in the same Court, this time on behalf of the Duke of York. The latter, who had returned from his unwilling exile in Scotland now that the political horizon was more favourable to his interests, was anxious to take vengeance on some of those who had most virulently traduced him in his days of unpopularity.   He proceeded first against Pilkington, the late Whig Sheriff, an "indiscreet man that gave himself great liberties in discourse."   His particular liberty on this occasion had consisted in his accusing the Duke of York to two of his fellow Aldermen as the man who had burnt the City and was now come to cut the throats of the citizens.   In face of an accusation of this kind it is not surprising that the Duke should have taken an early opportunity to bring an action for slander against Pilkington.   The latter, conscious by experience of the now Tory character of Middlesex juries, asked that his jury should be drawn from another county. The Court allowed him his choice, and he selected Hertfordshire.   But, alas for the uncertainty of human anticipation ! not even twelve Hertfordshire gentlemen could overlook the poverty of Mr. Pilkington's defence and the evasiveness of his witnesses ; and as things were being done on rather a broad scale just then, these same twelve gentlemen gave the royal plaintiff a verdict, and assessed the royal damage at £100,000. Burnet says that these were the most excessive damages ever given. Maybe they were, but it is not often that an individual is accused of having burnt the City of London and of an intention of cutting the throats of all the citizens in the immediate future !

This verdict with its swinging damages was Jeffreys' last achievement in the courts of law for the year 1682. The close of the year saw a great improvement in his position and influence at Court. As the King's power increased in security, the Duke of York obtained more and more weight in his counsels. James had always been a supporter of Jeffreys ; the dull, vindictive nature of the Duke, his grave and obstinate determination, inclined him to those whose bold and reckless principles would best serve his unscrupulous designs, while his devotion to his religion and the heaviness of his disposition blinded him to the extravagances or excesses of those who served him. Jeffreys was all he could desire. The Serjeant belonged to the extreme section of the Tory party, and it was in these men that James now placed his confidence. At the same time Jeffreys' friend Sunderland had been restored to office, and the two now worked together in close union, By the extreme character of their political principles they recommended themselves to the Duke of York, whose ultimate accession to the throne seemed now to be assured. At the close of the year Jeffreys, by the extent of his services, the force of his character and his opinions, and his interest with the brother and mistress of the King, stood an excellent chance of profiting by any changes that the Crown might see fit to make in the high places of the law. Circumstances brought him his reward sooner than he expected.

One important legal change had already taken place in the month of December, though it did not directly affect

Jeffreys. This was the death of the Lord Chancellor Nottingham. Finch had been ailing some time, and had left to Chief Justice North a great deal of the business of his office. During the Chancellor's illness the King had told North that he was to have the reversion of the place, and two days after Finch's death the promise was fulfilled. North left the soft cushion of the Common Pleas, for which his respectable character, his learning and intelligence pre-eminently fitted him, and, as Lord Keeper of the Great Seal, took upon him an office which was to prove the burden and distress of his declining days. At this period in the history of his country North was the wrong man to be Lord Keeper. The politics of the Court had passed beyond those limits which a cautious constitutional mind such as North's would have imposed upon them ; the manners and temper of the Court were such as to make the plain face, the smug manners, the timorous worth and desperate want of humour of the Lord Keeper the object of mockery and contempt to his associates at the Council board. In the hour of triumph when, as Ranke says, "from the fear of civil disorder the doctrine of passive obedience had achieved a momentary supremacy in social life," and the adherents of despotism were about to celebrate their Saturnalia, North was soon left behind in the march of excited progress, to die by the wayside despised and disregarded. "Here, my Lord, take it," said the King as he handed him the Seal ; "you will find it heavy." The words were prophetic, but the prophecy depended a good deal for its fulfilment on the fortunes of Mr. Serjeant Jeffreys.

IX

THE RYE-HOUSE PLOT—LORD CHIEF JUSTICE JEFFREYS

1683

AT the beginning of 1683 the Government was busy with its preparations for the attack on the City Charter. The case was to come before the Court of King's Bench for argument, and both parties were getting ready a formidable array of counsel, precedents, pleas and all the other arms employed in great legal battles. Not that the Government intended to leave anything to chance or the equally precarious fortunes of law. The parties might argue reams-full, as much as ever they liked, the more the better—it would lend greater gravity to the farce ; but there was to be no mistake as to the victor in this instructive contest ; and, as the decision would be in the hands of the Court of King's Bench, that Court would have to be doctored somewhat to prevent the possibility of an adverse judgment. Pemberton, the Chief Justice, and Dolben, one of the "puisnes," were considered insecure in a matter of this kind. The former had shown himself a Judge of some independence of character, but, it was feared, of insufficient loyalty. North, the Tory, attributes his removal on this occasion to his boldness, cunning and conceit, as a man who paid less regard to the law than to his own will ; Burnet, the Whig, says that he was not wholly for the Court ; and Evelyn, Whiggish, lauds his honesty. In any case, the Government did

not feel comfortable about him, and, as the Chief Justiceship of the Common Pleas was then vacant by North's
acceptance of the Seal, they took the opportunity of
sending Pemberton to preside over that Court. Dolben,
an "arrant, peevish old snarler," with a small body and
a large voice, was dismissed altogether, and retired to
terrorise over his servants and dependents until he was
reinstated in his judgeship at the Revolution. The
successors of these two Judges were Edmund Saunders in
the place of Pemberton, and Francis Wythens in the
place of Dolben. Wythens is already familiar to us
as sharing [with Jeffreys the honour of being the first
Abhorrer. " He was one of moderate capacity in the
law, but a voluptuary ; and such are commonly very
timid, and, in great difficulties, abject ; otherwise he
was a very gentile person, what was called a very honest
fellow, and no debtor to the bottle." This curious description North sustains by his account of Wythens's
snivelling behaviour, " his whimpering and wiping," when
the Parliament of 1680 called him to account for his
Abhorrences. The Crown, however, had continued to
employ him in its business after the dissolution, and the
hour of the " Quo Warranto " seemed a fitting and convenient one in which to reward his zeal.

Edmund Saunders was the very man to preside as Chief
Justice of the King's Bench over the trial of this important
issue; for it was he who had been chiefly instrumental in
preparing the case of the Crown against the City, and would
therefore have a peculiarly just appreciation of its merits.
The sweet disposition and fetid body of this singular man
have been admirably described by Roger North. Sodden
with ale, corpulent with want of exercise, his diseased body
stinking in the nostrils of the bystanders, there was yet in
the charm and amiability of his humour, his pleasant consciousness of his own defects, his readiness to help and
enlighten those younger than himself out of his copious
store of legal learning, and his genial good-fellowship,
something that won the affection and regard of those

about him, and made him, as North puts it, "a very Silenus to the boys." "Born but not bred a gentleman," Saunders had raised himself from obscurity by sheer talent and application. His days were strictly divided between his work at the Temple and the ale, pipe and garden with which he solaced his leisure hours at his house at Parson's Green. As a lawyer, Saunders stands high indeed, not only for the simplicity and precision of the Reports that bear his name, but for the dramatic interest he contrived to infuse into these generally dull epitomes, which won him the appreciative praise of Lord Mansfield as the "Terence of Reporters." The King, hearing of his fame as a lawyer, had long employed Saunders in his legal concerns. Now that those concerns were deeply involved in the success of this great issue of the "Quo Warranto," an assiduous lawyer, popular in the Courts, respected for his learning and friendly to the prerogative, would make a very much better Chief Justice of the King's Bench than Sir Francis Pemberton. The spirit was willing, but the flesh was weak ; Saunders accepted the office, but it was fatal to his poor carcase. The change of habits and the anxieties of his new position proved too much for his ruined constitution. However, he struggled manfully to do his duty. The hearing of the "Quo Warranto" began in February, but Jeffreys did not appear for the Crown ; Sawyer and Finch delivered the arguments, and the case was adjourned.

In May, Jeffreys took part in the prosecution of Pilkington, Lord Grey and a number of other eager Whigs, before the new Chief Justice, for rioting at the Sheriffs' election. Williams and Wallop appeared for the defendants, the latter making use of his "I humbly conceive," which Jeffreys rendered famous two years later at Baxter's trial. The proceedings are not very lively, though the case excited great public interest owing to its political character. Jeffreys complained of the horrid noise made by the audience, and Saunders was compelled to rebuke them for interrupting his charge to the jury by their humming. The Serjeant had one passage with his constant opponent, Mr. Williams. A Crown witness swore to his back having been so wrenched in saving the Lord Mayor from the rioters, that he spat blood for six or seven days after. "He took a surfeit," says Williams, facetiously, by way of explanation. "He took a surfeit of ill company, I am sure," retorted Jeffreys. The trial ended in a conviction ; but sentence was postponed, and it was not till June that the prisoners were sentenced to various fines.

On the 19th of the same month, the Government proceeded against another of the City Whigs. This was Sir Patience Ward, an ex-Lord Mayor. He was charged with committing perjury in the Duke of York's action for slander against Pilkington. There can be little doubt that he had done so. Jeffreys was one of the counsel against him. Ward was convicted, and sentence postponed ; but hearing in the interval that there was an intention of putting him in the pillory, he discreetly withdrew.

It will be gathered from the foregoing circumstances that these were sufficiently distressing times for the Whigs. Harassed in the law courts, cheated of their last resources against the legal manœuvres of the enemy, it only wanted the inevitable judgment in the "Quo Warranto" to complete their destruction. Evelyn gives a gloomy picture of the condition of the City after the surrender of their Charter : "Eight of the richest and chief Aldermen were removed, and all the rest made only justices of the peace, and no more wearing of gowns or chains of gold. The Lord Mayor and two Sheriffs holding their places by new grants as *Custodes* at the King's pleasure. The pomp and grandeur of the most august city in the world thus changed face in a moment, which gave great occasion of discourse and thoughts of heart, what all this would end in." That in this all but hopeless state of affairs the Whigs were rendered desperate is not a matter for astonishment ; and that, in the then barbarous condition of political warfare they were driven to desperate resolves and murderous plots, as the only weapons of offence left to them, is likewise not to be wondered at. Nor should it evoke painful and indignant surprise that the Government, on the discovery of these resolves and plots, proceeded to deal with the conspirators as they in their time had dealt with the so-called Popish plotters—but with this difference, that, in 1683, the Government gave the Whig prisoners a fairer trial and convicted them on much better evidence than ever fell to the lot of the luckless Papists of 1678. But in this very difference of treatment—galling as it is to the moral rectitude of the choicest Whigs—lies the secret of the extravagant canonisation of those who suffered for the Rye House Plot, and the violent abuse which many Whig historians have poured on those who executed judgment upon Russell and Sidney. The retributive element in the punishment of their heroes, the comparative decency with which they were tried and condemned, have been deliberately overlooked or misrepresented by Whig lawyers and Whig historians ; and, as the political principles of Russell and Sidney have now been generally accepted as wholesome by all political parties, no one has taken the trouble to do justice to those who in Charles II.'s day still preferred the despotism of a King to the despotism of faction, and whose eyes were fixed not upon the ultimate necessity of the Whig principles of Government, but rather upon the violence and injustice with which those principles had been contaminated by Shaftesbury and his followers. Dr. Johnson certainly had the courage to describe Russell and Sidney as " arrant rascals," a description which would have been considered horrible from the mouth of Jeffreys. Like most of Johnson's historical outbursts it is unjust and archaic ; but it is natural in an extreme Tory such as he was, to whom rebellion was the highest of political crimes. How much more natural in the minds of extreme Tories in a day when extreme Toryism was a possible and useful creed, and the murder of a King not forty years past ?

Can it be fairly said that in point of political morality

the Whigs of 1683 stood higher than their opponents?
The constitutional rhetoric of subsequent historians would
incline us to believe so ; but it is not the case. Socially,
domestically, Lord William Russell will always command
the respect that should be the portion of good husbands
and worthy gentlemen ; but his political career shows the
same fierceness of prejudice, the same violence towards
opponents, the same insensibility to justice and temperance,
that are the marks of these seventeenth-century politicians.
And Russell is the best of the lot, the rest very indifferent
as far as honesty, nobility, and their other imputed virtues
are concerned. Morally, there is no reason why the
political conduct of Russell and Sidney should be judged
more leniently or by a different standard than that of their
opponents, unless it be by the test of subsequent utility.
Legally, their much-vaunted wrongs are easily resolved.
We do not propose to discuss points of law which, as Sir
James Stephen remarks, have long ceased to have any
interest or importance. Whilst it is impossible to do
strict justice between the prisoners and their Judges, it is
now generally agreed that the law in these cases, if at times
harshly interpreted, was never violently strained, and
that the legal decisions of the Judges given in Russell's
and Sidney's cases can be legally supported, according to
the then existing state of the criminal law.

If these proceedings are to be judged—as it seems to us
necessary for the purpose of our work they should be—
from the point of view of conduct, the conduct and behaviour of " Judge Jeffreys," it is better to clear the ground at
once of those conventional causes of reproach which Whig
historians have levelled against the whole of these occur-
rences, against the disgraceful principles which could make
men regard Russell and Sidney as dangerous rebels and
punish them accordingly, and against the gross illegality by
which those punishments were inflicted.

Judgment had been given in the " Quo Warranto " on
June 12th, but in the absence of the Chief Justice through
indisposition. Five months of the ermine were sufficient

to destroy the poor remains of Saunders' constitution, and on June 17th he died.   As early as March the question of his successor had been discussed.   Sunderland had proposed Jeffreys, but he found the King unresolved and full of objections—the Judges would not like it, and Jeffreys had not law enough.   That Charles's objections at this time were quite sincere, his friendship for Jeffreys, and the favour he subsequently showed him, suggest a doubt ; he was probably inspired in his reluctance by the Lord Keeper.   To North the very mention of Jeffreys' name would be distressing, and he would use every endeavour to thwart the schemes of Sunderland.   At this period there were two parties in the Council of the King,—the extreme Tories headed by the Duke of York, Sunderland and Rochester, and the more moderate counsellors such as Halifax and North, who sought to prevent the King from making too violent a use of his opportunities.   If Jeffreys was to be admitted into the Council, he would be ranked in the van of the extreme section.   North was well aware of the treatment his cautious timorous measures would meet with at the hands of Sir George, to say nothing of the natural repugnance a heavy man always experiences towards one whose sense of humour was so insufficiently controlled as Jeffreys'.   North used every endeavour to recommend Sawyer to the King.   He was a connection of North's, and, as Attorney-General, had done much valuable work for the Government ; but in power, eloquence and all those qualities beyond mere legal accomplishments that are always expected in a Lord Chief Justice, he was in every way Jeffreys' inferior.   Certainly in March, when Sunderland first pressed Jeffreys' claims, which no one can deny to have been considerable, the "Quo Warranto" had yet to be tried, and Charles may well have looked at that time for a Chief Justice with such a reputation for legal profundity as would give the premeditated judgment an air of spontaneous sincerity.   According to one story, Charles considered Jeffreys to have " neither learning, law, nor good manners, but more impudence than ten carted whores." If this be true, he may well have hesitated to entrust the "Quo Warranto" to such a man, however in private life he may have esteemed him for these delightful traits. As Oates, however, is the only authority for this reputed saying of the King, it must be received with the same scrupulous care that should be extended to all the Doctor's reminiscences.

So the months wore on in suspense till Saunders died in June, Jeffreys no doubt burning with anxiety to receive the great prize within his grasp. But in the same month all considerations of this kind were forgotten in the discovery of the Rye House Plot. On June 23rd, Serjeant Jeffreys took the information of Mr. Robert West, barrister-at-law, and despatched him to Hampton Court, there to tell the story of the dangerous conspiracy that threatened the life of the King. It soon became evident that this time the Government was in presence of no pretended or bogus plot, and that the King had really by a happy accident escaped the danger of assassination. "The public," writes Evelyn, "was now in great consternation, his Majesty very melancholy and not stirring without double guards, all the avenues and private doors about Whitehall and the Park shut up, few admitted to walk in it. The Papists in the meanwhile very jocund and indeed with reason seeing their own turned to ridicule, and now a conspiracy of Protestants, as they called them."

This conspiracy resolved itself into two parts : there was the section of the desperadoes, headed by West and Ferguson, who had planned the actual assassination of the King and his brother at the Rye House, near Hoddesdon, on their return from Newmarket, and were only frustrated in their purpose by a change of date ; and there was the Council of Six, a body of Whig statesmen, Essex, Russell, Hampden, Sidney, Grey and Lord Howard, who had met and discussed plans of a projected insurrection, as the only means left to the baffled Whigs of checking the King's continued violation of the people's rights. No one who reads the evidence can doubt that these conspiracies were really existent, though independently of one another. If the second was less bloody and more dignified in its authors and its purposes than the first, the Government could hardly be expected to see any great difference between an attempt to provoke rebellion in the country, and an attack upon the person of the King. Accordingly, along with Walcot, Hone and Rumsey, arrested on the Rye House charge, Russell and Algernon Sidney were sent to the Tower ; proclamations were issued against Grey, Sir Thomas Armstrong and the Duke of Monmouth, who was deeply implicated in the more general conspiracy ; and on July 8th the King's messengers pulled Lord Howard of Escrick down frcm his chimney, whither he had fled for concealment. This last capture proved fatal to the hopes of those already imprisoned. Howard, who had wit and cynicism but no courage, made a full avowal ; and the Government, furnished with his revelations in return for a pardon, felt their case strong enough to bring the prisoners to the bar.

Four days after Howard's arrest the trials of the conspirators commenced at the Sessions House at the Old Bailey. As the Chief Justiceship of the King's Bench was still vacant, Pemberton came from the Common Pleas to preside. Walcot and Hone, two of the Rye House plotters, were condemned on the 12th and the 13th of July ; and, on the last named day at nine o'clock in the morning, began the trial of Lord William Russell. At five o'clock in the afternoon he was convicted of high treason ; and on the following day the Recorder, Treby, a leading member of his own party, condemned him to death. Sawyer and Jeffreys conducted the prosecutions in all these cases, and, on the whole, justified North's boast that "if ever trials in England were fair both in the private and public conduct of them, these were." As we have already observed, in the credibility of the evidence, the dignity of the proceeding and the justice of the verdicts, these trials are models of legal propriety compared with those of Oates's victims. Jeffreys could fairly boast that, in this instance, the Crown had not raked the gaols for their witnesses, or brought to the bar profligate persons that wanted faith or credit before this time. His behaviour towards Russell was uniformly considerate, however determined his advocacy ; and compares favourably with that of Sawyer, who seems at times to have rather lost his temper with the prisoner.

The trial of Lord William Russell was the occasion of Jeffreys' last important appearance as an advocate. His speech closed the case for the Crown. Burnet calls it " an insolent declamation, such as all his were, full of fury and indecent invectives." This description is untrue. As the duty of a prosecuting counsel was in those days understood the speech is in no way unusual in its tone, and is free from any of the mockery in which Jeffreys was sometimes too ready to indulge towards people in Russell's situation. The reason of Burnet's constant abuse of Jeffreys, unbecoming in a Churchman, is to be found in a later trial arising out of the Rye House proceedings, in which Jeffreys as Chief Justice had occasion to wound the Doctor's peculiar self-esteem. Jeffreys, like Charles Surface, had a happy knack of offending a good many worthy men ; but in the case of Burnet he has found a good friend in Dean Swift, whose spirited notes on Burnet's *History* enlighten us very satisfactorily on the self-sufficient character of the author and the doubtful reliability in many respects of the author's work.

Jeffreys' peroration delivered at the close of the case against Lord W. Russell may be taken as a fair specimen of his eloquence as an advocate and his principles as a politician. He is speaking of certain witnesses Russell had called to his general character.

" Gentlemen, I must confess this noble lord hath given an account of several honourable persons of his conversation, which is a very easy matter. Do you think, if any man had a design to raise a rebellion against the Crown, that he would talk of it to the reverend divines and the noble lords that are known to be of integrity to the

Crown ?   Do you think the gentleman at the bar would have so little concern for his own life to make this discourse his ordinary conversation ?   No, it must be a particular consult of six, that must be entrusted with this. I tell you, 'tis not the divines of the Church of England, but an independent divine, that is to be concerned in this ; they must be persons of their own complexion and humour; for men will apply themselves to proper instruments.

" Gentlemen, I would not labour in this case, for far be it from any man to endeavour to take away the life of the innocent.   And whereas that noble lord says he hath a virtuous good lady, he hath many children, he hath virtue and honour he puts into the scale ; gentlemen, I must tell you, on the other side, you have consciences, religion ; you have a Prince, and a merciful one too ; consider the life of your Prince, the life of his posterity, the consequences that would have attended if this villainy had taken effect. What would have become of your lives and religion? What would have become of that religion we have been so fond of preserving ?   Gentlemen, I must put these things home upon your consciences.   I know you will remember the horrid murder of the most pious Prince, the Martyr King Charles the First.   How far the practices of those persons have influenced the several punishments since is too great a secret for me to examine.   But now I say, you have the life of a merciful King, you have a religion that every honest man ought to stand by, and I am sure every loyal man will venture his life and fortune for.   You have *your* wives and children.   Let not the greatness of any man corrupt you, but discharge your consciences both to God and the King, and to your posterity."

" Incorrect, disagreeable, viciously copious," are the adjectives Burnet applies to Jeffreys' eloquence ; Swift applies them without hesitation to Burnet's.[1]   Whether in the latter case they are deserved or not it is bootless to inquire ; in the former they cannot be considered appropriate.   Jeffreys' eloquence was passionate, too strong and

[1] Ferguson.

excitable for these genteel times ; but it always preserves a certain dignity, and he has a power of language and a direct majesty of phrase which in his most heated moments always preserved him from vulgarity. "For men will apply themselves to proper instruments." "Let not the greatness of any man corrupt you." How well he contrives to give a biblical solemnity to a performance which in some of the greatest advocates has too often bordered on the meaningless inflation of a leading article ! If ever Jeffreys strays into the too copious, he invariably pulls himself together by some master-stroke of forcible expression.

As a cross-examiner Jeffreys would have held a high place had he been born in the nineteenth century. A knowledge of human nature, a strong personality and a nice sense of humour are the best passports to excellence in that art. But in the seventeenth century cross-examination had not yet become an art at all. Witnesses were examined in a confused, irregular fashion ; everybody concerned asked questions in no sort of order, and the truth was extracted in a very hap-hazard manner ; indeed, the only skill an advocate could show was in insisting, in the midst of all that was irrelevant or chaotic, on the facts of real moment that the witness had been called to substantiate. This Jeffreys invariably did with no little significance.

When the Courts rose for the Long Vacation no Chief Justice had been appointed, but events were hurrying a decision in the matter, and that favourable to the claims of Jeffreys. Whatever hesitations may have been instilled into the mind of Charles, the discovery of the Rye House conspiracy and the dangerous schemes of the Whigs convinced the King that the administration of justice must be placed in strong and reliable hands. The conduct of Pemberton at Lord W. Russell's trial showed how little he could be depended on for such a purpose. His summing up was short, unwilling and in very direct contrast to the decided tone he adopted in the other cases he tried arising out of the Plot. Neither a strong Tory nor a sufficiently determined Whig, his conduct was too hesitating for the

Government and too questionable for Dr. Burnet. Some may please to regard him as a martyr to impartiality at a time when impartiality was out of the question ; at any rate, in September he was removed from the Bench altogether ; and Mr. Justice Jones, a stern loyalist, succeeded him in the Common Pleas. The same month Sir George Jeffreys, knight and baronet, was appointed Lord Chief Justice of England.

The necessities of the situation called him to the office. As dangers increased from the desperation of the Whigs and Charles realised that his victory could only be secured by the rigorous punishment of his now openly declared enemies, the influence of his more moderate counsellors proportionately decreased. He lent a readier ear to the voice of his brother and those friends who advised him to severe measures. Above all, a strong judge was necessary who could instil awe from the Bench and impose a powerful will upon the reluctant. Jeffreys as Recorder of London had already given proof of the strength of his personality. If some said he had no learning, there were others who denied it and held him to be a man of great parts ; and, as things turned out, the latter were nearer the truth. If Jeffreys was impudent, a degree of impudence has never been held amiss in a successful advocate ; and, if he had no manners, it need only be said that good manners have never at any time been considered as essential in a judge. Charles was far too intelligent a man to have allowed Jeffreys' social faults, whatever they were, to have blinded him to the real abilities of his Serjeant and the many qualities he possessed that fitted him to hold judicial offices, qualities he shared with some of the most eminent of lawyers who have preceded or followed him. At the beginning of the Michaelmas Term, Jeffreys took his seat in the King's Bench as Lord Chief Justice ; and, on October 4th, he was sworn a member of the Privy Council, to the great sorrow and misgiving of the Lord Keeper North. The latter had been consoled by a peerage as Lord Guilford, but it must have been an empty consolation at such an hour. Ten days before Jeffreys took his seat, the fallen and forgotten Scroggs died at his house in London, before he could witness the coming eclipse of his own melancholy fame.

Among the Whigs, Jeffreys' appointment spread dismay, as well it might. "All people," says Burnet, "were apprehensive of very black designs" at the thought of this vicious drunkard raised to the ermine; "most ignorant but most daring," is the reputation of Jeffreys, according to Evelyn, "of an assured undaunted spirit, cruel, and a slave of the Court;" chosen, according to Lord Campbell, to be the "remorseless murderer of Algernon Sidney now awaiting trial." Three Judges, says Burnet, were placed in the King's Bench worthy to sit alongside of him. One of these was Wythens, whom we already know; another, Holloway, a very honest lawyer; the third, Walcot, who enjoys the precious reputation of having made no published remark during his two years on the Bench "indicative of his character or talents." Before this, according to Burnet, awful tribunal, Sidney appeared, on the 21st of November.

The conviction of Sidney was important to the Government, who regarded him as, what he assuredly was, the most daring, most unscrupulous and most revolutionary of their enemies. An avowed republican, he was prepared to go to any lengths in resisting the encroachments of the royal authority. As one of the Judges of Charles I. he owed his return to his native land after the Restoration to Charles II.'s pardon. But Sidney was far too theoretical a revolutionist to suffer anything so irrelevant as gratitude to deter him from the furtherance of his political principles. As this was Jeffreys' first experience in the conduct of a great State Trial, men must have looked anxiously to the deportment of the new Chief Justice; the character of the prisoner added to the public curiosity and whetted their excitement. When two men of violent character and extreme political opinions, diametrically opposed to one another in all but a marked acerbity of temper, are confronted in a matter of life and death, the one fighting with a weapon of which he hardly knows the use and which he can only wield in a clumsy fashion, irritating to the superior knowledge of his opponent; the other, seeing in the prisoner before him a determined revolutionary, prepared to achieve by murder and rebellion the triumph of "tragical principles," deeply shocking to every loyal supporter of Church and State—in the stress of such a conflict men might well be afraid lest the dignity of the martyr and the gravity of the judge should tumble into hopeless ruin. That such a catastrophe did not ensue must be a matter for congratulation to the admirers of both parties.

The trial commenced at ten o'clock in the Court of King's Bench. Before the Crown opened their case, Sidney renewed an application he had already made a fortnight earlier for a copy of his indictment. Jeffreys, at some length, recapitulated his reasons for declining Sidney's request which could not be granted, according to the practice of the times, and concluded : " Therefore arraign him upon the indictment ; we must not spend our time in discourses to captivate the people." He then cautioned the jury against certain gentlemen of the Bar, who, he had been informed, were in the habit of whispering to them. " Let us have no remarks, but a fair trial, in God's name."

After Sawyer had opened his case, he proposed to call general evidence to establish the existence of a Plot, before proving it directly against the prisoner. To this Sidney objected ; was it right any evidence should be given unless it directly concerned him or his indictment ? Jeffreys met the objection in a very convincing manner : " Mr. Sidney, you remember in all the trials about the late Popish Plot, how there was first a general account given of the Plot in Coleman's trial, and so in Plunket's trial, and others : I do not doubt but you remember. And Sir William Jones, against whose judgment, I believe, you won't object," (he was Attorney-General and a leading member of Sidney's party in 1678,) " was Attorney at this time." Sidney was silent. But at the end of the evidence he renewed his objection. Jeffreys comforted him : "I tell you all this evidence does not affect you, and I tell the jury so." "But it prepossesses the jury," answered the prisoner. That was true enough. But Whigs had the least right to grumble at such prepossession ; for the precedent was derived from the days of Whig supremacy.

Lord Howard was the first direct evidence against the prisoner. He swore to Sidney's attending meetings of the Council of Six, where risings were planned, and to his sending Aaron Smith into Scotland to concert with the Duke of Argyll in bringing about a general insurrection. It is significant that Sidney asked Howard no questions in cross-examination ; but contented himself with calling three or four witnesses, who deposed to Howard having, before his arrest, denied that there was any Plot at all. Jeffreys in his summing up, dealt very reasonably with this defence. " Do you believe, because my Lord Howard did not tell them, 'I am in a conspiracy to kill the King,' therefore he knew nothing of it ? He knew these persons were men of honour, and would not be concerned in any such thing. But do you think because a man goes about and denies his being in a plot, therefore he was not in it ? Nay, it seems so far from being an evidence of his innocence that it is an evidence of his guilt. What should provoke a man to discourse after this manner, if he had not apprehensions of guilt within himself? This is the testimony offered against my Lord Howard in disparagement of his evidence. Ay, but farther 'tis objected, he is in expectation of a pardon ; and he did say he thought he should not have the King's pardon till such time as the drudgery of swearing was over. I must tell you, though it is the duty of every man to discover all treasons, yet I tell you for a man to come and swear himself over and over again guilty in the face of a Court of Justice may seem irksome and provoke a man to give it such an epithet. 'Tis therefore for his credit that he is an unwilling witness ; but, gentlemen, consider, if these things should have been allowed to take away the credibility of a witness, what would have become of the testimonies that have been given of late days ? What would become of the evidence of all those that have been so profligate in their lives ? Would you have the King's counsel to call none but men that were not concerned in this Plot, to prove that they were plotting ? " Jeffreys was determined that Sidney and his party should not escape the consequences of their reckless support of Oates and his fellow perjurers.

Howard was a base person enough ; but his evidence is undoubtedly reliable, and was corroborated in this case by the flight of certain Scotchmen whom he had described as negotiating with Sidney in his rebellious schemes.

Two witnesses being by law necessary to convict a man of high treason, the Crown made their second evidence against Sidney a manuscript found on his study table at the time of his arrest. It was an answer to a book of Sir Robert Filmer's, the famous upholder of royal prerogative, and was written to justify, under circumstances very much akin to those of 1683, rebellion against royal authority and the deposition of the King himself. The arguments were supported by a wealth of historical and biblical parallels, such as Tarquin, Nebuchadnezzar, Nero and Mary Queen of Scots. The manuscript was proved by three witnesses to be in Sidney's handwriting, and Jeffreys and his brother Judges held it to constitute a second evidence against him. Their decision on this point is questionable and, in any case, hard upon the prisoner, but not clearly illegal.[1] Jeffreys had no hesita-

---

[1] Sir J. Stephen (*History of Criminal Law*, Vol. I., p. 411), remarks : " I do not think that the illegality of permitting the jury to treat the possession of the pamphlet as an overt act of treason was as clear as it would be at present," and cites a statute of 13 Charles I., in confirmation of his opinion.

tion in stretching the law as much as possible, if by so
doing he could prevent the acquittal of so notorious
a traitor as Sidney.   And in such a course he would have
had the approval and sympathy of all good Tories of his
day, even of one of the Seven Bishops, as we shall see
later on.

Sidney fought the point with his accustomed spirit.
He began by discussing over again his own arguments
against Filmer's doctrine; but Jeffreys soon stopped
that. "I don't know what the book was in answer to.
We are not to speak of any book that Sir Robert Filmer
wrote; but you are to make your defence touching a
book that was found in your study, and spend not your
time and the Court's time in that which serves to no other
purpose than to gratify a luxuriant way of talking that
you have.   We have nothing to do with his book; you
had as good tell me again that there was a parcel of
people rambling about, pretending to be my Lord Russell's
ghost, and so we may answer all the comedies in England.
Answer to the matter you are indicted for.   Do you own
that paper?"

Col. Sidney.—No, my lord.

L. C. J.—Go on, then; it does not become us to be
impatient to hear you; but we ought to advertise you
that you spend your time to no purpose, and do yourself
an injury.

Sidney then embarked on certain points of law, with
which he was not very successful, finishing up with a
logic-chopping argument that only aroused Jeffreys'
sympathy.

Col. Sidney.—Truly, my lord, I do as little intend to
misspend my own spirit and your time as ever any man
that came before you.   Now, my lord, if you will make
a concatenation of one thing, a supposition upon supposition, I would take all this asunder, and show, if none
of these things are anything in themselves, they can be
nothing joined together.

L. C. J.—Take your own method, Mr. Sidney; but I

say, if you are a man of low spirits and weak body, 'tis a duty incumbent upon the Court to exhort you not to spend your time upon things that are not material.

Sidney's next point was more satisfactory : " Then, my lord, I think 'tis a right of mankind, and 'tis exercised by all studious men, that they write in their own closets what they please for their own memory, and no man can be answerable for it, unless they publish it."

L. C. J.—Pray don't go away with that right of mankind, that it is lawful for me to write what I will in my own closet unless I publish it ; I have been told, " Curse not the King, not in thy thoughts, not in thy bedchamber, the birds of the air will carry it." I took it to be the duty of mankind to observe that.

Col. Sidney.—I have lived under the Inquisition——

L. C. J.—God be thanked we are governed by law.

Col. Sidney.—I have lived under the Inquisition, and there is no man in Spain can be tried for heresy——

Mr. Justice Wythens.—Draw no precedents from the Inquisition here, I beseech you, sir.

L. C. J.—We must not endure men to talk that by the right of nature every man may contrive mischief in his own chamber, and he is not to be punished till he thinks fit to be called to it.

Sidney protested against isolated passages being taken out of his manuscript and used against him. " My lord, if you will take Scripture by pieces you will make all the penmen of the Scripture blasphemous ; you may accuse David of saying there is no God, and accuse the Evangelists of saying Christ was a blasphemer and a seducer, and the Apostles that they were drunk.

L. C. J.—Look you, Mr. Sidney, if there be any part of it that explains the sense of it, you shall have it read ; indeed we are trifled with a little. 'Tis true, in Scripture, 'tis said there is no God ; and you must not take that alone, but you must say, " the fool hath said in his heart there is no God." Now, here is a thing imputed to you in the libel ; if you can say there is any part that is in excuse of it, call for it.   As for the purpose, whosoever does publish that the King may be put in chains or deposed is a traitor ; but whosoever says that none but traitors would put the King in chains or depose him, is an honest man, therefore apply *ad idem*, but don't let us make excursions.

Col. Sidney.—If they will produce the whole, my lord, then I can see whether one part contradicts another.

L. C. J.—Well, if you have any witnesses, call them.

Col. Sidney.—The Earl of Anglesey.

L. C. J.—Ay, in God's name, stay till to-morrow in things that are pertinent.

Sidney called those witnesses against Lord Howard's testimony already referred to, and a Mr. Wharton on the question of his handwriting.   This ready gentleman deposed that if his lordship would show him any of Sidney's papers he would in a little time so imitate them that " you sha'n't know which is which."   Jeffreys took no notice of this singular evidence until his summing up, when he remarked : " **He** (Mr. Wharton) says he could counterfeit any hand in half an hour.   It is an ugly temptation, but I hope he hath more honour than to make use of that art he so much glories in."

Jeffreys' charge to the jury was temperate in language, if unfavourable to the prisoner ; in the latter respect it only showed that degree of bias which is usually found in the summings up of strong Judges.   He could not, however, avoid expressing a general dislike of anything approaching religious pretence or assumption, and the dangers of such devices : "He (Sidney) colours it (his work on Government) with religion, and quotes Scripture for it too ; and you know how far that went in the late times ; how we were for binding our King in chains and our nobles in fetters of iron ! " . . . " So that as on one side God forbid but we should be careful of men's lives, so on the other side God forbid that flourishes and varnish should come to endanger the life of the King and the destruction of the Government."

At six o'clock in the evening, after a withdrawal of half an hour, the jury returned a verdict of " Guilty," and the prisoner was taken back to the Tower.

Five days later Sidney was brought to the bar of the King's Bench to receive sentence of death.   Asked if he had anything to say why judgment should not be given against him, he repeated certain objections he had made to the jury and the indictment which the Court had already overruled.   Jeffreys pointed out to him the duty of the Judges.   " Mr. Sidney, we very well understand our duty ; we don't need to be told by you what our duty is ; we tell you nothing but what is law ; and if you make objections that are immaterial we must overrule them.   Don't think that we overrule in your case that we would not overrule in all men's cases in your condition. The treason is sufficiently laid."

Sidney protested that there was no treason in the paper found in his study.   Jeffreys answered : " There is not a line in the book scarce but what is treason."

Mr. Justice Wythens.—I believe you don't believe it treason.

L. C. J.—That is the worst part of your case.   When men are riveted in opinion that Kings may be deposed, that they are accountable to their people, that a general insurrection is no rebellion, and justify it, 'tis high time, upon my word, to call them to account.

Sidney then asked that the Duke of Monmouth might be called.   Jeffreys replied that the case was over, and the Duke could not now be sent for.   Sidney insisted.

Col. Sidney.—I humbly think I ought, and desire to be heard upon it.

L. C. J.—Upon what ?

Col. Sidney.—If you will call it a trial.

L. C. J.—I do.   The law calls it so.

Mr. Justice Wythens.—We must not hear such discourses after you have been tried here, and the jury have given their verdict ; as if you had not justice done to you.

Mr. Justice Holloway.—I think it was a very fair trial.

Col. Sidney.—My lord, I desire that you would hear my reasons why I should be brought to a new trial.

L. C. J.—That can't be.

Col. Sidney.—Be the trial what it will?

Cl. of Cr.—Crier, make an O yes.

Col. Sidney.—Can't I be heard, my lord?

L. C. J.—Yes, if you will speak that which is proper; 'tis a strange thing, you seem to appeal as if you had some great hardship upon you. I am sure I can as well appeal to you. I am sure you had all the favour showed you that ever any prisoner had. The Court heard you with patience when you spake what was proper; but if you begin to arraign the justice of the nation it concerns the justice of the nation to prevent you. We are bound by our consciences and our oaths to see right done to you; and though we are Judges upon earth we are accountable to the Judge of heaven and earth, and we act according to our consciences, though we don't act according to your opinion.

Jeffreys, however, suffered him to go on with his objections. Sidney went over again the ground that had already been covered, reiterating those points on which the Court had already decided against him. The Chief Justice heard him with patience and, at the conclusion of his arguments, addressed him : " Mr. Sidney, if you arraign the justice of the nation so as though we had denied you the methods of justice, I must tell you you do what does not become you, for we denied you nothing that ought to have been granted. If we had granted you less I think we had done more than our duty."

Silence was proclaimed, and the Chief Justice proceeded to pass sentence of death. " Mr. Sidney, there remains nothing for the Court but to discharge their duty in pronouncing that judgment the law required to be pronounced against all persons convicted of high treason; and I must tell you, that though you seem to arraign the justice of the Court and the proceeding——

Col. Sidney.—I must appeal to God and the world. I am not heard.

L. C. J.—Appeal to whom you will. I could wish with all my heart, instead of appealing to the world, as though you had received something extreme hard in your case, that you would appeal to the great God of Heaven, and consider the guilt you have contracted by the great offence you have committed. I wish with all my heart you would consider your condition ; but if your own ingenuity will not provoke you, nothing I can say will prevail with you to do it. If the King's general pardon, in which you had so great a share of the King's mercy, will not, I could wish that, as a gentleman and as a Christian, you would consider under what particular obligations you lie to that gracious King that hath done so much for you. I should have thought it would have wrought in you such a temper of mind as to have turned the rest of your life into a generous acknowledgment of his bounty and mercy, and not into a state of constant combining and writing, not only to destroy him, but to subvert the Government ; and I am sorry to see you so earnest in the justification of the book, in which there is scarce a line but what contains the rankest treason, such as deposing the King. It not only encourages but justifies all rebellion. Mr. Sidney, you are a gentleman of quality, and need no counsel from me. If I could give you any, my charity to your immortal soul would provoke me to it. I pray God season this affliction to you. There remains nothing with the Court but to pronounce that judgment that is expected and the law requires, and therefore the judgment of the Court is :—

" *That you be carried hence to the place from whence you came, and from thence you shall be drawn upon an hurdle to the place of execution, where you shall be hanged by the neck, your head severed from your body, and your body divided into four quarters, and they to be disposed at the pleasure of the King. And the God of infinite mercy have mercy upon your soul.*"

No sooner had the Chief Justice concluded than Sidney broke into the following prayer :—

"Then, O God ! O God ! I beseech Thee to sanctify these sufferings unto me, and impute not my blood to the country, nor the city through which I am to be drawn. Let no inquisition be made for it ; but if any, and the shedding of blood that is innocent must be revenged, let the weight of it fall only upon those that maliciously persecute me for righteousness' sake."

Jeffreys was indignant, and we think rightly indignant from his point of view, at the sanctimonious vanity of this appeal, assuming as it does the entire concurrence of Heaven in the late proceedings of Colonel Algernon Sidney, and betraying a smug hesitation between the proper charity of the Christian martyr and a lurking desire for revenge on his enemies. "I pray God," exclaimed the Chief Justice, "work in you a temper fit to go unto the other world, for I see you are not fit for this." Sidney held out his hand : "My lord, feel my pulse and see if I am disordered ; I bless God I never was in a better temper than I am now." If Sidney's pulse had been less regular his prayer might have been forgiven as the indiscretion of excitement ; as it is, it wears an unpleasant aspect of premeditation. But Sidney was, we are told, perfectly calm throughout the whole trial ; "he smiled several times," says Luttrell, "and was not in the least concerned even after his conviction."

A study of Sidney's trial justifies on the whole Lingard's criticism : "On the one hand," he writes, "the cool judgment, the undaunted spirit and the eloquent defence of Sidney "—to which for want of space we have not been able to do justice—"excited admiration ; on the other, Jeffreys showed that he was able to control the impetuosity of his temper, adopting a courtesy of language and a tone of impartiality which no man would have anticipated from his previous character." Harsh at times the treatment of Sidney must certainly appear, but so was the treatment of every prisoner as the law served him in those days ; and

Judges in those days were less patient with prisoners than they are now. Sidney fought with great spirit, and laboured with tenacity the points in his defence which he had been instructed to make ; and Jeffreys cannot be accused of curtailing his opportunities in that respect, though he was obliged to use some determination to prevent his unduly protracting the proceedings. Of Sidney's guilt it is impossible to doubt ; and that Jeffreys did not mean to let him get off if he could help it is equally certain. Jeffreys succeeded in his object ; but it cannot be said that his success was as disreputable as succeeding writers have asked us to believe.

Lord Campbell treats Jeffreys with his customary injustice. He accuses him of taking over from his puisne the duty of passing sentence on Sidney for the mere satisfaction of pronouncing it with his own lips. Lord Campbell should have known better than to have made such an accusation ; both before and after the time of Jeffreys, in cases of high treason tried in the King's Bench, the Chief Justice did *not* leave to his puisne as in other cases, the delivery of the sentence.

On December 3rd, Jeffreys sent to Mr. Secretary Jenkins a draft of a warrant for Sidney's execution ; on December 7th, a fortnight from the date of his condemnation—not three weeks, as Burnet would have it—Sidney was beheaded, the King remitting the other odious accompaniments of the sentence. Sidney had petitioned Charles for an interview on the ground of the unfairness of his trial and the violence of the Chief Justice ; but the King, apparently satisfied with the proceedings, declined the opportunity. Though Charles is said to have considered Sidney " un homme de cœur et d'esprit," he may well have felt, that whatever their merits as men of intelligence, the hearts and heads of Sidney and his followers were turned to his own destruction ; and that, in spite of their many excellent qualities, he could hardly be expected to spare those who would not have spared him had he fallen into their hands. Neither could Charles easily forget the innocent blood these same men had driven him to shed in the cause of their anti-Popish fury.   If ever deeds of political violence recoiled on the heads of their authors, surely the fate of these Whig statesmen offers a most signal example.

Jeffreys' conscience would seem to have been little troubled by his work on Sidney.   On December 5th, two days before the latter's execution, Evelyn met the Chief Justice and his brother Wythens at a City wedding.   The great men danced with the bride, and were exceedingly merry ; dancing over, they stayed till eleven at night, drinking healths, taking tobacco, and, says Evelyn, " talking much beneath the gravity of Judges who had but a day or two before "—it was ten days past—" condemned Algernon Sidney."   It is a little difficult to share Evelyn's surprise. Whatever the character of their lordships' customary recreations, they can hardly be expected to have suspended them because, in the ordinary course of their duty, they had condemned to death a traitor who, they believed, had thoroughly merited his punishment.

Besides, if Jeffreys felt a momentary depression, had he not the glowing panegyric of the poet Settle, published at the close of 1683, to comfort and rejoice his heart? though his sense of humour must have been sorely tried by Elkanah's gushing rhapsodies.

> " Free from all meaning, whether good or bad,
>   And, in one word, heroically mad "

is Dryden's description of Doeg-Settle in his *Absalom and Achitophel.*   The poor poet had certainly gone quite heroically mad over the " loyal and honourable," the " brave and bold " Sir George Jeffreys, called by kind Providence to save the kingdom from falling.   Noise and lunacy, he writes, raged so high

> " That all men feared they knew not What nor Why.
>   Jeffreys alone waked their lethargic souls,
>   And from their lips withdrew the Enchanting Bowls."

Jeffreys had stopped the poison of the Popish Plot as it spread, " and looked the impudent delusion dead " ; he is " monarchies' great Solon," the " wise Ulysses of our Albion land," a " wondrous cloud by day and leading fire by night " to a lost people. But his work is only half over, he has plenty to do yet ; he has got, among other things, to " set the course of staggering Nature right."

> " To bind our world to Charles and Charles his laws,
>   He the First Mover, Thou, the Second Cause."

If all this was not quite convincing to Jeffreys' mighty soul, if the encomiums of the shady poet cannot be taken as a very accurate measure of the esteem in which the Lord Chief Justice was held by those of his own way of thinking, a letter he received at the commencement of the following year from Dr. William Lloyd, the Bishop of St. Asaph, gives a more correct idea of the appreciation his services had met with.   Dr. Lloyd was afterwards one of the Seven Bishops, a Churchman universally respected for the honesty, piety and simplicity of his character, and one who must have had exceptional opportunities in the past of judging the conduct of Jeffreys, for his diocese of St. Asaph had been included in Jeffreys' circuit as Chief Justice of Chester.   He thus writes to the Lord Chief Justice of England on his recent appointment and his trial of Sidney :—

" When I heard of your promotion, though I could not but rejoice at it for the public good, I regretted it for your private concerns.   I do truly rejoice at your prosperity, and I heartily pray for your long life and better health than you have had of late years.   I pray God you may live to have many such legacies as Algernon Sidney has left you in his printed will ; for I doubt not so long as you live you will deserve them in the same manner of such men as have the impudence to call themselves the best Protestants, though they do not own themselves Christians, or, if they do, are a scandal to the name.   You cannot be like to yourself in performing these great trusts you have received from God and his Majesty otherwise than in exposing yourself to the virulent hate of their enemies." [1]

The good Bishop then goes on to regret that Jeffreys is not still with them in Flintshire to exercise his " talent for converting fanatics ;" and begs his lordship to put "life in the secular arm" against a certain Edward Jones, a troublesome Dissenter in those parts, who had promised Jeffreys on his last visit to mend his ways, but had failed to keep his word.

Jeffreys could not well look for warmer commendation and encouragement in his new sphere of employment than that given by the Bishop of St. Asaph. If in time to come he was to disappoint the expectations and forfeit the regard of Lloyd and his brethren, at any rate for the present, his rigorous punishment of such enemies of Church and State as Algernon Sidney gave unmixed satisfaction and evoked spontaneous approval in the most respected quarters.

[1] The original of Dr. Lloyd's letter is in the possession of Mr. M. R. Jeffreys.

X

IN THE COURT OF KING'S BENCH

1684

THE year 1684 was to be a busy one for the Lord Chief Justice of England. Strengthened in the public estimation by the discovery of the Whig schemes for provoking a civil war, the Government set vigorously to the task of punishing all who, however indirectly, had been instrumental by word or deed in feeding popular discontent. Dissenting preachers, tract writers of the Whig faction, the remnant of the Plot witnesses, gentlemen who had so far as four years back slandered the Duke of York in the days of his unpopularity, all alike found their sins visited upon them ; and the Court of King's Bench, presided over by Sir George Jeffreys, was in most cases the scene of the visitation. The City of London was in a most depressed condition. The surrender of its Charter left it at the King's mercy, which would in this instance seem to have been Jeffreys'. The Chief Justice, in spite of his surrender of the Recordership, had remained a person of very great influence in the City. As soon as the Charter fell into the King's hands, Charles had apparently turned over to Jeffreys the administration of his new powers. Many are the complaints at this time of the violent authority which the Chief Justice exercised over the helpless Mayor and Aldermen, so that the high office of the former had become little more than a name. At the beginning of 1684 Commissioners were appointed by the

King to supervise all things concerning the City, and to turn out of all public offices those Whiggishly inclined. Besides Jeffreys, Halifax, Rochester and other Tories were of the Commission; but they seem to have left to the Chief Justice the greater part of the administration. It must have been an especial delight to the ex-Recorder to humble the proud spirits of some who but a short time ago had been pleased to do the same for him,—a delight only possible in the days when a charitable spirit towards depressed opponents was unknown in political life.

Certain scores still remained to be cleared off in connection with the Rye business. Mr. John Hampden, grandson of him of the ship-money, and one of the Council of Six, had fallen into the hands of the Government. He would have been tried for high treason, but the Crown could not find the requisite two witnesses against him. He did not, unfortunately, emulate Sidney by writing injudicious works on royal authority, though Burnet says he was the most learned gentleman he had ever known, but heated and over-zealous in temper. Accordingly, the Crown had to be content with putting him on his trial for misdemeanour in seditiously, &c., intending to disturb the King's peace. On such a charge one witness, if believed, would be sufficient to convict. In a case of misdemeanour the prisoner was allowed counsel. Hampden selected Mr. Williams and Mr. Wallop, thereby imparting to the proceedings that spice of political animus which increases the difficulty and excitement of a trial of this kind. Jeffreys disliked Williams and contemned Wallop who, considering that he had been nearly forty years at the Bar, certainly seems from his passage with Pemberton during Lord Grey's trial to have been tactless and unskilful in his profession. The Court of King's Bench promised lively work on the 6th of February to those interested in such matters.

The one witness on whom the Crown relied to prove their case against Hampden was the unfailing Lord Howard of Escrick. He gave the same evidence as in Russell's and

Sidney's cases, proving Hampden's active participation in the schemes for an insurrection and the consultations of the Council of Six.   The defence consisted in an attempt to disparage Howard's veracity, similar to that made by Sidney.   Williams, in opening the defence, suggested that what Howard had sworn was sworn only for his own sake, that by exposing Hampden and the blood of others he might procure a pardon for himself.   " What do you mean by that ? " asked Jeffreys.   " By being a witness against the defendant and others, he has procured his own pardon," replied Williams.   " That is a little harsh expression," says the Chief Justice.

Mr. Williams.—My lord, I explain myself thus——

L. C. J.—It is an harsh word, and too roundly expressed ; you had need to explain yourself : it is a little too rank, as though the King's pardon were to be procured by blood.

When Williams had finished, Mr. Wallop desired to make a speech also, but Jeffreys rightly considered that unnecessary.   " Pray," he said, " do not take up our time altogether in speeches, but go on to your evidence."   " I desire to observe one thing, my lord," urged Wallop. " Make your observations at last," replied the Chief Justice, " but spend not our time in speeches.   I know you will expect to be heard at last ; and so you shall, whatever you will say."

Among those called to invalidate Howard's testimony was Dr. Burnet, the eminent historian.   He said Howard had told him there was no Plot at all.   " Did you believe there was a Plot yourself? " asked one of the Crown counsel.   " Yes," replied Burnet ; " and he laboured to dispossess me of that belief."   " Pray, do you believe it now ? "   " I make no doubt of it, sir, as to the assassination."   But the Doctor carefully refrained from expressing any belief in the scheme for insurrection for which Sidney and his friend Russell had been sent to the scaffold.   Jeffreys in his summing up took sharp notice of Dr. Burnet's reservation.   " But now he (Burnet) is sufficiently satisfied there was a Plot; and I am glad he is, for I think it scarce does remain a doubt with any men that have any value for the religion and Government we live under." Burnet, who prided himself so particularly on his just estimation of men and things, cannot have listened to this with pleasure; but in his *History of his own Time* has taken ample revenge for any slight he may have felt by employing his not inconsiderable powers of partial criticism on the character of the Lord Chief Justice.

Williams wanted to call as a witness for the defendant a gentleman who was one of the defendant's bail. "Mr. Williams," said the Chief Justice, "I wonder you will insist on it; in every ordinary case it is every day's practice to deny the bail to be witnesses." "My lord, I tell you what we will do," replied Williams. "Tell me what you will do!" exclaimed Jeffreys; "answer my question! Will you render him in custody?" "We will change the bail, my lord, and find some other person to stand in his place, rather than lose our witness." Jeffreys was satisfied. "With all my heart," he said. The Attorney-General graciously agreed: "I am so fair, I'll consent to it. Let us hear what he will say." "We thank you, Mr. Attorney," retorted Williams; "I am afraid you won't live long, you are so good-natured." The Chief Justice closed the incident with a pleasing sneer at Williams. "But you are like to live for your good nature, Mr. Williams."

Williams soon drew down a more distinct rebuke from the Bench. He proposed to call a witness who should give evidence of the late Lord Essex's opinion of Lord Howard. "It is not a proper evidence in this case," said Jeffreys. "It is a sort of evidence," replied Williams; but the Chief Justice was not to be trifled with.

L. C. J.—Ay, 'tis a sort of evidence, but 'tis not to be allowed. If you will prove Mr. Hampden's opinion, you may; but you must not for him bring proof of what my Lord of Essex, a third person, thought of my Lord Howard.

Mr. Williams.—I only offer it thus——

L. C. J.—Offer what is evidence, man! You are a practiser, and know what is evidence; but you have offered two or three things to-day that I know you do at the same time know is not evidence; and I speak it that it may not be thought we deny you, or your client, anything that is according to the course of law. You that know the law, know 'tis so as we say. Mr. Attorney has gratified you in waiving three or four things already, but nothing will satisfy unless we break the course of other trials.

Mr. Williams.—My lord, what I take not to be evidence I do not offer, and where the Court overrules me I have not insisted upon it.

L. C. J.—No?

Mr. Williams.—No, my lord.

L. C. J.—But you would have insisted upon it, if Mr. Attorney would not have been so easy as to consent, and the Court would have let you. Pray, keep to the business and the methods of law ; you know the law very well.

Williams then proposed to call evidence as to Lord Howard's belief with regard to rewards and punishments in the world to come. Jeffreys very properly refused to hear it, and comforted Lord Howard who was much troubled by the insinuation of want of faith. "My lord," said the Chief Justice, "do you think that everything that a man speaks at the Bar for his client and his fee is therefore to be believed because he said it? No ; the jury are to take nothing here for evidence to guide them of what the counsel say but what is approved,"—an expression of opinion that will commend itself warmly to the litigants of all ages.

Williams and the Attorney-General at the close of the evidence for the defence agreed not to address the jury ; but not so Mr. Wallop : he had his one observation to make ; he was up and desired to make it. "Ay, in God's name, Mr. Wallop," answered Jeffreys, "make what observations you will. Mr. Wallop, I hindered you from making your observations at first, because I knew it would be desired after the evidence was over." "Then, my lord, I shall expect to be heard too," threatened the Attorney-General. But Mr. Wallop persisted in spite of Williams' endeavours to quiet him. "Go on then, Mr. Wallop, and say what you will," says Jeffreys, with suspicious affability. At last Williams prevailed with his indiscreet colleague.

Mr. Williams.—My lord, we will leave it here, I think.

L. C. J.—Take your own course; do not say we hinder you of saying what you will for your client. . . . I'll sit still; make speeches every one of you, as long as you will.

But in spite of Jeffreys' amiable forbearance, poor Mr. Wallop's "one observation" has not come down to posterity.

The summing up of the Chief Justice is very long, careful and elaborate. As the counsel had not made speeches, he felt it his duty to review the evidence with especial care. His defence of Lord Howard's reliability as a witness against his previous accomplices is just and convincing, and was apparently satisfactory to the jury. In half an hour they found Hampden "Guilty"; and on the 12th of February he was fined £40,000, to be committed to prison till payment, and find sureties during life for his good behaviour.

The day following Hampden's trial Jeffreys tried a cause which was not carried through with quite the same forbearance, and in which Mr. Wallop made rapid advance in the Chief Justice's displeasure. The case turned on the suicide of the Earl of Essex. That constitutionally melancholy nobleman had been one of the Council of Six and had been arrested, along with Russell and Sidney, on the discovery of the Rye Plot. Whilst imprisoned in the Tower awaiting trial, he had grown so depressed and miserable by the distress of his situation that, on the very morning when Lord William Russell appeared at the Old Bailey, he committed suicide in his closet by cutting his throat with a razor. There is practically no doubt that this was the manner of his death, and his own family believed it to be so. But in the excitement of the time a rumour spread that the unfortunate Earl had not died by his own hand, but had been murdered by the orders of the King and his brother who were that very morning seen in the Tower. Two children were found who told a story of a hand that was seen to throw a razor from Essex's window, and of a hooded lady who ran out and picked it up. Mr. Braddon, a barrister and an enthusiast of the Whig party, hearing of these tales, found out the children and with unbecoming officiousness did his best by all manner of persuasions to put the two stories together and formulate a distinct charge against the King and the Duke. In his efforts he was seconded by Mr. Speke, a West country gentleman of an untruthful and intriguing disposition, and a member of one of the leading Whig families in that part of the world. The Crown very properly determined to sift the matter ; and accordingly Braddon and Speke were put on their trial in the King's Bench for misdemeanour. Whatever may be thought of the motives of the defendants, the charge they endeavoured to lay against the King and the Duke was one that should never have been made except upon very much better evidence than they were able to bring in support of it ; nor, from what we know of the characters of Charles and James, is it likely that they would ever have instigated so atrocious a crime. They had many faults, the pair of them ; but these stopped a good way short of murder of this kind. And even supposing them to have had the mettle for such a deed, no adequate motive for the crime can be established.

The Crown rather took the wind out of the sails of the defence by calling as their first witness one of the children who had told the story of the razor thrown from a window. This was a boy of thirteen, named Edwards. The Crown called him to confess that he had told a lie, but called his father first to prove that he was a liar by habit. The failing must have been inherited ; for the father seemed to find a similar difficulty in telling the truth, much to Jeffreys' disgust. When the boy was put in the box and exhorted by his father to be sure and say nothing but the truth, it was too much for the Judge. "And, child," he added, "turn about and say, 'Father, be sure you say nothing but the truth'." When the boy had told his story, Jeffreys could not refrain from an expression of surprise at the character of such evidence on which to found a charge of contriving murder. "What a dust," he cried, "has such a trivial report made in the world! Admit the boy had said any such thing, what an age do we live in that the report of every child shall blow us up after this rate! It would make a body tremble to think what sort of people we live among; to what an heat does zeal transport some people beyond all reason and sobriety! If such a little boy had said so, 'tis not an half-penny matter; but presently all the Government is to be libelled for a boy, which, whether he speaks true or false, is of no great weight; and he swears 'tis all false."

The nature of the proof adduced by their counsel to justify the defendants' conduct fully merits the indignation with which the Chief Justice received it, if that indignation is at times too warmly expressed. The conduct of Wallop and Braddon was not calculated to soothe the Judge's anger. The latter, by flourishing his hands and indulging in other demonstrations of excessive zeal, incurred sundry rebukes. Wallop was surpassingly indiscreet. He asked the boy Edwards' sister whether she had not told her brother that if he did not deny his story about the razor the King would hang their father. "Why have you a mind to have it believed that it was true then, Mr. Wallop?" asked the Judge.

Mr. Wallop.—My lord, the boy best knows that.

L. C. J.—But do you believe that, if it had been true, the King would hang his father, or turn him out of his place, if he did not deny it, as though the King would force people to deny the truth?

Mr. Wallop.—My lord, I do not say nor believe any such thing.

L. C. J.—But your question seems to carry it so.

Mr. Wallop.—My lord, I ask the question of her, whether she did not say so to him. I ask questions according to my instructions.

L. C. J.—Nay, Mr. Wallop, be as angry as you will, you sha'n't hector the Court out of their understandings. We see plainly enough whither that question tends. You that are gentlemen of the robe, should carry yourselves with greater respect to the Government, and while you do so the Court will carry themselves as becomes them to you.

Mr. Wallop.—I refer myself to all that hear me if I attempted any such thing as to hector the Court.

L. C. J.—Refer yourself to all that hear you ! Refer yourself to the Court. 'Tis a reflection upon the Government, I tell you your question is ; and you sha'n't do any such thing while I sit here, by the grace of God, if I can help it.

Mr. Wallop.—I am sorry for that; I never intended any such thing, my lord.

L. C. J.—Pray behave yourself as you ought, Mr. Wallop ; you must not think to huff and swagger here.

After a few more passages of a similar kind, Jeffreys gave plain expression to his opinion of the whole business. " We have got such strange kinds of notions nowadays that forsooth men think they may say anything because they are counsel. I tell you, Mr. Wallop, your questions did reflect upon the Government as though the King had a mind to turn a man out of his employment if he did not swear a falsity. What can be a greater reflection than that ? But all the matter is, what has been done must be avouched and justified, though it be never so ill. But we plainly see through all. This was the design from the beginning ; the King and the Duke of York were in the Tower at that time, and it must be thought and believed that they had designed this matter, and so then all people must be ruined in case they would not say the Earl murdered himself, though indeed others had done it. . . . No ; let us hear the truth, but not in the face of a Court permit men to asperse the Government as they please by asking such questions.

Mr. Justice Wythens.—Truly, I do not see where there is any countenance for asking such a question.

L. C. J.—No; but some people are so wonderful zealous.

Mr. Wallop.—My lord, zeal for the truth is a good zeal.

L. C. J.—It is so; but zeal for faction and sedition I am sure is a bad zeal. I see nothing in all this cause but villainy and baseness. And I believe no man that has heard it but will readily acknowledge that it appears to be an untoward malicious ugly thing, as bad as ever I heard since I was born, on purpose to cast an indignity upon the King and Government, and set us all in a flame.

Jeffreys seems to have rather used Wallop as a peg on which to hang his remarks. The advocate by his indiscretion had offered every convenience for this purpose, though he does not appear from his language to have been so heated and hectoring as the Judge chose to represent him. But great men in their wrath are careless of their instruments.

The defence called the other child who had told the razor story, a girl of thirteen, of the name of Lodeman. It is probable that playing in the Tower grounds, which seem to have been a regular playground for truant children of the neighbourhood at the same time as the boy Edwards, and hearing the report of Essex's death, the one had told the razor story to the other. Both had reputations for lying, their stories are inconsistent with each other and certain of their facts provedly impossible. The girl herself said that there was a large crowd of people standing round when she saw the razor thrown and the woman in the white hood pick it up. If this be true, it is astonishing that out of all this crowd only two children of thirteen could be found to substantiate the story. The Crown replied by calling Essex's servant, the warder, the sentinel whom the children had spoken of as standing by when the razor was thrown from the window, and Captain Hawley, an officer in the Tower. The latter swore that it was impossible to have thrown anything from the window of Essex's closet so as to be seen from where the children were standing.

The defendants did not improve their case by some flimsy evidence they called to prove that before Essex's death there were rumours of his suicide in Hampshire and Wiltshire, rumours which, they insinuated, had been spread by the Government to prepare men's minds for the approaching catastrophe.

The determination of Braddon and his party to credit the Government with murderous designs was a fair subject for Jeffreys' ridicule. In a letter of the defendant Speke recommending Braddon to a friend in Bristol, he wrote : " More here do fear that he (Braddon) will be either stabbed or knocked on the head." The Chief Justice made very merry over these apprehensions for Braddon's security. " Ay," he said, " we live in such a stabbing age that such an extraordinary gentleman as Mr. Braddon, that is such an extraordinary good Protestant, can't walk the streets for fear of being murdered. . . . Being such a virtuous man as Mr. Braddon, there was great need of all circumspection and care to preserve him ; why did not he get his life guard (alluding to the Whig conspiracies) to keep him from the danger that was thought so near him ? "

Mr. Speke, who certainly seems to have been rather unwise than guilty in the matter, protested his innocence. " Would to God you were innocent ! " answered Jeffreys. "You are a man of quality, Mr. Speke, I know ; I should be glad you were innocent with all my heart. But when men forget their studies and their own business, and take upon them the politics without being called to it, that puts them into frenzies, and then they take all opportunities of showing themselves men of zeal."

The Chief Justice had quite recovered in his manner

towards Mr. Wallop at the close of the case, and invited him to make a speech ; but Mr. Wallop declined the offer, he would leave it to his lordship and the jury.

His lordship in his charge reflected severely on the conduct of Braddon and his party and the factious spirit of the age. "We live in an age wherein men are apt to believe only on one side ; they can believe the greatest lie if it makes for the advantage of their party, but not the greatest truth if it thwarts their interests ; " as good an account as was ever given of the politics of Jeffreys' time. Of Braddon himself he spoke in terms that might still be addressed with some propriety to many would-be social reformers. "He is a busy man, you see, a great reformer, that does mightily concern himself in the reformation of the Government. I never knew that Mr. Braddon had any great share in it : he has not such a prodigious estate, I suppose, that for fear of losing his great estate he should be so wondrous busy and active in reforming the Government ; but I have always observed it for a rule that your beggarly inconsiderable fellows are the warmest people in the business of reformation, and for defending liberty and property, as they call it ; and then they put it under the disguise of religion, when, alas, those that have no religion are generally the greatest pretenders of taking care of it ; and those that have no estates nor properties are usually the fullest of noise about liberty and property. But the meaning of it is plain : if they can but exasperate the people into a rebellion, that is the way to get a property ; and if they can but have liberty to do what they please that is all the liberty they contend for."

And of Braddon's business in gathering up the evidence against the King and his brother, his frequent examination of the boy Edwards and his desperate attempts to keep him to his story : "How came Mr. Braddon, what authority had he to take this examination ? He is no justice of peace, no magistrate that had any authority to take examinations. What concern had he in it more than other people ? The boy could tell him there were abundance of people there besides himself. Why did not he stay to have it confirmed by some of those people? Why did not he carry these children before some magistrate or justice of peace, somebody that had authority to take examinations? There was a spirit that prevailed with Mr. Braddon to engage and make a stir in this business; and you may easily guess what a kind of spirit it was which gave him this authority that he had not before."

The evidence he dealt with in the only possible manner, and the jury gave the only possible verdict, "Guilty"; but Speke they very properly acquitted on that part of the charge relating to the procuring false witnesses.

Though sentence was not passed on Braddon and Speke until April 21st, on Jeffreys' return from the Western circuit, it will be as well to finish with their case at this point. The interval of two months does not seem to have softened Jeffreys' sense of their guilt. Williams and Wallop moved in arrest of judgment: but the Chief Justice would not hear them; judgment had already been entered. "But," urged Williams, "it was put off by consent." "I know nothing of your consent, nor what you consented to," replied Jeffreys; "if you consent among yourselves at the Bar, that is nothing to the Court." "My lord, we conceive," says Wallop, "we have very good matter upon the verdict to move in arrest of judgment." "Yes, no doubt," answered the Judge, "what you have to say is extraordinary material; but you come too late, we cannot hear you." The unrepentant confidence of Braddon had not abated in the interval, and stirred the Judge's indignation. "Here he smiles," he exclaimed, "and seems as if he had done no harm." "My lord, I know my own innocency, and therefore have no reason to be troubled." "Your innocence! your impudence, you mean. I tell you, had you been in any country but this, the innocence you brag of would have sent you to the galleys," which is more than likely.

The court was full of Braddon's friends among the

Whig party, lurking in corners to escape the eye of the Chief Justice. "I see a great many of the party about you," said Jeffreys. "I can spy them out, though they think they are not seen ; but they shall know we will not suffer such monsters as these to go without due punishment." In a tone of irony the Chief Justice once more lauded the high repute of Mr. Braddon, and the care with which Speke had recommended him to his friend. "But, oh ! what a happiness it was for this sort of people that they had got Mr. Braddon, an honest man, and a man of courage, says Mr. Speke, a man *à propos* ; and pray, says he to his friend, give him the best advice you can, for he is a man very fit for the purpose ; and pray secure him under a sham name, for I'll undertake there are such designs upon pious Mr. Braddon, such contrivances to do him a mischief, that if he had not had his Protestant flail [1] about him, somebody or other would have knocked him on the head ; and he is such a wonderful man, that all the King's courts of justice must needs conspire to do Mr. Braddon a mischief ; a pretty sort of a man, upon my word, and he must be used accordingly ; men that arrogate and assume to themselves a liberty to do such kind of things must expect to fare accordingly."

In guilt Jeffreys could only compare him to Aaron Smith, the Whig solicitor, a deep plotter, who, according to Roger North, should share with Braddon the epithet of "monster." "And indeed I look upon Braddon to be the daringest fellow of the party, he and his brother Smith. If there were any reluctancy, or any sense of any guilt they had contracted, and would show it by acknowledging their being surprised into it, and testified repentance by a submissive and dutiful behaviour, that were something to incline the Court to commiseration ; but when we see, instead of that, they are more obdurate and steeled in their opposition to the Government, they must be reclaimed by correction, and kept within due bounds

---

[1] An allusion to the weapon invented by Colledge, the "Protestant joiner," during the agitation of the Popish Plot.

by condign punishment, otherwise it will be thought by the ignorant sort of people that all courts of justice are afraid of them."

That the public might draw no such unworthy inference, the Court fined Braddon £2,000 and Speke £1,000, both to find sureties for good behaviour for life, and to be committed to prison until these things had been performed.

Jeffreys had one other important case to try before he went on circuit. This was the trial of Sir Samuel Barnardiston, a noted Whig, for high misdemeanour in writing certain letters, in which he "scandalised and vilified" the proceedings and evidence in the Rye Plot. He speaks of it in his letters as the "Sham Protestant Plot"; he writes that it is lost and confounded, that Papists and High Tories are quite down in the mouth, that Monmouth is to come back into favour and that Sir George Jeffreys is "grown very humble." Unfortunately, Barnardiston's confident hopes were premature, and he found himself summoned to the King's Bench bar to answer for his incorrect anticipations. The trial was short; the proof of the letters conclusive; the mind of the Judge very clear. Seeing that Jeffreys was personally alluded to in the correspondence, it would have been better had he declined to try Sir Samuel; but, in the case of such "caterpillars" as these factious makers of "uproars, tumults and hubbubs," he did not apparently think it worth while to bother about the ordinary appearances of impartiality.

In charging the jury he descanted in a loyal spirit on the crimes of Russell and Sidney. His language may appear startling, even insulting, to those accustomed to regard the lately executed traitors as outraged statesmen. But to Jeffreys and a host of well-informed and upright persons they were nothing of the kind, and any attempt to canonize them was in their minds profane and ridiculous. " Then here is," exclaimed the Chief Justice, " the sainting of two horrid conspirators; here is the Lord Russell sainted, that blessed martyr; my Lord Russell, that good man, that excellent Protestant; he is lamented, and what an extraordinary man he was, who was fairly tried and justly convicted and attainted for having a hand in this horrid conspiracy against the life of the king, and his dearest brother, his royal highness, and for the subversion of the government.   And here is Mr. Sidney sainted !   What an extraordinary man he was !   Yes, surely, he was a very good man, because you may some of you remember to have read the history of those times, and know what share Mr. Sidney had in that black and horrid villany, that cursed treason and murder—the murder I mean of King Charles I, of blessed memory ; a shame to religion itself.   A perpetual reproach to the island we live in, to think that a prince should be brought by pretended methods of law and justice to such an end at his own palace.   And it is a shame to think that such bloody miscreants should be sainted and lamented, who had any hand in that horrid murder and treason, and who to their dying moment, when they were on the brink of eternity, and just stepping into another world, could confidently bless God for their being engaged in that good cause, as they call it, which was the rebellion which brought that blessed martyr to his death.   It is high time for all mankind that have any Christianity, or sense of heaven or hell, to bestir themselves to rid the nation of such caterpillars, such monsters of villany as these are."

He then alluded to Barnardiston's account of his own condition : " As for anything that he has said of me Sir Samuel Barnardiston shall write and speak of me as long as he pleases.   But though he says *I am down in the mouth*, it is true I have a little lost my tongue by my cold ; yet I hope I shall never lose my heart nor spirit to serve the Government, nor forbear to use my utmost diligence to see that such offenders as these persons, that entertain principles so destructive to the Government, be brought to condign punishment. And be they who they will, were they my own brothers, I should be of the same mind ; and so in that mind I hope in God I shall live and die."

Jeffreys refers elsewhere to his cold and a " little hoarseness he had contracted." This had been a hard term with him ; and as he never spared himself in either the length or vigour of his addresses to the juries, the cold had evidently attacked his voice. But the change of air derived from going the Western circuit set him up again ; and when on his return Barnardiston came up to receive sentence, the Lord Chief Justice was able to inform him that " Sir George is not yet so down in the mouth but he can tell Sir Samuel Barnardiston his mind." Through the mouth of Mr. Justice Wythens, his ever-ready assistant and chorus, the mind of the Chief Justice declared itself in a fine of £10,000, with the accompanying sureties and committal.

In the conduct of these three trials Jeffreys shows an increased and more violently expressed indignation since the time when he had tried Sidney. The approval of such as the Bishop of St. Asaph, the impudence of the popular party in questioning the truth of what all Tories believed to be a well-established conspiracy, the boldness of attacks which did not hesitate to accuse the King and his brother of murdering one of their prisoners, and, lastly, the early symptoms of a disease which was soon to torture him with suffering, and hurry him in four years to an early grave,—all these causes concurred to aggravate the natural heat of his disposition and the severities which he conceived it to be his duty to practise against the enemies of his royal Master. The fact that Jeffreys found the greatest alleviation of his sufferings in drinking punch, if it soothed his pain, would tend to inflame his already inflammable temper.

But it cannot be said that so far there is much to complain of in the Judge's conduct. In these latter trials he shows himself guilty of no actual injustice ; the convictions were, on the whole, properly obtained, and the punishments, according to the spirit of the loyal party, well deserved. The unscrupulousness of the Whig methods and the recklessness with which they were prepared to clutch at any accusation against the Government, however groundless or ill-supported, showed that they had profited by the training in thoughtless credulity which they had received at the time of the anti-Popish agitation. The plots of Russell and Sidney, established on evidence that is conclusive to any impartial mind, were declared to be sham plots, forsooth ! to be scouted and ridiculed ; but the plot of Charles and James to murder the martyred Essex,—that was real enough to be nursed and encouraged ! Thus argued the Whigs. But the facts point to the opposite conclusion : they are on the side of Jeffreys, and justify from the Tory standpoint the warmth of his indignation and the severity of his sentences. His mode of expressing his sentiments stands in no need of commendation. His humour, his eloquence, his good sense, his knowledge of human nature and the powerful originality of his character find their most pleasing and temperate exemplification in the trial of Braddon and Speke.

Jeffreys' treatment of the Bar was always firm, and impartially so ; he was not above telling the Attorney-General to have done with " descants." His own conduct and experience had perhaps acquainted him with the presumption of the successful advocate ; he knew by experience how a strong judge like Baron Weston was needed to effectually curb it. Williams and Wallop might well have tried the temper of a more patient judge than Jeffreys. His peculiarly animated treatment of the latter seems to spring from one of those personal antipathies which, as we cannot see and hear the two men, it is impossible to describe. Wallop we know to have been tactless and promiscuous in the sources of his legal authorities ; but Jeffreys imputes to him a hectoring and swaggering manner, of which there is hardly sufficient proof. Judges are human after all, and not infrequently form antipathies to those practising before them, which, if put to it, they might find a difficulty in satisfactorily explaining.

XI

CHIEF JUSTICE AND LORD KEEPER—THE TRIALS OF ARMSTRONG AND ROSEWELL

1684

JEFFREYS started on the Western circuit at the end of February, 1684. His first visit to these parts is of interest, if only for the fact that this circuit was the scene in the following year of the ever notorious " Bloody Assizes." Moreover, in travelling this circuit, Jeffreys was to pass through the wealthiest, busiest and most populated part of England ; the West was the seat of the chief manufactures, wool and serge, of the mining industries in Cornwall, and of a greater variety of employments than any other district in the land, whilst its port of Bristol was the second city in the kingdom. His present visit had more than a purely judicial object in view. The Chief Justice was to examine the condition of political feeling in the West of England and ascertain the disposition of the gentry towards the present Government. The trial of Braddon and Speke had revealed the presence of a good deal of ferment in these parts and a readiness to sympathise with those hostile to the King. Jeffreys found that the gentry was for the most part loyal and zealously inclined to the King's service ; but that Dissent was powerful among the middle and lower classes, and called for repressive measures. The West of England was at this time the principal stronghold of the Dissenters ; for which reason, among others, Monmouth and his advisers selected it in 1685 as the scene of their invasion. Jeffreys wrote to Secretary Jenkins from the various towns through which he passed, keeping him well informed as to the results of his observations.

Besides gauging the political feelings of the Western counties, the Chief Justice was instructed, by arts of persuasion and fair promise, to induce those towns that had not already done so to make a surrender of their old Charters to the King and receive new ones in their places. Like the magician Abanazar, the wily Judge persuaded the Corporations of the West to give up their old lamps, and in return promised them beautiful new ones, fresh from Whitehall. At Plymouth he encountered some difficulty in accomplishing the transfer, owing to the arts of the Recorder of that town, Mr. Serjeant Maynard. This astute old gentleman, over eighty years of age, of vast legal learning and political principles so elastic as to have carried him safely through the changes and chances of the last forty years, did his best to dissuade the Aldermen of Plymouth from acceding to Jeffreys' proposals. But the Chief Justice successfully combated his evil intentions, and returned to London with copies of Maynard's factious letters to lay before the Secretary of State.

There is an interesting sequel to this incident related in the *Verney Correspondence*; "May 4th, 1684. In private cause between Nosworthy and another for £1,000 per annum, Maynard was very sharp on my Lord Chief Justice Jeffreys; the manner is variously reported." The skull-faced Serjeant was a difficult one to tackle on a point of law. The story is told that in a discussion of this kind Jeffreys lost his temper, and told Maynard he was so old that he had forgotten all his law; to which the Serjeant retorted, "Yes, my lord, I have forgotten more law than you ever knew." This may have been on the occasion referred to by Verney. If so, it must have afforded Maynard a pleasing opportunity to clear off the old score at Plymouth.

By the middle of April Jeffreys was back again in

Westminster Hall. There he found two more of the Rye conspirators awaiting judgment. These were James Holloway, a Bristol merchant, and Sir Thomas Armstrong, the friend and counsellor of the Duke of Monmouth. The two men had fled the country on the discovery of the Plot. Failing to plead to their indictments, they had been outlawed, and agents of the Government abroad were instructed to use every effort to secure them. In a few months' time both were taken : Holloway in the West Indies, and Armstrong by a spy at Leyden in Holland. On their arrival in London, nothing remained but that the Court of King's Bench should award execution against them ; for trial, conviction and execution were already implied in the sentence of outlawry, which in cases of high treason was equivalent to a conviction. But Armstrong, when brought before the Court, pleaded that by a statute of Edward VI. he could claim a full trial ; the statute said that if the party outlawed *yielded* himself to the Chief Justice of England within one year after the judgment of outlawry, he could be tried, and, if found not guilty, his sentence of outlawry reversed. Jeffreys would not admit this plea in Armstrong's case, because he did not consider that Armstrong had *yielded* himself according to the statute, but had been brought as an unwilling prisoner before him. Though Jeffreys has been heartily abused for this construction of the Act, surely there is much to be said in favour of his view. True, it has not been upheld since, but that is no argument against its claim to decent consideration. Jeffreys took the view that the term *yielding* implied a voluntary surrender of the outlaw, and did not apply to a man who had been captured against his will and brought a prisoner before the Court ; and according to the wording of the Act this interpretation is as likely and reasonable as any other.

But it is further alleged against Jeffreys and the Government that a trial refused to Armstrong was offered under precisely similar circumstances to Holloway. Certainly a trial was offered to Holloway ; but both Jeffreys and the

Attorney-General who made the offer, were careful to insist over and over again that such an offer was an act of pure grace and mercy on the part of the King, and arose from no claim or right of the prisoners. The King, they said, could if he chose give the prisoner liberty to be tried by a gracious exercise of his authority ; but that was the King's concern, the Judges had no such power. That the King chose to show mercy in Holloway's case and not in Armstrong's was no business of Jeffreys or his brethren ; it was a matter solely for the King, who had himself the best of reasons for not showing favour to Sir Thomas Armstrong. If Jeffreys' conduct towards the latter is deserving of censure, it is not upon these grounds, although many historians have warmly abused him for the gross illegality of his decision on this part of the case.

The King was determined not to spare Armstrong, whom he regarded as the guiltiest of the conspirators. Apart from his share in the Plot, Armstrong had little in his character to command sympathy or indulgence. A "debauched, atheistical bravo" according to unfriendly testimony, "a lewd bully and gamester" according to Lord Ailesbury, he was at least a man of vicious life and turbulent passions, and had been driven from the Court for the murder of a gentleman in the play-house. But it was not for these reasons that he was peculiarly obnoxious to Charles, to whom violence of character or irregularity of life were always pardonable if accompanied by useful or congenial qualities. The King hated him as the would-be assassin of his brother and himself, and the principal seducer of his unfortunate son. Armstrong had offered his fellow conspirators to get admission to the Duke of York and kill him with his own hand ; and, after the failure of the Rye House scheme, he had been still prepared to assassinate the royal brothers. But in Charles's eyes even this murderous energy was pardonable compared with his fatal influence over the Duke of Monmouth. If Charles ever really cared for anybody, he looked with real affection on the firstborn of his irregular family. To find

Monmouth deep in the designs of those who plotted against his throne and life was the bitterest shock that ever fell upon the callous Prince. Armstrong's influence over the weak youth was known to the King; and upon Armstrong, therefore, descended the full weight of his indignation. Charles, with all his lightness of character, was not incapable of cherishing sincere resentments; he never forgave Lord William Russell for his implacable violence against the Papists, much less could he forgive Armstrong's horrid temptation of his son.

Jeffreys was no doubt acquainted with all these facts when Armstrong appeared before him for judgment on June 14th. The prisoner was accompanied by his daughter, a Mrs. Matthews, whom Lord Campbell in his gushing sympathy describes as a most interesting and beautiful young lady. Jeffreys pointed out to Armstrong the hopelessness of his case; and was proceeding to ask the keeper of Newgate what were the usual days for executions when Mrs. Matthews, in her eagerness to assist her father, exclaimed: "Here is a statute, my lord!" meaning the Act of Edward VI. already alluded to. "What is the matter with that gentlewoman?" asked Jeffreys. Armstrong told her abruptly to hold her tongue, and went on to press the statute she had cited on the attention of the Chief Justice. Once more Mrs. Matthews' zeal overcame her discretion: "Here is a copy of it," she said. "Why, how now?" exclaimed Jeffreys at this second interruption. "We do not use to have women plead in the Court of King's Bench: pray be at quiet, mistress." "Pray hold your tongue," urged her father, and resumed his argument. But the Judge explained to him that he had not yielded himself to the Court according to the terms of the statute he cited. Armstrong then begged that he might have counsel to argue to the point. Jeffreys answered: "For what reason? We are of opinion it is not a matter of any doubt. For you must not go under the apprehension that we deny you anything that is right; there is no doubt nor difficulty at all in the thing." "Methinks, my lord, the statute is very plain," urged the prisoner. "So it is very plain that you can have no advantage by it," retorted the Chief Justice. "Captain Richardson,"—to the keeper of Newgate,—"you shall have a rule for execution on Friday next." Armstrong desired to speak; Jeffreys assented readily. "Very freely, what you please." Armstrong referred to Holloway's case and the offer of a trial which had been made to him; but Jeffreys explained that such an offer had been made solely by the King's mercy, that the same mercy might have been extended to him if the King had pleased, but that it was not the Judge's business to interfere with the King's prerogative. At this Mrs. Matthews's indignation could restrain itself no longer. "My lord," she cried, "I hope you will not murder my father; this is murdering a man." "Who is this woman?" asked the Chief Justice. "Marshal, take her into custody. Why, how now? Because your relation is attainted for high treason, must you take upon you to tax the courts of justice for murder, when we grant the execution according to law? Take her away." "God Almighty's judgments light upon you!" from the lips of Mrs. Matthews. "God Almighty's judgments will light upon those that are guilty of high treason," from the lips of Jeffreys. "Amen, I pray God!" exclaimed the lady. "So say I," answered the Judge; "but," he went on, "clamours never prevail on me at all; I thank God I am clamour proof, and will never fear to do my duty." Mrs. Matthews was removed in custody. Once more Jeffreys explained to Sir Thomas his view of the law and the reasons of the indulgence shown to Holloway. "We are not," he repeated, "disposers of the King's grace and favour, but the ministers of his justice." Then there ensued the following dialogue, which, in fairness to the two men, must be given in full.

Sir Thomas Armstrong.—My lord, I am within the statute. I was outlawed while I was beyond sea, and I come now here within the twelvemonth. That is all I know or have to say in this matter.

L. C. J.—We think quite the contrary, Sir Thomas.

Sir Thomas Armstrong—When I was before the Council, my lord, they ordered that I should have counsel allotted me, but I could have no benefit by that order ; for when I was taken I was robbed of all the money I had, and have not had one penny restored to me, nor any money since.   I know not whether the law allows persons in my condition to be robbed and stripped.

L. C. J.—I know nothing at all of that matter, Sir Thomas.

Sir Thomas Armstrong.—My lord, I know lawyers will not plead without money, and, being robbed, I could not have wherewithal to fee them.

L. C. J.—Sir Thomas Armstrong, you take the liberty of saying what you please ; you talk of being robbed ; nobody has robbed you that I know of.

Sir Thomas Armstrong.—Nobody says you do know of it ; but so it is.

L. C. J.—Nay, be as angry as you will, Sir Thomas ; we are not concerned at your anger.   We will undoubtedly do our duty.

Sir Thomas Armstrong.—I ought to have the benefit of the law, and I demand no more.

L. C. J.—That you shall have, by the grace of God. See that execution be done on Friday next, according to law.   You shall have the full benefit of the law.

By giving partial extracts from the report of this trial writers have usually succeeded in making Jeffreys appear brutal and violent in his treatment of Armstrong and his daughter, and the two latter appear in the light of oppressed and amiable martyrs.   Public opinion was not at the time so sure on this point ; for in the *Verney Correspondence*[1] Jeffreys is commended for his honourable conduct in releasing Mrs. Matthews from custody the same afternoon, after the very " savoury curse " which the writer says she had given them all round.   Jeffreys certainly kept his temper and his dignity in the encounter with the heated lady, and showed proper judicial charity

[1] Hist. MSS. Comm.

in so soon pardoning her affront. On the other hand, he was undoubtedly guilty of harshness, if not illegality, in not allowing Armstrong to have counsel to plead his case on the Act of Edward VI. Jeffreys may have looked on such pleading as a waste of time—it would certainly have had no effect on his mind—and considered the guilty Armstrong unworthy of indulgence; but as a Judge he should have allowed him the full benefit which the law accorded to people in his situation. Both he and Armstrong lost their tempers at the conclusion of the hearing; but it will be admitted that Jeffreys as well as Armstrong had received some provocation. In spite of Burnet's extravagant account of Armstrong's wrongs and his beautiful endurance under their infliction, it can only be political prejudice or a nauseous sentimentalism that denies the guilty violence of his methods and character, and casts up its eyes to Heaven at the inhumanity of the Lord Chief Justice.

During May and June the Courts had been very active in enforcing the authority of the King, and Jeffreys had enjoyed some pleasing opportunities of paying off old scores against some of his former opponents. His friend Francis Smith was fined, pilloried and imprisoned for printing libels against the Government; an information was exhibited against the ex-Speaker, Mr. Williams, for printing, by order of the House of Commons, the narrative of Dangerfield, one of the Popish Plot witnesses; and Dr. Titus Oates was committed to the King's Bench prison, pending an action for slander brought against him by the Duke of York. It is impossible not to admire the Doctor's fortitude in the hour of adversity. His impudence and confidence were unabated. When the Duke's attorney called on the Doctor and asked him what he intended to do in the approaching action, Oates coolly replied, "I do not value the Duke nor his attorney neither; I neither love the Duke nor fear him. It may be I am in for one hundred thousand pounds here; but, if ever Parliament sits, I do not question but to have somebody else in my place." The attorney asked him to explain this mysterious forecast ; but Oates was not to be drawn out. "Do you come to trepan me?" asked the wily Doctor ; and away he went. He disdained to defend himself against the Duke's claim, so that the Court of King's Bench had nothing to do but to impanel a jury to assess the plaintiff's damages. Jeffreys presided over the enquiry, but the Doctor did not appear ; his presence was hardly necessary on this occasion ; these proceedings were but the prologue to the great day of reckoning. The Doctor's slanders against the Duke were fully proved. In the days of his supremacy, when, as the Bishop of Ely said, none dared talk with him, Oates had publicly loaded James with the coarsest abuse : he was " a traitor, the son of a whore, a man who ate with the devil, a scavenger and an incendiary." All the jury could do was to justify Oates's premonition that the affair would cost him £100,000, by a verdict for the plaintiff to that amount. Jeffreys gave a foretaste of the spirit in which he was likely to deal with Oates, if he ever got the opportunity, by denying him his title of Doctor, referring ironically to his claims as a Gospel preacher and man of eminence, and exclaiming in the course of his summing-up on the height of corruption to which an age must have reached that would have suffered such a fellow's insolence. As it was quite beyond the Doctor's means to pay the plaintiff's damages, he remained in the King's Bench prison after the conclusion of the trial, emerging a year later to meet fresh charges, which only his personal appearance could render useful or effective for the public good.

Before Jeffreys started again on circuit,—this time he had chosen the Northern, and was due at York in July—he tried a civil cause in the Court of King's Bench, remarkable alike for the magnitude of the claim involved and the impudence of the forgery by which it was attempted to substantiate the claim. A certain Lady Ivy, true to the encroaching propensities of the plant which bears her name, declared herself to be legally possessed of the greater part of Shadwell. She founded her title upon certain deeds dating back to Tudor times. These deeds on examination turned out to be nothing more nor less than elaborate forgeries, contrived and executed by the Lady Ivy with the help of certain rascally attorneys. Jeffreys saw through the imposture from the first, much to the disgust of the Attorney and Solicitor-General who appeared for the plaintiff. He told them plainly that one of their principal witnesses was an "arrant notorious knave," and, calling the immortal Shakspere to his aid, declared that he would never believe him if he swore as long as Sir John Falstaff fought. It is interesting to note Jeffreys' familiarity with the great poet. From his acquaintance with Shakspere's stupendous vocabulary, and his natural sympathy with such a character as Falstaff, the Chief Justice may well have derived in part that extraordinary wealth of language and quaint originality of expression which in his more awful moments of transported rage make him appear rather the creation of a powerful dramatist than a creature of flesh and blood.

A great array of counsel had been mustered on both sides, and their many dialogues and little heats sorely tried the temper of the Chief Justice. Mr. Bradbury, an intelligent junior, having been commended by Jeffreys for an ingenious discovery of the falsity of one of the reputed title deeds, was so elated that he could not refrain from enlarging on his observations. "Lord, sir," cried Jeffreys, "you must be cackling too ; we told you your objection was very ingenious, but that must not make you troublesome ; you cannot lay an egg but you must be cackling over it." Finally the Solicitor-General, angered and mortified by the breakdown of his case and the observations of Jeffreys, could not conceal his irritation from the Chief Justice. "Nay, be not angry, Mr. Solicitor," said Jeffreys ; "for, if you be, we cannot help that neither. The law is the law for you as well as me." "My lord, I must take the rule from you now," answers Finch. Jeffreys discovered some impertinence in the answer.

"And so you shall, sir, from the Court, as long as I sit here," he retorted ; "and so shall everybody else, by the grace of God. I assure you, I care not whether it please or displease ; we must not have our time taken up with impertinent things ; for I must say there have been so many offered in this cause to-day as ever were in any cause that ever I heard ; and if all be not as some would have it, then they must be in passion presently. The Court gives all due respects and expects them." Jeffreys showed himself no respecter of persons or parties in upholding his authority : it was not only on Wallops and Williamses that his wrath descended. It is almost needless to add that the Lady Ivy did not recover the greater part of Shadwell.[1]

Jeffreys' position at Court had been considerably enhanced since his accession to the Chief Justiceship, and the worst fears of the Norths seemed only too likely to be accomplished. With increasing mortification the Lord Keeper viewed the growing power of his rival. Apart from his conduct of judicial proceedings, Jeffreys gained credit and influence by the adroitness with which he

---

1 Lady Ivy, *née* Theodosia Stepkin, was a niece of Sir John Bramston, Chief Justice of the King's Bench, 1635—1642. Her story, says her cousin Bramston, the autobiographer, would take up a volume. She had three husbands. The second, Ivy, was a "trade fellow," knighted at the Restoration, but "merited whipping rather." Her father was a German by extraction, who made a fortune by draining Wapping marsh. The history of her lawsuits is curious, and illustrates the imperfect way in which cases were prepared and cross-examinations carried out in the seventeenth century. She had already had a trial as to her title previous to the present one before Jeffreys, when every one had been perfectly satisfied that her title was "as good as could be." At the second trial the contrary is as clearly proved as possible. Yet in 1687, on the validity of another lease, against which evidence of forgery was given similar to that in 1684, she recovered two verdicts, one in the King's Bench, the other in the Common Pleas. Bramston, who is of course friendly to her, suggests that in 1684 her Judges were prepossessed, but he gives no reason for their being so, and certainly the case against her seems from the report to be proved up to the hilt. Lord Campbell describes Jeffreys' charge on that occasion as "most masterly, lucid, and impartial."

had procured the surrender of Charters in the West of England and the peculiar authority he exercised over the City of London. With the fall of the Whigs his influence in the City seems to have become despotic in its character, the Mayor and Aldermen his fearful tools. They might murmur against his pride, but no attention would be paid to their complaints. And now, in a marked and public fashion, the King was to set the seal of his personal encouragement and approbation on the efforts of his Chief Justice ; he was to go forth to new conquests with the prestige of one whom the King delighted to honour. On a Sunday morning early in July, when Whitehall was thronged with courtiers, Charles took from his own finger a diamond ring, and, in the sight of all, presented it to the Lord Chief Justice as a mark of his signal favour and his gracious acceptance of Sir George Jeffreys' services. **Roger** North complains bitterly that no wonder Jeffreys, thus stamped as a favoured legate of the King, made all the Charters of the North fall before him like the walls of Jericho, and insinuates that any one could have done the same with a ring off the King's hands. There are not wanting at this time signs of great uneasiness among the North family ; "thus bad begins, but worse remains behind."

Durham and York were the principal cities visited by Jeffreys on this Northern circuit. At the former he arranged for the surrender of the city Charter into the hands of the Bishop ; at the latter he made himself very pleasant and bestowed upon the civic authorities amiable promises of the royal grace which he did not subsequently fulfil, at least to the satisfaction of Sir John Reresby. That careful courtier did his best to make Jeffreys' visit to York a pleasant one, partly from respect for his mission, partly as a mark of gratitude for the kindness with which Jeffreys had treated him in former days. He received the Judge with military honours, waited on him at his lodgings and invited him to dinner. Jeffreys, in return for these civilities, called on Reresby one evening incognito, and "being a jolly, merry companion when business was over," stayed with him over a bottle till one in the morning.

Jeffreys returned to London laden with surrendered Charters, "the spoils of towns," as Roger North calls them. On September 12th he attended the King, and gave him an account of his proceedings, at which Charles expressed his satisfaction—a satisfaction not shared by at least one of his Majesty's advisers.

With the return of Jeffreys from the Northern circuit opened that chapter of misery which closed the respectable career of the Lord Keeper North. The distresses of that worthy man as narrated by the ever-faithful and solicitous Roger, the mental suffering induced by the conduct of Jeffreys, to which his timorous desire to please all men rendered him painfully subject, his physical collapse before the ridicule and neglect of a Court that could see nothing to respect or pity in the forsaken Minister, tell a story to which a devoted brother has lent a glow of martyrdom, but in which posterity can only recognise the disastrous effects of a want of moral courage on even the most pronounced and self-conscious integrity.

As the reign of Charles drew to its close, the influence of the moderate section of his advisers, Halifax and North, declined, and that of the Duke of York, Sunderland and Jeffreys increased. To the dismay of those who, like North, considered the supremacy of the Church of England as part and parcel of the supremacy of the King, James was beginning to insinuate the claims of the Papists, and procure for them some measure of indulgence. These matters were discussed at the meetings of the Cabinet, a kind of inner committee of the Privy Council, consisting of the King's most trusted Ministers. The full Council met on Thursdays, the Cabinet meetings took place usually on a Sunday evening. Jeffreys, who had been sworn of the Privy Council on his appointment as Chief Justice, was admitted into the Cabinet after his return from the North,—a circumstance very unpropitious to the Lord Keeper. When one Sunday morning shortly after this undesirable event, the Duke of York requested North to assist him that evening in a business to be moved to his Majesty, that excellent man could not avoid a presentiment of something unpleasant, which the gravity of the other Ministers' faces did nothing to allay.

The same evening the King had no sooner taken his seat at the Council Board than Jeffreys rose to his feet, holding in his hand certain rolls and papers. These contained lists of various persons in the North of England then lying in prison or under commitment for refusing to take the customary oaths to observe the Protestant religion as by law established. They consisted of Papists and Nonconformists ; but the real design of the Duke of York was, through the mouth of Jeffreys, to obtain discharge or release for his co-religionists, and to further that object he was prepared to include the other classes of Dissenters if necessary. According to North's account, Jeffreys delivered a vehement speech, "letting fly his tropes and figures" on behalf of these unfortunate men "rotting and stinking in prisons." When he sat down, a painful silence ensued, North waiting to see if any one else would answer the Chief Justice. As nobody volunteered, North felt it his duty to intervene. In characteristic fashion he made no objection to the real cause of uneasiness, the proposed indulgence to the Papists, but blamed the proceeding as involving the release of a number of Protestant Dissenters, who would only go about turbulently stirring up sedition. His remarks were received in silence, and the matter was not further discussed. But the Lord Keeper returned home that night full of melancholy. "What can be the meaning? Are they all stark mad?" he frequently exclaimed. Then, taking out his pocket almanack, he soothed his troubled mind by entering against that day : "Motion which I alone opposed." Roger says that he accounted his action on this occasion as the most memorable in his life. It certainly furnishes an accurate notion of the extent of his virtue. North had intuition and conscience ; he saw the drift of Jeffreys' motion, and he knew it to be his duty to oppose it ; but he had not that courageous determination which should have prompted him to boldly declare the real danger of such a measure ; he rather grounds his opposition on an objection which can have deceived no one as to his real feelings, and can only have tempted his enemies to fresh attacks on his peace of mind.

This incident shows Jeffreys as the declared follower of James in his policy of indulgence for his fellow-Papists. If Sunderland or Jeffreys had ever realised how far and with what hopeless obstinacy James would ultimately endeavour to secure the triumph of his religion, they would, even with all their thirst for power, have hesitated to enter into his present designs. Had they done so, Sunderland would have saved himself from an unpleasant suspicion of treachery, Jeffreys from irretrievable ruin. But in all probability they did not foresee—who could ?—the depths of James's infatuation; they only saw in him the personification of absolute government of which they were ready to be obedient ministers. Jeffreys in particular looked upon the Duke as the engine by which he might hope to wrest the Seal from the apprehensive Lord Keeper. For Jeffreys did not intend the Chief Justiceship to be the ultimate goal of his ambition ; he must reach the highest summit of legal fame, and that summit seemed the more easily attainable for the dizziness that was overcoming its present occupant. If North's account is correct, Jeffreys was prepared to achieve his purpose by rendering the Lord Keeper's position so intolerable that he should be compelled to resign. But in choosing that course of action Jeffreys had not truly gauged the character of his opponent. Death alone released the Seal from a hand that clung to its empty trophy long after dignity and self-respect had perished in the attempt.

North soon underwent such experiences of the growing influence of the Lord Chief Justice as would have induced most men in his situation to reconsider their position and the possibility of continuing in an office the rights and privileges of which they had ceased to enjoy. One of the highest functions of the Lord Chancellor or Keeper, as the case might be, was to recommend to the

King new Judges whenever any vacancy occurred on the Bench; but even in this important duty North was obliged to bend to the will of the Chief Justice. In the October of 1684 Mr. Justice Wyndham had died on circuit. North designed to fill his place by the appointment of Serjeant Bedingfield, a grave, heavy lawyer, of loyal principles and a good Churchman. Bedingfield, overwhelmed with joy and gratitude, communicated the good news to his brother, a woollen draper in the City. The woollen draper, who happened, unfortunately, to be the friend and creature of Jeffreys, carried the intelligence to his patron. Jeffreys, desirous of some opportunity of wounding the power of the Lord Keeper, sent for the Serjeant, and told him plainly that as long as he relied on North's influence he should never be raised to the Bench; and that, if he really wanted to be a Judge, he must look to the Lord Chief Justice and not to the Lord Keeper for his promotion. Bedingfield, who, Roger North says, was not "formed for the heroics," yielded to the inevitable, and was content to wait for promotion until after North's death.

If the case of Bedingfield was a sufficiently painful slight to the Lord Keeper, the case of Serjeant Wright was a hundred times worse. Baron Street, from the Exchequer, had been sent into the Common Pleas to fill Wyndham's place; it therefore remained to fill up the vacant Barony. North went to the King to consult him as to a fit person to take the office, and was horrified when Charles suddenly asked: "My lord, what think you of Serjeant Wright? Why may not he be the man?" North replied that he knew Wright only too well, and that he was the most unfit person in England to be made a Judge. "Then it must not be," answered the King; and the matter was dropped. But it left food for much unpleasant reflection in the mind of the Lord Keeper. He knew Wright well indeed, knew him as a comely, airy, flourishing gentleman of a good Suffolk family, altogether attractive in person, but in habit an unprincipled voluptuary, on the brink of financial ruin. North had done his work for him when they were at the Bar together, and lent him money on many occasions,—services Wright had returned by dealing fraudulently with his benefactor over a mortgage on his estates.   And this was the man the King suggested to the Lord Keeper as his new Judge ! How could such a man have entered into the King's mind for such a purpose ? That question the Lord Keeper soon learnt to answer by the hated name of Jeffreys ; it was not long before he detected the malign influence of the Chief Justice in the proposed advancement of Wright.   The latter had gone to Jeffreys, who was his friend, and with tears begged his influence in obtaining the vacant Judgeship as a means of saving himself from utter ruin.   Jeffreys, seeing in Wright a pliant tool for himself and his party and a further means of humbling the Lord Keeper, had urged his claims to the King.   Charles had accordingly mentioned his name to North, with the result we have seen.   But the King's "Then it must not be" was as final an utterance as might be expected from the lips of the speaker.   In a very few days he returned to the subject : "Why may not Wright be a Judge ?" he asked of the Lord Keeper ;   "is it impossible ?" North saw the King's pangs as he asked the question, and pitied him as the unwilling tool of unscrupulous men.

Such is Roger North's account.   The idea of Charles II. suffering pangs over the appointment of Wright, and his acting as the unwilling tool of anybody, one would have thought too absurd for even the devoted Roger to stomach ; but apology makes a man acquainted with the strangest notions.   According to Roger, his brother was so touched by the agony of the King, that after once more fully recapitulating the unworthiness of Serjeant Wright, he ended by saying : "And now I have done my duty to your Majesty, and am ready to obey your Majesty's commands in case it be your pleasure that this man shall be a Judge."   "My lord," replied the King— and there seems a touch of irony in the brief reply—"I thank you."   Soon after came the King's warrant that Wright was to be a Baron of the Exchequer.

But the cup of the Lord Keeper's humiliation was not yet full. One morning shortly after Wright's appointment had been decided upon, North was sitting in Westminster Hall in his Court of Chancery. In these days the Courts were actually inside the Hall, and in sight of one another. Opposite the Chancery was a small bar within which the Judges of the King's Bench robed before going up to Court. Here on this same morning, Jeffreys was standing robing with his other brethren, when Serjeant Wright came walking up the Hall. Jeffreys saw him, and beckoned him to come to the bar. The Serjeant approached, full of crouching and humility ; on his reaching the bar the Chief Justice took him by the shoulders, whispered something in his ear, and then, flinging him off from him, kept his arms extended towards him for some short time. This, says North, was a public declaration on Jeffreys' part that in spite of "that man above there," *i.e.* the Lord Keeper, his excellent friend Wright was to be a Judge.

On another occasion we find the Lord Keeper complaining that in the matter of a dispute among the Wapping justices, Jeffreys came flaming drunk to the Council Board, and, staring like a madman, attacked North fiercely, under cover of a general denunciation of the "Trimmers."

Unfortunately, in his reduced circumstances the luckless North derived no comfort from the sympathy of his fellow courtiers. "The rising sun," writes his brother, "hath a charming effect, but not upon courtiers as upon larks ; for it makes these sing, and the others silent." As the sun of Jeffreys rose in its glory, an indifferent silence, to say nothing of openly expressed derision, was all the sympathy North received from the larks of Whitehall. Only at home, in the society of his devoted brother and his relatives and personal friends, could North find any consolation for his sorrowing spirit. But even the influences of home were not strong enough to prevent the broken Minister from sinking into a state of morbid depression, which ultimately developed into a fatal melancholy.

For these details of the rivalry between the Lord Keeper and the Chief Justice we are entirely dependent on the narrative of Roger North, which, from the very nature of the circumstances, must be received with great caution. But by this time we should have been able to form some estimate of Jeffreys' character, and of that of North we have the amplest material for judging.   On the one side we can discern an arbitrary disposition, reckless in its methods and principles, full of unsatisfied ambition, moved to contempt and mockery in the presence of unattractive moral worth ; on the other side, genuine integrity of character diseased and disfigured by moral cowardice, and an ignominious greed of office.   If, instead of yielding unwillingly at every point, and going home to lament over the hardness of his lot, North had fought openly and courageously against the schemes of Jeffreys and his party, he would not have been so completely deserted and despised by those around him, and the pity of posterity would have been mingled with some measure of admiration.

During the Michaelmas sittings of 1684 the activity of the Court of King's Bench in prosecuting the enemies of the Government was unabated.   On November 6th Jeffreys sat at the Guildhall to try an action for false arrest brought by the ex-Lord Mayor, Sir William Pritchard, against Mr. Papillon.   The case arose out of the old troubles in the Sheriffs' election of 1682.   There can be no doubt that Pritchard's arrest, which had been effected at the suit of Papillon, had been a party move, designed, the Crown alleged, to throw the City into a state of tumult, and further thereby the rebellious designs of the Whigs.   It is more than probable from the names of those concerned in it that some such object was in view.   At any rate, the trial of the action resolved itself into a party conflict, and stirred the wrath of the Chief Justice to unexampled indignation.   A prime actor in the events with which the trial was concerned, conscious of his authority in the City of London, and in former days one of the principal objects of the hatred of the faction, the

Chief Justice could not overcome, in spite of some praiseworthy attempts at impartiality, the temptation to give the City Whigs and their adherents some " licks with the rough side of his tongue."   He first fell foul of Mr. Ward, one of the defendant's counsel, a respectable lawyer, afterwards a Lord Chief Baron under William III.   Ward was pressing, with every respect, a point which Jeffreys considered unproved and irrelevant.   The Chief Justice charged him with speaking "ad captandum populum," denounced his " flourishes, enamel, garniture and ocean of discourse," and ended by accusing Ward of being angry and not understanding his business.   The audience added to the excitement by beginning a little hiss.   " Who is that ?" cried Jeffreys, remembering some former trials in which he had taken part as Recorder.   " What, in the name of God ! I hope we are now past that time of day that humming and hissing shall be used in courts of justice ; but I would fain know that fellow that dare to hum or hiss while I sit here : I'll assure him, be he who he will, I'll lay him by the heels, and make an example of him. Indeed, I knew the time when causes were to be carried according as the mobile hissed or hummed ; and I do not question but they have as good a will to it now.   Come, Mr. Ward, pray let us have none of your fragrancies, and fine rhetorical flowers, to take the people with."   At length old Serjeant Maynard intervened and succeeded in calming the Judge.

When, however, the defence called as witnesses Alderman Cornish and other of the City Whigs, the sight of them was too much for Jeffreys.   He ironically compared them to sucking children in innocence, and said it was his duty to let the world know what sort of men these were who pretended to saintship, whining fellows that snivelled at the Government ; the City, he said, had been quiet and happy until Bethell and Cornish, a couple of busy fellows, got into public offices.   " Let the whole party go away with that in their teeth, and chew upon it if they will," he concluded.   His summing up opened with a statement of the legal aspect of the case as fair and well expressed as possible, but he was soon aflame again when he came to the facts. In alluding to the Whig corruption of juries, he remarked how the Sheriffs got " this factious fellow out of one corner, and that pragmatical, prick-eared, snivelling, whining rascal out of another corner, to prop up the cause, which was tried not according to justice but demureness of look ! " As to the arrest of the Lord Mayor, he remarked, with truly Hohenzollern confidence, that if God had not put it into some one's heart to send for the City Militia, London would have been in ashes, the King's subjects wallowing in their own and one another's blood ; and all this damned hellish conspiracy the work of a lot of " notorious Dissenters or profligate atheistical villains that herd together." . . . . " This, gentlemen, is plain English, and necessary to be used upon all these occasions." A little of this plain English he conceived necessary for the good of Mr. Papillon. His conduct he described as canting and hypocritical, setting himself "cock-a-hoop" as the only true patriot in the City. "You had much better keep in your counting-house, I tell you, and mind your merchandise." This advice was timely ; for the jury, after half an hour's consideration, decided that Mr. Papillon was to pay the plaintiff £ 10,000 damages. " Gentlemen," said the Chief Justice, " you seem to be persons that have some sense upon you and consideration for the Government, and I think have given a good verdict and are to be greatly commended for it."

On November 18th Jeffreys sat in Westminster Hall to try Mr. Thomas Rosewell, an eminent Dissenting minister. With his accession to power the Judge's hatred of Dissent had increased in proportion to his opportunities for giving it greater play ; and though we must accept with caution such descriptions of his conduct as come from Dissenters themselves, there are collateral circumstances which go to prove the excess of his zeal in this direction. At any rate, over the case of Mr. Rosewell he experienced a check, deserved or undeserved, according as the Bishop of St. Asaph or Dr. Burnet might judge him. Jeffreys' initial error was in misjudging the character of the man with whom he had to deal. When Rosewell was pulled out of bed one early morning in the September previous to his trial and haled before the Chief Justice at his house in Aldermanbury, Jeffreys received him like a " roaring lion, or raging bear," in the language of Dissent, and was only rendered more furious when Rosewell answered him in Latin and Greek. The Judge was probably unaware that the prisoner before him had been a scholar of Westminster School under his old headmaster Dr. Busby, and that he was not now dealing with the type of ignorant and factious ranter which constituted his idea of the Dissenting preacher. However, certain marks of royal favour extended to Mr. Rosewell soon corrected any false impression on the part of the Chief Justice, and though not inclining him to mercy, made Jeffreys' reception of the prisoner at his trial in Westminster Hall facetious rather than terrible.

The Judge first displayed the humorous bent of his disposition by asking Mr. Wallop, whom he saw in court, what he was doing there. Wallop answered that he had come to hear the trial, and moved a little away from the bar. Jeffreys fancifully replied that the case could not proceed as long as Mr. Wallop remained in court, before which alternative Mr. Wallop was obliged to withdraw. Jeffreys then felt himself at liberty to go on with the trial.

The case against Rosewell was based on the evidence of three women who swore to having heard him preach a discourse at a house in Rotherhithe, in which he spoke of Charles II. and his father as two wicked Kings bent on bringing in Popery, compared them to Jeroboam, and exhorted his hearers to resistance with broken platters, rams' horns, and other biblical weapons. Rosewell in his defence denied the words quoted by the three women, and called evidence to show them to be mercenary informers of vile character and unworthy of credence. When the first of them was called, Rosewell was anxious to exhort her as a divine to speak the truth ; but Jeffreys would have none of his "preachments." "My lord," replied the prisoner, "I meant only to endeavour to convince her by putting some questions like a divine to her. For I pity them though they envy me, and I bless my God have prayed for them many times since my imprisonment." "Well, well, do not stand to commend yourself now," answered Jeffreys ; and turning to the witness bade her speak the truth, in quite as impressive terms as even the excellent Rosewell could have used on such an occasion. Jeffreys could not resist the pleasure of telling the prisoner what "frightful stuff" he thought his discourse to be, and praised his long-windedness in being able to preach from seven till two. He also delighted in the discomfiture of the Recorder Jenner, one of the Crown counsel, and, according to Rosewell, the "bloody contriver" of all his misfortunes. Jenner really was a despised and feeble sort of person, only raised from obscurity by the desperate necessities of the latter part of the reign of James II. Mrs. Farrar, one of the Crown witnesses, swore that Rosewell had said in his sermon that it was a fine sight to see fools in scarlet gowns, "for he had heard the Recorder was to be made a Judge." "He hears strange stories, it seems," Jeffreys slily remarked, "What do you make of this, brother Jenner ?" "God forbid, my lord, this should be true," ejaculated Rosewell. "You see, she swears it," urged Jeffreys ; but brother Jenner remained discreetly silent.

Rosewell in his defence called evidence to show that he had ever prayed loyally and heartily for the King. Jeffreys remarked significantly : "So there was praying in this Hall, I remember, for his late Majesty, for the doing of him justice. We all know what that meant, and where it ended." Some of the witnesses against the characters of the Crown informers excited the anger or irony of the Chief Justice. To one who prevaricated somewhat he remarked : "We know well enough you snivelling saints can lie ; " to another who had described one of the women as rash and ready to swear anything, he exclaimed : " Oh, dear sir ! and you seem to be a grave, prudential sort of man." In spite of Jeffreys' taunts, Rosewell did certainly succeed in destroying the credit of two of the women who reported his words. Against the third, Mrs. Farrar, he could bring no evidence. He explains in his *Life* that he did not know that she was to be called. He did not, however, mention this fact at the trial ; and Jeffreys in his summing up pointed out that the prisoner had not in any way impugned Mrs. Farrar's testimony. The Chief Justice's charge was unfavourable to the prisoner. He meant to get a conviction, and set about it as decently as possible. He reviewed the evidence, to all appearances impartially, and then dwelt at length on the dangers of rebellion, which, he said, were excited by the beating of the pulpit cushion quite as easily as by the beating of the drum ; and contrasted the prosperity which England then enjoyed with the troublous state of the Continent, where their neighbours were wallowing in blood and were reduced by the grievous necessities of war to eating base and filthy animals,—a prosperity which preachers like Rosewell were seeking to destroy.

Jeffreys was successful ; the jury convicted Rosewell of high treason, and he was put back to come up for judgment of death. Burnet says that the verdict caused shameful rejoicing. Shameful to Whigs certainly, but not to the Tories and extreme Churchmen ; they rejoiced at the victory, and, let us hope, Jeffreys received some more letters from grateful Bishops.

But these rejoicings were premature. When Jeffreys waited on the King with tidings of his success, he found his news coldly received. Sir John Talbot, one of Rosewell's witnesses, had gone straight to Whitehall on hearing the verdict, and told the King that a gentleman and a scholar had been convicted on evidence that would not hang a dog. " Sir," he said, " if your Majesty suffers this man to die, we are none of us safe in our houses."

The Church zealots had gone too far this time ; the King told Jeffreys he must undo his work as best he could. But even from this mortifying performance the Chief Justice managed to extract some amusement.   When Rosewell came up for judgment and moved certain objections to his indictment, the amazement of the Crown lawyers as the Chief Justice received the prisoner's objections with sympathy and encouragement afforded his lordship food for a great deal of malicious enjoyment. Before Jeffreys was called on to pronounce judgment on the points raised, Rosewell had received a pardon.

One other case of importance engaged the attention of Jeffreys in the year 1684. This was the case of Mr. Joseph Hayes, a City merchant, indicted in the King's Bench for high treason in assisting Sir Thomas Armstrong by sending him money during his outlawry in Holland.   The money had been sent in the form of a bill of exchange, and was proved by comparison with other writings to be in the handwriting of the prisoner. Hayes objected to such a method of proof. Jeffreys told him his objection was the "idle whim of an enthusiastic counsel," and that such proof had been allowed in Sidney's case.   Hayes also insinuated that he could have obtained a pardon if he would have betrayed certain things to the Government. Jeffreys rebuked him sternly for making such aspersions on the King, and warned him that if he was not silent, he might have some very unpleasant things to say about a certain 4,000 guineas which some indiscreet friends of Hayes had offered to the King in return for a pardon. The opening of Jeffreys' charge—the only portion reported—is unfavourable to Hayes, of whose guilt it is impossible to doubt ; but a jury of merchants, impervious alike to the powers of the Judge and the weight of evidence, acquitted the prisoner. The Attorney-General showed his opinion of the finding of the jury by asking that, as the evidence had been so strong, the Court should bind over Hayes to good behaviour for life ; but Jeffreys declined : " Mr. Attorney, that is not a proper motion at this time."

XII

THE DEATH OF THE KING—THE TRIAL OF TITUS OATES

1685

DURING the latter part of the year 1684 and the beginning of 1685 the Government showed no abatement of zeal in harassing notable Whigs. Dr. Burnet was silenced from preaching; and Gabriel Barnes, Esquire, of the Middle Temple, was clapped into the King's Bench Prison for speaking seditious words. The toils were drawing closer round Dr. Oates. In the December of 1684, two of his creatures were convicted of uttering scandal against the Government; by January of 1685 it had been resolved to bring the Doctor himself to his trial for perjury; and on the 23rd of the same month in the Court of King's Bench he pleaded "not guilty" to the charge. Hot words, says Luttrell, passed between the prisoner and the Chief Justice. Perhaps Oates would have borne himself more seemly if he could have foreseen an event that in two weeks time made his situation more desperate than ever.

"The 6th of February, being Friday, his Majesty, King Charles the Second died at Whitehall, about three quarters after 11 at noon."

However from private motives Jeffreys may have mourned the loss of the only English Sovereign who has succeeded in being disreputable and delightful at the same time, the Chief Justice must have felt that in exchanging the gay for the grave, King Charles for King James, his own position in the Government would be considerably strengthened, and his hopes of further advancement practically assured. As long as Charles II. was on the throne none of the parties, or sections of parties, that shared his counsels could lay claim to his entire confidence. Charles was far too astute and accommodating in his principles to allow himself to be made the slave of a consistent policy, or to throw himself obstinately into schemes which he knew to be futile and impossible under existing circumstances. He had to keep his throne, and was well aware that the best way to lose it would be to run into extremities. He must have seen from the first the dangers of going to those lengths which his brother would have urged upon him, and in which Sunderland and Jeffreys were prepared to follow him ; and therefore, whilst their influence was at the time of his death considerable, Charles had not cut himself entirely adrift from Halifax, North and his less arbitrary advisers. Some men are said to be open-minded, but Charles II. was far more than that. His mind kept open house ; to all comers it offered a genial reception and bright entertainment ; but there were secret chambers into which the most constant guests had never been invited.

Jeffreys was well aware that he was on no surer footing than any of the other guests, and quite as liable to be shown the door at any moment. But with the heavy brother his position was very different. Charles had resorted to the arbitrary measures which Jeffreys approved and encouraged, because for the moment it was only by such measures he could cope with the violence of his opponents, a violence he had suffered in silence until popular feeling had grown weary of it and turned to him for help. It was quite possible that as soon as his enemies had been awed and weakened by the rigorous punishments of their leaders, Charles would relax the severity of his Government, and strengthen his position by seeking to unite all parties under an amiable and indulgent Sovereign. Already at the time of his death there had been rumours

of a return of the Duke of Monmouth, which would have
meant a return to a more liberal policy.   Jeffreys would
have been one of the first to fall if such a change had
occurred.   The determined and passionate character of his
principles and proceedings would have made his removal
one of the most welcome signs of a merciful reaction.
Charles would not have hesitated to drop him as he had
dropped Scroggs before him, and Jeffreys would have
passed into the same obscure disgrace which has been the
portion of the former.

But James the Second King, Jeffreys could banish
all fears of a declining fortune.   James supported and
sympathised with the arbitrary notions of the Chief Justice, his hatred of faction and Dissent, not because he felt
such a policy to be at the moment necessary, but because
he loved the arbitrary for its own sake as the embodiment
of his idea of Kingship and the form of Government
prescribed by the authority of his Church.   He had no
open mind.   His was firmly closed to all but the privi-
leged few who would share in the dull enjoyments of that
solemn mansion ; there was no fear that its doors would
ever be thrown open to enlightened strangers.

To such a man Jeffreys' services would be more than
acceptable.   James loved severity, and no view of the
extent of his own prerogative could be too exaggerated to
satisfy his principles of government.   The dangers involved in allowing a free expression to such a temperament as that of the Chief Justice would not present
themselves to a mind destitute of political sanity and a
sense of humour.   Charles, whilst delighting in the force
and originality of Jeffreys, exercised during his lifetime a
restraining influence on the heat of the Welshman's disposition, and, as in Rosewell's case, was prepared to check
the Judge when his prejudices had led him into injustice.
With the death of Charles that restraining power was lost.
Jeffreys found himself encouraged rather than checked.
The first year of the reign of James II. may be considered
the crowning point of Jeffreys' career, the zenith of his

fame, the climax of his infamy. In that year he enjoyed in the security of royal favour a degree of power that has seldom fallen to the lot of a man of thirty-seven born outside the purple ; in that year he first fell a victim to the tortures of a disease, fortunately as rare as a Chief Justiceship in men of immature age ; and in the same year he was commanded by his royal master to perform a judicial duty fortunately never before or since imposed on a Lord Chief Justice of England. By the force of these singular circumstances and by a certain genius for the terrible which Jeffreys possessed in an almost fascinating degree, the year 1685 is to witness the stormy descent of the Lord Chief Justice into the dark realms of the historically accursed, where that familiarity which is the annoying and inaccurate accompaniment of historical disrepute, places "Judge Jeffreys" in the same circle with "Richard Crookback," "Bloody Mary," and other fanciful exaggerations of popular resentment.

The enthusiasm with which the accession of James II. was greeted by the nation at large is a commonplace of history. Addresses of loyal congratulation poured in upon him ; no reign could have commenced more auspiciously. The very day after Charles's death, Jeffreys and his brother Judges took their seats in Westminster Hall with fresh commissions from the new King continuing them in their offices.

So promising was the aspect of affairs that Jeffreys was able to leave London in March to go the Norfolk circuit with Mr. Justice Wythens, who was ever ready to act as his faithful creature and chorus when occasion offered. The exciting influences of the new *régime* on the temper of the Chief Justice were displayed at Bedford. The Sheriff's chaplain chose as the text for his Assize sermon, Shadrach, Meshach and Abednego that would not bow their knees. Jeffreys, seeing in this a covert sympathy with resistance to royal authority, rose up in a passion from his seat in the church and would have plucked the preacher out of the pulpit, if brother Wythens had not calmed his fury and the pliant preacher changed his tone.

As soon as the Chief Justice returned to town he was busily occupied with certain extra-judicial work. A Parliament was to be summoned, and every effort used to make it as thoroughly Tory as possible. The elections began in April. Buckinghamshire was to be the sphere of Jeffreys' influence. His country seat of Bulstrode was in that county, and thither he departed to work in the Tory cause. He found his presence very necessary indeed ; things were not promising at all well. He wrote to Lord Sunderland that Wharton and Hampden, the Whig candidates, had been very mischievous, spreading all sorts of false reports ; and that a certain Sir Roger Hill, a " horrid Whig," son of one of Charles the First's Judges and a fierce exclusionist, had been doing a great deal of mischief ; but the Chief Justice pledged himself to use every endeavour to " serve his master's interests " on the day of election.[1] A man called Hackett, described as a violent partisan, was put up in the Tory interest, and the fact that his cause was hopeless only made the struggle the more desperate. Jeffreys proved himself to be an election agent of more than ordinary skill. The polling was to take place at Aylesbury ; but on the very day fixed for it, without a minute's warning, Jeffreys suddenly appeared, and on his own authority adjourned the poll to Newport Pagnell. Here the Tories had previously engaged all the inns, so that when the Whig candidates arrived they could find no accommodation. However, in spite of the cunning and influence of the Lord Chief Justice, the Whigs won the day, and Jeffreys returned to London, where he furnished another public proof of his political sentiments by attending the funeral of Mr. Cradock, a Tory mercer of the City who had died of erysipelas. Luttrell, whose sympathies are unfeignedly Whig, describes Cradock as a " highflown spark," and Jeffreys' attendance at his funeral

---

[1] The original of Jeffreys' letter to Lord Sunderland on this occasion is among the Domestic State Papers in the Record Office.

as a " pretty employment " for a Privy Councillor. But Mr. Narcissus Luttrell need not be so shocked as all that ; there are possible bonds of union between mercers and Privy Councillors which the Councillor would be only polite in acknowledging by lending a hand with the mercer's pall.

In the general rejoicing and confidence evoked by the succession of King James, Dr. Oates was not forgotten. It was not likely that he would be ; for no amount of public acclamation could deter James from the methodical pursuit of his pre-arranged measures, one of the most cherished of which would be a prompt revenge on his scurrilous enemy. It is impossible not to sympathise with James in this desire. Oates, who really had a curious sense of the fitness of things, would probably have admitted that there was a certain element of propriety in some hostile notice being taken of him at this time. A prospect of possible martyrdom in the cause of religious perjury may have held out strange attractions to his perverted intellect. At any rate, whatever his motives, it was with a strange mixture of fatalism and pugnacity that the Doctor made his appearance before Jeffreys in the Court of King's Bench on May 8th. The Court was crowded with Papists, not unnaturally anxious to see judgment passed on the murderer of their co-religionists.

The trial of Oates may be accounted one of the most satisfactory and characteristic examples of Jeffreys at his best. Even those who knew his dangerous temper were surprised at the fairness and dignity with which he conducted the proceedings ; and though there are outbursts of indignation to be read in the report, one eye-witness, at least, did not seem to consider that they detracted from the admirable bearing of the Lord Chief Justice. Thomas Earl of Ailesbury happened to be in the Court of King's Bench on the day of trial, and was invited by Jeffreys to sit beside him. He has left in his *Memoirs* strong testimony to the Judge's good behaviour. " Knowing well," he writes, " the Chief Justice's unlimited passion, I expected he would show himself in his true colours ; but I was greatly surprised at his good temper, and the more because such impudent and reviling expressions never came from the mouth of a man as Oates uttered." Jeffreys was bound to be effective in dealing with such a man as Oates ; he was always a rare hand at smelling out a knave, and knew what to do with them when he had secured them in his clutches.

The first charge of perjury against Oates consisted in his having sworn at Ireland's trial in 1679 that he had been present at a Jesuit consult at the White Horse Tavern in the Strand, held on April 24th, 1678. The Crown, to prove their case, called a number of Catholic gentlemen, fellow students of Oates at the Jesuit College at St. Omer's, who swore that Oates had never left the College between the December of 1677 and the June of 1678, so that it was impossible he could have been in London at the time he had sworn to. These witnesses described Oates as an absurd and ridiculous person, notorious among them for his silly and quarrelsome disposition, so silly that the men made sport of him, and "a little boy beat him up and down with a fox's tail." His very foolishness made it impossible that he could have gone away at any time without being missed. Oates's cross-examination consisted in making each witness confess himself a Papist, whereby he laid himself open to great penalties, and in asking them what reward they had for coming to swear against him. Jeffreys allowed him every latitude, but Oates would not be contented. " My lord," he said, " I do find my defence is under very great prejudice."   " Why so ? " asked the Chief Justice ; " because we won't let you ask impertinent questions, or such as may render the witnesses obnoxious to a penalty ? "   " No, my lord," replied the Doctor ; " it is not fit they should, for there is a turn to be served." This was a little too impudent for Jeffreys. " What do you mean by that ? Ay, and a good turn too if the witnesses swear true ; it is to bring truth to light and perjured villains to condign punishment." Oates saw that he had gone too far, and tried to mollify the Judge. " Behave yourself as you ought," said Jeffreys, "and you shall be heard with all fairness that can be desired." Oates complained that the Judges made themselves pleasant with his questions. "I did not make myself pleasant with your questions," answered Jeffreys; "but when you ask impertinent ones, you must be corrected. You see, we do the same thing with them (pointing to the King's Counsel); I find fault with nothing but what is to the purpose."

Oates in his defence endeavoured to show with what credit he had been received by the House of Lords and courts of justice at the time of his discovery of the Plot, and to prove by certain witnesses that he had been in London in the April and May of 1678. Jeffreys strongly advised him to rely on the latter defence. As to the support he had received from the Judges, the Chief Justice told him that what Chief Justice Scroggs said at any of the Plot trials or what he (Jeffreys) or any other person, counsel or Judge, said, was merely to be considered as their opinions on the fact as it then occurred to their present apprehensions, but was no evidence binding on the jury. "Alack-a-day!" he exclaimed, "how many times in Westminster Hall have we causes wherein we have verdict against verdict!" And he went on to cite Lady Ivy's case, in which at the first trial every one believed her title to the greater part of Shadwell good; and at the second, the very witnesses who had proved her title at the previous trial were found to be notorious perjurers. "We give our opinions always according to the present testimony that is before us," he concluded. Such a conclusion cannot have been encouraging to the general body of suitors who relied on the courts of law for the bringing to light of truth and justice; but the examination and cross-examination of witnesses was at that time in so confused and inept a condition that injustice was only too frequent and unavoidable.

Jeffreys advised Oates: "if you did call two or three witnesses to prove that you were in town the 22nd, 23rd or 24th of April, it would be the best defence you could make." Oates agreed to this ; but the two or three he did call were very faulty, and directly contradicted each other. One, a Mrs. Mayo, sought to strengthen her deposition by declaring that what she spoke she spoke as in the presence of the Lord. The touch of Gospel was not lost on the Chief Justice. " Prithee, woman," he inquired with irony, " dost thou think we ask thee anything that we think thou dost not speak in the presence of the Lord? We are all of us in the presence of the Lord always." Mrs. Mayo was not to be outfaced by any one—" And shall answer before Him," she exclaimed, " for all that we have done and said, all of us, the proudest and the greatest here—" " But I would not have so much to answer for as thou hast in this business, for all the world," retorted Jeffreys. Mrs. Mayo somewhat excused her presumption by re-marking that she knew his lordship, though he did not know her, for she had been in Wales. " I am very glad of it, good woman," answered the Judge.

Oates persisted in calling certain Judges and Peers, and Mr. Williams, Speaker of the Commons in 1678, to depose to his credit at that time. He had better have taken Jeffreys' advice and let such evidence alone. He came sadly to grief over one of his witnesses, Lord Huntingdon, who, after describing the faith with which the House of Lords had at first received his story, added, " And I do believe most of the House of Peers have altered their opinion as to this man's credit, and look upon his evidence as I do to be very false." " Do you hear him, Mr. Oates ? " asked Jeffreys. " No, my lord, I do not very well." " Then, my Lord Huntingdon, turn your face to the jury ; and say what you said to us over again." Huntingdon complied with the Judge's request. Oates was disappointed, but not abashed. " Very well, my lord," he said to Hunt-ingdon. " I called you in to answer my question, as to somewhat that is past, and not to give your judg-ment how you are inclined to believe now." Jeffreys intervened, " Nay, but with your favour, it was to declare what opinion the House of Lords had of you ; and he says very well, and that is in truth the same answer that must be given for the Judges and the juries that tried the people on your evidence." "Well, my lord, I have done with my Lord of Huntingdon." "And he has done with you, as I perceive," put in Mr. Justice Wythens. Jeffreys closed the incident quite jauntily : "Yes, truly, methinks ye shake hands and part very fairly."

Lord Chief Baron Montagu cut a rather sorry figure in the witness box. As a Judge who had sat on most of the Plot trials Oates called him to depose to the convictions that had been obtained on his evidence and the support he had received from many of the Judges at that time. Montagu admitted these circumstances, but remarked that he himself had never had any great faith in Oates's testimony. Then why, Oates might have asked, had the Chief Baron suffered so many innocent men to be convicted on evidence he disbelieved, without uttering one word of protest from the Bench ?

Oates's case was concluded with Montagu's evidence. The Crown then called certain additional evidence by which they proposed to answer the prisoner's defence. First of all the Earl of Castlemaine and Sir George Wakeman were heard, both of whom had been tried on Oates's evidence but acquitted by the juries at the time when the Plot fury had begun to wane. Oates in cross-examining Lord Castlemaine went on his usual tack of trying to make the witness confess his religion, and so lay himself open to the severe laws against Papists. Jeffreys endeavoured to stop him. Oates declared the witness was malicious. The patience of the Chief Justice was exhausted : "Hold your tongue!" he cried; "you are a shame to mankind !" Oates was not to be dismayed. He offered to stand to his evidence and seal it with his blood. "It were pity," ominously replied the Judge, "but that it were to be done by thy blood." "Ah ! ah ! my lord, I know why all this is, and so may the world very easily too," replied Oates. "Such impudence and impiety was never known in any Christian's nature," exclaimed Jeffreys. The scene ended by Oates excusing himself on the ground that ill words provoke any man's passion. "Keep yourself within bounds and you shall be heard ; but we will suffer none of your extravagances," answered Jeffreys.

At certain of the Plot trials Oates had called witnesses to prove that he was in London at the time of the consult at the White Horse Tavern at the end of April, 1678. The Attorney-General now offered evidence to show in what fashion two at least of these witnesses had been procured by the prisoner. One, he said, a man called Smith, a schoolmaster at Islington, had been arrested by Oates on the first discovery of the Plot, but had been promised a free pardon by the Doctor on condition that he would swear that Oates had dined with him on the first Monday in May, 1678. Smith had consented to commit the perjury, for, as he said, he must have died if he had not done it. The Attorney-General now called Smith, who was prepared to forswear his previous forswearing, and was about to examine him when Jeffreys stopped him : "That is very nauseous and fulsome, Mr. Attorney, methinks, in a court of justice." Sawyer went on with his examination, but Jeffreys stopped him again. "I tell you truly, Mr. Attorney, it looks rank and fulsome ; if he did forswear himself, why should he ever be a witness again ?" Sawyer urged precedents. "I hate such precedents in all times," answered Jeffreys. The Solicitor-General came to the rescue, but the Chief Justice was firm : "for example sake, it ought not by any means to be admitted." Attorney and Solicitor being unable to move the Judge, Mr. Roger North, who was holding a junior brief for the Crown, thought he might succeed where his leaders had failed. "My lord," he began, "if a man come and swear"—but he was not allowed to finish. "Look ye, sir," came from the Bench, "you have our opinion ; it was always the practice heretofore that when the Court have delivered their opinion the counsel should sit down and not dispute it further." Poor Roger ! he soon realised the fact that his timid sensitive nature was not fitted for the rough atmosphere of Westminster Hall, and desisted from legal pursuits ; but in writing his brother's life he was able to give the Lord Chief Justice Jeffreys a much better answer than any he could have made him in the Court of King's Bench.

If the Crown had failed with Smith, they could produce a more satisfactory witness than he against the prisoner in one Davenport, who had been an inmate of the Gate House prison at Westminster at the time of the trial of Langhorne and the five Jesuits. He swore that shortly before the trials Oates had come to the prison with Sir William Waller and threatened to hang an old man of the name of Clay, imprisoned there as a Popish priest, if he would not swear in court that Oates had dined at his house in May, 1678. Clay, to save his life, had consented to commit the necessary perjury. With this dismal evidence the Attorney-General closed his case.

Oates could only reply by renewing his objection to Papists being received as witnesses against him. But Jeffreys would not hear of it : " a Papist, except you'll prove any legal objection against him, is as good a witness in a court of record, as any other person." Oates desired he might have leave to argue the question as a point of law. " No, sir, it is no point of law at all," replied Jeffreys. " Then," cried Oates, " I appeal to all the hearers whether I have justice done me !" This was a piece of impertinence Jeffreys, or any other Judge, could not have suffered to pass unnoticed : " What's that ? Why, you impudent fellow, do you know where you are ? You are in a court of justice, and must appeal to none but the Court and jury." " I do appeal to all my hearers," repeated Oates. Jeffreys ordered him to be removed, but relented on condition that he behaved with decency. Oates then cited *Bulstrode's Reports* to show that it was Lord Coke's practice not to admit Papists as witnesses. Jeffreys referred to the book, and answered: "That book says it was Lord Coke's practice ; and we think if that was his practice, his practice was against law."

The argument continued for some time until Oates began to reflect on the peers whom he had called as witnesses, and who had so bitterly disappointed his expectations.   Jeffreys thought fit to defend the noble lords against his aspersions, though, he added, " a slander from your mouth is very little scandal."   Oates, quite undaunted by his misfortunes, pertly replied, " Nor from somebody else's neither."   " But, sir, you must be taught better manners," answered the Chief Justice.   Even Mr. Justice Walcot, a silent Judge at ordinary times, felt bound to expostulate with Oates on his behaviour.   " Good Mr. Justice Walcot," pleaded the Doctor, " was there ever man dealt with as I am ? "   And then for the last time he declared the truth of his narrative and the injuries he was now suffering, concluding with the following prophetic utterance : " For my own part I care not what becomes of me, the truth will one time or another appear."   " I hope in God it will," echoed the Chief Justice.   " I do not question it, my lord," answered Oates.   " And I hope we are finding it out to-day," added my Lord Chief Justice.

Finch, the Solicitor-General, had hardly commenced to sum up the case for the Crown when Oates asked leave to retire.   He was very weak and ill, he said, suffering from the stone and gout.   In all probability the Doctor, whose infirmities had not prevented him from carrying on his desperate case with wonderful spirit and audacity, felt that the affair was at an end as far as he was concerned, and did not anticipate with any degree of pleasure having to sit and listen to the terrible summing up of the Chief Justice.   Jeffreys suffered him to depart.

When, after a careful review of the evidence by Finch, Jeffreys' turn came to address the jury, the Chief Justice began by deploring the manner in which the nation had been at first surprised into a belief in Oates and his crew, " a thing for which the justice of the nation lies under great reproach abroad."   And now, when such conclusive evidence had been given of the perjury of the man, his " blood was curdled and his spirits raised to see him brazening it out in a court of justice." " The pretended infirmity of his body made him remove out of court ; but the infirmity of his depraved mind, the blackness of his soul, the baseness of his actions ought to be looked upon with such horror and detestation as to think him unworthy any longer to tread upon the face of God's earth. You will pardon my warmth, I hope ; for it is impossible such things should come before any honest man, and not have some extraordinary influence upon him." Jeffreys might well speak, as many others besides himself, with warmth and bitterness of Oates's deception ; for on the strength of that deception he had, as Recorder of London, passed sentence of death on Ireland, Langhorne and the five Jesuits ; " and I am sorry to say it," he added when he came to speak of his own share in the Popish trials. Well he might exclaim against the hurry Oates had thrown men into at that time, so that all of the Romish persuasion were looked on with an evil eye, and Oates treated with greater respect than the branches of the royal family. " Nay, it was come to that degree of folly, to give it no worse name, that, in public societies, to the reproach and infamy of them be it spoken, this profligate villain was caressed, was drunk to and saluted by the name of the 'Saviour of the Nation.' O prodigious madness ! that such a title as that was should ever be given to such a prostitute monster of impiety as this is ! The prisoner has said he will venture his blood in confirmation of his impious falsehoods ; but to speak the truth he makes no great venture in it ; for when he had pawned his immortal soul by so perjured a testimony, he may very easily proffer the venturing of his vile carcase to maintain it." In spite of the foregone conclusion to which the trial pointed, Jeffreys reviewed the evidence at length. He terminated his review : " And sure I am, if you think these witnesses swear true—as I cannot see any colour of objection—there does not remain the least doubt but that Oates is the blackest and most perjured villain that ever appeared upon the face of the earth."

As the jury retired from the bar, Jeffreys offered them some drink before they went   They did not, however, think refreshment necessary, and in a quarter of an hour returned with a verdict of "Guilty" against the prisoner. Jeffreys expressed his entire concurrence and that of his brethren in what they had done, and his satisfaction that the days were now past when verdicts were received with hummings and hissings by the auditors.

On the following day Oates appeared to answer the second charge of perjury.   He had sworn in the course of the Plot trials that one of the prisoners, Ireland, had been in London between the 8th and 12th of August and on the 1st and 2nd of September, 1678.   The Crown now put into the box a number of witnesses who proved conclusively that Ireland was in Hertfordshire and Staffordshire at the dates sworn to by Oates.   Oates made practically no defence ; he was weary of playing a losing game two days running.   He complained once to Jeffreys that a barrister behind him was meddling with his papers. Jeffreys replied that the gentleman "had better do somewhat else if he found him out."   Oates asked that he might have seven days after the present trial in which to instruct counsel in certain points of law with reference to errors in the indictment.   Jeffreys allowed him such time, though, as he afterwards remarked, it was allowing him longer than usual, four days being the customary period. As on the previous day, Oates asked leave to withdraw before the Solicitor-General's speech, which Jeffreys accorded him.

The summing up of the Chief Justice, if shorter than at the first trial, was more heated.   Since the adjournment of the Court circumstances had occurred to swell his disgust.   Over the "Saviour of the Nation" he again waxed indignant.   "Oh, horrid blasphemy, that no less an epithet should be given to such a profligate wretch as Oates, than that which is only proper to our blessed

Lord ! As though Oates had merited more than all man-kind, and so indeed he has if we take it in a true sense. He has deserved much more punishment than the laws of this land can inflict." From this he passed to a long attack on the Whigs and their methods, which he held, not without reason, to be responsible for much of the past injustice. It was their Sheriffs' trickery and packing of juries that caused verdicts to be given by passion and prejudice, and not by merits of a case. If a man was blasted by the name of Tory he was sure to lose his case ; but if a whining rascal was sanctified by the name of Whig he was sure to have it on his side ; witness the famous cause of Mr. Loades about his lemons."[1] He said that Charles II. had remembered with concern to his dying day the fact that he had consented to Ireland's execution, as his royal father before him had deplored the signing of Strafford's death-warrant. The cause of the additional warmth of the Chief Justice's indignation was not long in appearing. After insisting once again on the admissibility of Papists as witnesses in a court of law, " Let the sober party," he exclaimed, " as they call themselves, make what reflections they please upon it ; I value them not, nor their opinion ; let them send as many penny-post libels as they have a mind to, two of which I received last night, about yesterday's trial." " Gentlemen," he con-cluded, " I have taken up much of your time, and detained you longer in this matter, because, I cannot but say with grief of heart, our nation was too long besotted ; and of innocent blood there has been too much spilt ; it is high time we ought to have some account of it. It is a mercy we ought to bless Almighty God for that we are pre-vented from spilling more of innocent blood ! God be blessed, our eyes are opened ; and let us have a care for the future, that we be not so suddenly imposed upon by such prejudices and jealousies, as we have reason to fear such villains have too much filled our heads with of late."

[1] Loades, a Dissenter, afterwards made City Chamberlain when James II. admitted the Dissenters to municipal offices.

In half an hour the jury had found Oates "Guilty" on the second charge, and was congratulated by each of the four Judges individually on the justice of its verdict.

A week later Oates was brought up for judgment. His exceptions to the previous proceedings, prepared by the indefatigable Wallop, were read and shortly disposed of from the Bench. Jeffreys then declared the sense of all the Judges of England as to Oates's punishment. They had, he said, all consulted together, and decided that in cases of perjury the law left the punishment to the discretion of the Court, provided that their judgment "did not extend to life or member." To his brother Wythens he left the duty of pronouncing that judgment, which was to be exemplary enough to punish this villainous wretch and terrify all others. In terms which strike the reader as insipid after some pages of Jeffreys, Wythens delivered the sentence : a fine of 1,000 marks on each indictment, a great deal of pillorying at different times, and, most urgent of all, next Wednesday a whipping at the hands of the common hangman, from Aldgate to Newgate, and on the Friday following from Newgate to Tyburn. "This," concluded Wythens, "I pronounce to be the judgment of the Court upon you for your offences. And I must tell you plainly, if it had been in my power to have carried it further, I should not have been unwilling to have given judgment of death upon you ; for I am sure you deserve it."

One would have thought that it was unnecessary for Mr. Justice Wythens to exercise his mind concerning the inadequacy of the sentence he passed on Oates ; it must have seemed to many who were not familiar with the Doctor's powers of endurance quite equivalent to a judgment of death. It was a delightful freak of legal subtlety that considered a sentence of whipping such as that inflicted on Oates as one that "did not extend to life or member !"

And so, to use Jeffreys' expression, the Chief Justice and the Doctor "shook hands and parted" in this life, whether "very fairy," to continue the Judge's words, may be a matter of opinion. It is singular that Oates survived the full measure of his deserts, and that on his release from prison at the Revolution his Judge lay dying in the Tower. Of the justice of his sentence it is impossible to doubt ; one cannot help concurring in the closing words of Wythens. Even the temperate Evelyn writes that some thought the punishment extraordinarily severe ; "but," he continues, " if he was guilty of the perjuries, and so of the death of many innocents, as I fear he was, his punishment was but what he deserved."

Little can be said against the way in which Jeffreys presided at his trial. To say, as Macaulay does, that the Judges browbeat and reviled the prisoner is to say what is untrue. Considering the exceptional atrocity of Oates's guilt, the stubborn impudence of his bearing, the reckless support which was still accorded him by the scurrilous fanatics of the Whig party, the judicial temper of the times, and the fact that the Chief Justice himself had been made a victim to his crimes by the sentences he had passed on innocent men, Jeffreys' treatment of him was none too severe.

His language may appear excessive to modern readers, but it impressed Lord Ailesbury as most dignified and judicial in its tone. It is to be observed that it was not until his guilt had appeared in very glaring colours that Jeffreys first addressed Oates in terms of reprobation ; he allowed him certain privileges and the full exercise of his rights, and stopped the Crown when they wished to bring improper evidence against him. If he did at times break out into stronger denunciation than seems to us now be-fitting in a judge, it must be remembered that at no time has it ever fallen to the lot of any judge before or since to try so monstrous and horrible a perjurer. Oates, singularly enough, did not bear that resentment to Jeffreys which might have been expected under the circumstances. In the *Western Martyrology*—a book written by Oates's most enthusiastic supporters, as may be judged from the fact that he is therein styled " the worst made man for a dissembler, an hypocrite or a secret villain of any man in the world,"—it is said that at Jeffreys' fall Oates was almost the only man who pitied him. It is more than likely that in Oates's peculiar nature there resided a certain respect for the man who had so thoroughly appreciated what a scoundrel he was, though there is little trace of any such respect in Oates's allusions to Jeffreys in the *Eikon Basilike*, his foul-mouthed life of James II. Perhaps in print the Doctor felt it his duty to be stirring and hide his feelings.

XIII

1685

BETWEEN the conviction and sentence of Oates, Jeffreys had been the recipient of an honour peculiar at that time, though it has since become almost customary. His grateful master created him a peer. It was the first occasion on which a Lord Chief Justice had been so rewarded during his tenure of office. Jeffreys selected as his title Baron Jeffreys of Wem, in the county of Shropshire. The same Gazette that contained the announcement of Jeffreys' peerage also announced the conferment of similar honours on two of the King's most intimate friends, Henry Jermyn and John Churchill, afterwards Duke of Marlborough.

On the heels of these new honours followed the rumour that the Lord Keeper North was to be dismissed and the new judicial peer to have his place. The shades of night were gathering around that unfortunate Minister. The death of Charles II. and the accession of his brother had proved indeed, as Roger puts it, a " funest alteration " in his affairs; "all his lordship's joys and hopes perished; and the rest of his life, which lasted not long after, was but a slow dying." He found himself neglected and supplanted, his advice rejected. The elaborate speech he had prepared to deliver at the opening of Parliament on the King's behalf he was never allowed to speak, and in the preparation of the speech which the King delivered in person he was not so much as consulted. His nominee for the

Speakership of the House of Commons was set aside in favour of Jeffreys' cousin, Sir John Trevor, his advice as to the collection of taxes before the meeting of Parliament disregarded. His enemies, chief among them Sunderland and Jeffreys, with that want of feeling common to the age, openly derided him and made him a butt for their jests. His morality, perhaps a little pretentious, was annoying to the courtiers ; so they sent one of their number to him to seriously advise him to keep a mistress as a sure way to recover his waning credit. He went one day with his brother, Sir Dudley, to see an enormous rhinoceros which had been brought to London. Sunderland and Jeffreys heard of this, and immediately spread a report that the Lord Keeper had taken to riding a rhinoceros. The joke is not a great one, but its authors were probably well aware of the anger it would cause to a man so smug in his propriety and so destitute of humour as North. And they were right in their conjecture. On hearing it, the Lord Keeper flew into a violent rage and quarrelled with his brother Dudley, because the latter laughed and would have taken the jest in good part. It is typical of North's character that no real slight, none of the greater injustices that were put upon him stirred him to any show of passion or resentment ; but the folly of the rhinoceros threw him into a transport of indignation. The real ignominy of his situation preyed on him in quite another fashion : he fell into a fatal depression of health and spirits, all that was good in his humour left him ; " sunk and spiritless " he went about " as a ghost with the visage of death ; " " all was chip," to use the fantastic expression of his biographer. He had hardly strength enough to get through the ceremonies of the Coronation. Conscious of his disgrace, he fancied that his face betrayed his sense of shame ; so that in the Summer Term, as he sat in Westminster Hall, he covered his face with the nosegay of flowers he used to take with him into court, that men might not see the dejection of his countenance. At length his state of health became so serious that he withdrew, in the company of the faithful Roger and a few friends and dependents, to his country seat at Wroxton, in Oxfordshire. But he carried the Great Seal of England with him.

North should have resigned the Seal as soon as he found that under the new reign his services were not required. There can be no question about that ; and it is his unsightly clinging to office which has made his fall pitiful and contemptible. Roger says that his pride and his consideration for his friends prevented his resignation. His pride ? but where was the pride that could stoop to such humiliation in its own defence ? His consideration for his friends ? But what friend would claim his consideration at the price of his honour ? He did not wish to see the Seal placed in unworthy hands, the hands of Jeffreys ? But did he imagine that when a suitable occasion offered James would hesitate to take the Seal from one whom he had openly slighted in every conceivable manner, and give it to another who, whatever his faults or his crimes, was likely to prove a lively instrument of the King's designs ? The Lord Keeper's conscious shame that made him hide his face from the people in Westminster Hall, is surely the most convincing answer to Roger's praiseworthy efforts in the cause of his brother's reputation.

When North departed for Wroxton, Jeffreys must have felt that the coveted Seal was nearer his grasp. On May 19th Parliament met, and Baron Jeffreys of Wem took his seat in the House of Lords. At the same time the general security was disturbed by the arrival of news that the Duke of Argyle had landed with a rebel force in Scotland ; and rumours soon reached London that the Duke of Monmouth was purchasing war ships in Holland. Many arrests were made of suspicious characters ; and addresses of loyalty poured in upon the King.

In the midst of these commotions Thomas Dangerfield and Richard Baxter stood their trials before the Lord Chief Justice on May 30th. That of Dangerfield began at eight in the morning in the Court of King's Bench. Though one of Oates's confederates and author of the Meal Tub Plot, Dangerfield was not tried for perjury, but for libels on the late and present King, contained in a narrative he had published in the days of his credit. The man was a thorough rascal. He had, when a boy, stolen his father's horses and afterwards taken to coining. But the Popish plot had set him on his legs, and a handsome presence increased his reputation. The only report of his trial is a contemporary sheet, wherein we are told that the prisoner began to reflect on several honest men, but was sharply reproved by Jeffreys, " which was observed to put him a little out of his Newgate rhetoric." He received the same sentence as Oates, but he did not survive it. In the midst of his sufferings an indignant Tory gentleman named Francis struck him in the eye with his cane ; and, as he died soon after, popular resentment ascribed his death to the Tory gentleman's rash act. The Government, confronted with Monmouth's rebellion and anxious to allay disturbance, had Francis tried and executed for murder.

The Court adjourned after the trial of Dangerfield. The same afternoon Jeffreys took his seat at the Guildhall, where, among the list of cases to be disposed of was that of the King against the eminent divine Richard Baxter, one of the most worthy and respectable of the Dissenting ministers of the day. Baxter had already arrived at the Guildhall with his friend, Sir Richard Ashurst, and Dr. Bates, a well-known Dissenting minister ; others of his friends filled the court. The charge was one of seditious libel, it being alleged that in his *Paraphrase of the New Testament*, published a little before, Baxter had reflected on the prelates of the Church of England in a scandalous and seditious manner. Baxter was furnished with a large array of counsel : Mr. Pollexfen, a leading Whig lawyer, afterwards Chief Justice of the Common Pleas under William III. ; the inevitable Mr. Wallop and Mr. Williams ; Mr. Rotheram, afterwards appointed a Baron of the Exchequer by Jeffreys ; Mr. Atwood ; and Mr. Constantine Phipps, afterwards Lord Chancellor of Ireland under Queen Anne. After waiting some time, the

Chief Justice came into court with a countenance full of indignation. A short cause was tried and the clerk was about to call another, when Jeffreys told him he was a blockhead, "the next cause is between Richard Baxter and the King."

There is no report of the case for the Crown. Baxter's friends—to whom we owe any account of the proceedings—did not apparently trouble themselves about reporting their opponents' case. At any rate, whatever its worth, it had convinced Jeffreys ; for no sooner had Pollexfen opened the defence than the Chief Justice hailed him as a "patron of the faction." His client was " an old rogue, who encouraged all the women and maids to bring their bodkins and thimbles to carry on the war against the King and Government." The more Pollexfen endeavoured to mitigate his client's guilt, the greater the fury into which Jeffreys was fast working himself. From denunciation he passed to mimicry and mocked the reverend defendant by throwing up his hands, and singing through his nose, in true nonconformist style, " Lord, we are Thy people, Thy peculiar people, Thy dear people." Pollexfen urged that the King had once thought Baxter deserving of a bishopric. " What ailed the old blockhead then that he did not take it ? " retorted the Chief Justice ; Baxter deserved a good whipping ; "This one old fellow hath cast more reproach upon the constitution and discipline of our Church than will be wiped off these hundred years."

Wallop then rose to argue that Baxter did not intend to allude to the prelates of the Church of England in the passages quoted in the indictment. Jeffreys soon silenced him. He told him he was in all these dirty causes, and he and his brethren should have more wit and honesty than to hold up factious knaves by the chin. Wallop " humbly conceived "—Jeffreys echoed his words : "Sometimes you humbly conceive and sometimes you are very positive . . . but in short I must tell you that if you do not understand your duty better, I shall teach it you." Wallop sat down. Then Rotheram tried his hand. He and Baxter endeavoured to assure the Judge that the latter was no enemy to Bishops. Jeffreys only laughed. "Baxter for Bishops! That's a merry conceit indeed! Turn to it, turn to it!" Baxter tried to intervene, but received an exhortation from Jeffreys for his pains: "Richard, Richard, dost thou think we will hear thee poison the Court? Richard, thou art an old fellow, an old knave; thou hast written books enough to load a cart; every one is as full of sedition (I might say treason) as an egg is full of meat; hadst thou been whipped out of thy writing trade forty years ago, it had been happy. Thou pretendest to be a preacher of the gospel of peace, and thou hast one foot in the grave; it is time for thee to begin to think what account thou intendest to give; but I leave thee to thyself, and I see thou wilt go on as thou hast begun; but, by the grace of God, I'll look after thee. I know thou hast a mighty party, and I see a great many of the brotherhood in corners waiting to see what will become of their mighty Don; and a Doctor of the party (looking at Dr. Bates) at your elbow; but, by the grace of Almighty God, I will crush you all."

Mr. Rotheram sat down after this, and Mr. Atwood [1] rose to his feet. He proposed to read some texts; but Jeffreys exclaimed: "You sha'n't draw me into a conventicle with your annotations, nor your snivelling parson neither." Atwood referred the Chief Justice to some words he had used in Rosewell's case. "No, you sha'n't!" cried the Judge; and then added, rather irrelevantly: "You need not speak, for you are an author already, though you speak and write impertinently." Mr. Atwood "having had his say," as Jeffreys fantastically termed it, sat down also. Williams and Phipps, seeing the case was hopeless,

---

[1] William Atwood, a staunch Whig controversialist, afterwards Chief Justice of New York, where he contrived to make himself unbearable. He may be relied on as another instance of the reasonableness of many of Jeffreys' antipathies towards people who have been usually regarded as glorious martyrs to Jeffreys' reckless temper.

did not trouble the Judge with any further remarks. Baxter offered to speak in his defence and call some witnesses, but Jeffreys would not hear him. In his summing up, the Chief Justice said that there was a design abroad to ruin the King and nation ; the old game of Charles I.'s time was being renewed ; " Gentlemen, for God's sake don't let us be gulled twice in an age by the cant of those who preach rebellion by texts." He charged the jury to find Baxter guilty. " Does your lordship think any jury will pretend to pass a verdict upon me on such a trial?" indignantly exclaimed the defendant. " I'll warrant you, Mr. Baxter," answered the Judge; " don't you trouble yourself about that."

Baxter was convicted and fined 500 marks, to be imprisoned till they were paid, and to be bound to his good behaviour for seven years ; but in November, by intercession to the King, he was discharged. James found it advisable, a little later in his reign, to conciliate the Dissenters.

As Baxter left the court he administered a parting rebuke to the Chief Justice. " My lord," he said, alluding to his friend Sir Matthew Hale, " there was a Chief Justice once who would have treated me very differently." Was he aware that Jeffreys also had been the friend of Hale? If so, his allusion was lost upon Hale's furious successor. " There is not an honest man in England but looks on thee as a knave," was Jeffreys' curt reply.

Jeffreys' treatment of Baxter exceeds in its furious resentment any previous instance of his judicial conduct. For that reason the reliability of the testimony on which that account is founded should be carefully considered. There is no full or official report of Baxter's trial ; the only descriptions of it are those written by the defendant or his friends. Now, with all respect for the integrity of these excellent people, the atmosphere of religious prejudice is so fatal to strict veracity that it is impossible to accept implicitly the one-sided narrative of even the most well-intentioned Dissenters. It would be only fair to

Jeffreys that we should have the entire proceedings verbatim, and thus be enabled to judge how far the words of Baxter or his counsel were calculated to irritate his feelings. Jeffreys hated all Dissenters ; he believed them to be hypocrites who made religion a cloak for treason and sedition, the descendants of the psalm-singing fanatics who had put their King to death. And certainly in many respects the Dissenters of his period justified his dislike. There was a great deal of God and Jesus and the Protestant religion in their mouths ; but they had as little mercy and Christianity in their hearts as their enemies in Church and State, whom they reviled with such godless fervour. It was among the Dissenters who formed the backbone of the extreme Whig party that Oates was regarded as a noble martyr, and Dangerfield as a great and bright soul. Even among the better class of Dissenters there was a suspicious familiarity with the designs of the factious. There was not, Monmouth declared to the King in 1683, any considerable Nonconformist minister who did not know of the existence of the Rye House Plot. Jeffreys, the Bishops, and all those who joined in the stern suppression of Dissent, did not do so from motives of religious persecution, but of revenge for the past, and dread of their resorting once more to civil war for the assertion of their rights. It may have been incorrect to take such a sweeping view of the conduct and responsibility of the Nonconformists, but it was a sincere view, and one which, by their recent conduct, the Dissenters had gone far to justify.

When a man takes a rooted antipathy to a whole class, when it has been his experience to see the worst side of a movement, he cannot help including in his condemnation a certain number of worthy men. In the cases of Rosewell and Baxter, Jeffreys allowed his hatred of a class to prejudice him against two very respectable persons. He was probably the fiercer against Baxter because Baxter's trial occurred at a time when a rebellion was imminent which found its strongest support among the

Dissenters. Monmouth's rebellion was a rising encouraged by the extreme section of the Protestants, who were shocked at seeing a Papist on the throne, and had not the good sense or the moderation to wait and see how the Catholic King would behave himself. They selected the West as their scene of operations because it was the stronghold of Nonconformists. In such a rebellion, the rumours of which were spreading at the end of May, Jeffreys saw a confirmation of his worst fears—the "snivelling saints" were at the old game of 1640. He was accordingly only too ready to regard Baxter as one of the fomenters of the coming disturbance, and to pour out on his venerable head the vials of his wrath. Baxter too sympathised with the "Trimmers," and Jeffreys hated "Trimmers" as cordially as he hated Dissenters. Though Baxter might plead that he did not allude to the English Bishops in his *Paraphrase*, it looks very much as if he did. Macaulay admits that his book was a bitter complaint against the then treatment of Dissenters. It is therefore permissible to infer that his allusion to the Bishops had a more than purely historical interest.

If Jeffreys' indignation can be excused, his manner of expressing it, if correctly reported, cannot ; though it requires a little hypocrisy to deny that it is amusing, and it must have delighted the heart of the Chief Justice to watch its effect on a Court full of the brethren. Even Bishop Lloyd, who so admired Jeffreys as a converter of the stubborn Nonconformists, must have considered that Richard Baxter did not stand in need of quite such extreme arts of persuasion as those made use of at the Guildhall, and that the Chief Justice was on this occasion somewhat exceeding the limits of the Bishop's well meant encouragement. Perhaps Dr. Lloyd was aware that the Judge's health, for which he had once expressed such tender solicitude, was about this time beginning to be fatally affected and his temper inflamed by repeated attacks of the stone.

On June 11th the Duke of Monmouth landed at

Lyme, in Dorsetshire. On the 15th the King issued a proclamation against any who should be guilty of spreading the Duke's Declaration. On the 25th Jeffreys, under a Special Commission of Oyer and Terminer for the county of Surrey, condemned to death at the Marshalsea in Southwark, one William Disney, Esquire, for printing and publishing the said Declaration. The Battle of Sedgmoor was fought on the 6th of July, and nine days later Monmouth was beheaded on Tower Hill. The rebellion was soon at an end. It only remained to punish the rebels.

The method of punishment had not been decided on by the 11th of July ; for on that day Jeffreys was gazetted to go the Home Circuit with Mr. Justice Street, to hold the ensuing Summer Assizes from August 31st to September 15th. But in the meantime the Western Assizes for this summer had been prevented by the rebellion ; and it was therefore decided that a Special Commission should be issued to five Judges to hold these Assizes and at the same time try the captured rebels. At the head of the Commission was the Lord Chief Justice Jeffreys. With him were the Chief Baron Montagu and Mr. Justice Levinz of the Common Pleas, both respectable Judges ; and Mr. Justice Wythens and Mr. Baron Wright, who can only be regarded as followers or creatures of the Chief Justice. Wythens had been the obsequious echo of "the Chief" ever since he had sat under him in the King's Bench ; Wright was the questionable gentleman for whom Jeffreys had secured a Judgeship to mortify Lord Keeper North. A second Commission invested Jeffreys with the rank of Lieutenant-General, and gave him the command of the body guard that accompanied the Judges as a protection from the fury of the populace.

The Commission was late in setting forth, as the Chief Justice had been detained at Tunbridge Wells. He was suffering from the stone, and had left the Wells before the completion of his cure. Afflicted by this painful malady, he started on the Western Circuit.

XIV

THE "BLOODY ASSIZES"

Aug.–Sept., 1685

If a man of passionate temper, suffering the agonies of a peculiarly cruel disorder, is appointed in his capacity as Judge to try, by the comparatively slow process of law, more than a thousand rebels against the Government of which he is himself an ardent member, at a time when mercy to rebels and mercy in the administration of the law were no part of the ethics of political strife, it is more than likely that from a combination of such circumstances results will ensue very shocking to modern notions, and all the more appalling if treated by writers whose political prejudices tempt them to forget the differences of thought and spirit that divide one century from another.

On landing in England the Duke of Monmouth issued a Declaration, the work of Ferguson, a Dissenting minister of more than doubtful character. This Declaration must have been pleasant reading to the King and Jeffreys, and must have furnished them with a nice opinion of those who fought in its justification. In it James "Duke of York" was openly declared a fratricide and an assassin, the murderer of his brother King Charles II. and the unfortunate Earl of Essex ; he was to be pursued as a "mortal and bloody enemy," and was to be mercilessly prosecuted and punished for these execrable facts. To James's grave disposition the humorous side of these slanders would not present itself. Jeffreys and his brother Judges were "suborned, forsworn, men that

were the scandal of the Bar, ignorant and mercenary"
—true or false, statements not calculated to soothe the
irritated feelings of the Lord Chief Justice. No mercy
was to be shown to such as Jeffreys and other members of
the Government by these God-fearing men, going forth to
battle in the name of the Lord of Hosts. "And we
would have none that appear under his (James, Duke of
York's) banner to flatter themselves with expectation of
forgiveness ; it being our firm resolution to prosecute him
and his adherents, without giving way to treaties and
accommodations, until we have brought him and them to
undergo what the rules of the Constitution and the Statutes
of the realm, as well as the laws of nature, Scripture and
nations, judge to be a punishment due to the enemies of
God, mankind and their country, and all things that are
honourable, virtuous and good."

In spite of the "meekness and purity of their principles
and the moderation and righteousness of their ends,"
mercy towards their enemies was evidently not part of the
creed of these champions of the reformed Protestant religion ; nor was their language calculated to inspire mercy
in the bosoms of the victorious Government. If the
servants of the Lord of Hosts were prepared in the hour
of victory to inflict stern retribution on the idolatrous
tyrant, what treatment could they look for at the hands
of the said idolatrous tyrant should things turn out
contrary to their expectations ?

The suppression of a revolt in the age of Jeffreys was
accompanied by severities very shocking to modern notions,
but which were the commonplace of victory at that period,
and had been so for centuries past. Extermination for
the sake of example, in a more or less complete form, was
the principle adopted by a successful Government within
the area of an unsuccessful rebellion. It was usual, as in
the case of the Northern rebellion in Elizabeth's reign, to
leave it to the victorious general to hang up a few hundred
of the common sort, besides those actually taken in the
field, to serve as a warning to others. These were selected

so that each hamlet in the district which had to be impressed with a sense of its guilt furnished its quota of examples. Thus, by a plentiful scattering of well-filled gibbets, the rebellious neighbourhood was cautioned not to do it again.

Under the auspices of Feversham and Kirke the punishment of the Western rebels made a spirited commencement after this fashion. But just as the gibbeting had got thoroughly under way, orders from London interrupted this method of proceeding, and stayed the energies of the Colonel. With the advance of civilisation it had been perceived that there was a commercial side to the joys of victory as well as a didactic, that profit could be drawn from extermination as well as example. Kirke had realised this by beginning a small trade in selling pardons, and it was for this reason that he was suddenly stopped in his exemplary functions and rated by Jeffreys on his return to London. The Court, from the King downwards, had determined that it was no use embarking on a system of wholesale correction without some prospect of remuneration. Enemies had to be punished, but friends had to be rewarded ; and it would never do if Colonel Kirke anticipated all the benefits. It was accordingly with a view to regulating the traffic, as well as the performance of their punitive functions, that the Commission headed by Jeffreys was despatched to the West.

But in their desire to deal generously by themselves and friends—laudable enough as far as it goes—the Government in sending Jeffreys to the West did a clumsy thing. It would have been much wiser to have allowed Feversham and Kirke a free hand in the hanging. They would have expeditiously strung up a few hundreds of rebels or those notoriously sympathetic to the rebellion ; there would have been little or no attempt at a trial ; the affair would have been carried out on martial lines, and, coming directly after the Battle of Sedgmoor, would have formed part of the immediate consequences of defeat ; and whatever cruelty had accompanied the proceedings would have been attributed to the habitually ruthless character of victorious soldiery. But instead of such prompt and decided action, the Government preferred, more than a month after the battle, when the prisons were crammed with unpunished rebels, to send down a Commission of Assize to try by ordinary legal process some two thousand prisoners. Within the limited space of time allotted to the Assize it would be impossible for the Judges to have given these men such a trial as the law allowed them ; the thing was physically impossible ; and, unless the Judges were prepared to relax considerably the provisions of the law or use some method of force or cajolery to shorten the proceedings, they would be engaged on the Western Circuit all through the winter. But however it might have been justifiable under the circumstances for the Judges to curtail the trials, Judges are not the proper people to do that sort of thing ; it comes badly from them ; and whatever excuse may be offered for their conduct, they are guilty of a violation of their duty in acting in such a manner. Accordingly the King and his Judge must bear the blame attaching to the mistaken system which they adopted in order to terrify their enemies, and secure to themselves the bountiful harvest that was to be reaped from a shady administration of the law. To Kirke should have been left the work of hanging the bulk of the prisoners, and only a few of the more important have been reserved to take their trials at the Assizes, when there would have been sufficient time to have given them the full benefit of law allowed to persons in their condition. But a King who calls his Assize a "campaign," and a Lord Chief Justice who is at the same time a Lieutenant-General,— these are anomalies in something more than name.

In calling this Western Circuit a "campaign" James was not merely perpetrating a heavy and improper jest. It is its militant character in other respects than the Judge-General and the body guard of soldiers, that makes the term Assize deceptive and ridiculous. Besides the punishment of those actually implicated in the rebellion, the Commission was intended to teach a lesson to certain Whig gentlemen in the West of England, who, though too wise or cautious to join Monmouth, were known to be friendly in spirit to any designs against the Government, and whose influence would have been immediately exerted in Monmouth's favour if he had met with any degree of success.   The Prideaux, the Spekes, the Trenchards,—these were the men whose names smelt in the nostrils of the Government, and who, by fair means or foul, were to be made to suffer for the reckless conduct of such of their baser adherents as Rumbold and Ferguson. Some, as Mr. Charles Speke, had gone so far as to shake hands with the Duke of Monmouth ; that was sufficient to hang them.   Others less effusive, as Edmund Prideaux, had done nothing that could be construed into an overt act of sympathy ; these were to be arrested on suspicion, and, if no evidence could be offered against them, to pay so heavily for the privilege of release as might impoverish them and enrich some staunch adherent of the King. By these means the Government intended to take advantage of the rebellion to inflict lasting discomfiture on the more wealthy and influential of their opponents, as well as on the ignorant and misguided peasants who had flocked to the Duke's standard. The Whigs and the Nonconformists of the West were the enemies to be struck down and terrified by a signal punishment. A wide net was to be cast that should draw in the wary and unsuspecting, and Jeffreys was the great fisher. He, unfortunately, happened at the same time to be Lord Chief Justice of England.

So much for the singular functions the Chief Justice was expected to perform. These will in some measure account for the odium that has fallen on the Western transactions ; but not entirely. Above all these considerations there looms the spectre of the hideous and drunken Judge bawling his victims to death, making his Court a hell of indecency and injustice, reviling men in coarse and brutal terms, jeering at suppliant women with foul and unmentionable jests. "Humanity could not offend so far as to deserve such punishment as he inflicted. A certain barbarous joy and pleasure grinned from his brutal soul through his bloody eyes, whenever he was sentencing any of the poor souls to death and torment ; so much worse than Nero, as when that monster wished he had never learned to write because forced to set his name to warrants for execution of malefactors, Jeffreys would have been glad if every letter he writ had been such a warrant, and every word a sentence of death. He observed neither humanity to the dead nor civility to the living. He made all the West an Aceldama, some places quite depopulated, and nothing to be seen in them but forsaken walls, unlucky gibbets, and ghostly carcases. The trees were laden almost as thick with quarters as leaves. The houses and steeples covered as close with heads as at other times frequently in that country with crows and ravens. Nothing could be liker hell than all those parts, nothing so like the devil as he. Caldrons hissing, carcases boiling, pitch and tar sparkling and glowing, blood and limbs boiling, and tearing, and mangling ; and he, the great director of all, and, in a word, discharging his place who sent him, the best deserving to be the late King's Chief Justice there, and Chancellor after, of any man that breathed since Cain or Judas."

Such is the spectacle presented to posterity by the author of the *Bloody Assizes*, the book on which almost entirely rests Jeffreys' claim to exceptional disgrace. Into the truth of the latter part of his description it is needless to enquire. A considerable quantity of executions, carried out according to the letter of the usual sentence in cases of high treason, was not likely to improve the aspect of the neighbouring country, more especially as it was the custom to hang people in their own particular part of the country, where the example of their swinging bodies or mouldering quarters might appeal as an awful example to their awe-stricken friends. And if those friends happened to be Dissenters or Whigs, as the author or authors of the

Bloody Assizes undoubtedly were, the natural consequences of such a mode of punishment would be viewed in the light of a true Aceldama.

It is the first part of the description with which this work should concern itself. The manner in which Jeffreys carried out his difficult and unpleasing duty,—this is the burden of the great accusation laid to his charge. The number he condemned to death—a very vexed question—seems to me immaterial. If he made up his mind to accept the Commission, he would be bound to inflict the only possible sentence for high treason on a considerable number of rebels who had been taken red-handed. Clemency was not in Jeffreys' day the accepted spirit in which to greet the vanquished adherents of an unsuccessful rising. The gaols were crammed with prisoners from Monmouth's army, and these gaols it would be his duty to deliver of their inmates. As soon as it was decided to punish them by the ordinary courts of law, an enormous array of gibbets and cauldrons was inevitable. The question which concerns the biographer of Jeffreys is not so much the nature of his functions as the degree in which the Chief Justice by his fierce and brutal demeanour aggravated the horrors of an unpleasant situation. How far did he deride and exult over the prisoners? What innocent men did he condemn? Was his progress marked by drunkenness and shameless immorality? Was he venal as well as brutal? Was he a raging wild beast rather than a man? These are the questions that have to be answered for or against Jeffreys, if we would see the man " truly limned and living " before our eyes, and not the distorted creation of his enemies' caricature.

Now, the evidence from which the details given in Locke's *Western Rebellion*, and consequently Macaulay's and all the accepted narratives of the Bloody Assizes, are derived, is a book called the *Bloody Assizes*, published in London, 1689, by one John Dunton, and republished at subsequent dates under other titles, such as the *New or the Western*

Martyrologies. These books, besides containing the lives of Oates, Dangerfield and many of those executed for complicity in Monmouth's rebellion, include also a life of Jeffreys, and various scurrilous attacks levelled against him at the time of his fall. Though unquestioningly accepted by Macaulay and other historians, though the instances of Jeffreys' villainy with which they abound have been treated as if they were unimpeachably authentic by scrupulous writers, these books must be unhesitatingly pronounced unworthy of more than a most limited and suspicious credence.[1]

Dunton was a low-class publisher of obscene and sensational literature, a man who, to use his own words, " had been infested with the itch of printing and had indulged his humour to excess." This excess, which in the department of the obscene had transcended the polite obscenity of his period, in political literature associated him with the violent and scurrilous section of the Whig party, and led him to publish such works as would excite the fanaticism of the sectaries or the violence of the Whig mobsmen. Accordingly, the *Bloody Assizes* is full of a kind of rampant salvationalism that finds expression in voluminous prayers of the most assured character, and heated attacks on the Popish murderers of Sir Edmundbury Godfrey and the Earl of Essex.

The author of the greater part of these books was John Tutchin, "a man who was no better than a cheap penny-a-liner of the day." More than that, he was a writer whose venom cost him his life—he was thrashed to death by some Tories he had vilified in 1707—and whose fate Jeffreys had endeavoured to anticipate by sentencing him during the Bloody Assizes to be whipped through all the market towns in Dorsetshire, a sentence which even in the hour of his fall the Judge saw no cause to regret. It would be idle to pretend that at the hands of such an

---

[1] Mr. A. L. Humphreys fully discusses the quality of these books in an article on the "Sources of History for Monmouth's Rebellion and the Bloody Assizes," published in vol. xviii of the *Proceedings of the Somersetshire Archæological and Natural History Society.* 1892.

author, Jeffreys, whatever his guilt, could be expected to receive anything but the most unfair and perjured treatment. This he received more particularly from Tutchin, in a book called ironically the *Merciful Assizes*, which is entirely devoted to Jeffreys, and, on the authority of certain "secret memoirs" of an undivulged source, loads him with the coarsest abuse under a clumsy affectation of irony. The *Bloody Assizes* is a more decorous work than this, but no more reliable. If for our judgment on Jeffreys' conduct we were entirely dependent on the *Bloody Assizes* and its kindred publications, it would be impossible to form a rational idea of the man who struck such terror into the hearts of the Western prisoners. A work dictated by obvious motives of personal vengeance, and written for the delectation of religious and political enemies, cannot be allowed, even in the case of a Jeffreys, to possess any authentic value whatever.

What we do know for certain at the opening of the Assizes amounts to this—Jeffreys was charged with a difficult task, unfitting in many respects to the office which he held ; his instructions were severe, mercy out of the question ; and he had left the Wells with a fit of the stone still on him, which increased in its violence as he proceeded on the circuit. The effect of this disorder upon Jeffreys' bearing as a judge becomes apparent for the first time at the trial of Baxter. Jeffreys' tone and language were always those of a passionate and irritable man, easily stirred to indignation by the presence of those he disliked, and regarding his seat on the Bench as a suitable eminence from which to defend his convictions and denounce those who were too openly opposed to them. But at Baxter's trial he passes the ordinary limits of his judicial excitement. If his treatment of Baxter be contrasted with that of Rosewell, the difference is manifest. Equally prejudiced against both, to the latter he is severe and sometimes sneering, but he hardly passes the bounds of judicial propriety as then understood. But to the former he is outrageous, he revels in denunciation, he mocks at the old man's worth, and taunts his respectability ; he delights in thrilling the hearts of the fearful Dissenters, and watches their horror-struck faces as he pours down his wrath on the head of their venerable leader. Allowing that Jeffreys' conduct may be somewhat exaggerated in the partisan reports of Baxter's trial, there still remains a peculiar change of tone, an increased wildness of fury of which hitherto we have merely seen the possibility, but which, in subsequent reports of unquestionable authenticity, we can contemplate in the perfected state. This change in Jeffreys is coincident with the acute development of the disease which brought him to an early grave; and it is the agony of the disease, acting in conjunction with great powers of mind and a striking personality, that have made Jeffreys vivid and terrible where others would have been horrible and vulgar.

The Assize commenced at the end of August, when Jeffreys opened the Commission at Winchester. Here there was only one serious case to be tried in connection with the rebellion, and that was the case of Alicia Lisle, who was indicted for high treason in harbouring and concealing one John Hicks, a Dissenting minister and follower of the Duke of Monmouth. Hicks had been with the Duke's army, and escaping after the defeat at Sedgmoor had been taken about three weeks later in Lady Lisle's house. With him at the time of his capture was a man called Nelthorp, also an adherent of Monmouth, who had been outlawed in 1683 for his connection with the Rye House Plot, but had returned to England under the Duke's standard. The prisoner, Lady Lisle,[1] was the widow of one of Charles the First's Judges. She was seventy years of age and had, since the Restoration, conducted herself with becoming loyalty.

Lady Lisle was indicted before Jeffreys and his four brethren on August 27th. Mr. Pollexfen, the advocate of Baxter and a noted Whig, led for the Crown. He had been appointed, presumably by Jeffreys with whom he was on terms of intimacy, to conduct the prosecutions of

[1] Her title as "Lady Lisle," by which she is generally known, is a courtesy one.

the Western rebels. A man of sour disposition but a sound and honest lawyer, he has been severely censured by writers of both parties for consenting to act as leading counsel for the King on this occasion ; but it is difficult to see on what grounds. Whig though he was, he may well have disapproved of Monmouth's rebellion, and as an advocate he may just as well have prosecuted a large assortment of traitors as any other kind of offender.

Pollexfen having opened the case, and Jeffreys having assured the prisoner that as they were all accountable to the Great Judge of Heaven and earth, so should she have a just and legal trial, the King's evidence was called. First came three witnesses who had been taken prisoners by Monmouth's soldiers. They swore that Hicks had visited them in their confinement and reasoned with them as to the legitimacy of the Duke's title to the throne. Hicks's complicity in the rebellion thus satisfactorily established, Pollexfen passed on to the evidence relating to Lady Lisle's guilt in harbouring the rebel.

The principal witness the Crown relied on to prove Lady Lisle's complicity was a man of the name of Dunne. He had acted as Hicks's messenger, had carried his request for shelter to Lady Lisle, had brought back her invitation, and had then conducted Hicks and Nelthorp to Moyles Court, the residence of the prisoner. But Dunne was an unwilling witness. The Crown counsel were acquainted with the fact ; and, accordingly, Pollexfen, before putting him in the box, humbly desired his lordship to examine the witness with more than the customary strictness. He knew well enough the skill of the Chief Justice in wresting the truth from the recalcitrant ; and Jeffreys was not slow to prove himself worthy of the confidence reposed in him. Before Dunne had opened his mouth, Jeffreys in awful language exhorted him to speak the truth. " For, I tell thee," he concluded, " God is not to be mocked ; and thou canst not deceive Him, though thou mayst us." His warning delivered, Jeffreys listened patiently while Dunne told, by the help of the Judge's questions, his own version of the affair. On Friday, July

26th, he said, a short man with a black beard came to him at Warminster, where he lived, and asked him to go to Moyles Court, some twenty-six miles away, and desire Lady Lisle to entertain one Hicks. Dunne consented, and rode to Moyles Court the following day, Saturday. There he saw the prisoner, who consented to receive Hicks, and appointed the Tuesday evening following for his arrival. On Sunday Dunne returned to Warminster, and sent word to Hicks of Lady Lisle's invitation. Accordingly, at eleven o'clock on the Tuesday morning, Hicks, "a full, fat, black man," Nelthorp, "a thin, black man," and Dunne, set out for Moyles Court, which, with the help of a man called Barter whom Dunne had employed on the previous Saturday, they reached between nine and ten o'clock the same night. On arriving at the house a girl opened the door, Hicks and Nelthorp went in, and Dunne never saw them again till they were arrested. He himself, after eating some cake and cheese which he had brought with him from home, withdrew to the stable. And he swore that all the reward he had received for his pains in the affair had been a month's imprisonment.

This was all Dunne said that he could remember. Jeffreys was quick to point out the absurdity of the story. "Thou seemest to be a man of a great deal of kindness and good nature; for by this story, there was a man thou never sawest before, and because he only had a black beard and came to thy house, that black beard of his should persuade thee to go twenty-six miles, and give a man half-a-crown out of thy pocket to show thee the way, and all to carry a message from a man thou never knewest in thy life to a woman thou never sawest in thy life. That thou shouldest lie out by the way two nights, and upon this Sunday get home and there meet with the same black-bearded little gentleman and appoint these people to come to thy house upon the Tuesday; and when they came entertain them three or four hours at thy house, and go back again so many miles with them, and have no entertainment but a piece of cake and cheese that thou broughtest thyself from home ; and have no reward, nor so much as know any of the persons thou didst all this for—is very strange." So strange that Jeffreys prepared to discuss the matter a little more closely with Master Dunne. In the most approved style of cross-examination the Chief Justice commenced by taunting Dunne with his peculiarly obliging disposition. He got from him that he was a baker by trade, and asked him if he baked bread at such easy rates as those at which he led rogues into lurking-holes : "But, I assure thee, thy bread is very light weight : it will scarce pass the balance here." Dunne had said that the black-bearded man lent him the horse on which he first rode to Lady Lisle's. If he never knew Dunne before, "how came he to trust thee with his horse ?" asked Jeffreys. "The Lord knows, my lord," replied Dunne. "Thou sayest right," answered the Chief Justice, "the Lord only knows, for by the little I know of thee I would not trust thee with two pence."

The first lie that Jeffreys detected in Dunne's evidence turned on the connection between Hicks and the black-bearded man. " Did not the black-bearded man first come to you," asked Jeffreys, " and employ you to go on this message ? and did not he know Hicks ?" "I cannot tell, my lord," answered Dunne. Jeffreys pressed him. " Did not he tell you Hicks desired you to go, and that he was in debt, and therefore desired to be concealed ?" " Yes, my lord," blandly replied the witness, giving the lie direct to his first answer. " How came you to be so impudent then," exclaimed the Judge, "as to tell me such a lie ?" " I beg your pardon, my lord." " You beg my pardon ! That is not because you told me a lie, but because I have found you in a lie."

Jeffreys soon found him in another. Dunne had sworn that, on arriving at Moyles Court with Hicks and Nelthorp, he had seen no one but a young girl, and that he had gone to the stable and unlatched its door by himself. He now admitted that Carpenter, Lady Lisle's bailiff, met them in the courtyard, and that it was Carpenter who had conducted him to the stable and opened the door for him. On the discovery of this second falsehood the pent-up rage of Jeffreys, till now confined to a few brief exclamations of anger, broke out in the fulness of its power. " Why, thou vile wretch, didst thou not tell me just now that thou pluckest up the latch ? Dost thou take the God of Heaven not to be a God of truth, and that He is not a witness of all thou sayest ? Dost thou think, because thou prevaricatest with the Court here, thou canst do so with God above, Who knows thy thoughts ? And it is infinite mercy that for those falsehoods of thine, He does not immediately strike thee into hell ! Jesus God ! there is no sort of conversation or human society to be kept with such people as these are who have no other religion but only in pretence, and no way to uphold themselves but by countenancing lying and villainy ! " Turks, he said, had more title to an eternity of bliss than such people as these. " See," he cried, " how they can cant and snivel, and lie, and forswear themselves ; and all for the good old cause ! They will stick at nothing if they think they can but preserve a brother or sister-saint forsooth ! " For the moment Jeffreys had done with him : " Thou art a strange, prevaricating, shuffling, snivelling, lying rascal. Will the prisoner ask this person any questions ? " She answered : " No." " Perhaps her questions might endanger the coming out of the truth," sneered Jeffreys ; " but it carries a very foul face, upon my word."

Barter, the man to whom Dunne had given half-a-crown to show him the way to Moyles Court, was the next witness. He did not prove unwilling. He said that when he showed Dunne the way to Moyles Court on the Saturday the latter brought a letter from Hicks to Lady Lisle ; that he went into the kitchen while Dunne delivered his message, and that, while he was waiting there, Lady Lisle came in with Dunne and spoke to him : and that then she turned away with Dunne, and he saw them laughing together and looking at him. When they got outside he asked Dunne what Lady Lisle had been laughing at ; Dunne replied that my lady had asked him if he, Barter, knew anything of the "concern," and that he had answered in the negative.

Eventually the mystery of the affair had so weighed on Barter's mind that he had told all he knew to Colonel Penruddock, one of the King's officers, who, acting on his information, entered Lady Lisle's house early Wednesday morning and discovered the fugitives. Dunne, he swore, also informed him that he was to have a large booty for his services to Hicks, and that before the fugitives went to Moyles Court they had been ten days in his house. Both these facts Dunne strenuously denied.

But the most important point in Barter's evidence, as going to show that Lady Lisle was aware from the first of the circumstances of her visitors, was the question which Barter swore that she had asked Dunne as to the former's knowledge of "the concern" that had brought Hicks to seek the shelter of her house. What concern did she mean ? Did she know that Hicks and Nelthorp were fugitives from Monmouth's army ? If the Crown could prove that she did, it would very materially strengthen their case. Jeffreys knew this well enough, and directed all his energies to getting from Dunne an admission that Lady Lisle knew her visitors to be fugitives from Sedgmoor. "Let my honest man, Mr. Dunne, stand forward a little," said Jeffreys at the conclusion of Barter's evidence. "Did not you tell him (Barter) that you told my lady, when she asked whether he was acquainted with the concern, that he knew nothing of the business ?" Dunne admitted it. "Did you so ?· Then you and I must have a little further discourse. Come now, and tell us what ' business ' was that ? and tell it us so that a man may understand and believe that thou dost speak the truth." Dunne only repeated the Judge's question. "Does your lordship ask what that business was ?" Jeffreys asked the question again ; Dunne paused. Twice Jeffreys repeated it ; Dunne only mused in silence. Jeffreys thought that perhaps he did not understand : "I will repeat it to thee again ; for thou shalt see what countryman I am by my telling my story twice over " (alluding to his Welsh extraction). Dunne at last answered that he could not remember what the business was that Lady Lisle had spoken of. "Be ingenuous ; tell the truth," urged Jeffreys. "Oh, how hard the truth is to come out of a lying Presbyterian knave !" Then the Chief Justice dwelt at some length on the love of God for the truth which the witness had sworn to speak, and concluded : " I charge thee, therefore, as thou wilt answer it to that God of truth, and that thou mayest be called to do, for aught I know, the very next minute, and there thou wilt not be able to palliate the truth ; what was that business you and my lady spoke of ?" For eight minutes after this last appeal Dunne continued silent ; at length he declared that he could not give an account of it. Jeffreys was aghast : "Oh, blessed God ! was there ever such a villain upon the face of the earth ? To what times are we reserved ! Dost thou believe that there is a God ? " Dunne protested that he did. Jeffreys assured him in solemn language how that God's all-piercing eye looked into the hearts of all men, that God was omniscient and omnipresent, all-mighty and all-knowing, the searcher of hearts and trier of the reins, to whom all hearts are open and from whom no secrets are hid. " Now tell us what was the business you spoke of." But the witness made no answer. The Lord Chief Baron joined in the exhortations of the Chief Justice ; but Dunne only averted his head. Jeffreys was beside himself. He turned to the jury and asked them to observe the strange and horrible carriage of this fellow : " Oh, blessed Jesus ! " he cried, " what an age do we live in, and what a generation of vipers do we live among ! . . . . Thou wretch ! all the mountains and hills in the world heaped upon one another will not cover thee from the vengeance of the great God for this transgression of false witness bearing !" "I cannot tell what to say, my lord," answered Dunne, at his wits' end before the wrath of the Judge. Jeffreys, seeing his confusion, put aside his anger and repeated his question as calmly as he could. Twice he asked it, and twice the witness remained silent as before. Jeffreys pleaded with him in a tone of mild remonstrance. Did he think he was serving the prisoner's interest by his obstinacy? "Sure thou canst not think so; such a sort of carriage were enough to convict her, if there were nothing else." When at length Dunne showed some signs of yielding, Jeffreys became quite gentle and fatherly: "It is not in my nature to desire the hurt of anybody, much less to delight in their eternal perdition; no, it is out of tender compassion to you that I use all these words. . . . If that soul of thine be taken away, what is the body fit for, but, like a putrid carcase, to be thrust into and covered with the dust with which it was made?" At last anxiety for his soul or the fatigue of long resistance opened the lips of Dunne, and the long-expected, eagerly-awaited reply came forth: "She asked me," he said, "whether I did not know that Hicks was a Nonconformist."

Oh, lame and impotent conclusion! Was ever mountain delivered of a smaller mouse? "Dost thou think," exclaimed Jeffreys, "that after all this pain that I have been at to get an answer to my question, that thou canst banter me with such sham stuff as this?" It was now late on this August evening. The candles had been lit in the court. "Hold the candle to his face," cried the Judge, "that we may see his brazen face." "My lord, I tell you the truth," urged Dunne. "Did she ask thee whether that man knew anything of a question she had asked thee, and that was only of being a Nonconformist?" asked Jeffreys. "Yes, my lord, that was all." "That is all nonsense; dost thou imagine that any man hereabouts is so weak as to believe thee?" "My lord, I am so baulked," pleaded Dunne, "I do not know what I say myself; tell me what you would have me say, for I am cluttered out of my senses." "Why, prithee, man," answered Jeffreys, "there is nobody baulks thee but thine own self; thou art asked questions as plain as anything in the world can be; it is only thy own depraved naughty heart that baulks both thy honesty and understanding, if thou hast any; but I see all the pains in the world and all compassion and charity is lost upon thee, and therefore I will say no more to thee." But Jeffreys was careful to charge the Crown counsel to see that an indictment for perjury was preferred against Mr. Dunne.

Pollexfen then called Colonel Penruddock, an officer in the King's army, whose father had been executed for organising a Royalist rising during the Protectorate. The Colonel had arrested Hicks, Nelthorp and Lady Lisle on the Wednesday morning, on information received from Barter. He had, he said, beset the house with soldiers, but could get no answer to his summons. At length Carpenter, the bailiff, came out and in reply to questions admitted that there were strangers in the house. Penruddock commenced a search. Hicks and Dunne were found in the malt-house, the latter covered over with some sort of stuff. When Lady Lisle appeared Penruddock told her that she had done ill in harbouring rebels. She answered that she knew nothing of the matter. He asked her to deliver up any other who was concealed in the house. She denied that there was any other. The search was resumed, and Nelthorp discovered in a hole by the chimney.

Barter, it also appeared, had told Penruddock that he believed Hicks and Nelthorp to be rebels, because Dunne had told him as much. This statement quite revived Jeffreys' interest in Dunne: " Did you say to Barter you took them to be rebels?" he asked. Dunne, thoroughly bewildered by this time or assuming to be so, could only repeat the question. " I take them to be rebels!" he exclaimed. "You blockhead, I ask you, did you tell him so?" "I tell Barter so!" echoed Dunne. " Ay, is not that a plain question?" "I am quite cluttered out of my senses; I do not know what I say." Jeffreys replied by ordering the candle to be held nearer to his nose; "but to tell the truth would rob thee of none of thy senses, if ever thou hadst any; but it would seem that neither thou nor thy mistress, the prisoner, had any, for she knew nothing of it neither, though she had sent for them thither."

If ever there had been any hope for Lady Lisle from the mercy of the Judge, that hope was fast dwindling away. Jeffreys had treated her with dignity and forbearance at first, as he treated even Oates before her. But the Chief Justice always decided on the merits of a case in the middle of it ; and if he was aggravated into a decision by perjury or impertinence, and that decision unfavourable to the accused, from that moment he treated those before him as already convicted, and it was not his fault if they did not get a very clear and immediate appreciation of what was passing in his mind. That in this particular case the prisoner happened to be an old lady of seventy was nothing to him ; all considerations of age or sex were lost in his raging disgust at the perjury of Dunne.

Carpenter, the bailiff, and his wife were the last witnesses called by the Crown. Pollexfen described them both as unwilling ; and all that could be got from them of any importance was the fact that Lady Lisle had been in the room with Hicks and Nelthorp while they partook of supper.

Hardly had Carpenter concluded his evidence when the Court was startled by the announcement that Dunne had at last decided to tell all he knew. Whether on reflection he had decided to save his soul, or some of the Crown counsel had been painting to him the awful consequences of an indictment for perjury, founded on the misfortunes of Dr. Titus Oates in that respect, it was through a Mr. Rumsey, presumably one of the King's advocates, that the announcement came of Dunne's repentance. " Let him tell the truth and I am satisfied," remarked the Chief Justice. The material facts now revealed by Dunne were these : that when he went to Lady Lisle with Hicks's message, she asked him whether Hicks had been in the army, to which he replied that he did not know ; and that, on arriving at Moyles Court on the Tuesday night, Carpenter took Dunne to the stable where he put up his horse, and then conducted him to a room where he had supper with Hicks and Nelthorp in Lady Lisle's presence. Pressed by Jeffreys, he also admitted that during supper the prisoner and her guests had talked of the army and the fighting. But Dunne insisted very strongly that he himself had never known that these men had been in the army, nor had kept them so much as one night in his own house. Jeffreys vainly tried to drag from him more precise details of the conversation during supper. Dunne said that he could only hope to remember more if he was given till the following morning to collect his bewildered thoughts.

During his cross-examination of the witness, Jeffreys divulged the fact that he had himself examined Nelthorp in London before starting on circuit ; and that it was on the strength of some of the latter's admissions that he was in a position to appreciate the heinousness of Dunne's lying. "I would not mention any such thing as any piece of evidence to influence this case; but I could not but tremble to think, after what I knew, that any one should dare so much to prevaricate with God and man as to tell such horrid lies in the face of a Court." He assured Dunne that he prayed with as much earnestness as he would for his own soul that God would forgive him and the blessed Jesus mediate for him, and he was of opinion that all people "should be pressed to join with him " in his prayers ; though in the same breath he declared that it filled him with horror that such wretched creatures as Dunne should live upon the earth. But pity and indignation were equally wasted ; not a word more would Dunne utter, and Jeffreys was fain to give him up as a bad job. " Well, I see thou wilt answer nothing ingenuously ; therefore I will trouble myself no more with thee ; go on with your evidence, gentlemen." But the Crown had no more evidence. " What have you to say for yourself?" he asked, turning to Lady Lisle.

The old lady began by protesting that she never knew that Hicks had been in the army, but had thought him to be a Presbyterian minister absconding to avoid warrants that were out against private preaching. At the word " Presbyterian " Jeffreys broke into an access of rage. " But

I will tell you there is not one of those lying, snivelling, canting Presbyterian rascals but, one way or the other, had a hand in the late horrid conspiracy and rebellion . . . Presbytery has all manner of villainy in it ; nothing but Presbytery could lead that fellow Dunne to tell so many lies as he has told here ; for show me a Presbyterian," he concluded, " and I will show you a lying knave." Lady Lisle pleaded that she abhorred the late rebellion. " I am sure you have great reason for it," sneered the Judge. She would have been ungrateful, she urged, for King James's kindness to her, if she had acted disloyally towards him. There is an incoherence of fury in the taunt Jeffreys flings at her in reply : " Oh, then ! Ungrateful ! Ungrateful adds to the load which was between man and man, and is the basest crime that any one can be guilty of." She protested that she had only come into the country five days before her arrest. " Nay, I cannot tell when you came into the country, nor do I care ; it seems you came time enough to harbour rebels." However, he allowed Lady Lisle to finish what she had to say ; but the poor lady might as well have addressed the furniture of the Court for all the impression she could make on the relentless Judge.

Jeffreys' charge to the jury is extraordinary—even for him. He always considered a summing up as an opportunity for dwelling at length on general topics suggested by the circumstances of the case, and invariably prefaced his review of the evidence by a vigorous declaration of his general sentiments in regard to the parties concerned. In Lady Lisle's case he follows the same course, but in an exaggerated fashion. Whilst his language is fierce and heated to an unwonted degree, a tendency to repetition, which was always with him, is developed to an alarming extent, his appeals to God and Christ he utters at every turn with an intensity of passion that makes them appear rather a desperate summons to his aid than a reverend desire to co-operate in Their service. Over and over again, with growing fury, he denounces the connection between Dissent and rebellion ;

and when at last he does come to the evidence he reviews it, contrary to his custom, hurriedly and confusedly, introducing irrelevant and prejudicial topics and then telling the jury to disregard them. It never seems to occur to him to dwell on the one point that might cause a difficulty in the minds of the jury, viz., the fact that Lady Lisle, was accused of harbouring a traitor whilst the alleged traitor was as yet unconvicted of treason. He ended by telling the jury that the guilt of the prisoner was "as evident as the sun at noonday." Now, whatever may be the opinion as to the guilt of Lady Lisle, hers was one of those cases in which there were a good many clouds to be dissipated by the help of the Judge before the jury could see the truth shining out in noontide brilliancy.

It is almost impossible to convey an accurate impression of Jeffreys' charge by extract ; it should be read in its entirety. He repeatedly blessed God for His mercy in frustrating the rebellion, lauded the King for the declaration he had issued on his accession in which he had promised to preserve safe and inviolate the rights of the Established Church, lamented the impudence and profligacy of the Duke of Monmouth, and denounced the "gilded bait of religion and conscience" by which those hypocrites the Nonconformist parsons had deluded ten thousand into rebellion, to the ruin of their families, leaving in many cases their widows and babes in want and desolation. In such fashion had that wretch, Hicks, "whose soul was blacker in the eyes of God than ever his coat was," deluded the poor unfortunate gentlewoman at the bar. But, he concluded, after commenting on the evidence against her, "neither her age nor her sex are to move you, who have nothing else to consider but the fact you are to try. I charge you therefore, as you will answer at the bar of the last Judgment, where you and we must all appear, deliver your verdict according to conscience and truth."

Before leaving the box the jury asked Jeffreys if it was equally treason to harbour an unconvicted traitor. "It is all the same, that certainly can be no doubt," (*sic*) answered the Judge; " for if Hicks had been wounded in the rebels' army and had come to her house and there been entertained, but had died there of his wounds, and so could never have been convicted, she had been nevertheless a traitor."

But even with this assurance the jury seemed to find some difficulty in returning a verdict. As they did not come back into court immediately, Jeffreys grew impatient. He wondered that in such a plain case they stayed away so long; if they did not come quickly, he should shut them up all night. In half an hour they returned; but only to ask a question of the Court. They were not satisfied, the foreman said, that Lady Lisle ever knew Hicks to have been in the army. Jeffreys reminded them of the conversation during supper about the army and the fighting which Dunne had sworn to; "and," he added, "did she not inquire of Dunne whether Hicks had been in the army? And when he told her he did not know, she did not say she would refuse him if he had been there, but ordered him to come by night, by which it is evident she suspected it." This was certainly clear enough; but it did not resolve the minds of the jury. Lady Lisle endeavoured to seize the opportunity to say something more. "My lord, I hope"—she began. Jeffreys stopped her: "You must not speak now." For another quarter of an hour the jury laid their heads together, and then they gave in their verdict, "Guilty." "Look to her, gaoler," said the Clerk of Arraigns; "she is found guilty of high treason, and prepare yourself to die." And then from the lips of Jeffreys there fell on the ears of the Court the awful words addressed to her reluctant jury: "If I had been among you, and she had been my own mother, I should have found her guilty."

On the following day, being Wednesday, the 28th of August, Alice Lisle was brought up to receive judgment of death. The Lord Chief Justice, in passing sentence, lamented to find a gentlewoman of quality and fortune involved with a herd of canting and whining fanatics, and deplored that in this little case so many perjuries had been added to the crime of treason; "you ought to reflect upon whose account those perjuries were committed, and to lay them seriously to heart; for ere long, in a few hours—deceive not yourself—you are to give an account at a greater bar for all your thoughts, words and actions. You would likewise do well to bethink yourself with all seriousness and remorse of your own false asseverations and protestations: that you upon your salvation should pretend ignorance in the business, when since that time, even since last night, there has been but too much discovered how far you were concerned." "No," he went on, alluding to information that had reached him since the adjournment of the Court; "it is not unknown who were sent for upon the Monday night in order to have that rebellious, seditious fellow to preach to them, what directions were given to come through the orchard the back and private way, what orders were given for provision, and how the horses were appointed to be disposed of." Let her make some recompense to public justice by discovering the truth. Then she was sentenced to be burnt alive, according to the law in such cases.[1]

"But," added Jeffreys, "when I left his Majesty, he was pleased to remit the time of all executions to me; that wherever I found any obstinacy or impenitence, I might order the executions with what speed I should think best; therefore, Mr. Sheriff, take notice you are to prepare for the execution of this gentlewoman this afternoon." Yet, he should not be leaving Winchester for an hour or two; the prisoner should be given pen, ink and paper, and "if in the meantime you employ that pen, ink and paper and this hour or two well—you understand what I mean—it may be you may hear farther from us, in deferring the execution."

Lady Lisle did not avail herself of the opportunities afforded her by the Judge for a full confession; but, at the intercession of some divines, her execution was respited

---

[1] Until 1790 burning alive was the legal punishment for women convicted of higher or petty treason.

for a week.   That week was employed in efforts to obtain a remission of the sentence.   On Sunday, the 30th, Lady St. John and Lady Abergavenny, both friends of the prisoner, addressed a letter to Lord Clarendon, the Lord Privy Seal.   In it they assured him of Lady Lisle's constant loyalty, and begged him to represent it to the King in the hope of a reprieve.   Clarendon did as he was requested, but James refused to have anything to do with the matter, " having left all to the Lord Chief Justice." On the following day a petition from the lady herself was presented to the King, praying him to alter the sentence from burning to beheading, and grant another four days' respite.   But James was obdurate ; he would not reprieve her as much as one day, and would only alter the sentence if a precedent could be found for doing so.   The precedent was found, and it was to the block and not the stake that Lady Lisle was led out on the following Wednesday afternoon.   She died forgiving all her enemies, at the same time making certain accusations against some of them which, if founded, considerably enhance her charitable disposition.

On the facts as given in evidence against her, few will deny that Lady Lisle was guilty of the offence laid to her charge.   If she did not know that Hicks had been in Monmouth's army when Dunne brought her his message, which, as Jeffreys pointed out to the jury, is very unlikely, she certainly learnt it at supper on the Wednesday evening.   It then became her duty either to send them away immediately from her house, or, if harshly inclined, to send word to the authorities that she had rebels under her roof, and to detain them till the arrival of the soldiers.   But she preferred to do neither of these things. She concealed them during the night, and when the soldiers arrived in the morning, twice denied any knowledge of their whereabouts.   In this she may have acted from sudden fear or surprise ; but Dunne's determined perjury, his obstinate endeavours to avoid telling all he really knew, would certainly make it appear as if the discovery of the whole truth would have been very detrimental to the prisoner. His second story, incomplete as it was, told more against her than the first, and might have told still more if Dunne had not been so anxious to save his own skin. If Barter is to be believed, Dunne well knew and had himself harboured the fugitives, and, from his whispering with Lady Lisle in Barter's presence, would seem to have acquainted her with their real circumstances. But without Barter's evidence, Dunne's admissions, coupled with Lady Lisle's suspicious conduct, were quite sufficient to justify in the mind of a Judge and jury a verdict of "guilty." To justify, but not to recommend. The nature of the offence and the circumstances of the prisoner were such as, we should think, ought to have inclined a Judge and jury to a proper exercise of mercy. The jury was evidently desirous of taking such a view, but the Judge would not allow it. He was determined to carry the case to its bitter end, and refused to be turned aside by any humane considerations.

In this Jeffreys was not less merciful than any of his brethren would have been. As soon as Lady Lisle was placed in the dock on a charge of treason, her conviction and sentence were certain at the hands of any Judge on the bench. The evidence was quite strong enough to warrant a verdict of "guilty"; and her age and sex were not such potent considerations in those days as they are now. Women fared no better, if not worse, than men at the hands of the law, and Judges saw no reason to treat them with any less severity. The reluctance of the jury in all probability arose from the fact that they were previously acquainted with the high character of the lady in her own county, and were the more inclined to sympathise with her by the harsh conduct of the Judge. The actual conviction of Lady Lisle, apart from its inadvisability and his personal bearing at the trial, cannot be charged as a crime against Jeffreys, as Hallam and others would have us believe. Whatever his personal conduct, he did not procure the conviction of a woman innocent of the crime for which she was indicted.

But it has been said that he deliberately violated the

law in order to obtain a conviction, by directing the jury to treat Hicks as a traitor, though he had never been legally convicted as such. Sir James Stephen demurs to this. After carefully examining the authorities that have been cited against Jeffreys, and which he shows to have been rather unfairly used by one writer, he says : "I think that this is another of the numerous instances in which there really was no definite law at all, and in which the fact that a particular course was taken by a cruel man for a bad purpose has been regarded as proof that the course taken was illegal." A process of reasoning similar to this suggested by Sir J. Stephen may have led Lord Campbell to assert that "there was the greatest difficulty even to show that Hicks had been in the rebellion "—the fact was never even questioned at the trial, and three witnesses were called who proved it beyond a doubt—may have persuaded Hallam to declare that Lady Lisle's conviction was *without evidence*, and induced Burnet, who was absent from England at the time, and whose account of the trial contains glaring misstatements, to state that the jury brought her in three times "not guilty."

It was certainly a cruel severity that selected Lady Lisle as a fitting object for exemplary punishment, and a blind severity also ; for such a punishment must have aroused horror and disgust rather than wholesome fear. If there was reason for such an act, that reason lay in the fact that at the commencement of Jeffreys' "campaign," the King desired to give signal and alarming proof of his determination to visit the sin of rebellion not only upon the poor and ignorant, but upon the gentry of the West who had aided or encouraged the rebels. Not having in their hands any person of birth or influence in the neighbourhood whose guilt could at that time be satisfactorily established, the Government was obliged to make the best use they could of the old gentlewoman of seventy, whose sympathy with the rebel fugitives had been so unfortunately discovered.

Her fate had been determined before Jeffreys left

London; she had been marked out as the first victim; and Nelthorp had been already examined before the Chief Justice in order to prepare the case against her. Fully convinced of her guilt, Jeffreys took his seat on the bench at Winchester. He knew what Dunne could say if he chose, and anticipated the case would be a "little" one, as he phrased it. But suddenly he found himself confronted with gross and obstinate perjury; the agonies of his disease, of which we shall find him openly complaining at Dorchester, were upon him; his aggravated temper saw in Dunne a very type of the impious hypocrisy of Presbyterianism; he smelt out a conspiracy of "the saints" to baulk truth and justice, and in the comatose old lady in the dock discovered a secret participator in their lies and their rebellions. With the religious violence of some mediæval tyrant butchering in the name of God and Christ, he called on Heaven to witness the canting villainy that beset him at every turn, and in an access of physical and mental torture carried out with superfluous brutality the superfluously brutal task that had been allotted to him.[1]

[1] Woolych, in his *Memoirs* of Judge Jeffreys, says that Jeffreys' frequent exclamations to God and his imprecations of Divine wrath against Dunne for his perjuries were deliberately used by the Judge for the purpose of frightening the witness by the repetition of expressions he would have heard in the Dissenting places of worship he was in the habit of attending. I cannot agree with this tribute to the Judge's ingenuity. Jeffreys' religious outbursts have little kindred with the familiar terms in which the Dissenters of his day addressed God and Jesus. Jeffreys calls upon God as a great and awful Power, far removed from the knowledge and familiarity of men, and not as a kind friend who is waiting to shake him by the hand as soon as he can get free of his body and reach that blessed paradise which a fortunate inability to conform has made his joyous birthright for all eternity. Jeffreys' appeals to Heaven are often terrible, sometimes shocking to the ears of a milder generation, but never impertinent or ludicrous. Jeffreys was not ignorant of his weakness in this respect. He once remarked in the course of a trial at which he presided: "God knows how often all of us have taken the great name of God in vain, or have said more than becomes us and talked of things we should not do."

XV

THE "BLOODY ASSIZES" (*continued*)

THE report of the trial of Lady Lisle is the only reliable account left to us of any of the trials at which Jeffreys presided on this Western Circuit. Henceforth we have to depend almost entirely upon the accounts of the various prisoners and their sufferings given in the *Bloody Assizes* and the *Western Martyrology*, works of no authority, written to consecrate the glorious lives and deaths of those who fought and died for the true Protestant religion, and to denounce the followers of Antichrist who shed their innocent blood. It is obvious, as has been already pointed out, that little or no reliance can be placed on works of this kind, except so far as they are corroborated by external evidence, of which, unfortunately, we possess very little.

From Winchester the Judges went on to Salisbury. There they found little work to detain them ; and on Thursday, September 3rd, they arrived at Dorchester, where some three hundred prisoners were awaiting trial. In the life of Jeffreys attached to the *Bloody Assizes*, we have a more detailed account of the proceedings at Dorchester than at any other town on the circuit ; for it was here that John Tutchin, alias Thomas Pitts, the author of the *Bloody Assizes*, was tried and sentenced to be whipped by Jeffreys.

On Friday, the 4th, he tells us, the Chief Justice attended Divine Service ; and when the Sheriff's chaplain in his sermon spoke of mercy, the Judge was seen to laugh. From church Jeffreys proceeded to the court, hung all in red by his orders, and delivered his charge to the grand jury. To the general dismay, he declared the scope of his Commission was to prosecute not only those who had actually served under the Duke's banner, but all those who had abetted, aided and assisted him. We can well believe that some of the Somersetshire and Devonshire gentry who had accompanied the Judge on to the bench and were expecting a visit from him in a week's time, did not relish this intelligence. As soon as Jeffreys had finished his charge, he adjourned till eight o'clock on Saturday morning.

At Dorchester, Jeffreys and Pollexfen, seeing the large number of prisoners that had to be disposed of, conceived it necessary that some steps should be taken to shorten the length of the proceedings. If every prisoner pleaded "not guilty," they would never get away in time for the next Assize. The Judges now began to experience the ill effects of the clumsy procedure which the sending of a judicial Commission involved in such cases as they had to try. Most of the prisoners were men taken red-handed in the act of rebellion, who might just as well have been shot or hanged straight away ; but once they came before a court of law, they had the right to plead "not guilty" and put themselves on their trials, and if deprived of that right, they were being unjustly dealt with. But Jeffreys was not going to be bothered about that ; in the cases of such notorious villains, the strict rules of law might well be waived in favour of the public convenience. Accordingly, on Saturday morning, the Chief Justice, on taking his seat, informed thirty prisoners against whom the grand jury had found true bills, that if any put themselves on their trials and were found guilty, they would be executed immediately, and insinuated that those who pleaded guilty at once might expect favour. But the thirty preferred to be tried, with the result that twenty-nine were found guilty, sentenced to death, and thirteen ordered to be executed on Monday. Tutchin says, that of these thirteen two were innocent men, convicted on worthless evidence by the menaces of the Chief Justice. We have only his evidence for this statement ; and as he was in prison at the time, he could not have been present at their trials, though he may have heard about them from other prisoners. One, Matthew Bragg, an attorney, was, he says, convicted on the evidence of a woman of ill fame, "to whom the Lord Chief Justice was wonderfully kind," [1] and, what would be little better to Tutchin, that of a Roman Catholic gentleman. Bragg was of the true persuasion. He said on the scaffold he was not the first who was martyred, but he was so much a Christian as to forgive his enemies ; and was then " translated," as Tutchin has some hope to believe, from earth to Heaven. Smith, constable of Chardstock, was convicted on similar evidence to Bragg. Having reflected on the nature of the evidence given against him, Jeffreys thundered at him : " Thou villain ! methinks I see thee already with a halter about thy neck ; thou impudent rebel, to challenge these evidences that are for the King ! " And so the narrative is filled out with other instances of Jeffreys' fury and the glorious carriage of the martyrs too numerous to repeat. It is difficult to know which to wonder at the most,—the pointed brutalities of Jeffreys, about smelling Presbyterians forty miles off and easing the parish of aged almsmen, or the prolific prayers and dying speeches of the Protestant martyrs. Though executed in different localities, there would seem to have been a very complete staff of reporters at the service of their friends, to take down in full the martyrs' utterances ; and if there is a suspicious similarity of style in all of them, this must be set down to the unanimity of sentiment induced by a common fate and a common religion.

Whether Tutchin's account is truthful or not, those prisoners who were tried on that Saturday at Dorchester,

---

[1] In the *Merciful Assizes* Tutchin gave scurrilous rein to his purely imaginary ideas of the Chief Justice's private morality.

came before a Judge almost prostrate with the agony
caused by a severe attack of the stone. If their carriage
was as confidently godly as their speeches would almost
invariably imply, woe betide them ! the crown of martyrdom so earnestly desired, would be theirs with a vengeance.
Late in the evening the Judge returned to his lodgings
almost incoherent with pain. He had to write to the
Secretary of State, Sunderland, an official account of his
day's work. With that he encloses a private letter to the
Minister, with whom he was on terms of close friendship
and alliance. It is written at ten o'clock at night, in an
unsteady and illegible hand that tells its own story.

"I most heartily rejoice, my dearest, dearest Lord, to
learn of your safe return to Windsor. I this day began
with the trial of the rebels at Dorchester, and have despatched ninety-eight ; but am at this time so tortured
with the stone, that I must beg your Lordship's intercession to his Majesty for the incoherence of what I have
advertised to you and his Majesty and the trouble of ;
and that I may give myself for much ease by your Lordship's favour as to make use of my servant's pen to give a
relation of what has happened since I came here."

And then he concludes with this agonised declaration of
his devotion to his friend—

"My dearest Lord, may I ever be tortured by the
stone if I forget to approve myself, my dearest Lord,
"Your most faithful and devoted servant,
"JEFFREYS.[1]
"DORCHESTER. 10, night."

Once more the wretchedness of the suffering man finds
vent in a postscript.

"For God's sake make all excuses and write at leisure
a word of comfort."

This letter is dated September 5th ; but in a day or

---

[1] The originals of these letters written by Jeffreys on the western
circuit are preserved in the Record office. See Appendix III.

two such comfort was to come to my Lord Jeffreys as should go a mighty way to relieve, if anything could, his body's agony. For on that same September 5th, at his house at Wroxton in Oxfordshire, the Lord Keeper North had passed away. At six o'clock on the following evening his faithful brothers, Dudley and Roger, coming to Lord Sunderland's house where the King was dining, delivered up into his Majesty's hands the great Seal of England. The King rose immediately and went to the Council, and Mr. Evelyn and Sunderland's other guests fell to guessing who should succeed the dead Minister. There were few among them who did not make their guess in favour of the afflicted judge at Dorchester.

It was not till the 7th that Jeffreys received the good news. He immediately wrote off to Sunderland asking him to press his interests with the King, though, from the expressions in his letter, he had apparently already received from the Secretary some intimation of James's intention to confer on him the vacant office.

" Give me leave, my dearest Lord, with more opportunities than ordinary to beg your Lordship's patronage and protection ; it's that station that (next to his Majesty) I will owe to your Lordship's favour, and desire no longer to continue in any condition than to show my gratitude more than I can speak it. I heartily beseech your Lordship to render my most humble duty and thankfulness to his Majesty for his most gracious thought of me, and assure him I will to the utmost approve myself his most loyal and faithful servant, and my dearest Lord,

" Your Lordship's most entirely devoted "
" JEFFREYS."

In the meantime the Chief Justice was doing all he could to show his devotion to his master's service by his proceedings at Dorchester. Pollexfen had hit on a surer way of curtailing the King's business. Jeffreys' insinuations proving hardly effective, two officers were sent into the prison with instructions to tell the prisoners that those of them who pleaded guilty might expect mercy. The names of those who consented to do so were taken down, so that, if in the meantime they relented of their decision, the officers could give evidence to the Court of their previous plea. This method proved most effective; few preferred the certain fortune of a trial, and Jeffreys was able to dispose by sentence of death of some 292 rebels. The promises of mercy were not fallacious, however; of these 292 only 74 at the highest calculation actually suffered.[1]

Among the 74 were two prisoners whose cases have aroused a good deal of sympathy, not because there was any doubt about their guilt, but on account of their youth and personal attractions. One was Mr. Christopher Battiscomb, the other William Hewling. Hewling and his brother Benjamin had both held commands in Monmouth's army. William was twenty years of age. He is the very type of the misguided youth, bursting with uncontrollable religious excitement, who easily falls a prey to the exhortations of unthinking or unscrupulous fanatics. His description of how he came to join Monmouth is characteristic. "God by His Holy Spirit did suddenly seize upon his heart when he thought not of it, in his retired abode in Holland, as it were secretly whispering in his heart 'Seek ye My Face,' enabling him to answer his call, and to reflect upon his own soul, shewing him the evil of sin." With an assured spirit he sends word from the scaffold to his brother and sister that he is gone to Christ and will quickly meet them again in the glorious Mount Sion above. When one finds useful young men in such a state of mind as this, it is easy to sympathise with the indignation felt by Jeffreys towards the ministers of religion who had wrought upon their feelings to such a deplorable extent; and it becomes easier still if we bear in mind the fact—which cannot be too strongly insisted upon, even at the risk of repetition—that to Jeffreys, to all Tories and

---

[1] In quoting the figures of those tried and sentenced during the "Bloody Assizes," I have relied on those given in Roberts's *Life of the Duke of Monmouth*, which seems to be on the whole the most trustworthy.

to the prelates of the Church of England, this language, this fanaticism had only forty years past gone hand in hand with civil war and sanctified in glory the murder of a King. To-day, if not rhetorically or sentimentally minded, we can regard the fate of the Hewlings and other promising young men with a melancholy equanimity. Some few may be still inclined to shed tearful periods over their sad fates, a pleasure from which no one would willingly debar them ; but whatever we do, we must not forget that two hundred years ago most sensible men would consider the punishment of the Hewlings as well-merited and necessary, whilst to a vigorous hater of cant and sedition like Lord Jeffreys, it would give, to put it mildly, satisfaction.

Mr. Battiscomb, who suffered with William Hewling, had also served in the Duke's army. He was " very much a gentleman," according to his friends, but " not that thin sort of animal that flutters from tavern to play-house and back again all his life " ; he was not unlike Monmouth in appearance, and not displeasing to the fair sex ; in short, a most exemplary and altogether perfect young man. He was a barrister and had been arrested on suspicion at the time of the Rye House conspiracy. Jeffreys, according to Tutchin, railed and foamed at him, and he was condemned. He was very spiritual at the last, equally certain that a celestial paradise and a heavenly Jerusalem were awaiting him. Jeffreys is accused of having repulsed with a foul jest a young woman who came to beg Battiscomb's life. This incident gives Tutchin the opportunity for penning some indifferent lines, beginning—

> " Harder than thine own native rocks !
>   To let the charming Silvia kneel
>   And not one spark of pity feel ;
> Harder than senseless stones and stocks ! "

Later on Jeffreys is described as " by some Welsh wolf in murders nurst," and the poem dies meaningless away.

Like some of the stories about Kirke and his treatment of women, this anecdote of Jeffreys is either a modernised version of some older anecdote, or the invention of Tutchin's prurient mind which could never find one single fact worthy of the name to establish the charges of personal immorality or indecency he was perpetually levelling against Jeffreys. The only authentic testimony of the Judge's behaviour to suppliant women comes from Hannah Hewling. When she came to him to beg her brother's life, Jeffreys treated her with the greatest politeness and respect.

One other notable prisoner was tried at Dorchester, a youth of very different kidney from Hewling and Battiscomb. This was John Tutchin, who has been already described as the author of *The Bloody Assizes*. He had come over from Holland with Monmouth, but had escaped prosecution by calling himself "Thomas Pitts." Jeffreys, however, found out his real identity. Angry at being so outwitted, and well aware of all the particulars of his past conduct, the Chief Justice put him on his trial. Tutchin says he could have escaped if he would have given evidence against certain Hampshire gentlemen whom the Government desired to implicate in the rebellion. In any case, on his appearance at the bar, Jeffreys hailed him as a rebel from Adam, one of a family that never had any loyalty : "I understand you are a wit and a poet ; pray, sir, let you and I cap verses !" But Tutchin discreetly declined the invitation. He knew, he said, upon what ground he stood, and when he was overmatched. That he most certainly was. Jeffreys sentenced him to be imprisoned for seven years, and once a year to be whipped through every market town in Dorsetshire. On hearing the sentence many ladies in court burst into tears. Jeffreys turned to them : "Ladies, if you did but know what a villain this is as well as I do, you would say this sentence is not half bad enough for him." The Clerk of Arraigns represented to the Judge that there were so many market towns in Dorsetshire, that the sentence would amount to whipping once a fortnight, and that the prisoner was very young. "Aye," replied Jeffreys, "he's a young man but an old rogue ; and all the interest in England sha'n't reverse the sentence that I have passed upon him."

But Jeffreys did ultimately mitigate the sentence of

whipping, when the Deputy Sheriff of Devonshire assured him that there were many market towns by charter which were in reality little better than villages. In the meantime Tutchin petitioned the King in a rather impertinent fashion that he might be hanged instead of receiving such a whipping. "He must wait in patience," was Sunderland's answer. At length a timely attack of small-pox procured him a pardon, for which, he adds, his friends paid money to Jeffreys. But the account is not very clear on the latter point, and in his subsequent interview with the Judge in the Tower of London, Tutchin did not mention the circumstance, though he discussed the justice of his sentence. Tutchin's version of his sufferings in the *Western Martyrology* is curiously confused and lacking in precise detail considering how fully he should have been able to relate the circumstances and how great the ills he pretends to have endured.

It is, perhaps, on the whole a misfortune that Tutchin was not executed according to his request, along with so many better men. He was in every way a contemptible character, and only used his life to write a vile play and scurrilous attacks on the Tories, for one of which he was thrashed to death at the age of forty-four. His only public service was to afford by his pamphlet *The Foreigners* the opportunity to Defoe for his *True-born Englishman*, for which service Pope has sufficiently rewarded him in the couplet—

> "Careless on high stood unabashed Defoe,
>   And Tutchin, flagrant from the scourge, below."

Tutchin had the good taste to visit Jeffreys when the dreaded Chancellor was a prisoner in the Tower, and, in a Christian spirit that comes well from such a true Protestant martyr, to tell the fallen minister that he was glad to see him there. But it is satisfactory to know, on Tutchin's own authority, that, even in the hour of his humiliation, Jeffreys did not regret the sentence he had passed upon him. "You were a young man," he said, "and an enemy to the Government, and might live to do abundance of mischief." In taking such a view of his character, Jeffreys was perfectly correct, and he was not the only person who considered whipping to death none too little for John Tutchin. As to the actual sentence passed on him by Jeffreys, it is to be remembered that whippings of extreme severity were, as Lingard points out, frequent in those days, and gave a good deal of pleasure to the public, especially if the culprits were women. But it was, perhaps, a mistake to bestow on so poor a rascal as Tutchin a punishment that would have raised him to the dignity of an Oates.

From Dorchester about September 12th, the Judges set out for Exeter. During the journey the accidental discharge of a pistol among his suite is said to have considerably infuriated the Chief Justice, but in the county of Devonshire he found few prisoners on whom to vent his wrath. The deficiency of business at Exeter was more than atoned for at Taunton, where Jeffreys found 526 prisoners awaiting trial. Somersetshire had been Monmouth's principal recruiting ground, and Taunton and Wells between them could make up a calendar of over a thousand prisoners.

At Taunton, out of the 526, some 144 were executed, and 284 transported. On the subject of transportation Jeffreys wrote to the King. In those days it was considered lawful that prisoners taken in rebellion who had been spared the extreme penalty and sentenced to transportation, should be given to favoured individuals as gifts or rewards for loyalty, to be either ransomed at their profit, or sold by them to West Indian planters as little better than slaves. James had bestowed quantities of these prisoners on his friends at the Court, and Jeffreys now wrote to put in a humble plea on behalf of the loyal gentry of the West, who would seem to have been sadly neglected in this respect. "If," he wrote, " your Majesty orders these prisoners to be disposed of as you have already designed, persons that have not suffered in your service will run away with the booty, and I am sure your Majesty will be perpetually perplexed with petitions for recompenses for sufferers as well as rewards for servants." And he continues : "Had not your Majesty been pleased to declare your gracious intentions (in the matter of these prisoners) to them that served in the soldiery, and also to the many depressed families ruined by this late rebellion, I should not have presumed to have given your Majesty this trouble." Setting aside the unpleasantness of this method of rewarding adherents, Jeffreys is to be commended for his attempt to turn the stream of reward into its proper channel, and for his courage in remonstrating with the King himself, however submissive the terms he employed. It is also to be observed from his letter that Monmouth's adherents were not the only sufferers by the rebellion, as most historians would seem to persuade us. The true Protestant rebels had managed in their short reign of glory to do a good deal of damage to the property of the Papists and the loyal Churchmen and Tories in their neighbourhood.

At Taunton Jeffreys condemned the elder Hewling, Benjamin. He went to his death exuberantly joyful and with full assurance of the eternal heaven awaiting him. So great was the confidence of these martyrs in their ultimate salvation, that "some of the most malicious in Taunton, from whom nothing but railing was to be expected," were heard to say that "these persons had left a sufficient evidence that they were now saints in heaven." The fact that the horses refused to draw the sledge which was to convey Hewling to the scaffold, was accounted by many a miracle.

Another sufferer was one Simon Hamlyn. He was said to have been convicted on perjured evidence concocted against him by a Justice who hated him for a Dissenter. After his conviction the Justice repented of his sin, and told Jeffreys that the conviction had been wrongly obtained. "You have brought him on," replied the Judge, "if he be innocent, his blood be upon you ;" and the Justice departed into outer darkness.

One other case at Taunton deserves notice. A youth named William Jenkins was condemned and executed for having fought in Monmouth's army. Sunderland had written to Jeffreys on September 12th, asking him to show favour to Jenkins if he could do so without prejudice to the King's service. Apparently Jeffreys did not see his way to accede to Sunderland's request, and Jenkins was hanged. Roberts, in his *Life of Monmouth*, a very careful and useful work in many respects, observes : " It really appears that Jeffreys delighted in blood," and quotes Jenkins's execution, in spite of Sunderland's intercession, as the illustration of the Judge's bloodthirsty disposition. Why Jeffreys should have imperatively yielded to Sunderland's request does not appear. He may well have considered that Jenkins's pardon would have been an unfair exercise of clemency prejudicial to his Majesty's service ; and in the absence of all details as to the merits of the case except that Jenkins had fought in the rebel army, the case may quite as well be cited as an example of Jeffreys' unwillingness to allow any personal consideration to interfere with the strict administration of justice according to his principles. But to say that because he refused to oblige Sunderland, he appears a rejoicer in blood, is a childish inference.

It is generally stated that after leaving Taunton, Jeffreys went on to Wells, but in his letter to the King, quoted above, and written from Taunton, September 19th, he writes that he leaves for Bristol on Monday, and then goes to Wells. Monday was the 21st, and the same day, after a long and tiresome journey, he opened the Commission at Bristol. The 21st of September was a terrible day for the Mayor and Aldermen of that fat city. There were no prisoners to be tried for the rebellion, but there was a mighty ill-reckoning to be settled between the Corporation and the Lord Chief Justice. Not only were most of the Aldermen factious Whigs enough, who were only restrained by want of numbers from opening their gates to Monmouth, but a practice of kidnapping had grown up among these greedy merchants. Not content with the customary profits to be made out of such criminals as had their sentences of death commuted to transportation, the Mayor and Aldermen had increased their gains by terrifying petty criminals whose offences were not legally punishable by death, into an idea that they would be hanged, and so inducing them to pray for transportation as a merciful alternative.   By this device the city merchants were enabled to send out annually large consignments of prisoners to work their West Indian estates.   Jeffreys, hearing of this practice, had made inquiry into it, and fully resolved of its prevalence, determined to teach these avaricious magistrates a wholesome and never-to-be-forgotten lesson.   As he left Taunton a fit of the stone had seized on him with increased violence.   His torments being cruelly aggravated by the unevenness of the road from Taunton to Bristol, the Chief Justice by the time he arrived at his destination was in a condition of temper, which the sight of the kidnapping magistrates, coming out to receive him in their red robes of office, soon worked into a state of raving fury. No sooner had he taken his seat on the Bench, the court thronged with an expectant audience, the red-robed kidnappers seated apprehensively on each side of him, than he flew at the throat of the city of Bristol.   By the mercy of God, he began, he was come to this city, the second in the kingdom.   " Gentlemen, I find here are a great many auditors who are very intent, as if they expected some formal or prepared speech ; but assure yourselves, we come not to make neither set speeches, nor formal declamations, nor to follow a couple of puffing trumpeters, for, Lord, we have seen these things twenty times before."   All the stately efforts of the Corporation to be summed up as a " couple of puffing trumpeters " ! A woful day indeed for Bristol !   After casually remarking that women governed and bore sway in the city, he continued ominously : " For points and matters of law I shall not trouble you, but only mind you of some things that have lately happened, and particularly in this city—for I have the kalendar of this city in my pocket ; " and, he went on, if he did not express himself in formal and set terms, they might put it down to the pain of the stone and the bad roads.

Then, in violent and disjointed language, full of parentheses and repetitions—five times he uses the expression " rebellion is like the sin of witchcraft "—he denounced the conspiracies of the past and praised the excellence of the King, though he went so far as to describe James " as a King, I will assure you, that will not be worse than his word—nay (pardon the expression), that dare not be worse than his word." If this expression was carried to Whitehall, it cannot have been very much to James's liking.

The Chief Justice then addressed himself to Bristol in particular. He told the city he was afraid there were too many rebelliously inclined within its walls—" your Tylys, your Roes and your Wades—men started up like mushrooms—scoundrel fellows, mere sons of dunghills ! these men, forsooth, must set up for liberty and property. . . . I have brought a brush in my pocket, and I shall be sure to rub the dirt wherever it is, or on whomsoever it sticks. Gentlemen, I shall not stand complimenting with you, I shall talk with some of you before you and I part. I tell you, I tell you I have brought a besom, and I will sweep every man's door, whether great or small." First he fell upon the Trimmers of the City. Trimmers, he said, were merely base-spirited Whigs. " These men stink worse than the worst dirt you have in your city ; these men have so little religion," he sneered, " that they forget that he that is not for us is against us. But enough of complimenting ! Come, come, gentlemen, to be plain with you, I find the dirt in the ditch is in your nostrils. Good God ! where am I ? In Bristol ? I find you need a commission once a month at least. The very magistrates, that should be the ministers of justice, fall out with one another to that degree that they will scarce dine with each other ; whilst it is the business of some cunning men that lie behind the curtain to raise divisions amongst them, and set them together by the ears and knock their loggerheads together ; yet I find they can agree for their interests. Or if it be but a *kid* in the case (for I hear the trade of kidnapping is in much request in this city), they can discharge a felon or a traitor, provided they will go to Mr. Alderman's plantation at the West Indies. Come, come, I find you stink for want of rubbing."

He then reprimanded the Aldermen for showing favour to Dissenters in the administration of justice. He did not spare the clergy, " amongst whom he heard there were differences," " those that ought to preach peace and unity to others." "Gentlemen, these things must be looked into." Then, turning to the Mayor and Aldermen, who sat by his side : " Sir, Mr. Mayor, you I mean, kidnapper, and an old Justice of the Peace on the Bench (alluding to one of the Aldermen), I do not know him, old knave ; he goes to the tavern for a pint of sack, he will bind people servants to the Indies in the tavern. A kidnapping knave ! I will have his ears off before I go forth out of town. Well, read that paper ! " (addressing the Town Clerk, who read a case in which the Mayor had tried to send a pickpocket to Jamaica). Jeffreys resumed : " Kidnapper, you, I mean ! Sir, do you see the keeper of Newgate ? If it was not in respect of the sword which is over your head, I would send you to Newgate, you kidnapping knave, you are worse than the pickpockets that stand there (pointing to the bar). I hope you are men of worth. I will make you pay sufficiently for it." With that he charged the Grand Jury to find true bills for kidnapping against the Mayor and certain of the Aldermen, and as soon as the jury had done so, ordered the accused to come from the Bench in their robes and their fur, and plead at the bar like common criminals. If the astonished Mayor hesitated on the way, or slackened his pace, the Chief Justice bawled and jeered at him, " See how the kidnapping rogue looks ! " with other taunting expressions. When finally he departed from Bristol, he took with him a list of the offending citizens, with a view to their further prosecution.

Among the proscribed was Sir Robert Cann, a loyal Alderman, who, without participating in the illegal traffic of his colleagues, had sat by in silence whilst it was carried on.   The old gentleman hurried up to London after the Chief Justice in great trepidation, and went at once to the house of his son-in-law, who happened to be Sir Dudley North, the brother of the late Lord Keeper, to beg him to intercede with Jeffreys.   This Dudley consented to do.   Taking with them Roger, who, being at the bar and a King's Counsel, might the better plead with the Judge, the three went to Jeffreys' house.   They were shown into his presence, and Roger did his best to extenuate Sir Robert's share in the matter.   For some time Jeffreys stared at them and dwelt on the enormity of the offence and the necessity of exemplary punishment.   At last, however, he was melted and, turning to Sir Robert, said : " For these two gentlemen's sakes I pardon you for this time ; but go your way and sin no more lest a worse thing come unto you."

Poor old Sir Robert never really recovered the distress of mind induced by his alarming predicament.   He gave up sherry for small beer at a time when his constitution was too matured to endure such a signal change of diet, and died soon after his return to Bristol.   But being a Tory, he has not been accounted among the martyrs to Jeffreys' cruelty.

The fact that a loyal Tory like Sir Robert Cann was included in the intended prosecution of the Bristol kid-nappers goes to show that Jeffreys' attack on them was not a purely political move.   The Chief Justice was well known for his skill in detecting abuses and for the vigour he always showed in denouncing those whom he found guilty of trickery or dishonesty.   But he was not often in the habit of using such language as that in which he rated the Mayor and Aldermen.   He has himself, however, furnished the explanation for his peculiar freedom of expression on that occasion, which those who have ever suffered as he did will thoroughly appreciate.   Those who have not, must exercise their imaginations.

On September 22nd, Jeffreys wrote to Sunderland an account of his proceedings at Bristol.

" I am just now come," he writes, " my most honourable Lord, from discharging my duty to his most sacred Majesty, in executing his commission in this his most factious city, for, my Lord, to be plain, on my true affection and honour to your lordship and my allegiance and duty to my Royal Master, I think this city worse than Taunton." Though " harassed by the day's fatigues and mortified with a fit of the stone," he acquaints the King with his proceeding against the Mayor and Aldermen, and begs his Majesty not to be surprised into a pardon to any man though he pretend much to loyalty—this looks like an allusion to Cann—but to wait until he himself has the honour to kiss his hand. " I will pawn my life," he goes on, " and what is dearer to me, my loyalty, that Taunton and Bristol and the county of Somerset too shall know their duty both to God and their King before I leave them, and in a few days don't despair to perfect the work I was sent about." For the particulars of Taunton Assizes he refers Sunderland to Lord Churchill who was present there. He has received his Majesty's commands as to the disposal of the transported convicts, and they were evidently not to his liking, for, he adds, " the messengers seem to me too impetuous for a hasty compliance. And now, lest, my dearest Lord, you should be afflicted by further trouble as I am at this time by pain, I will only say that I am "—and then he is Lord Sunderland's most dutiful, grateful, &c., &c. servant, Jeffreys.

There now remained but one city that required to be further taught its duty to God and the King, and that was the city of Wells. Here there were some 500 for trial, of whom 99 were executed and 283 transported. Here also Jeffreys is said to have frightened to death one of the maids of Taunton by the fierceness of his glance. Among the condemned prisoners was Mr. Charles Speke, brother of Hugh Speke whose trial before Jeffreys with Laurence Braddon has been already described. Coming of a Whig family who had received Monmouth with encouragement—his brother

John fought in his army—the fact that Charles Speke had shaken hands with the Duke was quite enough to hang him. It is also said that Jeffreys and Jones, the Chief Justice of the Common Pleas, coveted the disposal of a legal office held by Speke. Not that, in suffering death for so small a trespass, Speke was being treated with exceptional severity. At Taunton one man was tried for saying he would not go to church till Monmouth came, another for expressing a hope as a well-wisher that Monmouth was not dead, another for saying he was for Monmouth and God and would fight for the former as long as he lived. I do not find that any of these men were hanged, but shaking hands is a step further than mere lip worship.

One other case of importance was tried by Jeffreys at the city of Wells. The culprit was John Coad, described by Macaulay as an "honest God-fearing carpenter" This honest God-fearing man had deserted from the King's army and joined the Duke's colours, "less than which argument" he says in his *Memorandum of God's Wonderful Providence* to him "was enough to make the lion's whelp, Jeffreys, to roar against, yea, to damn me." He was not unreasonably condemned to death by the "bloody hero" of a Judge; but, not being of the stuff of which martyrs are made, he tried to bribe an officer to get him transported instead. The attempt failed; but, "Jehovah-Jireh being on his side" he contrived to change sentences with a fellow prisoner who was tired of life and willing to exchange transportation for death. And so this honest God-fearing man was preserved from the fury of "the bloody Popish Judge, the merciless monster Jeffreys." A carpenter of this vehemently religious type might nowadays be esteemed honest and God-fearing among intemperate sectarians, and would certainly be considered a harmless nuisance among sober people, but in the seventeenth century he was, in the eyes of the Government, a dangerous rebel who was better out of the way. In either century he deserved to be hanged or shot as a deserter.

So ended the "Bloody Assizes." From Wells Jeffreys

returned to London, and on October 3rd, he and his brother Judges kissed the King's hand and publicly received his thanks for their services. In the meantime, on September 28th, his Majesty, "taking into consideration the many eminent and faithful services which the Right Honourable George Lord Jeffreys of Wem, Lord Chief Justice of England, had rendered the Crown, as well in the reign of the late King of ever blessed memory as since his Majesty's accession to the throne, was pleased this day to commit to him the custody of the great Seal of England, with the title of Lord Chancellor." Charles II. had told North when he gave him the Seal that he would find it heavy. The story goes that a boon companion over a bottle of wine, gave Jeffreys a similar warning, to which the new Chancellor jestingly replied : "No, I'll make it light." Perhaps, if Charles had given the warning, Jeffreys would not have laughed it aside so easily ; at any rate, as things turned out the King's prognostication would have been nearer the truth than the Judge's thoughtless jest. Jeffreys had coveted the seal as eagerly as North ; both were comparatively young when they received it, North forty-five, Jeffreys thirty-seven ; but they both died within four years of taking office, considerably the worse for their precious trophy.

Before leaving the "Bloody Assizes," one or two facts remain to be considered.

The Government was vastly strengthened in public estimation by the suppression of the rebellion. To all sensible men it had appeared as the vain and unworthy adventure of a weak man, led on to his doom by a set of mischievous fanatics. The Church viewed it with bitter hostility and publicly rejoiced in its destruction ; they called it the "Dissenting Rebellion" and warmly supported the civil authorities in taking severe measures against the Nonconformists. The Bishop of Exeter, Dr. Lamplugh, a devoted loyalist, directed his clergy to publish a document drawn up by the county magistrates, in which the Dissenters are spoken of as a "pestilent faction, as impenitent, hardened sectaries, schismatics or rebels," the mischievous seducers of the unwary; the sword of justice is to be kept still unsheathed—this was in October—that the nation may not again experience the fatal effects of too much lenity. It would be instructive after this to know the Bishop of Exeter's opinion of Jeffreys. If the *Bloody Assizes* is to be as implicitly believed as it has been hitherto by the most distinguished historians of the period, the parsons were no whit better, in fact rather worse, than Jeffreys, and should have been included in their indignant censures. " But the greatest persecutors and insulters of these poor people," writes the author of the *Martyrologies*, " were the country parsons." They did not preach to the spirits in prison, but they reviled them. One of them, when he heard some condemned persons in prayer just before their execution, said : " These fellows will pray the devil out of hell ; and the prison was seldom free from black-coats." Another clergyman of the Church of England, he writes, ordered a boy, whom Jeffreys had condemned to be whipped, to be flogged a second time over because a merciful gaoler had not laid it on hard enough the first time ; and on the second occasion the boy was nearly beaten to death.

But it is really better on the whole, considering the many respectable interests involved, that the *Bloody Assizes* should not be treated as too serious an authority, even at the risk of over-indulging "Judge Jeffreys." It would be wiser to accept the testimony of Archdeacon Echard, who admits that the conduct of the Western prisoners tended rather to exasperate their Judges than to move them to compassion. The comment of an anonymous author of a pamphlet written against the Whigs, is also instructive. " I have indeed sometimes thought that in Jeffreys' Western Circuit, justice went too far before mercy was remembered, though there was not a fourth part executed of what were convicted. But when I consider in what manner several of these lives then spared were afterwards spent, I can but think a little more hemp might have been usefully employed upon that occasion."

A question that has been warmly discussed is the relative share of the King and Jeffreys in the cruelties of the Western Assizes. Jeffreys, at the time of his imprisonment in the Tower, pleaded that he had not been severe enough according to his instructions, and was snubbed on his return to London for being too lenient. James, on the other hand, when he was anxious after his flight to conciliate public opinion, said that he was not aware of the lengths to which Jeffreys had gone, and had suffered in the public estimation from the excessive conduct of the Chief Justice. As to Jeffreys' plea it may be said, that if by his acts he fell short of the royal commands, by the severity of his personal behaviour he more than atoned for any remissness in other respects. That he did act on very particular instructions is proved by his own letters and his frequent reports of his proceedings. James's plea is easily disposed of. A King who writes delightedly of his Judge's assize as a "campaign," who will only remit the burning of Alice Lisle if he can be satisfied of a precedent for doing so, and whom Lord Churchill described to Hannah Hewling as the equal in compassion to a piece of marble, was not likely to be very distressed at any of Jeffreys' proceedings. But Thomas, Earl of Ailesbury, is the most damaging witness against James. A loyal Tory, the Earl was shocked at the severities practised in the West, and personally protested against them to the King himself. James's replies not being very satisfactory, the Earl bluntly remarked : "Your Majesty ought to turn out the Justice (Jeffreys) and Mr. Percy Kirke, and that will show the world your true abhorrence." Better advice could not have been given ; but Kirke remained a Brigadier-General and the Justice was made Lord High Chancellor of England. Comment is superfluous. James's plea of ignorance is either a falsehood on his part or a myth invented by his friends.

The truth is that James II. and Lord Jeffreys were a most unfortunate combination to be entrusted with the suppression of a rebellion ; they reacted fatally on one another. The cold implacability of the one was supplemented by the "great and fiery passion" of the other ; the still resentment of the King was augmented by the loud and mocking virulence of the Judge. Those who escaped the fiery darts of Jeffreys were shattered against the marble of James's heart.

And what rewards, as an earnest Judge and loyal servant, did Jeffreys receive for his work in the West ? He received £1,416 10s. from the Crown Solicitors, presumably as circuit expenses, the office of Lord Chancellor, and Mr. Edmund Prideaux. Mr. Prideaux was given to Jeffreys, as Azariah Primly was "given" to Mr. Nephir, and the Taunton maids to the Queen's maids of honour—that is to say, as a prisoner whose friends could ransom him by paying the money to the person to whom he had been "given." Prideaux was an ardent supporter of the country party and the Dissenters ; but, though no doubt fully sympathising with Monmouth he had remained peaceably at home during the rebellion. His house had been visited by some of the Duke's soldiers, one of whom drank a health to his leader ; but nothing more could be proved against him. However, he was arrested, released on heavy bail and then re-arrested and lodged in the Tower in close confinement. Jeffreys had threatened to hang him, and the Judge's agents did all they could to rake up evidence against him. Jeffreys was determined to make the most of his gift ; the stronger the evidence against Prideaux, the heavier could be the price demanded for a pardon. In vain Mrs. Prideaux applied to the King. The answer came back that the "King had given him to Jeffreys." £7,000 were offered to the Judge ; he only replied that he wondered how any one could speak for so vile a person who deserved to be hanged. £10,000 were offered and declined. At last £15,000 were paid, subject to £240 discount on prompt payment ; and Prideaux was released. Jeffreys purchased some property in Leicestershire with the profits of the negotiation.

The immorality of Prideaux's treatment is so obvious and has been so repeatedly dwelt upon, that there is no need to enforce it. It was the natural outcome of the prevailing idea that injustice was fair dealing towards those disaffected to the Crown, an idea which causes a painful impression when it is found upon the judgment-seat. Ministers and courtiers and maids of honour may traffic in pardons with comparative decency ; but a Lord Chief Justice, whatever his political antipathies, should avoid such incongruous barter. If, however, his financial position is in any way difficult, the sense of incongruity would no doubt become less obtrusive.

Jeffreys should have remained in his doctor's hands, instead of going the Western Circuit. He was not in a fit state of health to administer justice, especially on such a rough and extensive scale as that designed in the King's Commission. Though, substantially, little injustice may have been done, and one may be inclined to agree with the author of the *Caveat*, that none too much hemp was employed in the proceeding, Jeffreys, by the awful intensity which his passionate disposition acquired in the agony of his body, so aggravated the well-merited distresses of the rebels as to make it easy for such as Tutchin to bestow on them the crown of martyrdom and load the Chief Justice with coarse and virulent abuse. This abuse has lived and been his portion for two hundred years ; it has been literally and authoritatively accepted by the most popular historians, and out of it has sprung the Jeffreys of still more popular romance. It is not the object of this work to demolish this figure, to destroy one of the most cherished bogies of fireside history ; but if there exists a real and living Jeffreys, a human being and not a monstrous puppet dressed up to frighten children and confiding adults, the true purposes of history may be in some slight measure served by an attempt to reduce the monster to human proportions.

XVI

THE LORD HIGH CHANCELLOR

1685, 1686

THE conferment of the Chancellorship on Jeffreys was the zenith of his career. He had reached the highest honour in his profession, his power was feared and acknowledged, and he belonged to a Government that recent events had made the strongest since the Restoration. How in three years that Government fell, its opportunities wasted by a rash and obstinate King, how his Chancellor fell with him to die in misery and disgrace, these are well-known facts of history. The period has been treated by more than one master of the art of historical narrative ; and nothing but a painful sense of inferiority is likely to accrue from any attempt to reproduce more than its general features in so far as they may concern the career of Jeffreys. In his history these years are a period of anti-climax. To a certain extent the Chancellor passes behind the curtain, his acts and thoughts are hidden from our view. The nature of his new office does not bring him into the same public prominence as that of the Chief Justiceship ; his appearance in the pages of the *State Trials* are few and far between ; his performances as a Judge are entirely limited to his equity jurisdiction in the Court of Chancery, and his part in the Government is played in the Council Chamber or the King's closet. Contemporary memoirs and the despatches of Barillon afford an occasional evidence of the Chancellor's share in the counsels of the King ; but under his own hand or out of his own mouth there is the scantiest testimony to his motives or his conduct.

If it were possible to describe briefly the policy pursued by the Chancellor during the reign of James II., it would be that of absolute obedience to the King's conception of his own prerogative, even when that obedience conflicted with his most cherished principles. He has himself said that in pursuing this line he did his best to serve as much as possible the interests of the Church of England, to which with his last breath he protested his devotion ; but so far these assurances have met with little credit. No doubt, like Sunderland, with whom at first he seems to have worked, he aimed at keeping his own power above all things, and hoped by devotion to the King to secure it. But at the end of the reign he certainly used his influence to persuade James to restore things to the condition in which they were at his accession to the throne ; and on more than one occasion he is found withstanding or openly disapproving some of James's extreme measures. Perhaps for that reason his position was frequently insecure, for James always expected the blindest obedience from his followers. Rumours of his fall were frequently abroad throughout the reign. But he weathered the storms, and, if James had not been so thoroughly irrational, might have ridden safely into port and died quietly in his bed, Lord Chancellor of England. But, hopelessly committed to the King's cause, the King at his flight left him behind ; and, baulked in his own efforts to escape, he fell into the hands of his enemies, from whose resentment he was only extricated by a timely death.

The voices of Jeffreys' admirers were not silent on his elevation to the Chancellorship. The contemplation of his picture threw one poet into signal raptures. He sings—

> "An aspect open and a brow that's clear,
> Without the flattering, sly, insidious leer,
> A front that's awful ; yet a friend may see
> The truest signs of affability."

Jeffreys as Lord Chancellor,
after a Painting in the possession
of the Earl of Tankerville.

And then in lines that might have been well applied to the prisoners in the West—

> "An eye so keen, what villain can have sense
> Pierced by its terror to plead innocence?"

Jeffreys is the "bulwark of the nation's laws" and has done more for England than Solon or Lycurgus did for Athens or Sparta.

But to Joshua Barnes, M.A., a Senior Fellow of Emmanuel College, Cambridge, may be allotted the highest place among Jeffreys' worshippers. His Pindaric *Congratulation* begins—

> "Great Jeffreys, yet not half so great as good,
> How little was thy worth once understood,
>   How lay it unrevealed
> Like a rich gem in dirty mines concealed,
> When by the mobile so much abused!"

But Mr. Barnes had not gone far enough in simile, he corrects himself to some purpose—

> "Or rather then, how was thy virtue known
> And dreaded by the vice-empoisoned town,
> Who thee (as sinful Jews the Saviour once) refused."

Not satisfied with invoking the story of Christ as a fitting comparison for Jeffreys' want of public recognition, he next addresses the King, and informs him that in spite of his many noble qualities his greatest praise will be that he was Jeffreys' friend. Then he returns to the Chancellor, with a metaphor borrowed from the destruction of the octopus—

> "Well did thy wisely pruning hand,
> Lop off the suckers of the Western land."

And concludes by declaring that monarchy shall endure against all storms, "till Jeffreys' fame's asleep and Time itself is past."

It would be interesting to know what snug preferment Joshua Barnes received for these modest compliments to the Lord Chancellor, and what the latter thought of a production of this kind. An anonymous and violently hostile writer says that Jeffreys loved flattery, and enjoyed nothing better than to be surrounded by sycophants to whom he could hold forth on Philosophy and Mathematics. Jeffreys on Mathematics strikes one as rather a pleasant conceit !

But Jeffreys' Chancellorship was not celebrated only in terms of congratulation. The author of *The Dream* writes in a very different strain ; the Jesuits are caballing to root out English heresy—

> "Immediately they pitch'd upon a rule,
> How to suppress it by a forward fool,
> A bawling, blundering, senseless tool,
> Whose mouthing at Whitechapel first began,
> Who regularly to his greatness ran
> Thro' all the vile degrees of treachery,
> And now usurps the Court of Equity."

Or the author of the *True Englishman*, 1686, possibly Mr. Tutchin, whose denunciatory style is always conspicuous for a certain merciless vigour—

> "Let a lewd Judge come reeking from a wench
> To vent a wilder lust upon the Bench ;
> Bawl out the venom of his rotten heart,
> Swell'd up with envy, over act his part.
> Condemn the innocent by laws ne'er framed,
> And study to be more than doubly damn'd."

Tasteful productions of this kind were always present to remind the Chancellor that he was not universally beloved and admired, whatever his sycophants might assure him.

But there were things more serious than flattering rhapsody or frantic abuse awaiting the attention of the new Chancellor. Early in October Jeffreys issued his first batch of judicial appointments. A new Chief Justice of the King's Bench had to be appointed in his own place, and a puisne Judge in the same Court to supply the place of Mr. Justice Walcot, recently deceased. The man selected as Lord Chief Justice of England was Sir Edward Herbert, son of a former Sir Edward Herbert who had been Lord Chancellor to Charles II. during his exile. Herbert was not a strong lawyer, but he was honest and loyal, highly respected by those politically opposed to him, and known to have strong views as to the extent of the royal prerogative. The second appointment, in which Jeffreys would have had more influence, was not so respectable. Mr. Baron Wright, the Chancellor's shady dependent, was promoted from the Court of Exchequer to fill Walcot's seat in the King's Bench. Sir Edward Nevil, a loyal Tory, succeeded Wright in the Exchequer.

According to custom, on October 23rd Jeffreys took his place in the Court of Chancery with the usual pomp. Rochester and Clarendon, the Lord Treasurer and Lord Privy Seal, Sunderland and other peers accompanied the new Chancellor into court, and stayed while he heard his first motion. Later in the day the new Chancellor delivered the customary address to the new Chief Justice on admitting him to his office. He first thanked the Bar for the kind assistance they had always given him while he had held that office ; "they did not," he said, " prate impertinently to please the audience ; for if we met any such, they were sure to meet with a rebuke." He then exhorted Herbert : " Be undaunted and courageous ; be sure to execute the law to the utmost of its vengeance upon those that are known—and we have reason to remember them—by the name of Whigs ! and you are likewise to remember the snivelling Trimmers ! For you know," he continued, reverting to a quotation he had already used in his address at Bristol, " what our Saviour Jesus Christ says in the Gospel, that ' They that are not for us are against us '." Herbert was also to be kind and affectionate to the Bar and the inferior magistrates, " though, perhaps," with regard to the latter, they have not arrived to that perfection in the knowledge of the law which is a good fortune of a particular education in the profession." " In fine, sir," he concluded, " as the sum of all your duty, fear God and honour the King; but," with one last stroke at the Whigs, " use your utmost authority for the suppression of those that are given to change." His duty discharged, the Chancellor afterwards dined with the new Chief Justice at Serjeants' Inn.

A few nights later he had the pleasure of dining with his old friend Alderman Sir Robert Jeffreys, the "Great Smoker," who had so kindly helped his young namesake in his early days and had just been elected Lord Mayor of London for the ensuing year. The Chancellor's influence had probably helped to secure Sir Robert's election. His power in the City appears to have been unlimited. The outgoing Mayor, Sir James Smith, had complained bitterly to Reresby of Jeffreys' haughtiness and authority ; he said that the City had no access to or communication with the King save through the medium of the powerful favourite ; but, he added, his haughtiness would undo him, for Smith meant to acquaint the King in due season with his Chancellor's arrogant behaviour.

In the Court of Chancery Jeffreys soon discovered a great deal that was unsatisfactory or dishonest, for in November he committed to the Fleet prison a registrar, two or three clerks and a lawyer or two, and suspended a Master in Chancery from his place. It may be that the lawyer in question was the same of whom Roger North relates an amusing anecdote. A petition had been presented in Chancery against a City attorney, charging him with some abuse of his functions, and an affidavit was produced before Jeffreys in which it was stated that the attorney, on hearing that he was to be brought before the Chancellor, had exclaimed : "My Lord Chancellor ? I *made* him ! " meaning thereby that he had given Jeffreys work in his early days. The affidavit was read to Jeffreys. "Well," said my Lord Chancellor, "then I'll lay my maker by the heels ; " and the attorney was immediately sent to gaol. About the same time his lordship gave the College of Physicians a bit of his mind for not surrendering their Charter into the King's hands with becoming zeal.

On November 20th Jeffreys, at the King's direction, prorogued the Parliament, which had not proved satisfactory, and never met again during the reign ; so that in this Parliament, Jeffreys made his only appearance as a member of the House of Lords. Ralph, a very hostile historian, says that Jeffreys was a complete failure as a parliamentary speaker, because he adopted an Old Bailey style of oratory which the Lords resented. But there is no report of the debates from which we can form any judgment of Jeffreys' style; he was probably sensible enough to adapt it to the occasion. His conduct at Lord Delamere's trial before the peers in the following year showed him very well able to hold his own with dignity and firmness before that august body.

That trial had been fixed to take place in January, 1686. Delamere, the Mr. Booth of the Parliament of 1680, is described by Lord Ailesbury as a "man of implacable spirit against the King and Crown, and of a most sour temper of mind." There can be little doubt that he was deep in the Whig designs, and that he was ready to utilise his influence in Cheshire against the Government, if a suitable opportunity occurred; in 1688 he was one of the first to join William of Orange with an armed force drawn from that county. The Government determined to include him in the prosecutions they instituted against one or two of the most dangerous Whigs, after the suppression of Monmouth's rebellion. Cornish had already suffered, and Delamere was, if it were legally possible, to share a similar fate. As a peer he had the right to be tried by his peers; but since Parliament was not sitting in January he was summoned before the Court of the Lord High Steward, which, for judicial purposes, took the place of the full House of Lords when Parliament was prorogued or dissolved. This Court consisted of a certain number of peers who were summoned by the Lord High Steward to act as "triers" on the particular occasion. The Lord High Steward was himself appointed only for the purpose of the trial, at the conclusion of which he broke his staff as a sign that his Commission was at an end. He did not vote with the lords "triers" in giving their verdict, but acted as Judge of the Court, with the assistance of the ordinary common law Judges. The Lord Chancellor was almost invariably the peer chosen to act as Steward, and in this case the King appointed Lord Jeffreys. It was singular that Jeffreys should have been Delamere's Judge. It will be remembered that it was Lord Delamere, then Mr. Booth and a member of the House of Commons, who, in 1680, had described in such indignant terms Jeffreys' conduct as Chief Justice of Chester, declaring that he behaved like a jack-pudding, and blessing God that he, Mr. Booth, was not a man of such principles and behaviour. The strange chances of seventeenth-century politics had oddly reversed the positions of the two men. Booth had been Jeffreys' Judge five years before, when the Recorder was punished by the indignant Commons; now, Jeffreys, Lord High Chancellor of England and a peer of the realm, sat in judgment on Lord Delamere.

And Jeffreys bore himself worthily in these altered circumstances. He neither forgot the dignity of his high office nor the respect due to himself as holding that office. His enemies have said that he was overawed by the presence of his fellow peers, and behaved well because he was afraid to behave otherwise. On the contrary, he showed equal firmness in dealing with the prisoner or his peers when thy attempted to usurp or meddle with his proper functions. The trial itself is not interesting. Delamere was charged with organising a rising in Chester to co-operate with Monmouth on his landing. The evidence against him depended almost entirely on the testimony of a witness named Saxon, who was shown to be clearly perjured ; and Delamere was acquitted.

At the beginning of the trial the prisoner put in a plea to the effect that, as Parliament was only prorogued and not dissolved, it was still " continuing " and so he ought to be tried by the whole House of Peers, and not in the Court of the Lord High Steward. After hearing Lord Delamere and the Attorney-General argue the point, Jeffreys as Judge of the Court pronounced the plea to be "frivolous." Delamere cunningly endeavoured to insinuate that Jeffreys was slighting the privilege of the peers. "My Lord, I hope the privilege of the peers of England is not frivolous." Jeffreys answered him : " Pray, good my lord, do not think that I should say any such thing that the privilege of the peers is frivolous. As I would not willingly mistake you, so I desire your lordship would not misapprehend or misrepresent me, I spoke not at all of the peers' privilege, but of your plea." Jeffreys' patience encouraged Delamere to be presumptuous. " I hope, your Grace," he went on, " will be pleased to advise with my lords the peers here present, it being upon a point of privilege." But Jeffreys was quick to teach his lordship his place : " Good my lord, I hope you, that are a prisoner at the bar, are not to give me direction who I should advise with or how I should demean myself here." Delamere was wise enough to see his mistake and made suitable apologies. However, as he still tried to continue the argument, Jeffreys was obliged to silence him : " My lord, you must pardon me ; I can enter into no further interlocutions with your lordship."

Later in the course of the trial the question arose whether the Court could adjourn in the middle of the case until the following morning. Jeffreys consulted the Judges, and came to the conclusion that he could not allow an adjournment, as the legal right to do so seemed doubtful. The peers claimed the right to decide the question for themselves, as it was a matter concerning their privilege. Jeffreys positively refused to admit their claim. " My lords, I confess I would always be very tender of the privileges of the peers wherever I find them concerned ; but truly I apprehend, according to the best of my understanding, that this Court is held before me. It is my warrant that convenes the prisoner to the bar. It is my summons that brings the peers together to try him, and so I take myself to be Judge of the Court." Lord Campbell quotes this very proper assertion of the High Steward's authority as an instance of Jeffreys' habitual arrogance.

In concluding his short charge to the peers, Jeffreys expressed his dissatisfaction with Saxon's evidence. The King, who was present during the trial, was much enraged against the lying witness, and threatened him with Oates' fate. The same month Parliament was further prorogued till May.

James was now bent on getting the judgment of his courts of law in favour of his power of dispensing with the penal laws against the Catholics. He wished, when next he met the Parliament, to be fortified with a legal decision in his favour. Accordingly, Jeffreys was instructed to sound the Judges as to their opinions on this question, and, following out the " reductio ad absurdum " method in judicial decisions which had always been employed as long as the King held the right of dismissing his Judges at will, to remove those whose opinions were contrary to the royal claim. Two puisnes, Levinz and Gregory, were already known to be unfavourable, and were removed without being consulted at all. Their places were filled by Serjeant Bedingfield, the timorous person who had been scared by Jeffreys out of accepting a judgeship at the hands of Lord Keeper North, and Thomas Jenner, the Recorder of London, of whom Rosewell at his trial had spoken with not unmerited contempt.

In the midst of these proceedings the Lord Chancellor was temporarily incapacitated for work by a severe and almost fatal attack of the stone, from which he was only delivered by some kind of operation ; for, says Luttrell, " he is since, by the use of means, pretty well recovered." The peculiar severity of the attack was partly due to hard drinking, in itself a consequence of the disease. Jeffreys once admitted that he was compelled to drink a good deal of punch to alleviate his sufferings. But about this time he seems to have passed the strict limits of punch. A round of entertainment had followed his acceptance of the Seal, and entertainments in those days were no light matter to a hard drinker in indifferent health. One or two of the Chancellor's guests on these occasions are familiar to posterity, and have left records of their visits to his house. Twice we find Jeffreys inviting Evelyn to dinner, for the two seem to have been on excellent terms, although the diarist entertained an unfavourable opinion of the Chancellor's public character. Sir John Reresby also dined with him twice. On the second occasion Sir John was rather scandalised because the Chancellor, after "having drank smartly at table, which was his custom," called into the room, Mountford, the handsome actor, who was afterwards murdered by Lord Mohun. The Chancellor made Mountford, who was an excellent mimic, plead a feigned cause in which he gave imitations of all the most celebrated lawyers to the intense delight of their distinguished head. Any form of mockery was always a pleasure to Jeffreys ; and, the more successful he became, the more he indulged in his love of it. But it was an imprudent indulgence, as his friend Reresby thought, "since nothing can get a man more enemies than to deride those whom he ought to support."

But the climax to Jeffreys' round of conviviality occurred at a party or "debauch of wine," as Reresby terms it, at Alderman Duncomb's, where the Lord Chancellor and Rochester, the Lord Treasurer, a son of the great Clarendon and the chief supporter of the Church of England in the Ministry, drank to such an extent that they stripped to their shirts and were only prevented by an accident from getting on a signpost in their semi-nude condition to drink the King's health. As this was in the month of January, a chill probably put the finishing touch on Jeffreys' indisposition. Little wonder that at the beginning of February his life was despaired of. Barillon writes that the King was deeply troubled at the Chancellor's illness, saying that the loss of such a Minister would be hard to repair ; Jeffreys was certainly not declining in favour at this date. But James was spared so serious a loss. By the 12th of February Jeffreys was sufficiently recovered to take his seat again in the Court of Chancery. That day he heard his friend Mr. Evelyn's great cause, and granted him a re-hearing. Six lawyers appeared for Evelyn and three against him, of whom one was Finch, "the smooth-tongued solicitor." Jeffreys never liked the "smooth-tongued" gentleman, and had had some smart passages with him as Chief Justice. On this occasion, writes Evelyn, Jeffreys reproved Finch in a great passion, on a very small occasion. But, the virtuous diarist continues, " Blessed be God for His great goodness to me this day."

During March Jeffreys retired to his country house at Bulstrode, to regain his strength, which, he writes, has been very much impaired by his long and severe illness, the cause of which is still troubling him. He was back in London by the 25th, when he writes a very friendly letter to Lord Clarendon, the Lord Lieutenant of Ireland. Clarendon and his brother Rochester were at the head of the Church party ; and for that reason, Jeffreys was no doubt anxious to retain their esteem and support. Clarendon seems to have rather mistrusted the Chancellor's friendly sentiments, though he was not above making pretty considerable use of him in his legal affairs when it was convenient to do so. In the letter of the 25th, Jeffreys informs Clarendon of the King's intentions as to some of the Irish Judges, and concludes : " I would be glad to receive your lordship's commands how to steer myself and those affairs as may be most suitable to your Excellency's inclinations," and sends his and his wife's humble duty to Lady Clarendon.

The King was now fully occupied with the preparations for the Dispensing judgment ; and in April Jeffreys sounded the Judges as to their intentions. He was in all probability not sorry to find that one of the first to prove unwilling was Jones, the Chief Justice of the Common Pleas. He was a fellow-countryman of Jeffreys, and they seem to have been jealous of one another. Jones had hitherto been a firm and severe supporter of the Government, but he could not stomach the Dispensing power. He told the

King he might find twelve judges of his opinion, but not twelve lawyers. He was dismissed. Montagu, the Chief Baron, and Nevil, a "puisne," shared the same fate. Another of the Judges was only too glad to find in the Dispensing power a good cause for retiring from the Bench. This was old Sir Job Charleton, who, in 1680, had been consoled against his will for giving up the Chief Justiceship of Chester to Jeffreys by a Judgeship in the Common Pleas. He took his quietus with peculiar satisfaction, for he was at the same time restored to his old place at Chester and given a baronetcy. He lived until 1697, to the age of 83, in full enjoyment of his honours.

Mr. Justice Bedingfield was promoted to Jones's place, Baron Atkyns to Montagu's, and the other vacancies were filled up by the faithful and reliable. The most interesting of the new appointments was that of Christopher Milton, the younger brother of the poet, as a Baron of the Exchequer. He had been all his life as consistent an adherent of the royal house as his brother of the Protector, and later in life he had gone to the extreme of Roman Catholicism. His religious belief was, in all probability, the chief cause of his elevation to the Bench, for he was seventy-one at the time of his appointment, and in two years was given a writ of ease in consideration of his age. A quiet easy man, he survived some five years in retirement in the country.

Another dismissal, brought about by the Dispensing affair, must have given the Chancellor considerable satisfaction. "Smooth-tongued" Mr. Solicitor Finch was removed, and Thomas Powys, an able and faithful lawyer, succeeded to his place.

As soon as everything had been conveniently settled, Sir Edward Hales, a Roman Catholic officer in the army, defended the test action as to the King's right of Dispensation, before the Court of King's Bench ; and Chief Justice Herbert gave judgment in his favour. He said he had consulted the twelve Judges, who, with one exception, were in favour of the King's right. The one exception was Mr. Justice Street ; but it has been suggested, though on no very clear evidence, that his dissent from his brethren was collusively given, in order to lend an air of spontaneity to the judgment.

James now turned his attention to the Church of England, and with that began the real difficulties of Jeffreys' position. As a lawyer and a Tory he had good grounds for believing in and upholding the right of Dispensation. Jones's reply to James about *judges* and *lawyers* sounds well, but it is by no means irrefutable. In strict law there was quite as much to be said in favour of the Dispensing power as against it ; and the refusal of some of the Judges to assent to it was imputed by many to a fear of being called to account by a future Parliament for such an assent, rather than to their loyalty towards what they conceived to be the true principles of English law. But when James, as head of the Church of England, began to exercise his power in a way detrimental to the welfare of that Church, Jeffreys was thrown into an uncomfortable state of hesitation between his devotion to his King and his devotion to his Church. On the one side stood Sunderland, on the other Rochester, both friends of the Chancellor, and statesmen with whose respective aims he had sympathised. But Sunderland had now thrown in his lot with the Jesuitical cabal that ruled the King, and was bent on driving Rochester from office. Jeffreys must either stop with the Lord President or go with the Lord Treasurer. He preferred to stop. Office was a protection to him ; he had hosts of enemies, whom his mocking tongue and violent opinions had made him ; he knew that, if he fell, his fall would be deep and complete. As long as he retained some sort of power he could keep them at bay. Therefore, resignation was impossible to him ; he must continue to act obediently and entirely in the service of the King, for there was no half obedience with James. All he could do for that Church, from whose communion he never departed for one instant, greatly as such a step might have served his interests with the King, was to mitigate as much as possible the excesses of the King's obstinacy, and hope in time to be able to prevail with saner measures when James should have realised the hopelessness of his attempt. But such a line of policy, if necessary and the best in his circumstances, could have been neither pleasant nor satisfying to his self-respect, though it can hardly be called perfidious. Much as he himself would have loathed the appellation, Jeffreys " *trimmed* " at this critical juncture, and continued " trimming," till James, too late, partially came to his senses. But trimming is not perfidy, or what would become of many honourable reputations ? In not resigning his office at this time, Jeffreys was violating no principle of ministerial responsibility ; for, as Lingard puts it, " it did not enter into the minds of the statesmen of this period that it might be a duty to resign office, rather than lend the sanction of their names to measures which they condemned." And his office was at no time made intolerable to him, or his person slighted, as in the case of North. He had to perform many unpleasant duties, but he was always well treated ; and, if his place in the King's favour was at times imperilled, he received continued marks of the royal esteem throughout the reign.

But it must not be imagined that Jeffreys was merely the submissive instrument of his master. In the Council on more than one occasion he withstood the King, and for the time proportionately declined in his good graces. It is significant that rumours of his fall are always coincident with these occasions.

The first of these is in the April of 1686, when Clarendon writes from Dublin that he hears the Chancellor is tottering in favour. Now, about this time, Herbert, the Chief Justice, had declared to the King his views as to the Dispensing power, whereupon Jeffreys, whether from a desire to discredit the Chief Justice, in whom he saw a possible rival, or on purely professional grounds, stated certain legal objections to Herbert's view. Ultimately he dropped his objections, and the affair proceeded ;

but his momentary hesitation was quite sufficient to shake him in the King's esteem.

In May he is found again resisting his Majesty. Much to James's annoyance the Protestant refugees who had left France on the revocation of the Edict of Nantes had, on their arrival in England, been warmly welcomed by the prelates and clergy of the English Church. The King now declared to the Council that a paper, written in French by Claude in favour of the reformed Protestants and widely read in England, was to be publicly burnt at the hands of the common hangman. Jeffreys rose and opposed this senseless insult, on the ground that though it would be legal to prosecute any one who had printed the paper in an English translation, it was an extra-ordinary measure to burn a paper, written in French and printed in a foreign country, which contained nothing against the English Government. James interrupted him : " I have made up my mind to this ; dogs defend each other if one is attacked, says the English proverb. I think Kings should do the same ; besides, I have my own reasons for not allowing a libel of this kind against the King of France." The Councillors were silent. But, says Barillon, " I have no doubt they would all have supported the Chancellor's objections." Louis XIV. was of the same opinion, and considered James's act needlessly indiscreet and dangerous.

In spite, however, of this act of resistance, Jeffreys could count on the Royal favour within certain limits. In July he obtained for his elder brother Thomas, who was the King's Consul at Alicant in Spain, the honour of knighthood. Thomas seems to have been a very worthy man, with a real affection for his brother, which the latter did not sufficiently repay, at least in the matter of letter-writing. Soon after his knighthood Sir Thomas returned to Spain, where he was regarded with great awe and respect on account of his ancient Welsh descent. On his way back he sends the Chancellor a letter of farewell from the " Three Kings," Deal. He writes that he has been in a storm so terrible and tormenting that " it was by God's infinite mercy I did not burst." Luckily, the captain put in to shore, and Thomas was able to go to bed. " For God's sake," he writes, " let me have a line from you now and then, which will be the only comfort of my life." He sends his duty to his father, and adds : " My hearty thanks for all your favours, and I shall daily pray the Almighty God to grant you perfect health." [1]

A service which Jeffreys tried to do his younger brother, James, was not so successful. The latter had been made, in 1682, no doubt through the then Serjeant Jeffreys' interest, a Prebendary of Canterbury Cathedral, though at the time only thirty-three years of age. About June of 1686 the bishoprics of Chester and Oxford fell vacant by the deaths of their holders. As early as the October of the previous year, Dr. James Jeffreys had been speculating on the possibility of succeeding to the former see. Mr. Shakerley, a confidential agent of the Chancellor's in the county palatine, writes to Jeffreys, October 24th, 1685, that the Bishop is now very ill and not expected to live, asks him to acquaint Dr. James with the income of the see, and promises to keep the Chancellor informed of the changes in the Bishop's condition. When at length the Bishop died, both the Archbishop of Canterbury and the Lord Chancellor did their best to bring about the nomination of Dr. Jeffreys ; but the King, if he could not appoint Papists to the vacant sees, was determined to appoint those Popishly inclined. To Chester he declared his intention of appointing the very questionable Cartwright, Dean of Ripon ; to Oxford, Dr. Parker, the Archdeacon of Canterbury, a dignitary of very suspicious orthodoxy. Dr. Jeffreys, fearing that Chester might slip through his grasp, centred his hopes on the less exalted dignity of Archdeacon of Canterbury, which would be vacant by Parker's promotion. But the Chancellor felt it his duty to discourage even these more modest

---

[1] The domestic correspondence quoted in the latter part of this work is in the possession of Mr. M. R. Jeffreys.

aspirations. "As to your desire on the promotion of Dr. Parker," he writes to his brother, "there will be no opportunity offered. As to other hopes"—he alluded no doubt to Chester,—"which I guess you are more often saluted with, I hope you will be wise enough to leave them to my management and discretion, and not to be too much corrupted by your own humour, or that, that you know I think is worse, of your guardian the D———, thereby to prevent that advantage that your friends think you deserve, and I shall always be willing to promote." He adds that his brother Thomas, who had been lately troubled with his own unhappy distemper, is better, and hopes to see James at Tunbridge Wells whither he goes the next week.

Dr. Jeffreys' hopes were finally crushed by the official nomination of Cartwright to the vacant see of Chester, at the end of the month. The Chancellor was sufficiently annoyed by the nomination to make certain formalities of the Bishop's appointment, over which he had some control, as tedious and troublesome as he could, until reproved by the King ; and Sancroft, the Archbishop, who had warmly espoused the cause of Dr. Jeffreys, tripped and fell down at Cartwright's consecration. It was mortifying to good Churchmen to see that in his ecclesiastical appointments James was going to consider the interests of Romanism before those of the Church of England. In the meantime poor Dr. Jeffreys was persistently pressing his brother to do something for him in the general distribution of perferment ; but his efforts were uniformly unsuccessful. In September the Chancellor wrote to him, through Sprat, the Bishop of Rochester, what he called a " peremptory answer " to the Doctor's importunity, told him the King had promised him a bishopric soon, but that he must be content and submit to his hard fortune in the Chester affair, "as some of his friends had had to do before him." To console him, he added that his successor at Canterbury was already nominated. But it all came to nothing, and Dr. James never profited further by his brother's advancement. The Chancellor was far too orthodox to be allowed much influence in the King's ecclesiastical appointments.

During the affair of the Bishopric of Chester, Jeffreys was fully occupied with the institution of the Ecclesiastical Commission. According to Burnet, Jeffreys originally suggested the Commission to James as a means of reviving his sunken favour. Lord Campbell has blindly followed Burnet's lead, and succeeded in making his account of this part of Jeffreys' life a remarkable instance of historical distortion. Quoting from " King John " the King's rebuke to Hubert, " How oft the sight of means to do ill deeds makes ill deeds done ! " he places Jeffreys in the character of Hubert, and declares that if James had only been resisted by a firm and virtuous Minister, and not unscrupulously supported in his insane measures by a slave of the Court, he might have continued to reign prosperously. Anybody with the slightest knowledge of James's obstinate and arbitrary disposition will see how false is such a caricature of the situation ; and there is enough evidence that Jeffreys, far from inciting and hounding the King on to his ruin, was rather a reluctant follower who would have gladly got out of the business, if any other agreeable course had been open to him. Burnet's account is a misstatement, because, in the first place, as far as we know, Jeffreys was not at this time sunk in favour ; and in the second place, the King was the first to decide on making use of an Ecclesiastical Commission. Jeffreys, when it was first mooted, doubted its legality, and twice took the opinions of the Judges on the question.

But as soon as the Commission was decided upon, Jeffreys certainly entered into it with complete devotion, and accepted the principal place upon it. Whether he knew that he would be dismissed if he refused to comply, or whether he hoped, by sitting on it, to be able indirectly to make it as little objectionable as possible, it is impossible to say ; he was in all probability swayed by a variety of motives. A seat on the Commission was an awkward predicament for a friend of the Church of England, though Rochester himself was one of its original members.   The others were the Archbishop Sancroft, who never took his seat, Sunderland, the Bishops of Durham and Rochester, and Chief Justice Herbert.   But Jeffreys was the essential member ; no sitting, no quorum was complete without him ; he was, as Ranke puts it, in some sort a Vicar-General of the Church, but Vicar-General under a Roman Catholic King ; and there lay the absurdity of the whole proceeding.

The first case before the Commission was that of Dr. Henry Compton, Bishop of London.   James had issued an order, as head of the Church, forbidding the English and Romish priests to preach on controversial topics relating to their respective beliefs.   Dr. Sharp, rector of St. Giles's, had disobeyed this order.   Accordingly James, who wanted to test the loyalty of the Bishop, ordered Compton to suspend the preacher.   Compton replied that he could not do so until he had heard and examined into Sharp's case.   For this act of disobedience he was summoned before the Commissioners on August 4th.

The Bishop began by asking the Chancellor for a copy of the Commission.   Jeffreys replied the Commissioners could not grant that, and added : " It is upon record, all the coffee-houses have it for a penny a piece, and I doubt it not but your lordship has seen it."   The Bishop apparently took offence at the remark about the coffee-houses, for Jeffreys afterwards assured the Bishop that he had never intended to imply that his lordship was a haunter of coffee-houses : " I abhorred the thoughts of it, and intended no more by it but that it was common in the town."   The Bishop asked for an adjournment to prepare his defence, and suggested the beginning of the next legal term.   " Ha ! that is unreasonable," answered the Chancellor.   " His Majesty's business cannot admit of such delays ; methinks a week should be enough !   What say your lordships ?   Is not a week enough ? "   Their lordships agreed that it was ; and the Commission adjourned till Monday, the 9th.

After a week spent by Jeffreys at Tunbridge Wells, the Bishop met the Commissioners again in the Council Chamber at Whitehall. As he showed a further inclination to quarrel with the legality of the Commission, Jeffreys told him that such a course was futile ; " we are well assured of the legality of it, otherwise we would not be such fools as to sit here." The Bishop asked for a further postponement, and was given a fortnight.

On the 23rd, counsel were heard on behalf of the Bishop, and on September 6th he was suspended from exercising his functions by order of the Commissioners. Rochester and Jeffreys were both in favour of giving the Bishop time to carry out the King's orders in his own fashion, but Sunderland insisted that they must first ascertain the King's wishes in the matter. It is needless to guess what these were, and Compton was accordingly suspended. But it is evident from his conduct that Jeffreys was not prepared to go to the same lengths as Sunderland in seconding the dangerous measures of James, and that he did not wish to make an arbitrary use of the powers given to him by the Commission, to the detriment of the Church of England. If Jeffreys had possessed any real control over James's policy, it would have been at least wiser. But Jeffreys never had any real influence with the King. A blind and unquestioning obedience and a readiness to embrace the Romish faith were the only things that impressed James with a man's value as a counsellor.

The year 1686 closed in a full tide of Roman Catholic prosperity. As Lord Chancellor, Jeffreys had to lend a hand in the advancement of the King's co-religionists. Richard Allibone, a fiery Romish barrister, who had boasted that he was going to do fine things in a great place, took his first step in that direction, by his appointment as one of the King's Counsel, accompanied by the honour of knighthood, in October. In November, orders were sent to the Inns of Court to call nine Roman Catholic gentlemen to the Bar, and in the same month Allibone and a Papist named Brent were made justices of the peace. It must have been with very mixed feelings of pleasure that Jeffreys carried out the King's commands in these respects. But what if he should be ordered to perform similar services in the course of Nonconformist advancement? That would be a sore trial indeed to the doctrine of passive obedience that was the unavoidable keynote of his Chancellorship.

XVII

THE BEGINNING OF THE END

1687

THE year 1687 was the most harassing period of Jeffreys'
political career. It was the year in which James gave wildest
scope to his unfortunate principles of government ; it was a
year of slight and oppression to the Church of England,
and the year in which the hopeless Whigs and the
despondent Tories were driven to seek the aid of William
of Orange. Jeffreys was obliged to bow to the will of
the King in co-operating in measures odious to his convictions and his prejudices, and could merely wait and
watch for the hour when James should to some extent
awake to the impracticable folly of his schemes. The
Chancellor saw clearly the fatal drift of the King's policy ;
but he knew that no counsel, however sincere or disinterested, could prevail over James's set purpose, until
a stern necessity should compel him to turn back. All
Jeffreys could do was to cling to the Seal through thick
and thin, until a time should come when he might regain
power and influence by some new shuffle of the cards.

Jeffreys lost a strong supporter in the Cabinet by the
dismissal of Rochester at the beginning of the year. An
argument by opposing divines in the King's presence had
failed to wean the Treasurer from his allegiance to the
English Church, and James felt it his painful duty to
dispense with his services. Rochester's departure left
Jeffreys practically the only adherent of the Church in the

Cabinet, and he had neither power nor influence enough to be of much avail.

About this time the Chancellor moved from his house in Queen Street to one which he had built in Westminster, overlooking the Park. He added to it a cause-room, where he could hold his judicial sittings without going to Westminster Hall. Certain rather significant circumstances attended the Judge's change of residence. Mr. Pitts, who built the house for him, was never paid a farthing of his money. He had built it on a promise from Jeffreys that the latter would obtain for him from the King a grant of the land on which the house was erected, at a nominal rent. But Jeffreys had promised more than he could perform. It appears that Sir Edward Hales, the Catholic officer who had defended the test case on the Dispensing power and was later appointed Lieutenant of the Tower, had rented a small portion of the same land from Pitts, and had only paid him half a year's rent. Hearing that Pitts only held the land on Jeffreys' promise, Hales saw a good way of getting out of paying any rent at all. He went to the King, and, being a greater favourite than the Chancellor, prevailed on James to refuse Jeffreys the grant of the land. If Jeffreys ever intended to indemnify Mr. Pitts for his disappointment, his fall occurred before he had time to carry his good intentions into effect. Accordingly the unfortunate Pitts lost by his own account some £2,006 15s., cost of building Jeffreys' house, and at the end had neither the land nor the house to show for it. There can be no doubt that in the latter part of the reign, Jeffreys occupied a very secondary position among the King's friends, due to his continued adherence to the English Church. Apostasy was the way to the King's heart, and that was a way Jeffreys never would follow. Perhaps if he had, Mr. Pitts would not have been so severe a loser by the royal caprice. Hales's behaviour does not appear so glorious an instance of the moral regeneration wrought by conversion as to induce many followers.

The greatest blow to Jeffreys' self-esteem fell in April,

with the publication of the Declaration of Indulgence. James, anxious to secure support in his schemes for his fellow Catholics, determined to grant to the Dissenters the same reliefs and privileges as had been already accorded to the Papists. By his declaration of April 4th he suspended all penal laws relating to ecclesiastical affairs, and allowed freedom of worship to every form of religion in the country. Not content with granting religious freedom to the Nonconformists, James admitted them to municipal offices and the Privy Council. The very men whom Jeffreys had denounced and punished were now put into places of consequence, and the men of his own party politely expelled. In the City of London, the seat of his power, the Chancellor saw his old Tory friends and supporters, Sir William Pritchard, Sir John Moor and Sir Robert Jeffreys, turned out of their places as Aldermen. Sir Peter Rich, the Tory candidate in the famous Sheriffs' election, was removed from the office of Chamberlain, and Mr. Loades, of the lemons, reigned in his stead. Men who had been put in by royal prerogative at the time of the " Quo Warranto " now made way, by royal prerogative, for the factious and the fanatic. Anabaptists and Quakers held civic office ; the City Companies were filled with hot Dissenters, whilst violent Tories were coldly left out ; and, greatest horror of all ! a Presbyterian was chosen Lord Mayor for the ensuing year. The bestowal on the Chancellor of the Lord Lieutenancy of Shropshire can have afforded little consolation to his spirits amidst so much that was heartrending and ignominious.

Further legal changes, some of them not quite so sorrowful to Jeffreys, had become necessary early in the year. Herbert, the Chief Justice of the King's Bench, and the pliant Wythens had hesitated before ordering the execution of one of James's soldiers, who had been condemned to death for desertion from the colours. The King would tolerate no hesitation even among his most devoted or slavish adherents ; Herbert and Wythens were quickly made acquainted with the royal displeasure. Very opportunely Bedingfield, the Chief Justice of the Common Pleas, had died while receiving the Sacrament in Lincoln's Inn Chapel (February), and the office had only been filled up five days by the promotion of Mr. Justice Wright. Herbert and Wright now simply changed places, and Wythens received his quietus. The latter had not expected that his independence would meet with such a summary reward. He was unbuttoning his doublet one night, " very well content with himself and his conscience," when his quietus came to disturb his self-congratulation and remove him from the Bench. Beyond being excepted from the Bill of Indemnity at the Revolution, his public career ended on this eventful night. His domestic troubles brought him as a suitor before the Courts in 1690, and he died at his seat in Kent, in 1704.

In Herbert's removal men saw the strong arm of Jeffreys, for Herbert had been high in the royal favour, and was just as well out of the Chancellor's way. The Chief Justice himself expected that his removal to the Common Pleas was only a step in his descent back to the Bar ; but he was happily deceived, holding his new office during the remainder of James's reign. Jeffreys' strong arm was likewise shown in the appointment of Mr. Justice Wright to succeed Bedingfield in the Common Pleas, and afterwards as successor to Herbert in the Chief Justiceship of the King's Bench. Whatever the political exigencies, Jeffreys' patronage of Wright cannot be justified, for the man was as incompetent as he was disreputable. Jeffreys originally favoured him as a means of slighting North, and probably continued his patronage because he saw that Wright had neither the character nor the ability to become a possible rival. From the point of view of Jeffreys' security in the Chancellorship Wright was a more comfortable Chief Justice of the King's Bench than Herbert. And as the Judges were daily becoming more and more automatic, Wright was as good as anybody else. Barillon says that Wright was appointed because there was no

Papist fit to hold the office, a reason not very complimentary to the Papists. Wright was perhaps aware of the uncertainty of Protestant tenure, for he soon began to hold out signs of becoming a Roman Catholic. He had also married as his third wife a daughter of Scroggs, a circumstance that may have been considered in his favour.

One of the vacancies in the King's Bench was filled by the Papist Allibone, so that now he had got his opportunity of doing fine things in a great place ; and it is only fair to add that he did his best to keep his word, proving a most vehement advocate of arbitrary measures and a public and punctual attendant at mass. But he made a very poor Judge, or he might have had still greater opportunities for doing fine things.

At the end of April, Jeffreys, as President of the Ecclesiastical Commission, had the Vice-Chancellor and Delegates of his old University of Cambridge before him. They had been summoned for refusing to obey the King's mandate to grant academical degrees to a Benedictine monk. Peachell, the Vice-Chancellor, made a poor defence, which evoked smiles from Jeffreys. Some of the Delegates were too eager to assist the Vice-Chancellor by interruptions. Dr. Cook was particularly zealous. " Nay, good Doctor," says Jeffreys, stopping him, " you never were Vice-Chancellor yet ; when you are, we may consider you ; " and to a young Delegate who suddenly made quite a long speech : " Nay, look you now, that young gentleman expects to be Vice-Chancellor too ; when you are, sir, you may speak ; but till then it will become you to forbear." Dr. Smoult was also reproved : " Is that Dr. Smoult in court ? " asked Jeffreys. Smoult had been alluded to as the representative of a body of petitioners against the mandate. Smoult appeared : " And pray, sir, who are you," asked Jeffreys, " that you should be thought fit to represent a whole House ? Why should they choose you rather than anybody else ? " to which Smoult could give no very convincing answer. In the end Peachell was deprived of the Vice-Chancellorship and the headship of his College ; " and because," added Jeffreys, " the Commissioners have a tenderness for the College for which all along you have shown little regard, my lords are pleased to appoint that the revenues of your headship shall go to the College." The Delegates he dismissed with his favourite caution : " Go your way and sin no more, lest a worst thing come unto you."

In June the University of Oxford was represented before the Commission. The Fellows of Magdalen College, ordered by the King to elect one Farmer as their President, rejected him as a man of disreputable character, and chose instead Dr. Hough, one of their own number. Summoned before the Commission they justified to the Commissioners their rejection of Farmer, but were told they ought not to have elected any one else without the King's permission. One incident occurred which roused something of the old Jeffreys. One of the Fellows, Dr. Fairfax, a " grave " Doctor, says Macaulay, " hinted some doubts as to the validity of the Commission," whereupon the Chancellor " roared at him like a wild beast." But in this instance Macaulay's account is rather inflammatory, and the facts are better left to speak for themselves. The great historian's treatment of the affair is instructive. It would be interesting in the first place to know what evidence there is for the "gravity" of Fairfax. Instead of his " hinted doubts " as to the Commission, Luttrell says Fairfax was " very bold there." " In the *Verney Correspondence* Fairfax is described as " arguing with great heat : " and the only report in the State Trials gives his " gentle hint " as expressed in an abrupt desire to know by what authority the Commission sat. At the hands of Macaulay and others, Jeffreys has more than atoned for his own bad character by the beautiful traits and characteristics which these authors have generously bestowed on his victims or opponents in order to heighten his own iniquity. It is not said in the report that Jeffreys " roared like a wild beast." His words are perfectly coherent, and in no way justify a comparison which, unless it be suitable to the occasion, becomes an unmeaning effort at sensationalism.

The real circumstances of the Fairfax incident are these. The Fellows had put in a kind of half-submission to the King, from which Fairfax alone dissented. He desired to give his reasons for doing so to the Commissioners. Jeffreys seems to have thought that Fairfax meant to submit fully, and readily gave him permission ; " ay, this looks like a man of sense and a good subject ; let's hear what he'll say." But Fairfax, instead of submitting, began a legal argument. Jeffreys, annoyed at his disappointment, snubbed him by telling him he was a doctor of divinity, not of law. Fairfax lost his temper, and asked by what authority the Commission sat, which was a bold question, to say the least of it. Then Jeffreys lost his temper, but not his sense of humour, and cried : " Pray, what commission have you to be so impudent in court ? This man ought to be kept in a dark room. Why do you suffer him without a guardian ? Pray, let the officers seize him." Fairfax's question certainly deserved a reprimand as an impertinence, and, if it was academically urged, would go a long way to account for Jeffreys' irritation. But, be that as it may, an account which puts all the blame on the Lord Chancellor is manifestly unfair.

The affair of Magdalen College was the occasion of Jeffreys' last recorded appearance as President of the Ecclesiastical Commission. Except in his passage with Fairfax Jeffreys acted with conspicuous moderation towards those who appeared before the Commissioners. He always asserted, even with his dying breath, that he had accepted his place on the Commission with a view of reviving and not destroying the Church. If that was the case he was making a most impossible attempt to reconcile principle and interest, and one foredoomed to failure as long as James II. was in the enjoyment of unrestrained authority. But his conduct in the past and his wavering influence in the present obliged the Chancellor to make the best of a state of affairs which he may well have hoped would soon prove too extravagant even for James.

In August the King and Queen went on a progress

through the West, and Jeffreys accompanied them part of
the way. At Marlborough some unpleasantness occurred
over the royal lodgings ; and Jeffreys was said to have
taken down the Queen's bed and put his own into her
room. When they got to Bath the Queen told her
husband, who sent Lord Dover to Jeffreys, to discharge
him from his office and the Court. A good deal of this is
probably gossip, and that exaggerated ; but the Queen was a
bad-tempered lady, and some misunderstanding about the
beds may have arisen. In any case, Jeffreys was declining
in favour, and at the end of the year his position was
becoming one of great anxiety.

His own conduct must partially account for it. He
had let it be known that he had not signed the Declaration
of Indulgence. He had been put with Sunderland and
others on a Board of "regulators" for municipal elections
and the appointment of magistrates. As the Board was
expected to act in the interests of the Papists and Dissenters
he showed little zeal in the enterprise, and evaded as much
as possible the orders given him. This behaviour brought
down a reprimand from the King, and he promised to be
more careful in future. The rumour spread that Jeffreys
was to be turned out of the Cabinet, that he was to be
shelved as a Vicar-General, and Allibone of all people to be
Chancellor in his stead.

In December, in the midst of these difficulties, an
incident occurred as surprising as it was odious to the
Lord Chancellor. Sawyer, not being considered thorough-
going enough, had been removed from the Attorney-
Generalship, and Powys, the Solicitor, promoted into his
place ; while to the astonishment of all men the vacant
office of Solicitor-General was conferred on William
Williams, Esquire, of Gray's Inn, late Speaker of the
House of Commons. This man had been the Whig
Speaker of the Parliament of 1680, and the ardent Whig
advocate who defended all the Whig prisoners and causes
from 1680 until the death of Charles II. As recently
as the May of 1686, he had been fined by the Govern-

ment £10,000 for publishing Dangerfield's *Narrative* during his Speakership. And yet this same man was now James the Second's Solicitor-General, sworn to support the King at the most arbitrary period of his reign. There has been seldom in the history of political apostasy a case so glaring. Barillon writes of it quaintly. Williams "wishes to atone for his past conduct. There are people who think that it is not a thing to be proud of." The appointment filled Jeffreys with misgiving. The proximity of this unblushing Welshman to the Great Seal, his old opponent sprung up all of a sudden to confront him, evidently prepared to stop at nothing to accomplish his ambitious aims,—disturbing considerations of this kind were an awful addition to the discomforts of his present situation. A severe attack of the stone, which entirely prostrated him at the end of the year, may have been in some part a fruit of his mental troubles.

While the Chancellor is lying sick of the stone and the strangury, the days of his life and his power already numbered, it may be well to sum up what is known to posterity of the personality of this remarkable man. As an introduction to the subject one cannot do better than quote Roger North's description of the Chancellor in its entirety. North was an eye-witness of Jeffreys' conduct on the Bench, a prejudiced witness certainly and very un-reliable where his prejudices are concerned. But, when he writes of what he must have seen with his own eyes and when he succeeds in presenting us with one of the most vivid contemporary portraits that have ever been handed down to posterity, it is safe to assume that the singular intensity of the picture is to a large extent due to the realism of its details.

"I will subjoin," he begins, "what I have personally noted of the man, and some things of indubitable report concerning him. His friendship and conversation lay much among the good fellows and humourists, and his delights were accordingly drinking, laughing, singing, kissing, and all the extravagances of the bottle. He had a set of banterers for the most part near him ; as in old time great men kept fools to make them merry. And these fellows abusing one another and their betters were a regale to him. And no friendship or dearness could be so great in private which he would not use ill and to an extravagant degree in public. No one that had any expectations from him was safe from his public contempt and derision, which some of his minions at the Bar bitterly felt. Those above or that could hurt or benefit him, and none else, might depend on fair quarter at his hands. When he was in temper and matters indifferent came before him, he became his seat of justice better than any other I ever saw in his place. He took a pleasure in mortifying fraudulent attorneys, and would deal forth his severities with a sort of majesty. He had extraordinary natural abilities, but little acquired beyond what practice in affairs had supplied. He talked fluently and with spirit, and his weakness was that he could not reprehend without scolding ; and in such Billingsgate language as should not come out of the mouth of any man. He called it 'giving a lick with the rough side of his tongue.' It was ordinary to hear him say : 'Oh, you are a filthy lousy knitty rascal !' with much more of like elegance. Scarce a day passed that he did not chide some one or other of the Bar when he sat in the Chancery ; and it was commonly a lecture of a quarter of an hour long. And they used to say : 'This is yours ; my turn will be to-morrow.' He seemed to lay nothing of his business to heart, nor care what he did or left undone ; and spent in the Chancery Court what time he thought fit to spare. Many times on days of causes at his house, the company have waited five hours in a morning, and after eleven he hath come out inflamed and staring like one distracted. And that visage he put on when he animadverted on such as he took offence at, which made him a terror to real offenders, whom also he terrified with his face and voice, as if the thunder of the day of judgment broke over their heads ; and nothing ever made men tremble like his vocal inflections."

If this is a true description of Jeffreys he must have possessed a very genius for the terrible. Many men before and since have been strong in their language, passionate in their characters, loving and exulting in the sense of power ; but there is not one who by a singular combination of mental and physical attributes has risen to such a height of majestic violence, scaring the hearts of men by an awfully brilliant and wayward exercise of voice, language and demeanour, as George Lord Jeffreys. North's description is of course exaggerated in parts ; for instance, he says " filthy, knitty and lousy " were words frequently used by Jeffreys. In the many verbatim reports of Jeffreys' language which are preserved in the volumes of the " State Trials," I doubt if any of these words are to be found in his mouth. His frantic charge at Bristol is the only approach to anything like unpleasantness in his style of oratory. As to the details of his private life, North admits that he writes by report ; and therefore requires corroboration. Moreover, to a man of North's timid, proper, almost effeminate character, Jeffreys would appear very much more terrible in his moments of excitement than to men of more robust constitution, accustomed to judicial strong language and judicial displays of temper when they were less restrained in their expression than they are now. His judgments on Jeffreys' personal character are even less reliable than his testimony to his personal bearing ; for the man who failed to perceive the moral defects of Lord Keeper North would hardly detect the better qualities of Lord Chancellor Jeffreys. It must also be borne in mind that North's account describes Jeffreys in the last years of his life, when he was suffering with ever-increasing frequency the torments of a disease which powerfully affected his temper, and emphasised to a painful degree the less pleasing features of his character. As to the more pleasing features the entire absence of friendly testimony either from relatives or friends leaves us in darkness. Charitable surmise, however, will be a safer guide in this respect than Roger North. And if ever there was need of charity, if ever that virtue was required to display its utmost fortitude, would it not be in the service of " Judge Jeffreys " ?

But whatever North's exaggerations, there can be no doubt that the Court of Chancery was an anxious place to barristers and solicitors during the Chancellorship of Lord Jeffreys—more particularly to such barristers or solicitors as had been neglectful or dishonest in their duties. Jeffreys took a stern view of the duty of a Judge towards those who practised before him, and was always prepared to give very good reason for exercising a sharp authority in his courts. Some measure of his unpopularity was probably due to the many rogues he had exposed and the abuses he had checked. There was a great deal of the Augean stable about the Court of Chancery in Jeffreys' day, and he undertook the ungrateful rôle of a raging Hercules at his own peril. He added to the unpopularity of his conduct by meting out to Trimmers and other of his political *bêtes noires* the same denunciations that he poured on the heads of fraudulent attorneys. But, whatever he did in the way of terrifying and denouncing his fellow men, he did well ; and that is the best that can be said for him.

Jeffreys' reputation as a lawyer has never been seriously disputed, and may be safely left in the hands of those competent to judge. Sir James Stephen, in his careful review of the State Trials, has done more, perhaps, than any one to relieve it from unjust aspersions, and to reduce to the category of exploded shells Mr. Justice Foster's assertion that he was the worst Judge that ever disgraced Westminster Hall. Sir Joseph Jekyll, the Master of the Rolls, a weighty and learned lawyer, who was a student at the Temple during Jeffreys' time as Chief Justice and Chancellor, denied to Speaker Onslow the truth of Burnet's statement that Jeffreys was not learned in the law ; and Onslow himself—also a contemporary—says " he had great parts, and made a great Chancellor in the business of that Court. In more private matters he was thought an able and upright Judge wherever he sat," though he admits his violence where Crown or party was concerned. Such of Jeffreys' legal decisions as are preserved bear out the opinions of these excellent judges, if confirmation was necessary in the face of such authorities.[1] And that he should have done equally well as Chief Justice and Chancellor, in the Courts of Common Law and Equity proves that, if his reading was not extensive, his genius as a lawyer more than atoned for any deficiencies in his early studies.

The domestic life of the Chancellor was careless and extravagant. His second wife seems to have shared her husband's laxity in household expenditure ; and his eldest son, on his death, soon dissipated the remains of what should have been 'a fine estate. In spite of the large sums of money that passed through his hands and the quantity of landed property he had acquired, Jeffreys died with mortgages on some of his lands for money lent. The Chancellor was a Bohemian in his tastes, for most of his money was presumably spent in entertainments. He loved conviviality, and that of the boisterous and inebriate kind that prevailed amongst the fast livers of the day. Like many great men he preferred the society of his inferiors in mind to that of his equals ; he loved to reign among a company of dependents who fed and drank at his table, and who would swallow his wine and his sneers with equal composure. From his tongue the servile guests learnt to reckon in jibes and mocks the price of what his hand had given. But behind his back the sponging crew snuffled their resentment, and, in the hour of his fall, unanimously deserted him. Bitterly enough in that day Jeffreys learnt to reckon his true friends ; for, strange to say, these lavish hosts never quite realise that the way to the hearts of their guests, if they have any, is never found through their stomachs, and are surprised in the evil hour to find that the spongers have moved on like the immortal Hatter from the exhausted board to a

<hr>

[1] See his judgment in the case of the East India Company *v.* Sandys. *State Trials*, Vol. X.

fresh cup and platter at another man's table. In the hour of his prosperity, Jeffreys, impetuous and wilful, would never lend an ear to any word of caution, or he might have listened to the sage counsel of his good brother Thomas. Shortly before the Chancellor's ruin, Sir Thomas writes from Spain to the Prebendary at Canterbury : " I wish he (the Chancellor) would trust less to those who so much frequent his table, who are but mere spies and promoters of debauchery, and thereby dive into such things as may prove his overthrow. But who dare to give counsel when that of a brother is despised ? I pray continually to the Amighty to direct him and to defend him against their malice." Surely if prayers could have averted the evil day in the Chancellor's career, they would have been those of this good brother.

Jeffreys' personal appearance at this time is thus described : " He was of stature rather above a middle sort than below it ; his complexion inclining to fair ; his face well enough, full of a certain briskness, though mixed with an air a little malicious and unpleasant." His later portraits bear out this description. The young and handsome face that belongs to the picture in the National Portrait Gallery has become rather fuller with the natural changes of ten years' difference in time, ten years of hard living and political excitement ; the expression, perhaps, slightly mocking and sinister. But there remains the same attractive refinement of face and figure; and the large full eyes with their long marked eyebrows one can imagine capable of dire expressions. There are no traces of the bloated looks of the habitual drunkard which have been so long associated with the mention of Jeffreys' name, no marks of the suffering of four or five years of his painful disorder, unless they have been politely filled in by the courtly artist. It is a face which contradicts the extreme malice of his enemies, but at the same time, by the not altogether pleasant curl of the lip and a certain staring hardness in the eye, affords some reason for the virulence of their hate.

XVIII

THE DOWNFALL OF JEFFREYS

1688

THE Chancellor lay sick and ill at the beginning of the new year. In February, Clarendon, who had left office at the same time as his brother but was still bent on an endeavour to reconcile the King and the Church, called at the Chancellor's house, but could not see him. He was asleep, his servant said ; he had been in the Court of Chancery a little while in the morning, but was still much indisposed in health.

The sickness and apparent disfavour of the Chancellor stirred his enemies to open attacks on his peace of mind. But he still had sufficient vigour to resist them. The estimable Bishop of Chester, Cartwright, in a drunken humour, revenged himself on the Chancellor for his opposition to his election by calling him a traitor in the King's presence ; but he found Jeffreys was not so sunk as to be unable to vindicate himself, and received a stern rebuke from James. In a less exalted sphere nine men were prosecuted in the courts of law for speaking words reflecting on the Lord Chancellor.

And now, with his recovery to health, began the real tussle between Jeffreys and the apostate Williams. At the end of May the Seven Bishops petitioned the King that he would not insist on their reading the Declaration for liberty of conscience in their churches. On the 8th of June they appeared before the Privy

Council and were committed to the Tower charged with delivering and publishing a seditious libel against the King. Jeffreys all along opposed these proceedings; Williams vehemently supported them. It was said that if they were successful, the latter would receive the Seal as the reward of his apostasy. James always rejoiced more over the recovery of one lost sheep than all the faithful of the flock put together, and Williams was more than a lost sheep; he had come in spontaneously from a hostile fold, a cause of great rejoicing and worthy of all confidence. The trial of the Bishops was to be a measure of James's strength. He had now gone so far in his arbitrary career that it seemed as if nothing could stop him; and if a verdict was secured in this case, he might regard his power as a thing assured. The birth of the Prince of Wales at which Jeffreys with the other Councillors was present at the foot of the poor Queen's bed, only determined James in his rash course, instead of inclining him to forbearance. But Jeffreys saw the danger of the step; he hated these attacks on the Church, which he believed must end in disaster, and hoped, for more reasons than one, that Sir William Williams might be wrong and my Lord Chancellor right as to the issue of the approaching trial. The acquittal of the Bishops would check the King's folly and Sir William's advance upon the Seal. The partisans of the King, however, have accused Jeffreys as the instigator of the proceedings against the Bishops. Jeffreys certainly advised the King in the matter of the prosecution in his official capacity as Lord Chancellor, giving his opinion as to the best legal means for effecting his purpose. But according to the conception of ministerial ethics prevalent in Jeffreys' day, such counsel in his official capacity would be quite consistent with a private disapproval of the proceeding. And there is strong evidence that Jeffreys did disapprove and was suspected of doing so by the King. On June 14th he told Clarendon how much he disliked the business, and sent through him his professions of service to the Bishops. He said that James had at one time thought of dropping the affair, but had been advised to the contrary ; " some men would hurry him to his destruction." Two days before the trial Clarendon called on the Chancellor and found him much troubled ; he said the Bishops being brought to a public trial would be of ill consequence to the King's affairs; but it would be found that he had acted an honest part in the matter. " As for the Judges," he characteristically added, " they are most of them rogues."

On the 27th the famous trial took place in the Court of King's Bench, and Williams did all he could to obtain the conviction of the Bishops. After the Judges' charges, the jury retired for the night to consider their verdict. It was ten o'clock when the Court sat again the following morning. Jeffreys had already taken his seat in the Court of Chancery, which was on the opposite side of the Hall to the King's Bench. As the verdict of " Not guilty " was given, a shout was raised in the Court which soon spread throughout Westminster Hall. Jeffreys heard it, and quickly learnt the cause. He was seen to smile and hide his face in his nosegay ; it had happened as he had prophesied, and Mr. Solicitor would not receive the Seal. On July 5th he was able to tell Clarendon that the King was a little troubled that the Bishops had been brought to trial, and seemed in a milder temper. Now, he said, was the time when all honest men should come back to Court.

Not that Jeffreys had entirely recovered favour by the issue of the trial. Williams had been made a Baronet, and the Chancellor experienced some further unpleasantness from the conduct of his cousin, Sir John Trevor. Trevor, it will be remembered, had alone defended Jeffreys before the Parliament of 1680, and Jeffreys had not forgotten his services. Soon after his appointment as Chancellor he had procured for Trevor the Mastership of the Rolls. But " Squinting Jack," who was not an amiable or attractive person, was supposed by many to be scheming to supplant his benefactor. In July matters came to a head, and hot words passed between the Master and the Chancellor. But the difference was patched up, and a better understanding arrived at between the two heated Welshmen.

So anxious and harassed had the Chancellor been of late that he had quite forgotten his brother in Spain. Sir Thomas had written to Jeffreys asking him to get him appointed Envoy Extraordinary to the King of Spain in succession to Lord Lansdowne, but had received no answer. On July 5th he writes to Dr. James complaining bitterly of his neglect. He knows, he writes, my lord is busy and worried, but in the nine months of his absence he might have found time to write a word; he has been " snubbed in his affairs," and all because he had trusted to my lord. Whether James expostulated with the Chancellor or not, Jeffreys did at last write to Sir Thomas and told him a piece of family good news. On July 21st Jeffreys' eldest son, John, the heir to his title, had married a daughter of the Earl of Pembroke. Her mother had been a De Querouaille and a sister of the Duchess of Portsmouth, Charles the Second's mistress. The Duchess had been one of Jeffreys' early patrons, so that the union of his son with her niece was peculiarly fitting. Jeffreys was much cried out against at the time, because, just before the marriage, he gave judgment in the Court of Chancery in favour of his future daughter-in-law in a suit instituted to determine whether a certain sum of money was to go to Lord Pembroke's creditors or to his daughter. Lord Pembroke was very angry at Jeffreys' decision, and said he had done a scandalous thing in judging the case at all under the circumstances. But Jeffreys had purposely at the hearing of the cause called in to his assistance the Master of the Rolls and two of the best of the common law Judges, Powell and Lutwyche; and his decision was twice confirmed after the Revolution in spite of strenuous efforts on the part of the Pembroke family to upset it.

Sir Thomas was delighted at the Chancellor's letter

and the news it contained, which, he writes to Dr. James, will strengthen my lord's interest at Court and the establishment of his family. The following passage would suggest that Jeffreys' second wife had not been a very good mother to his family by his first, or that at any rate one of them did not hit it off with her stepmother : " There is only wanting that poor Sally (Jeffreys' daughter Sarah by his first marriage, who afterwards married a Captain Harnage in the Marines) be accommodated, which I hope you will be assistant in, for she is a mighty modest pretty girl, and I daresay will make a good wife ; and if this were effected I should be much at ease, and so would my lord, I am sure ; for the rest, I know the mother will take good care of them and thereby lessen ours." Thomas goes on to express his grave misgivings as to the future. The Chancellor's failing health, the uncertainty of the royal favour, and the political outlook combine to make him anxious. He realises that my lord has a very difficult game to play, and hopes he has settled his estates on " Jacky " (the eldest son John, afterwards Lord Jeffreys).

Sir Thomas's letter was written at the end of September, but in the meantime his gloomy prognostications had been partially dispelled, and the Chancellor's position at Court considerably strengthened. Sunderland shared Jeffreys' opinion that things had been carried too far, and after the acquittal of the Bishops the two Ministers had begun to urge on the King the advisability of summoning the Parliament. James heard their advice unwillingly, for he knew that such a step would involve the surrender of those cherished objects for which he had fought so determinedly in the past. But the pressure of external events forced him to listen to more moderate counsels, and to restore to favour the Minister whom he had previously been ready to remove in favour of the blushing convert, Williams. Jeffreys' idea that " the King should set all things on the foot they were at his coming to the Crown," was the only possible remedy for the King's affairs, and if James had acted promptly on this advice he might have saved his throne. But his fatal want of pliancy—the saving characteristic of his brother—his clumsy adherence to an impossible conception, made him shuffle and waver where he should have moved with obedience and decision, and the opportunity was lost. Three months of fatal irresolution destroyed his cause, and with it his Chancellor.

At first, Jeffreys was full of hope, and much was expected from the King's altered demeanour. In July he received a mark of royal favour in being recommended to the University of Oxford as their new Chancellor. Unfortunately, or fortunately, the recommendation arrived too late, and the University had already chosen the Duke of Ormond. With many protestations of respect and devotion, the Vice-Chancellor wrote to Jeffreys deeply regretting the accident. At another time the matter might have been pressed further, but at this juncture it was allowed to drop. In August Jeffreys was so far restored in the royal grace that the King and Queen accepted an invitation to dine with him on the 22nd, at Bulstrode. Clarendon dined with him there a few days before their Majesties, and Jeffreys told him how great his hopes were that the King would be moderate when Parliament met. Driving back with his guest after dinner, the Chancellor let out freely on public affairs. He abused the Judges, of whose capacities he would be only too well aware, calling them a thousand fools and knaves, and his *protégé* Wright a " beast." Justifiable as may have been the Chancellor's indignation against the unfortunate gentlemen, it was not kind to upbraid them in this unruly fashion, especially as a few months before they had shown their gratitude for their appointments by presenting the Lord Chancellor with their portraits. How Wright had particularly offended him, except by his general unworthiness, it is difficult to tell ; perhaps he had been designing for the Chancellorship. However, Jeffreys' after-dinner utterances must not be taken too seriously. Later in the drive he grew merry, and told Clarendon that he had to be cautious at home, as there were Papists and spies among his own servants.

As the rumours of the Dutch preparations against England assumed a definite shape, the King yielded further to Sunderland and Jeffreys. On September 21st he published a declaration that in the new Parliament to meet in November, the Church of England should be made secure again and Roman Catholics excluded from the House of Commons. This declaration was penned by the Chancellor himself. Jeffreys was at the same time commanded to restore all the " honest old aldermen," his friends in the City who had been turned out for Dissenters, and many Deputy-Lieutenants and Justices of the Peace who had shared a similar fate. Jeffreys was delighted at these measures, but they proved less significant than he had hoped. The King still wavered. Three days after James had told the Chancellor that all things were to be as at the beginning of his reign, the latter complained to Clarendon that some rogues had changed the King's mind, that he would yield in nothing, and that now, as Jeffreys sneeringly remarked, " the Virgin Mary was to do all." Father Petre still held the King in the grasp of his false subtleties.

But there was no time to be lost if James would listen to reason. William of Orange had set sail for England with fleet and army. The London mob was up and attacking the Popish chapels. Sir William Williams' windows were smashed, and reflecting inscriptions fixed over his door. To quiet the City, Jeffreys persuaded the King to restore to it its old Charter; and in his state coach and full robes of office, attended by his mace and purse, the Lord Chancellor drove to the Guildhall on October 4th, amid the huzzas of the populace. There he delivered the Charter to the Aldermen. On his way back, however, he was hooted. The mob was quick to let him know that it was the Charter not the Chancellor they had huzzaed a little while before. On the 6th he again went into the City, and ordered Sir John Chapman to act as Lord Mayor until a new one should be chosen according to the Charter. On the 11th Chapman was duly elected to the Mayoralty, and on the 29th Jeffreys dined with him at the customary banquet. Chapman had a great awe for the Lord Chancellor, which well nigh proved fatal to the unfortunate man the next time Jeffreys partook of his hospitality. On October 23rd the new legal term began, and the last Judge appointed by Jeffreys took his seat on the Bench. This was Thomas Stringer, whose son had married the Chancellor's daughter Margaret.

On the 30th of October Sunderland, finding his advice unacceptable to the King, resigned his office. But Jeffreys remained. He must stand or fall with James. There was no hope for him otherwise. If he could still fix the reluctant King to a Parliament and join with Clarendon in bringing about some arrangement between James and the party of William of Orange, he might escape from the graver difficulties of the situation ; and, though he can hardly have hoped to have continued to hold office, he might have been gently laid aside in return for his present services in the cause of peace. But it would only be as the representative or under the protection of James that he could hope for a prosperous issue to his embarrassments. As soon as the protection of the King was withdrawn from him, he would be at the mercy of countless enemies who thirsted for his disgrace. He must try all he could to force the King to keep his promise of a Parliament. But at the beginning of November in the midst of growing alarms, the Chancellor was again prostrated by another severe attack of his old complaint. Meanwhile events were hurrying to a conclusion.

On November 5th William had landed at Torbay. With each fresh news of the Prince's good fortune the violence of the mob increased. Popish monasteries and chapels were broken into, and the soldiers had to be sent for to disperse the rioters. On the 17th James left for Salisbury. He had some plan of resisting the Prince by arms, but he found his troops disaffected and unreliable, his most trusted officers treacherous. On the 26th he returned to Whitehall. On the 27th he held a Council, when Jeffreys and Clarendon urged the calling of the Parliament. On the 28th, the last day of term, Jeffreys announced in the Court of Chancery the King's intention to summon Parliament, the writs for which were to be issued immediately. But Jeffreys could place no firm reliance in the King's unwilling promises. He had learnt by this time that nothing could be hoped from James's good sense. A courtier meeting him asked him what were the heads of the Declaration recently issued by the Prince of Orange. He answered that he did not know. "But," he added, "I am sure mine is one, whatever the rest are." He had already begun to pack up his things and interview his tradesmen. Thirty-five thousand guineas and a great deal of silver were already shipped on a collier that they might be ready to be carried beyond the sea.

In the early days of December the King sent for the Chancellor to Whitehall, for he wanted to have the Seal near him. Jeffreys was to leave his house at Westminster and occupy Father Petre's lodgings in the Palace. Disappointed in the hope of French aid and unable to endure the consequences of his rashness, James had now resolved on flight. On Saturday, December 8th, Jeffreys sat for the last time in the Court of Chancery, and the same day delivered up the Seal to the King. At two o'clock in the morning of the 11th (Tuesday) the King and Sir Edward Hales secretly left Whitehall, carrying with them the Great Seal, but not its Keeper

Jeffreys had been left behind, to shift for himself as best he could. In the course of Monday he had disappeared, no one knew whither. His plans had probably been already laid in anticipation of the need of sudden flight. Whether he had actually secured a vessel to carry him from England is uncertain ; the accounts differ. He had at any rate laid aside his gold frog-button gown which he wore as Chancellor, and his beaver hat with its diamond-buckled hatband, and was dressed in fur cap, seaman's neckcloth and a rusty coat.   He is also said to have shaved his eyebrows. Disguise was imperative ; the news of the King's flight had spread like wildfire. The same night the mob, several thousands strong, gutted a chapel in Lincoln's Inn, and attacked the house of the Spanish Ambassador.   Jeffreys well knew the peril in which he stood if he should fall into the hands of the excited rabble. In his seaman's attire he reached Wapping sometime during the Tuesday, and bargained with the master of a coal vessel bound for Hamburg to take him with him on his voyage. The master agreed, and Jeffreys went on board to wait for a favourable tide. The delay was fatal. The mate of the vessel guessing his identity, or suspicious at the more than ordinary treasure which had been brought on board with the stranger, gave information to the authorities. Some constables were sent to search the ship, but the fugitive fearing discovery had changed to another vessel. They followed him thither, only to find that he had gone ashore. Landing at King Edward's Stairs, they traced him to a peddling alehouse, the "Red Cow," in Anchor and Hope Alley, kept by a Mr. Porter, presumably the master of the collier in which Jeffreys was to have sailed. It was between one and two on the Wednesday afternoon that the constables arrived at the alehouse. They searched the lower part of the taven without result. They went upstairs, and there, on a bed between two blankets, begrimed and in a seaman's habit, lay the Lord Chancellor of England. They asked him if he was the Chancellor. He answered, " I am the man." [1]

[1] It may have been that among those who discovered him in this sorry plight was the solicitor whom, according to North's story, Jeffreys had so terrified in the Court of Chancery that he could never forget the awful face of the Judge, and who on this eventful 12th of December was said to have recognised the Chancellor as he sat drinking in the Wapping tavern. The *London Mercury* is the only one of the contemporary broadsides describing the Chancellor's capture which mentions this incident of the solicitor, and gives his name as Burnham. Very possibly Mr. Burnham was present at the taking of Jeffreys,

From the "Red Cow," the constables took their prisoner to the house of a Captain Jones, master of a ship. Jones sent for a coach. Jeffreys was put into it, and, guarded by blunderbuses and followed by a howling mob, carried to the house of Sir John Chapman, the Lord Mayor, in Grocers' Hall. As they drove along Jeffreys begged the chief of the constables to keep him from the fury of the people, and a man was put in front of him on his lap to receive the mire and dirt flung by the angry rabble. One who stood by as the coach passed said : "There never was such joy ; they longed to have him out of the coach, had he not had good guard." By the time they reached the Hall, Jeffreys had been given an old hat in place of the seaman's cap. As he alighted from the coach, he hung his head and seemed to be weeping. The Lord Mayor was at dinner when they brought to him the fearful and dishevelled prisoner. The sight of the fallen man, the once great and awful Chancellor now a terrified and weeping suppliant at his feet, is said to have so shocked the unfortunate Mayor that as he knelt in an access of sympathy to kiss the hand of the once powerful Minister he was seized with some kind of convulsion or fit, of which he soon died. "But yet," says Bramston, with some humour, "he committed the prisoner to the Tower." In any case the frightened Mayor had not lost his power of speech. A clamouring mob filled the courtyard, crying that Jeffreys should be brought out to them. Some even broke into the Hall, and with drawn swords threatened the Lord Mayor that he should answer with his life if he suffered the prisoner to escape. Three times Chapman had to go out and plead for patience, while he sent to the Lords of Council to know their pleasure as to Jeffreys' disposal. Jeffreys himself, anxious to escape his raging enemies, offered to help the Mayor in his distress by drawing a warrant for his own committal to the Tower. At length an order came from Whitehall. It began : "Whereas the Lord

and was able, from his terrible experience in Chancery, to identify him immediately.

Jeffreys was seized and brought to the house of the Lord Mayor, and was there in great danger by the insults of the people; to secure him, therefore, from the said violence, and at his desire, to the Lord Lucas (the Lieutenant of the Tower) to remove him to the Tower, the following order was made, &c., &c."   Under this warrant and the guard of two companies of the trained bands, and amidst fierce cries of "Vengeance! Vengeance! Justice! Justice!" from a raging mob, George Lord Jeffreys was conveyed that same afternoon from Grocers' Hall to the Tower of London.

" That evening," writes Sir Edmund King, " the mobile extremely violent and ungovernable. Dr. Oates, I am told, is dressed in all his doctor's robes again, and expects liberty quickly."

XIX

THE TOWER OF LONDON

LORD JEFFREYS on arriving at the Tower was lodged at the house of a warder named Bull. On the Sunday following his capture, the Tower church was thronged with people anxious to catch a sight of the fallen Minister, "but he came not out." It was rumoured that the prisoner had pen, ink and paper, and was busy drawing up petitions and disclosures for the Prince of Orange. A deputation of lords was sent to examine him. They asked him certain questions as to the fate of the Seal and the formalities connected with the discharge of his office. Jeffreys answered them briefly, and at the same time took the opportunity of returning his humble thanks to the lords for the care they had taken in preserving him from the violence of the rabble. The *Mercury* of the 15th informed the public that the Lord Chancellor's portrait had been taken down from the place it occupied in the Guildhall, and that the Lord Mayor was pretty well recovered again. But the timid Chapman died three months later of apoplexy.

And now that the fierce Judge, the unholy terror of the Whigs and the Dissenters, was safely lodged within the walls of the Tower, the pent up fury of his enemies broke forth in streams of abusive literature. Discoveries and Confessions, Examinations and Preparations for his Trial were issued by various publishers ; some dully ironical, others, after a feeble attempt at restraint, coarsely defamatory. One gives a facetious sketch of Jeffreys' last will and testament, in which he gives orders for $1\frac{1}{2}$ ells of cambric to be cut up into handkerchiefs to dry all the wet eyes at his funeral, and half a pint of burnt claret for all the mourners in the kingdom. The hand of Tutchin is traceable in a letter to the Lord Chancellor, exposing to him the sentiments of the people. The author advises Jeffreys to cut his throat, and concludes with an offer of kind assistance : "I am your lordship's in anything of this nature. From the little house over against Tyburn, where the people are almost dead with expectation of you."

Another probable emanation from the pen of Tutchin is the humble petition of the widows and fatherless children in the West of England,[1] in which the widows and fatherless children repeat the foul answer said to have been made by Jeffreys to the lover of Mr. Battiscomb, when she begged his life at the Judge's hands. The elegy upon Dangerfield, which is bound up with these two in the *Western Martyrology*, is more vigorous ; it opens with an exhortation to the perjurer's ghost :—

> "Go then, mount on ! Wing through the midway air !
> And Godfrey's hovering shade shall meet thee there !"

> *   *   *   *

> "No well-wrote story, no romance can yield,
> A greater, nobler name than Dangerfield."

The good Protestant author compares the punishment of Dangerfield to that of Christ :—

> "Thy master thus, thus thy Lord Jesus died,
> He must be scourged before he's crucified ;
> Though milder Jews far more good nature have,
> They forty stripes, Jeffreys four hundred gave."

---

[1] Woolrych and Lord Campbell have treated this as a genuine petition, but the tone of its language altogether contradicts such a supposition. As it is found in Tutchin's books, I should conclude it to be the work of that author or another of Dunton's scribblers.

Lucifer, "shaking the scaly horror of his tail," is represented as participating with Jeffreys in his cruelty to the martyr. At the conclusion of the elegy, Dangerfield's ghost addresses Jeffreys personally. He comes to haunt and plague the fallen Judge, his body putrid with gore, his "dangling eyeball," alluding to Francis's attack on him, "rolling about in vain, never to find its proper seat again." Behind him follows the ghastly train of the Western victims ; hovering o'er him they " fright back the sickly day "—

> " Each at thy heart a bloody dagger aims,
>   Upward to gibbets point, downward to endless flames."

The *Triumph of Justice* gives a disgusting account of Jeffreys' deposition at the birth of the Prince of Wales. But the Chancellor's " Address and Confession to both Houses of Parliament " is spirited and amusing. It is in the form of a soliloquy by the imprisoned Chancellor —" What a damned fool I was that I did not run away in time ! Could not I have had the wit of Petre, and put my ten thousand pound bag of guineas under my arm and troop to Brussels ? A dull beast to stay to be thus noosed ! Now, Petre, Pope and Judges, with your dispensing scarlet, where are you to assist me ? You will be damned before you'll help me at a dead lift. I see, I see now, I was a dull ass. Out upon it, to be thus outwitted ! . . . . Was it for this I perverted justice, and did things contrary to the law of God and man ? Oh, Hub ! Bub ! Bub ! Boo ! What shall I do now ? A PARLIAMENT ! A PARLIAMENT ! . . . . Curse my fortune that ever I should have been born in a time of printing ! They put my name in capital letters, they have out my titles too, and seem to care no more for me than for Balaam's ass ! My purse and mace will not protect me ; my purse will serve to put my head in, after it is off ; and my mace will serve to stick it on afterwards ! " Visions of his sins rise before his eyes ; he thinks on Job iv. 8. " God Almighty will be my Judge, from whom there is no appeal.

I have little to say in vindication of myself, for if I did never so much, there is none would believe it, my crimes are so evident plain and notorious."

The following delicately expressed sentiments, conveyed in a " Letter of Advice " to Lady Jeffreys, will fittingly conclude the literature of Jeffreys' downfall. " Though his lordship is provided with two or three suits of stout armour, these rebels are plaguy impudent fighting fellows, and will not fall before his lordship's usual shot of rogues, rascals and villains.   Therefore he had better make other preparations, not a suit of armour for his conscience, for that is so hardened to be as proof against all bullets as against honour, justice, religion or humanity."   Lady Jeffreys is exhorted to provide her husband with a large quantity of clean linen, " lest he should stink in his Majesty's nostrils as he does already in God's."

The vulgar malignity of these effusions not only testifies to the extraordinary sentiments of hatred felt by a certain section of the populace towards Lord Jeffreys, but they help us to appreciate how thoroughly well-deserved was the severity with which Jeffreys invariably treated factious scribblers whilst he sat on the Bench.

The silence and solitude of his deserted chamber in the Tower tell a far more tragic story of the Chancellor's fall than the noisy scurrility of the hack writers.   The passionate gratitude which the prisoner evinced towards the few who visited him in his affliction, the sense that he was coldly forsaken by many of those on whose friendship he thought he might have counted in the hour of distress,—sentiments such as these betray the anguish of his soul, and afford to posterity some idea of the man's misery.   Whatever his errors or his sins, he now suffered an atonement bitter enough to have satisfied all enemies, save such a stony and untruthful Whig as Old-mixon [1]   The griefs of his mind were augmented by the mortal ailment of his body.   His days were clearly numbered, and to the few who visited him he spoke as

[1] See his account of Jeffreys in his *History of England.*

one prepared to die.   There were some members of that
Church to which, whatever his guilt, he had always adhered,
who sought him out in his loneliness, and spoke to him of
the forgiveness of the God whose name had been ever on
his lips when mercy was farthest from his heart.   Not that
Jeffreys' religion had been ever insincere, the cant of an
oily hypocrite.   His Christianity was mediæval in its
spirit, a Christianity that exercised no controlling force
over his passions and desires, but which went along with
them as a rather unpleasing handmaid in their accomplishment, and was only transformed into a moral power when
the things of this earth had been dissolved in hopeless
ruin.   To all who came he expressed a sense of his guilt.
Some things, such as the punishments of Tutchin and
Lady Lisle, he could not acknowledge to be undeserved.
He protested that in the West he had not acted up to the
severity of his instructions ; whilst in other matters he
complained that he had to bear the guilt of those who
were at that very moment the idols of the nation.

Of the real measure of the responsibility of Jeffreys and
of his partners in these transactions that have been so
shocking to later generations, posterity will never be in a
position to judge.   Nor is it important to be able to decide
on the respective guilt of the several participators.   In
the hour of retribution, those who are accused are always
curiously ready to apportion blame among their confederates.   But the testimony of such is worthless.   Widely
different characters, acting from a variety of motives and
under circumstances of thought and time which we can
with difficulty reconstruct, brought about an alarming
crisis in the history of the nation.   To the accomplishment of this crisis the Whigs and Tories, by the intemperance of their political conduct, were equal contributors.
As far as political morality goes, in the choice of means
and an enlightened appreciation of their opponents, in
freedom from prejudice and the grievous assaults of party
passion, Shaftesbury and Russell and Sidney can hardly
be accounted more temperate and scrupulous than Charles

or Sunderland or Jeffreys. Fortunately for England, the uncompromising fatuity of James II. put a speedy end to the most merciless party struggle recorded in the history of our country.

This struggle was accompanied by actions so appalling to the modern mind that it gave up trying to understand them, and wrote them down as the deeds of human monsters, or " wild beasts." Calmer views have at length prevailed. The complexity of motives, frequently so trivial and momentary as to elude not only the investigation of the historian but the recollection of the actor himself, will on impartial reflection be admitted to have played its customary part in the actions of the so-called good and bad men of history alike, and the " wild beast " school of moral investigation has been relegated to the religious tract. In order to judge the real moral obliquity of such a man as Jeffreys and the real infamy of his deeds, one can but reduce him to human proportions, endeavour to enter into the spirit of his age and present him by the side of and in his relations with the other characters in his story, and leave to those who can more fitly determine than his biographer the exact degree of moral reprobation of which he is deserving. But men should not be too swift to pass a sweeping condemnation even on such a man as Jeffreys ; for if they do so by modern standards and without a due appreciation of the difference between the present and the past, they may commit an impertinence.

The career of Jeffreys ended in disastrous failure. That it should have so ended was wholesome and necessary, wholesome because Jeffreys was the incarnation of a glaring vice in our political constitution, inevitable because he was a man of excessive character placed in a preposterous situation. The judge-politician is a contradiction in terms. The coldest and most subtle of men would have found it difficult in times of revolution and the violent alternations of party victory to have saved himself from disaster in so anomalous a position. But a judge whose genius lay in transport, in the unmeasured denunciation and mockery of political opponents, in the unsparing flagellation of cant and scurrility, at a time when cant and scurrility were encouraged to do their worst, was foredoomed to perish in the fray.

In Jeffreys' circumstances a judge could only be an instrument in the hands of a higher power, to be used as an executioner to emphasize a political victory, and to be got rid of as soon as he had performed his unpopular office. If Charles II. had lived, he would in all probability have thrown Jeffreys overboard as soon as the Whigs had been sufficiently punished and intimidated. James adhered to his Chancellor not only because he was his brother's intellectual inferior, but because the two men had become necessary to each other in the throes of a desperate situation. Jeffreys' part in the drama of history has been that of a dependent. But by the sheer genius of his personality, by that great gift of character by which alone, whatever their moral excellence or infamy, men can hope to survive in the pages of history, which unites in the interest of posterity a Savonarola and a Borgia, he has raised his transgressions out of the dull obscurity of ordinary misbehaviour, and lent to the deteriorating circumstances of his situation an eloquence, an intensity, and a vigour of performance that exalt him above the fleeting mediocrity of a Scroggs, a Laubardemont or a Fouquier-Tinville.

One of Jeffreys' earliest visitors in the Tower, not a divine nor bent on a charitable mission, was Mr. John Tutchin. According to his account, he got a glass of wine out of the prisoner, but no expression of regret for the sentence Jeffreys had passed upon him. Tutchin made up for his disappointment by a revenge worthy of his character and his intelligence. He sent the Judge a barrel which looked to be full of oysters, but on being opened was found to contain a halter. No doubt a very good joke to Mr. John Tutchin!

Two Bishops visited Jeffreys, White of Peterborough

one of the Seven Bishops, and Frampton, the pious and eloquent Bishop of Gloucester. Besides these, Dr. Sharp, then Dean of Norwich and afterwards Archbishop of York, took pity on his loneliness. "What! dare you own me now?" asked Jeffreys of the Dean as he entered his room. Frampton has left a striking picture of his first interview with Jeffreys. Though scarcely acquainted with the ex-Chancellor, the Bishop out of a Christian friendliness went to see him in his prison. "I found him sitting in a low chair, with a long beard, and a small pot of water, weeping with himself; his tears were very great ones. I told him not to weep for hardships, but for past sins, in which case his tears were more precious than diamonds." Jeffreys replied: "My lord, all the disgrace I have suffered hitherto I can bear, and by God's grace will submit to whatever more shall befall me, since I see so much of the goodness of God in sending you to me; you, that I never in the least deserved anything from, for you to visit me when others who had their all from me desert me. It can be no other than the motion of God's spirit in you. I thank you for your fatherly advice, and desire your prayers that I may be able to follow it; and beg you would add to this the friendship of another visit at what time I would receive the Sacrament."

When Frampton paid his first visit to Jeffreys the end was very near. Four months of suffering had done their work on a sick body and a mind as morbidly sensitive to the miseries of disgrace as it had been in the past weak to yield to the over-confidence of a too easy success. His utter desolation, the fury of his enemies, the neglect and treachery of many of those he had thought his friends, entirely shattered the remains of his enfeebled constitution. In the infatuation of his principles and his power he had not realised how terribly after his fall he would be made to suffer the utmost miseries of disgrace; and how his passionate conduct in the past made him a convenient peg on which others, as responsible as himself, might hang their responsibilities. Now that he was shut up in the Tower, a victim to popular resentment, so mortally sick that he might be safely left to die without a hearing, he found that some of his colleagues, taking advantage of his enforced silence, were making their peace with the new Government at the expense of the imprisoned Chancellor. On the back of the sinking man, already overweighted by his own burden, they cast the load of their transgressions, and Jeffreys was too weak and helpless to resist the outrage.

From his first entrance into the Tower he had been tormented with stone and rheumatism ; all human aid was powerless to check the progress of his maladies. He was seen by those around him to be fast wasting away ; he could take little or no food ; nothing but small quantities of sack or punch gave him any comfort in his sufferings. Men said in the town that he was drinking himself to death ; but one who was always with him during his imprisonment told Archdeacon Echard that this was untrue. Jeffreys himself complained to Dr. Sharp that people said he had given himself up to drink ; whereas he assured the Doctor he had only taken punch to alleviate the pressure of the stone and gravel. At the beginning of April he was unable to digest a bit of salmon for which he had expressed a fancy ; indeed, a poached egg was the only form of nourishment he could retain.

It must have been early in April that Dr. Frampton first saw him. A few day's after Frampton's visit, on Monday, April 15th, Jeffreys made his will, and received the Sacrament at the Bishop's hands, in the presence of his wife and children. His will is preserved in Somerset House, and is an important document, for it contains the only words written by Jeffreys himself in defence of his past conduct that remain to posterity.

It begins :—

" I, George Lord Jeffreys of Wem, being heartily penitent for my sins, and begging forgiveness for the same, I give and submit my soul to God who gave it, and my body to the grave to be decently and privately buried."

Jeffreys had apparently already executed a deed poll in which he disposed of all his property in favour of his wife and children. But in his will, " for many reasons " he curtails the allowance he had given by deed to his eldest son, John, during his minority to any sum not exceeding £80. John, a brilliant but reckless youth who dissipated his inheritance, may have offended his father, or perhaps, under the influence of his new wife and relations, had neglected him during his confinement. It may be that the following passage in one of Sir Thomas Jeffreys' letters refers to some misconduct of John's. Writing of the Chancellor's many troubles, he says, " And I have heard that the nearest relation hath been much wanting in his obligation ; so he hath, poor man, a very hard game to play." [1]

He bequeathed forty shillings to all the men and maids in his service over and above wages due.

And then comes a list of those few of his friends who visited him in his distress, to whom he makes small bequests as a mark of his gratitude for their devotion. To the Bishops of Gloucester and Peterborough, forty shillings to buy them rings ; to Dr. Sharp, Dr. Scott, the Dean of St. Asaph and Mr. Hesketh of St. Hallows, twenty shillings for the same purpose. To his executors and trustees, of whom the chief were Sir Robert Clayton, one of his oldest friends and a noted Whig, whom Jeffreys is said to have saved from prosecution at the time of the Rye House Conspiracy, and Henry Pollexfen, the eminent advocate, ten pounds to buy mourning.

His wife's relatives had not been wanting in kindness, for there are three Bludworths among the recipients of these tokens of his gratitude, and forty shillings are also bestowed on Lady Moor, presumably the wife of the Lord Mayor who had served the Court so loyally at the time

---

[1] John, second Lord Jeffreys, died without male issue, in 1702 when the title became extinct. The Judge's five other sons had died in infancy. His only child who reached maturity besides those already alluded to was his daughter Mary by his second wife, who married Charles Dive, Esq.

of the Sheriffs' elections, and on Sir Thomas Stringer, the last Judge appointed by Jeffreys before his fall.

Whatever coldness may have arisen between Jeffreys and his cousin Trevor, the former seems anxious that it should be forgotten. He leaves his cousin forty shillings to buy a ring, "which I desire his kind acceptance thereof." And if he has omitted to mention any of those who have shown him kindness in his affliction, he begs his executors to make good his omission, as they shall think fit. He desires to be buried in Aldermanbury Church, " as near as may be to my former wife and children, and at about ten of the clock at night, without escutcheons and all funeral pomp and show, and with few persons thereto."

And then he adds the following words, which speak for themselves, and must be left to the judgment of his fellow men :—

" I was in hopes, notwithstanding my long indisposition of body, I might by the blessing of Almighty God have recovered so much strength as to be able to have vindicated myself if called to account, and made out that I never deserved to lie under the heavy censures I now do. I am sure I would have excused myself from having betrayed that Church of which I have lived and died a member, I mean the Church of England, which I take to be the best Church in the world ; and in the words of a dying man, I declare I never contrived the Ecclesiastical Commission, and never acted thereon save in order to the service, not overthrow of that Church. And I do charge all my children, upon the blessing of a dying father, they be steady to the commands I have given them of being firm even to death to the principles of that holy Church."

Jeffreys had three more days to live. Dr. James Jeffreys had been unable to see his brother in the Tower. He was himself lying mortally sick at Canterbury, where he died in September. On April 18th Edward Jennings, one of his lordship's executors, wrote from the Tower of London to the Prebendary at Canterbury : " And it happened according to my expectations ; for this morning, about four o'clock, it pleased God to deliver him out of all his troubles and miseries. He was taken with a looseness on Saturday, which continued upon him till yesterday with great violence. And I did not think it was possible for him, when I came in to him on Monday, to continue so long. He was very sensible to the last, and had his speech till a quarter of an hour of his death, which he was apprehensive on Monday was approaching. And then he made his will, which was prepared by his directions. This being over he gave his family many pious admonitions and exhortations in moving and passionate expressions, and continued very devout to the time of his death. I suppose he will be interred privately Saturday or Sunday night in the Tower. So it will be necessary you should come up Saturday if possible."

On the Saturday or Sunday the body of Lord Jeffreys was buried in the Tower of London. Three years later Queen Mary ordered the remains of George Lord Jeffreys to be delivered over to his friends and relations, to bury him as they should think fit ; and the following year, 1693, the body of the Chancellor was laid by the side of his first wife in Aldermanbury Church, according to the directions in his will.

APPENDIX I

A LIST OF THE PRINCIPAL AUTHORITIES RELATING TO THE LIFE AND TIMES OF "JUDGE JEFFREYS"

Woolrych's "Memoirs of Judge Jeffreys." 1827.
"Life and Death of George Lord Jeffreys," prefixed to the "Bloody Assizes."
"An Impartial History of the Life and Death of George Lord Jeffreys." 1693.
"The Unfortunate Favourite." 1689.
"Life and Character of the late Lord Chancellor Jeffreys." 1725. (Very abusive.)
There are lives of Jeffreys in Campbell's "Lives of the Lord Chancellors," Foss's "Judges of England," and Roscoe's "Eminent British Lawyers."
The general histories of Macaulay, Ranke, Lingard, Hallam, Ralph, Mackintosh, Burnet, Echard, Oldmixon, Dalrymple.
Diaries and Memoirs of Pepys, Evelyn, Reresby, Luttrell, Lord Clarendon, Lord Ailesbury, Henry Sidney, Bramston, Kiffin, Bishop Cartwright.
Hatton Correspondence (Camden Society).
The Ellis Correspondence and the Clarendon and Rochester Correspondence.
Sir James Stephen's "History of the Criminal Law," vol. i.
Howell's "State Trials," vols. vii.—xii.
Campbell's "Lord Chancellors" and "Chief Justices."
Foss's "Lives of the Judges."
Pike's "History of Crime," vol. ii.
Roger North's "Lives of Sir Francis and Dudley North," his "Autobiography" and "Examen."
Clarke's "Life of James II."
Roberts's "Life of the Duke of Monmouth."
L'Estrange's "Brief History of the Times."
Willis-Bund's "State Trials," vol. ii.
Lives of Rosewell, Archbishop Sharp, Baxter, Philip Henry.

B B

The "Bloody Assizes," "Western Martyrology," and "Merciful Assizes." 1689—1705.

Locke's "Western Rebellion."

Journals of House of Commons—Prideaux's Petition, March 1, 1689.

Appendices to Reports of Historical MSS. Commission (Morrison, Verney, Dartmouth, Throckmorton, Duke of Rutland, Beach, Pine-Coffin).

London Gazette.

Pennant's Wales.

Nicholl's Leicestershire.

Lipscomb's Buckinghamshire.

Burke's "Extinct Peerages."

Seyer's Memoirs of Bristol.

Harleian Miscellany.

Grey's Parliamentary Debates.

Sydney's "Social Life in England, 1660—1690."

Account of the Flight, Discovery and Apprehending of George Lord Jeffreys, 1688. (In British Museum.)

An Account of the Manner of Taking the Lord Chancellor. (In the Bodleian Library.)

A Full Account of the Apprehending of the Lord Chancellor at Wapping. (In the Bodleian Library.)

London Mercury, December 15, 1688.

Ballad Society Publications.

Poems on Affairs of State, 1702.

In the British Museum Library a great number of pamphlets will be found under the general headings of "L'Estrange," "Popish Plot," "Oates," and "Rye House Plot."

It is hardly necessary to add that in a work of this kind the "Dictionary of National Biography" has been of constant service. Other authorities will be found to be referred to in the text.

APPENDIX II

A LIST OF THE PRINCIPAL JUDGES, &c., DURING THE CAREER OF LORD JEFFREYS

LORD CHANCELLORS, OR KEEPERS OF THE GREAT SEAL.

Heneage Finch, Earl of Nottingham (L. C.) . . . . . . 1673—1682
Sir Francis North (L. K.), (created Lord Guilford, 1683) . 1682—1685
George Lord Jeffreys (L. C.) . . . . 1685—1688

LORD CHIEF JUSTICES OF THE KING'S BENCH.

Sir Matthew Hale . . . . 1671—1676
Sir Richard Rainsford . . . . 1676—1678
Sir William Scroggs . . . . 1678—1681
Sir Francis Pemberton . . . . 1681—1683
Sir Edmund Saunders . . . . Jan.—June, 1683
Sir George Jeffreys (created Lord Jeffreys of Wem
    1685) . . . . 1683—1685
Sir Edward Herbert . . . . 1685—1687
Sir Robert Wright . . . . 1687—1688

LORD CHIEF JUSTICES OF THE COMMON PLEAS.

Sir Francis North . . . . 1675—1682
Sir Francis Pemberton . . . . Jan.—Sept., 1683
Sir Thomas Jones . . . . 1683—1686
Sir Henry Bedingfield . . . . 1686—1687
Sir Robert Wright . . . . April 16—April 21, 1687
Sir Edward Herbert . . . . 1687—1688

LORD CHIEF BARONS OF THE EXCHEQUER.

Hon. William Montagu . . . . 1676—1686
Sir Edward Atkyns . . . . 1686—1688

Recorders of London.

Sir John Howel	1668—1676
Sir William Dolben	1676—1678
Sir George Jeffreys	1678—1680
Sir George Treby	1680—1683
Sir Thomas Jenner	1683—1686
Sir John Holt	1686—1687
Serjeant Tate	1687
Sir Bartholomew Shower	1687—1688
Sir George Treby (re-appointed)	Dec., 1688

Attorneys-General.

Sir Francis North	1673—1675
Sir William Jones	1675—1679
Sir Creswell Levinz	1679—1681
Sir Robert Sawyer	1681—1687
Sir Thomas Powys	1687—1689

Solicitors-General.

Sir Francis North	1671—1673
Sir William Jones	1673—1674
Sir Francis Winnington	1674—1679
Hon. Heneage Finch	1679—1686
Sir Thomas Powys	1685—1687
Sir William Williams	1687—1688

APPENDIX III

Fac-simile of a letter from Lord Jeffreys to the Earl of Sunderland, written from Dorchester, September 5, 1685, and preserved in the Record Office.

[*See page* 289.

THE END

www.ingramcontent.com/pod-product-compliance
Lightning Source LLC
Chambersburg PA
CBHW032143110726
47902CB00003B/673